The Pebble
and
The Man

Connie N. Hart

Copyright © 2019 Connie N. Hart
All rights reserved
First Edition

PAGE PUBLISHING, INC.
New York, NY

First originally published by Page Publishing, Inc. 2019

ISBN 978-1-68456-106-3 (Paperback)
ISBN 978-1-68456-107-0 (Digital)

Printed in the United States of America

From diaries, letters, and declassified files,
From memories of those who were involved
Come the pieces of this story.

It is not a story of espionage.
It is the story of a man.
It is my father's story.

—Anna

PROLOGUE

1969

Eddy Street, San Francisco—the small man walked the dirty sidewalks, passed doorways that reeked of human waste. From across the street, the barker shouted, luring him with peep shows and nude dancers, his voice harsh against the sweet bells of cable cars.

The street was lined with broken-down hotels and broken people. The man stepped over a bum lying on the sidewalk and pulled his collar up against the wind. He was cold, sick, and empty.

Pushing his hands deep into his pockets, he sought the warmth that was gone from him now. But there was none, only the timid prostitute who approached.

"Hi," she said.

He stopped to watch her awkward attempt at seduction. The new girl on the street. Yes.

He followed her up the narrow stairway into the dirty room, and money changed hands. The sheets were stained with other men's semen and sweat, and it made him sick. But this was what he wanted. Instead of pleasure, it was the whore's wretchedness he paid for, a wretchedness to match his own. With each turn of her body, with each moan she faked, he pumped into her his anger, his hate…his grief.

He had no name because who he was didn't matter anymore. He raised himself off her, and for a brief moment, she caught his eye.

"Hey, are you all right?"

But the man didn't speak. He was gone moments later, stumbling off curbs and across streets, down finally to the sandy beach, where he could go no farther. It was there he fell, facedown, on the sand. The roar of the ocean pounded into his ears, drowning out all thought as the evening tide came in.

*****

"Pavlova…"

Leslie Fairchild opened her briefcase and looked at the photograph clipped to the manila folder. "Anton Pavlova. Yes, it's him. The USIB will take over his security. And, Nurse…" Leslie paused, looking up. "Why is this man restrained?"

"It's standard procedure on attempted suicides, ma'am."

Leslie flipped through the medical chart, then looked down at the pale man. His wrists were strapped to the rail of the hospital bed, his face bruised and swollen. The chart described an ugly gash on his forehead, left by the relentless waves that had battered him against the coastal rocks off the bay.

Paul Sanderson had called her in a panic during the night. His best man had been pulled from the sea and now clung to life in a hospital bed in San Francisco. Paul had asked her to stay with Pavlova until he could arrive from New York. Leslie had promised she would.

So, this is him, she thought. *This is the one.* She'd expected someone bigger than life. It was hard to imagine that this broken man was the one Paul had bragged about.

"I'm Dr. Fairchild, psychiatrist with the USIB. According to the Coast Guard, if this man had wanted to die, he would have. From what I see here, he put up a hell of a fight to stay alive. Has he been awake?"

"On and off. He's been delirious most of the time."

"Has he spoken?" she asked.

"No, ma'am." The nurse bent over him and adjusted the tube in his nostril. Anton's eyes flew open. He rattled the bars of the bed, mouthing frustrated screams that wouldn't come out—the tube blocked his throat.

THE PEBBLE AND THE MAN

"It's okay, Anton," Leslie said. She laid her hand on his shoulder, and a moment later, he closed his eyes. "Nurse, I want the restraints removed."

"It's standard procedure on attempted—"

"I want the tube removed too," Leslie continued. "I need to talk to him."

"That would take an order from the doctor."

Leslie leveled her cool gray eyes on the nurse. "From this point forward, I *am* the doctor."

The nurse closed the door quietly behind her, and Leslie sat on the orange vinyl chair to watch over Anton in his fitful state of sleep. She spent the night reading the Coast Guard report and the file on his personal background. But it was the photo and police report on his wife's suicide that left Leslie numb.

She held an eight-by-ten photograph showing a butcher knife stuck deep into Catherine's stomach, her hand still on its hilt. In the background, wrapping paper and bows lay in evidence of hastily opened gifts. A teddy bear, seemingly tossed into the corner, lay sprawled ironically in the same position as Anton's young bride.

Leslie looked at Anton now resting quietly. His fair skin had been ravaged by the salt and sun. He and his partner, Scott, had returned home from an assignment only to find Catherine dead. According to Scott, Anton had bolted. He'd been missing for ten days.

Leslie sighed. It was seven in the morning when she closed the last of the files. She stood and stretched, then smoothed Anton's blond hair. *How does one put back together the pieces of a broken man?* she wondered. *How does one unscramble an egg?* He had fought to stay alive, of that she was sure. Now it was up to her to make him want to live again.

*****

A familiar voice drifted through the fog. It was Paul Sanderson, Anton knew, but he couldn't open his eyes to confirm it.

My name is Anton. My name is Anton, he repeated to himself. It was the one thing of which he was certain through the drug-induced haze. Couldn't Paul see him? Couldn't he hear the waves rush toward them? He wished he could move his hands and push the tangle of seaweed from his face. *Paul, I'm drowning!* He coaxed the words from his throat, but they only surfaced as a pathetic moan.

He hated it. He hated being drugged. He wished he could open his eyes. If he could open his eyes and focus on something, he was sure the words would follow.

"What do you think, Leslie?" Paul asked, his voice distant.

"The Coast Guard had to pry him off a rock. That doesn't sound like a man who wanted to die. I'll know more when I can talk to him," she said.

Leslie, Anton thought. He tried to remember if he knew a Leslie. Whoever she was, Paul knew her.

"Did you receive the report on Catherine?" Paul asked.

"Catherine…" It surprised Anton to hear his own voice. He opened his eyes. The tube had been removed, leaving his throat scratchy and sore. "Paul, where's Catherine?"

Paul came to Anton's bedside and pushed a button to summon a nurse. "Pavlova, do you know where you are?"

Anton coughed and felt a crushing pain in his lungs. The drugs were wearing off.

Leslie pulled the chair beside him and reached through the railing, taking his hand.

"Where's Catherine?" he managed.

Paul and Leslie exchanged glances, and Anton felt a wave of grief course through him. The nurse bustled into the room and injected something into his IV, and his pain began to ease almost immediately. He knew he would soon slip away. "Paul, I have to know. Where is Catherine?"

"You have to tell him," Leslie said, looking up at Paul.

Paul hesitated as Anton's eyelids grew heavy. "We buried her for you three days ago," he said. "It's done."

It's done? "I didn't say goodbye," he whispered, spiraling back into unconsciousness. "I never said goodbye…"

*****

"Amazing grace, how sweet the sound…"

Barely aware of mourners singing softly at a nearby grave, Anton lay over Catherine's entombed body, choking back tears, the cool grass his only comfort.

Sanderson stood vigil beside him. When the singing finally stopped, the strangers began to filter passed on their way to the awaiting cars. Paul stooped protectively and put his hand on Anton's shoulder, silently reminding him that for them, too, it was time to go.

Anton looked up, reluctantly acknowledging the gesture, knowing his superior didn't really understand. No one did. No one had ever believed he truly loved Catherine.

Slowly he became aware of his surroundings: the beautifully maintained plots, thousands of them, fragrant with fresh-cut flowers, the gentle breeze that flowed over him as he gazed past Sanderson to the blue sky stretching over the vast sea of tombstones.

He was glad when the crowd of strangers thinned. He couldn't help resenting the intrusion. This was Catherine's resting place, the only spot in the world where he could feel close to her. He wished Sanderson had chosen a more private location, a secluded area that belonged solely to her, and to him. A final bed they eventually would share. It would have been little comfort, but now he didn't even have that.

He glowered as the final interloper ambled by. The man was old, withered, just as a man should be when death takes a loved one. Their eyes met and Anton saw a reflection of his own grief. The old man's eyes were different from his; the grief so frighteningly similar.

A young woman took the old man's arm and nodded a silent expression of sympathy before she led him away.

Anton rose to his feet. "Put me to work," he said, watching the cars pull out one by one.

"It's too soon. You'd get yourself killed."

"I speak Russian. I know you can use me. So, use me."

"It's suicide."

Anton turned, piercing him with his eyes. "Paul…I'm already dead."

The Years Before

CHAPTER 1

1944

Fewer than one hundred people were allowed to emigrate from Russia to the United States in 1944, the year Anton Pavlovich Vishnyakov turned three. After all, there was a war going on. But Anton knew little of war and cared less. His life was filled with other things, rides on his father's broad shoulders and games with his mother in the afternoons. What he remembered of her were golden hair, piercing blue eyes, warm gentle hands, and her laugh. It was a merry, gladdening laugh, one that brought hope to those who whispered the misery of war in the darkened halls of their flat.

"Anton, come." He awakened to the whispers of his grandmother as she lifted him and covered him with her shawl. He wrapped his little legs around her girth, then fell back to sleep on her soft, warm shoulder. "Yasha, are we doing the right thing?" Her troubled voice hardly fazed the sleeping child.

Yasha pushed Anton's blond hair away from his face and whispered to his wife, "It's his only chance for a better life, Mariya."

"They'll hate us," she lamented.

Yasha measured his words. "Yes, they will. But we will be giving freedom to him, to his children, and to theirs. Mariya," he continued in a gentler tone, "Anton won't hate us. He is young. I doubt he will ever know."

The arm around Anton tightened anxiously.

"Hurry," Yasha urged, and in the stillness of the night, Anton was taken from the only home he had ever known.

*****

Anton would remember little of the freighter that brought him to the United States, for he saw little. He only knew that each time he heard the word *purser*, he was whisked into the musty darkness of the travel trunk, onto a bed of freshly laundered garments his grandparents had brought with them. They should have brought more. A lifetime of cold Russian winters had taught them that too few clothes often meant a miserable existence—but too much baggage would have looked suspicious.

After the lid closed over him once again, Anton heard his grandmother lock it. It creaked when she sat down, as the purser knocked at the cabin door a second time.

"I've come for your trunk. We dock in half an hour," he said, and Mariya settled down heavier still, spreading her worn brown skirt around her.

"It's unnecessary. We will keep the trunk with us," she said.

Tears ran down Anton's cheeks as he pressed his small hands upward in the darkness to feel the confines of his surroundings. But he uttered no sound. *Always be silent,* his grandfather had told him. Even at three, Anton knew obedience could mean life or death. Suddenly he wondered if it was all right for him to cry.

The door opened, and the man's voice became clearer. "Why? What's in it?" he asked.

"Clothes…a few books," his grandfather said.

"Maybe we should have a look."

There was a long silence, and Anton instinctively held his breath.

"No. It's not necessary," his grandmother said.

He felt the weight of her body lift from the trunk, then slid with the other contents as the man lifted it. He pressed his palms even harder against the lid to steady himself, and when he looked through the air hole, the sight of his grandparents clinging to each other burned itself permanently into his mind.

CHAPTER 2

New York
1958

"Pavlova!" Mr. Delvardis growled.

Anton started, turning his attention to the front of the room.

"Repeat my last question." The instructor bristled behind black horn-rimmed glasses, his eyebrows sticking out of the top like the quills of a porcupine.

Anton's stomach knotted when he realized he'd been caught daydreaming, his eyes on the now-giggling Mary Ellen Habersham. The golden-brown tendrils of her hair teased more than the soft tops of her round breasts, and now she giggled with delight at his discomfort.

"Pardon?" he asked, buying time, wishing the ache in his groin would go away.

"My last question. What was it?" Delvardis demanded. The corners of his mouth curled like a cat's, and Anton could almost see a tail twitch with excitement.

He'd spent his entire life trying to be invisible. The hours of silence spent in the confines of the dark trunk had been a harbinger of the silent years to follow, years of not making waves, years of not being noticed. But now in his senior year of high school, Mr. Delvardis noticed.

Delvardis often told stories of Crimean seizures of his family's farm and of his professor father, who had been executed in Riga because he represented a certain school of thought. To Delvardis, a Russian was a Russian; wherever, whoever.

Anton's mind raced. "You asked who would be in charge if both the president and the vice president were killed," he said, praying he had caught the question.

He had. Delvardis's sardonic expression dissolved into one of frustrated anger. He pressed a finger against his dry lips. "And who would be? Do you know *that*, Mr. Pavlova? Or is it Pav…lo…vich?" He paused. "Or Vishnyakov?"

Anton blinked impatiently at his instructor. "The Speaker of the House."

"What house?"

"The House of Representatives."

The class grew still as Mr. Delvardis shuffled papers on his desk. It was no secret he hated Anton, though few clearly understood why. Anton had been a straight-A student from the start. The language barrier had forced him to study religiously for even the simplest of assignments. Those early years had been difficult, but by eighteen he'd found all his hard work had paid off. His excellent grades had secured him a scholarship, and even the prejudices of people like Delvardis couldn't deny him access to the college of his choice.

"Is he right, Mr. Delvardis?" Mary Ellen asked, giving Anton a wide grin.

The dismissal bell rang, and Anton rose from his seat, gathering his books slowly while the other students filed out. To bolt would prove, in his instructor's eyes, that he had something to hide.

"*Pav…lo…va*," Delvardis enunciated. "A variation of the name *Pavlovich*. Did your grandparents think changing your name would make you harder to trace?"

"The war in Europe does not involve me," Anton replied.

"You're Russian."

"I'm American."

"Not for long." Delvardis smiled wickedly as he walked out of the room.

Mary Ellen reentered as soon as he was gone. "What did he mean by that?" she asked.

"I don't know. Don't worry about it." Anton drew her close. "You almost got me into trouble," he said, and kissed her lazily. It was strange kissing a girl taller than him, but then, they were all taller. He hated it, but Mary Ellen didn't seem to mind. It was she who had taken his virginity only three months before. She had seduced him under the bleachers during a football game. It had been cold that night. He remembered the steam rising from their damp skin.

"I have to go," he said, still smiling at the thought.

"Want me to walk to the studio with you?"

"No."

"Do you still think someone's following you?" she asked.

"Of course not. See you tomorrow. We'll catch a movie or something."

Anton left and walked across the courtyard, then crossed the street. He turned left, glancing over his shoulder as he had for months.

There he was. Not Delvardis, but another. He was never clear enough to be seen, but he was there nonetheless. Anton had been aware of the shadowy presence wherever he went—to school, to the dance studio. Even on dates with Mary Ellen, he was aware of the presence, like an unwanted guest awaiting an invitation to dinner.

America teemed with Soviet paranoia. But the "Red Scare" no longer raged in Europe as much as it raged inside of Delvardis's head, Anton thought. That he was now being followed seemed only another part of the same insanity that made people bury bomb shelters in their backyards.

There was no part of him that *felt* Russian. As a kid growing up on New York's Lower East Side, he had assumed that everyone spoke two languages: one for home, another for school. He remembered all too well the day he had first been called a Russian. It had come as a shock, like playing cops-and-robbers and being told you weren't the cop. He'd run all the way home, where his grandfather shook him, trying to snap him back into reality long enough to see if he'd been hurt.

No, he hadn't been hurt. He had been brutalized.

"You know we are Russian," Yasha had said, "you, me, your grandmother. Many of our friends are Russian, and we are good people."

"Yes, we are all good people." *The good ones got out and the bad ones stayed. Like Mama and Papa,* he thought.

"Didn't they want me?" he had asked once when he was thirteen.

"We told them we wanted to take you with us," Yasha replied.

"Didn't they try to stop you?"

"No. They never tried to stop us."

From that time on, he never mentioned his parents to Yasha again.

*****

By the time he arrived at the studio, the tension in his neck and shoulders was almost unbearable, making the routine of warming up painful. He sat on the scuffed wooden floor and stretched, folding almost in half as he grasped his left foot and pulled. The tension in the back of his leg reared up in an unwarranted cramp. "Damn," he muttered. He laid his head against his knee with his eyes closed, willing the pain away.

It had been hard at first, taking ballet lessons. He had begun at ten. At first, even the smell of the old building, moldy from a leaky roof that had worsened over the years, frightened him. Then came the bullying, the taunts of "fag" and "queer," the black eyes he'd hidden behind books. But nothing came more naturally to him than dance.

Yes, the early years had been difficult, but the ritual went on. Each day he stretched, hoping his muscles wouldn't bunch up into the hardened masses he saw on so many of the young athletes on campus. Each day he did his barre, practiced each position and transition until he did them with satisfactory grace. By fifteen, he knew this was what he wanted more than anything in the world. He competed fiercely, always watching his reflection for the smallest mistake.

Then it happened. One day during trials, just before advancing to the next level, Anton was doing pirouettes in front of the class. His small, compact body was perfect for speed and precision. With each turn, he focused on his own image in the mirror for a fraction of a second, the blurred panorama of his vision stopping just enough to focus on that face.

Her face.

He had never seen a picture of his mother, but the face in the mirror had shaken his memory. He stopped and stared at the sharp features, the slightly large aristocratic nose and wide-set blue eyes. It seemed like a dream until his fingertips touched the cold glass. As the class looked on, he tried to touch the image, the finely etched mouth, the chiseled jaw, the straight white teeth.

With a shudder, he realized Aleksandr Terekov, his instructor, himself a Russian émigré, stood beside him. "I look like my mother," Anton said.

"Don't worry, you will change soon. You are later than most, but it will happen." In his benevolence, Terekov had misunderstood.

*****

Terekov was right, Anton thought now as he rose and looked in the mirror. His face and body had changed, although he was still sorely aware of how long the other dancers' legs were in comparison to his own. He prayed his meager five foot five wasn't the end of his growth. Surely, he would be taller. The other boys at school were gangling giants, while he was small, compact, and lean. His broad, muscular shoulders were what had attracted Mary Ellen, rescuing him from ridicule, but there was little he wouldn't give to be a few inches taller.

He stretched, then bent at the waist and placed his palms on the floor.

"My name is Paul Sanderson. I'm with the United States Investigative Branch."

Anton shot upright. There, in the mirror behind him, stood the mysterious shadow who had followed.

CHAPTER 3

Paul Sanderson slid a thin file across Dave Chatfield's desk. "I think this guy Delvardis has a hair up his ass," he said. "I've watched this kid for six months, and the worst thing he's done was get laid during a football game."

"Delvardis says he's subversive," Chatfield said in a noncommittal tone. As the newly appointed chief of the United States Investigative Branch, he didn't want anything to slip through his fingers, and if a Russian spy could be brought in under his new command, all the better. He hated to let the case drop, even though there had been no actual evidence against Anton Pavlova. "He's Russian."

"When did that become a crime, for chrissake? There's not a subversive bone in the kid's body!" Paul sat down on the corner of Chatfield's desk. Chatfield lifted his dark brows, and Paul moved reluctantly to the chair.

"How in the name of decency did we ever get involved with putting surveillance on an eighteen-year-old?" Paul asked. "It makes no sense."

"No. Not now, but it did at the time," Chatfield said. "Delvardis fingered the kid, who is certainly sharp enough, as a contact for the KGB. He had a point. Who'd ever suspect a clean-cut, completely Americanized high school student? A kid like that could get into places that no agent could, and it just happened to dovetail with a case we were working on at the time."

"You know, this could be a bonus for us," Paul said.

"How do you mean?" Chatfield asked.

THE PEBBLE AND THE MAN

"Because of those same reasons…he might be perfect material for the Branch," Paul said. "With a little work, I could really make this kid into something in a couple of years."

"You groomed Scott Bauer."

"Yeah. Then he got married, and that makes him worthless in my book."

Chatfield laughed. "So, you're telling me we should hire a guy we've been tailing for half a year? What about the case against him?"

"What case? There is no case! Delvardis is just an SOB that's trying to squash the kid's scholarship because the kid pisses him off!" Paul got to his feet and jabbed an emphatic finger at the file in front of Chatfield. "You said you were looking for a good man. I'm telling you, this is the one!"

Chatfield leaned back in his chair and pressed his fingertips together in careful contemplation. An offshoot of the Defense Department, the United States Investigative Branch trained and maintained covert agents for the government's use. They generally worked in pairs, though not always, and it was up to the senior partner to accept or decline assignments. It was extraordinary that a man of Paul Sanderson's reputation would look twice at a man outside the department.

Man? No. Boy, Dave Chatfield decided, wondering how Sanderson thought he could talk him into something so outrageous.

After giving him a few moments, Paul continued. "You said you'd assign me a new partner after Jack died. I realize you meant within the ranks. But I talked to Pavlova this afternoon. He told me everything, how he got here, who he was. He was locked in a goddamn trunk for six hours and didn't make a peep because his grandparents told him to keep quiet." Paul paused to let it sink in before continuing in a quieter tone. "He's disciplined, Chief. He's a ballet dancer, and I've watched him bandage his feet when they were so sore they bled. He has drive and discipline!"

Finally, Dave cleared his throat. "There are lots of ballet dancers. They all have bleeding feet."

"This one speaks perfect Russian."

"He's too young."

"If you wait until he's in college, the CIA will tag him. You know that. That's why they always wind up with the best men. The time to move is now."

"What makes you think he'd even work for us?"

Sanderson grinned. "That's the best part. The kid's a fucking patriot."

CHAPTER 4

It was 1968 when Anton returned to his grandparents' house in New York, his ten years of college and intense training finally over. He set his bag on the worn living room carpet, and Hamlet, the cat, eyed him curiously from behind the chair. "Here, kitty," he said, but Hamlet scampered through the nearest doorway.

"Grandpa?" he called. "Grandma?"

He followed the sound of clattering dishes to the kitchen, where Mariya stood at the sink. He pulled the string of her faded gingham apron and laughed when she swatted behind her, annoyed. Yasha had always done that, untied her apron while she worked. But now, the sound of Anton's laughter spun her around.

"Anton! My Anton, you're home!" She threw her sudsy hands around his shoulders.

"How's my old girl?" he asked and kissed her withered cheek. Tears of joy came to her eyes as she began checking him over like a valued object reluctantly loaned.

"Anton, how are you?" she bubbled and hugged him again.

He had written to them often, but visits had been few. The USIB had taken her boy, her darling grandson, and turned him into a man. "You've filled out. Look at you!" She pushed him around in a little circle, looking him over. There was something different, something unfamiliar about him. Perhaps it was the cut of his shirt, or the way his shoes shined; something. "You're taller," she decided.

"Not much," he laughed. His high school prayers for growth had yielded only two more inches. At five foot seven, he was still a small man. But compared to Mariya, he was a giant. "Where's Grandpa?" he asked.

"Oh, he went to Yuri's," she said as they took seats at the kitchen table.

"Who is Yuri?"

"He bought the grocery down the block. Yuri, his wife, and their twelve children. They all live upstairs. What a mess. Twelve kids!" she muttered, and Anton smiled. "I've never seen his wife, mind you," she went on. "She's always in bed, pregnant or just getting over having a baby. Yasha says she has trouble having babies, that's why she has to stay in bed." She gave Anton a cutting glance. "Doesn't look like she has trouble to me!"

Anton laughed. "How are you, Grandma? You look thin."

Yasha had called him about her illness, and he had known she'd been in the hospital by the bills he paid. Although he didn't begrudge their financial dependence, it had been the key factor in his decision to work for the government instead of going into dance. But now his grandmother appeared frail. She had always been a plump, sturdy woman. It had been her strength and determination that had held them together during times of hardship. He smiled a little now. How could he begrudge her anything?

"I'm all right," she answered. "I helped Mary Ellen's mother pack last week. They moved, you know."

Anton frowned. After he and Mary Ellen had graduated from high school, she and her mother had gone to San Francisco. "I thought Mrs. Habersham moved when Mary Ellen did," he said.

"She did. Mary Ellen started nursing school. I helped them pack."

Anton leaned forward and took his grandmother's hand. "Grandma, what year is this?" he asked.

"Nineteen fifty-nine, of course."

"And that would make me…?"

She thought for a moment. "That would make you eighteen."

Anton patted her frail hand affectionately. Mary Ellen had moved to San Francisco nine years ago. It was now nineteen sixty-eight, and he was twenty-seven years old.

"You should go to Yuri's," she said. "Your grandfather waits for you there."

She stood and went back to the dishes. He watched her for a full five minutes before he realized she was no longer aware he'd even come home.

*****

Within months of his homecoming, Mariya died, and Yasha followed her two months after that. *I've been gone too long,* he thought miserably as Yuri Ivanov handed him another glass of bourbon.

"If you were a real Russian, you'd drink vodka," Yuri said.

"I am a real Russian," Anton said. "Vodka gives me a headache."

"Has anyone ever told you you have a split personality?" Yuri pointed an incredulous finger while refilling his own glass.

Anton didn't answer.

"I'm sorry about your grandparents," Yuri continued as he settled down in the tiny living quarters of his upstairs apartment.

Below them, the grocery store was being closed by his eldest daughters, Clarisa and Lana. Around them was the clutter of toys, papers, coloring books, and empty baby bottles soured by the summer heat. Above them was the third floor. There, Anton surmised, were the sleeping quarters. But just now it was the clomping of children's feet he heard and the cracking voice of a pubescent boy begging privacy from his younger brothers. Anton smiled inwardly, remembering those awkward years.

"Thank you," he said, sipping the bourbon.

"It often happens like that, one dying right after the other. Your grandfather was a good friend. I will miss him..."

In the kitchen, somewhere between the mountain of unwashed dishes and mounds of dirty laundry, was Yuri's only other daughter, Catherine. *The queen of the kitchen,* Anton had come to think of her, for that was her domain. There she cooked and cleaned, even diapered the three youngest children. He could see her through the doorway from where he sat, and as Yuri continued in Russian above the din of the children, he watched her tiny, aproned frame take charge of the impossible.

*****

It had been late the last time he'd visited Yuri with his grandfather. "Yuri has pretty daughters, yes?" Yasha had said pointedly as they'd strolled home.

"Yuri's daughters are on the make," Anton had answered under his breath, causing Yasha to stop.

"On the make? What is this 'on the make'?"

"They're looking for a husband," he said.

"Yes, and so should you be looking for a wife! After I am gone, you will have no more family. *Family*—do you know what that means?"

"Every time I go there, they look at me like hungry she-wolves."

"Yuri says you can have one. He'll give you one of his daughters."

Anton laughed. "I see. Like he said he'd give me one of the homing pigeons he raises out back." He thought it was funny, but his grandfather bristled.

"You shouldn't make fun. It was a nice offer. The girl *and* the bird," he added.

"It's not so generous," Anton said. "He's just looking for some poor guy to take one of his children off his hands."

Yasha ignored him. "Catherine is out of the question, of course. She's only fifteen. But Clarisa and Lana are nineteen and twenty, and very pretty!"

"I don't like them."

"Why?"

"Because—"

"Because they're poor immigrants, like us? But then, you are no longer a poor immigrant, are you?"

"I didn't say that."

"No, you wouldn't." Yasha's voice had softened. "But don't you think I see you've changed? Look at how perfect you dress. Look at your haircut and your hands. This man Sanderson turned you into a gentleman."

Anton looked down at his manicured nails. His hands were strong and clean. Immaculate. He was perfect from head to toe. Mariya had seen the change, too.

"It's okay," Yasha said, waving it off. "Don't you think that's what I want for you? I only mean, while you make for yourself a better life, where is harm in taking one of your own kind with you?"

*****

Under the drone of Yuri's voice, Anton sat on the couch and continued to get drunk. He had come home to spend time with his grandparents, not to bury them. For the first time in his life, he felt very alone.

"Catherine!" Yuri shouted toward the kitchen. Her sullen brown eyes turned to her father. "Go and see what is taking Clarisa and Lana so long. Tell them Anton is here."

The house was miserably hot and smelled of unbathed children. When Catherine returned, she continued her chores as the older girls arrived and enthusiastically flanked Anton on the couch. Two boys walked through, arguing over whose turn it was to ride the motorbike as Clarisa slipped her arm through Anton's.

"I have beautiful daughters, yes?" Yuri boomed in Russian, indicating the girls on either side of Anton.

"Very pretty," he said, venturing a glance into the kitchen. Catherine's eyes were cast downward, her face thin.

"More to drink?" Yuri asked as he held the bottle toward Anton.

"I'll pour!" Lana snatched it before Clarisa could disengage from Anton and in her triumph sloshed bourbon over his hand.

"Stupid," Clarisa snorted.

Anton stood, grateful for the excuse. "I'll be right back."

He went into the kitchen, where Catherine stood, and nodded. "Do you mind if I wash my hands?" He picked up the bottle of soap and turned on the faucet.

Catherine stood three feet away, silent and shy. Finally, "I'm sorry about your grandparents," she said.

"Thank you, Catherine. That's very sweet."

She handed him a towel.

"You know, my grandmother had several nice antique dolls. I can't think of anyone I'd rather give them to," he said, drying his hands. "Stop by the house after school sometime. I'll give them to you. Would you like that?"

She nodded happily, but said nothing. He smiled at her before joining Yuri and the girls in the living room.

*****

Catherine returned to the dishes as Anton ensconced himself between her sisters. She was sure he hated them. How could he feel any other way? Beneath the layer of suds, in the depths of the dishwater, her small hands curled into fists.

She had always been the runt, the skinny little girl who could never be attractive to a man. When she was ten, the fever had kept her from school for almost the entire year, and she had never quite recovered. At the age of twelve, her menstrual cycle had begun and Clarisa and Lana had hooted and laughed at her "trying to be a woman."

Still they hooted. From the other room she heard it in their laughter: "We are with Anton, and you are not!"

Someday the scales will be balanced, she thought. *Someday God will make it right.* Each time Anton looked at her, she felt the searing touch of his gaze. But when his drunken laughter mingled with that of her sisters, she hated even him in a way she had never thought possible.

She closed her eyes and let the anger pass, glad when he finally went home.

*****

The following week, Anton knocked at the Ivanovs' door for the last time. "I've come to say goodbye," he said when Yuri greeted him.

"I thought you were settling Yasha's estate," Yuri said, inviting him in.

Anton sat on the couch, and like trained seals, Clarisa and Lana joined him.

"There wasn't much to settle," he said. "I'm being reassigned to San Francisco."

There was a crash in the kitchen. When Anton looked up, Catherine stood in the doorway with shards of glass at her feet. Without a word, she ran out the back, allowing the screen door to slam behind her.

"What's the matter with her?" Yuri asked, and the girls giggled.

"She's in love with Anton," Clarisa said. "She writes about him in her diary."

Anton scowled.

"It's only puppy love," Lana tittered.

"Puppy love is real to puppies," he said. He would have never put up with them if Yuri hadn't meant so much to his grandfather. Letting Clarisa's hand fall from his knee, he rose and followed Catherine out the back door.

He'd been to the loft only once, the first time he'd met Yuri. Yuri had been proud to show off his prize pigeons and had taken him down the back steps to the little wooden shack that butted into the alley.

It was hot and dusty as he entered. The birds flew in every direction, stirring dust, feathers, and bits of straw into a cloud. The whirring of their wings sounded as mournful as Catherine looked. She stood in the corner, anguished and humiliated.

"Catherine—"

"Oh, please don't say anything!"

"They should be jealous of *you*," he said gently.

"Oh, Anton, why do you have to leave?"

"I have to go back to work, little one," he said quietly. "I've been assigned a new partner, and he is stationed in San Francisco. He has an excellent reputation, and it's an honor that he requested me."

"Take me with you!" she cried, wrapping her arms around him. "I love you. Please take me with you!"

"My dear girl."

He enfolded her in his arms even though reason told him not to. He wanted to comfort her, to hold her, to protect her. She was like a frail flower, too weak to bloom. He kissed her forehead and wondered what it would be like to kiss her lips, to touch the silk of her skin beneath cool sheets.

He cursed the unbidden thought, but she was so soft and unspoiled, so needy. No one knew how he cherished the secret guilt of wanting her. Her innocence hung around her like an amulet, like sweet perfume.

The back door slammed, and Yuri's heavy boots tromped down the wooden stairs. "Little whore!" came his muffled shout.

Anton looked to the loft entrance, then back at Catherine. The worship in her eyes had turned to terror. The door of the loft burst open, and the pigeons scattered a second time. Yuri's eyes locked on his youngest daughter in Anton's embrace, his trembling fist clutching crumpled pages torn from her diary.

"Son of a bitch!" he shouted. "Son of a bitch!"

The First Year

CHAPTER 5

1979

Anton opened his eyes and turned to the pillow beside him. There was no indentation where Catherine might have been, no rumpled blankets on the far side of the bed. There was only the vague memory of the girl who had once been his wife. Like fresh water cupped in the hands of a thirsty man, Catherine's life had somehow been spirited away. More than memories, it was an endless, aching wound she had left behind.

He would be thirty-eight soon. Leslie had promised moments like these would pass. They hadn't.

The scent of fresh-baked bread and the early-morning sounds of the Iranian marketplace filtered their way to the second-story window of the stone house. Nezar and Mohammed, the brothers who owned the house, no longer asked questions. They were subversives of the Shah, supporters of the deposed Ayatollah Khomeini, and having a Russian as a boarder sent a clear message to others just which side they were on. As tensions between Iran and Soviet-backed Iraq continued to mount, this defector, this traitor, had value. The brothers were students at the University of Tehran, where hostility toward Americans grew stronger every day. It had taken Anton two years to arrive at this position, but finally he had finagled his way into the movement and was now being accepted and informed about underground plots, not to mention given access to reams of documents.

The USIB had become his refuge, his bride. It was his food, his air, his lover, his whore. An exclusive branch of intelligence-gathering, it had become a world where there were no attachments.

Anton rose and dressed, then went into the market, where he bought bread, fresh fruit, and goat cheese. He walked along the *jube*, where a man relieved himself and, half a block farther, a woman washed her small child it its same filthy waters. The stench of the open sewage ditch invaded his senses, as did the harsh, guttural sounds of Farsi, the native Iranian tongue. There was something about the language that grated him, and although he spoke enough to get by, he preferred his native Russian.

The weak February sun cast thin shadows across the alley as Anton let himself through the iron gate to the house, but when he did not hear the familiar clang of the gate behind him, he turned. Scott Bauer awaited him with a grin. The curly brown hair and deep-cleft chin were unmistakably Scott's. Anton would recognize him anywhere.

"Breakfast," Anton muttered in Russian, indicating the groceries.

"How the hell are you?" Scott asked.

Anton didn't speak. He climbed the stairs to his room, and Scott followed him inside.

"You should be more careful," Anton said disapprovingly. "They think I'm Russian."

Scott laughed. "You are! Good heavens, you should hear your accent. When's the last time you spoke English?"

Anton thought. "Six years, maybe seven, except for brief messages." The words felt foreign to him, shockingly so. "Just because I was born there doesn't make me Russian. I'm American, Scott. You know that."

"And still touchy, I see." Scott smiled.

Anton could tell Scott expected him to be happy to see him after so many years. They had been close during his brief marriage to Catherine. They had been partners then. But Catherine had left him gaping open, and he had long since filled that void with ice. He had nothing to give Scott Bauer. "It's good to see you," he said finally.

"How are you? I swear you don't look a day older," Scott said, offering his hand.

"Definitely older," Anton said. He met Scott's hand with his own. "How are Faye and the girls?"

"Great." Scott dug for his wallet and withdrew a picture, handing it proudly to Anton. "It's an old picture, but I think you'll still recognize the kids. Except that one." He pointed at the youngest child. "Another girl. You never saw her."

Anton grew anxious to get the small talk out of the way. He meant only to glance at the photo, but something about it drew him in. He had had ten years to convince himself he had no need of women—except for this. He looked again at the five angelic faces that stared, unblinking, back at him. He could hear their laughter, feel them crawl over him like puppies at the end of a hard day. Yes, he envied Scott his children and, therefore, his wife. He ran a fingertip languorously over the smiles of the pretty woman and the five little girls, then handed the photo back to Scott.

"You're a lucky man," he said.

"It's not too late, Anton. What you need is a family…" Scott said, but Anton's dark expression cast a shadow over the unspoken words.

*****

Scott Bauer looked him over. Anton's head and hands were large for a small man. His five-foot-seven frame and graceful demeanor had worried him when they'd first met. But Scott had learned quickly that Anton was very good at what he did, and now it was shocking to see how short he actually was. Funny, after knowing the man, Anton had seemed very tall.

Even then, Anton's angular features had seemed to carry a warning. To whom, Scott had never been sure. After Catherine's death, Anton's hospitalization had forced reassignments, and Scott felt oddly separated from him now. Only he, Paul, and Leslie knew the violent way Anton's young bride had taken the life of their unborn child, and in the process, her own. Leslie had admonished him not to speak of it to Anton. *How could he not know?* Scott wondered. *How could he have forgotten?*

He had looked forward to seeing his old partner but now realized that he was too much a part of the past, too much a part of that grand, gaping hole in Anton's memory, and he took little pleasure in seeing him.

"What are you doing in Iran?" Anton asked.

"Is it safe to talk?" he asked, and Anton nodded. "You sure?"

Anton had only to look at him. *Of course, he's sure.* Scott shrugged apologetically. "Chatfield's out. Sanderson is now Chief of Operations."

Anton smiled. "He finally got his promotion."

"Because of you. You've worked your ass off out here and he sits in New York and gets promoted."

"Whatever Paul gets, he deserves. I owe him."

"You've paid him," Scott said cautiously. He had learned over the years never to speak against Paul Sanderson. That was one thing Anton Pavlova would not tolerate, even from a close friend. Scott knew Anton no longer had any real friends in the division, if at the Branch at all, and there was no one outside the Branch he was aware of. That left Anton with nothing. He had become precise, articulate. Cold.

Scott pitied him. Anton's cobalt eyes were lifeless. The only glimmer of life in him was pain. *I'd rather be dead,* thought Scott.

Anton eyed him cautiously. "You haven't said why you've come."

"They want you back in the States. I'm taking over your assignment," he said flatly.

There was a knock on the door, and Anton moved toward it in one seamless motion, his snub-nose .38 poised before Scott had even reached a position.

"Yes. What is it?" he asked in a drowsy Russian voice.

"There is a meeting at the university tonight. Will you be there?" the young Iranian said.

"I'm sending a friend, an American." Anton glanced in Scott's direction.

"An American!"

"Don't ask questions," Anton continued through the door. "He can get into the American Embassy. He will be an asset, that's why I've chosen him."

There was a long silence outside the door, and Scott held his breath. "All right, my Russian friend. I'll trust you," the voice said finally. His retreating footsteps told them he was gone.

"You're in," Anton said, turning back to Scott, "but Nezar's going to be suspicious, so watch yourself." He paused.

"Tell me, what do they say about me back at the Branch? The truth, Scott. I want to know what I'm going home to."

Scott hesitated. "Most say you're the best operative the Branch ever had. To most, you're a legend. But to some, you're too ambitious."

"Is that what Paul says?"

"Of course not."

"Then why are they sending me back?"

This was the bad news he had been sent to tell Anton. "The USIB is being dismantled, Anton. Most of our men have already gone to the CIA or the FBI. Paul wants me to finish this job so you can have a cooling-off period. You're being partnered up with some guy in California, Dan Philips. You'll be debriefed in New York, then sent to San Francisco. Leslie still has an office there, and she wants to see you. The rest of the time, they want you in Three Rivers with Philips. Frankly, the USIB isn't concerned about a bunch of militant Iranian college students."

Anton stared, livid. "This place is ready to explode! Haven't they read my communiqués?"

"They don't think it'll come to anything. As I said, some think you're too ambitious. Besides, the Company is on it."

"Damn!" Anton paced the floor. "I've spent years over here putting myself into position for just such an event, and they send in the CIA!" He looked at Scott incredulously. "You're with them, aren't you? You've sold out."

"I'm with the Company now, yes. Sooner or later, everyone will switch over. Carter's administration has decided the Branch is 'redundant.' They're only leaving about a hundred operatives, and most of those are with security."

"Some promotion for Paul. He's finally given the reins just to close it down!"

"Who's this guy, Philips? What's he involved in?" Anton forced himself to cool down.

"Nothing, as far as I've seen. He's been with the Branch only six years. Has a brother named Clayton and was a football hero at the local college. Far as I could tell from his files, he's nobody. You're the senior partner. You'll call the shots."

By the time Scott finished, Anton had regained his composure. "You have a family. Why can't they send someone else?"

"I'm only here 'til year's end," Scott said, knowing the concern was Anton's way of apologizing. "Is there anyone you want me to say goodbye to?"

"You know I make it a point not to get involved with the locals."

"It's a lonely business we're in, you know," Scott said.

"Why don't you quit?"

"The truth?"

Anton nodded.

"I need the excitement," Scott said. "You?"

For the first time, Anton cracked a smile, and Scott Bauer saw a remnant of the man he had once known. "The diversion."

CHAPTER 6

1979

The Noisy Water Café wasn't busy in March. The mountains were still cold, and Three Rivers saw few visitors. The small California town lay along the middle fork of the Kaweah River, pinched between the rocky gorge and the Mineral King Highway. Higher up were Kings and Mineral Canyons and the Wolverton ski lodge. This much Anton learned from listening to Myrt, the waitress, chat with delivery drivers at a nearby table.

Through the plate-glass window, Anton watched hummingbirds dart back and forth through the fog to the row of feeders the owner had placed along the eaves. Beyond, he could hear the river rage against the boulders that lay in its path. The sound was hardly discernible from the distant thunder, only more constant, more urgent.

"Coffee?"

Anton turned toward the voice.

"More coffee?" Myrt repeated, and he nodded.

"Live here long?" he asked.

"All my life," she answered, wiping the counter with a damp cloth. "I like it when visitors come. We get a lot of skiers. Do you ski?"

"No."

"Oh? I can usually tell. So what brings you to Three Rivers?" she asked. "You're not here to fish or see the big trees."

"How can you tell?" he asked. He had been with the USIB over twenty years, had watched people, read people...stayed alive by knowing what they would do next. And here was a waitress claiming she could read people too.

"Your hands are too soft for a fisherman's," she said. Drying her hands on her apron, she took his hand and turned it over in her own. "Probably never held a pole." She clicked her tongue. "Too bad."

"Maybe I'm going up to see the redwoods."

"No. You're not the type," she said. "Where're you from?"

"New York."

"My ass."

He chuckled. She was an abundant woman somewhere in her sixties, with a thick neck that wobbled when she talked.

"Okay. You tell me," he said.

"Slavic origin, I'd guess. But you've been in the States a long time. Am I right?"

"Russian," he conceded. "Raised in New York, but we spoke Russian at home."

"Yeah, we get a lot of you fellas in here," she said, unaffected as she returned to wiping the countertop with the rag.

Anton laughed quietly. "Myrt, you seem like a knowledgeable woman, and I need a favor," he began in his friendliest voice. "I'm looking for a place."

"There are lots of hotels…"

"A more private place."

She raised a brow. "Why?"

He pulled out his identification and laid it on the counter.

She hovered over it for a few moments, still swiping at the counter with her rag. "Humph." The rag went still, and she lifted her gaze to meet his. "What exactly are you looking for?"

"Someplace quiet. I need someone to do my laundry, clean occasionally. Someone who can be discreet," he said, pocketing his wallet. "You seem like someone who might know of a situation."

"Well, there's an apartment above my garage. I had it built for my son when he went to Vietnam. I thought he'd like something more private to come home to. He didn't come home."

"I'm sorry," he said. "Is it occupied?"

"It's full of junk…"

THE PEBBLE AND THE MAN

The little bell over the door jingled, and one of the two truck drivers let out a shrill whistle. Myrt looked at them nastily. "Suppliers," she hissed under her breath and went to attend to the young woman who had seated herself at the other end of the counter.

The woman wore dark glasses, and the rain had matted her blond hair. Her sweater and jeans clung, exposing the bony frame beneath. Thin as she was, she was still beautiful, and both truckers stared.

"Lordy, Lordy, child," Myrt mumbled and set a cup of coffee on the counter.

Shivering, the woman wrapped her hands around it gratefully. "Myrt, don't tell him you've seen me."

Myrt said something inaudible, and the woman began to cry. At her feet was a small suitcase, and Anton wondered why she didn't have a coat. Outside, only his new black Corvette and the supply truck could be seen. Evidently, she'd come on foot.

Myrt reached across the counter and lowered the woman's dark glasses. She leaned away and pushed them up before anyone but the waitress got a clear view. Myrt frowned.

"Hope, I heard you'd gone back, but I just couldn't believe it. Why do you keep doing this? One of these days he'll kill you!"

"This is the last time." Tears spilled down her cheeks. "I called Uncle Nate and he said I could stay at the old house. He said you have a key."

"Honey, I can't leave the restaurant. I'm working alone this afternoon. You'll have to wait 'til I close up before I can take you."

"I'll walk."

"You'll never make it up the canyon before dark," Myrt said.

"I made it this far. Do you have the key?"

Reluctantly, Myrt went into the back, and Anton watched the young woman sip her coffee. Finally, Myrt returned and placed an oddly shaped key on the counter.

"Thanks," the woman said, picking up her bag to leave.

"What should I tell him if he comes in?" Myrt asked.

"Nothing, Myrt. You never saw me." With that, the woman left.

One trucker went to the window to see the direction she had taken as the other called for their check.

"Just hold on," Myrt said, casting a worrisome glance in Anton's direction. She licked the lead of her pencil and pretended to check her addition while the two men grew impatient. Anton rose from his stool and went to Myrt.

"I'll pay a year in advance," he said quietly.

One of the truckers went outside, while the other hovered over Myrt's shoulder. "C'mon, Myrtie, we're running behind."

Myrt looked into Anton's eyes, studying him. "When would you need the apartment?"

"As soon as you can have it available."

"My friend needs a ride," she said.

Anton smiled. "Keep my dinner warm. I'll be back."

Myrt bumped the woman's leftover coffee, and it spilled on the driver's check. "Damn," she said. "I'll have to write out a new one."

*****

Rain pelted Anton's windshield. The woman was barely visible in the deluge as he pulled to the side of the road. "Get in!" he shouted, pushing the passenger door open.

She slid into the seat beside him and closed the door. "Thanks," she said, brushing the excess water from her face.

"Where's your coat?" he asked.

"I left in a hurry," she said. Seeing him glance down at the suitcase between her feet, she added, "It's been packed a long time."

He nodded slightly and put the car into gear. "It's a lousy day to run away," he said, making note of the gold band on her finger. "Where to?"

"South Fork Road. It's on the left a few miles ahead."

He pulled onto the road and headed west. "I heard Myrt call you Hope. Is that your name?" he asked. She nodded. "Anton," he said without her asking.

After a few miles, Anton turned onto South Fork Road, which immediately began to wind its way up Horn Mountain. Within minutes, the rocky slope fell away to a vast canyon, and for a moment he could see between the trees to the top of the mountain range. There, a huge outcropping dominated the sky.

"That's Moro Rock," she said.

They came to a small concrete bridge that passed over the south fork of the river, and Anton pulled the car to a stop.

"It's still a couple more miles," Hope said.

Anton turned on the interior light and unfastened his seat belt.

Eyes widening, Hope reached for the door handle and threw her weight against the door. It opened only a few inches before crashing against the guardrail.

Anton winced. He took a deep breath and removed his jacket. "I just stopped to give you my coat," he said quietly.

By the glare of the overhead light, what he saw made him sick. In her panic, her sunglasses had fallen off, exposing pale, delicate features punctuated by dark, plum-colored bruises. She shivered as he helped her on with his coat, and he wondered if it was from fear or the cold. Her jaw was set, and she lifted her chin defiantly as he pulled the jacket around her.

"You put yourself in a dangerous situation," he said. "Those truckers were after you the minute you left the café. If Myrt hadn't been such a quick thinker, who knows where you would have wound up."

Hope turned her face away from him and struggled not to cry.

Finally, he turned off the light and continued to drive. An overgrowth of trees canopied the narrow road and blocked out the little light that remained of the day. The river lay on Anton's left, down the rocky gorge, then disappeared altogether as they turned away from the canyon. Once they were out of the trees, it reappeared, rapid and angry, colliding against the huge boulders. Anton hugged the side of the mountain until they passed over a narrow wooden bridge. On the other side, the trees thickened once again, blocking the river from sight. The blacktop turned to gravel as they skirted the mountain, ascending rapidly until they could see the deep canyon below.

"About half a mile," Hope said. She sat forward in the seat, like an anxious child, but slumped back when Anton pulled in front of the abandoned house.

It had been built in the twenties, he guessed. Behind it, a decaying barn squatted in the small meadow like a horse going down for the last time. The front porch was sorely in need of repair, and Anton could only guess at the roof.

Hope got out and stood beside the car, looking at the old house.

"Looks deserted," he said, pulling the keys out of the ignition. "Was your uncle expecting you?"

"It's been empty for a while," she said. "Uncle Nate went to a retirement home in Monterey after Aunt Stella died."

"How long ago?"

"Ten years," she said, not taking her eyes off the house. Finally, she crossed the porch and went inside.

Anton followed.

*****

She remembered the ranch like it was yesterday, twenty-three acres tucked high in the foothills of the Sierra Nevada. She also remembered the house. But not like this.

Inside, dust and grit covered everything. The once-sunny kitchen was dirty and dark, the gray linoleum tiles buckled and cracked. Plaster hung precariously from ceilings, and the living room rug stank with mold and the droppings of some creature that had taken up residence through a broken window.

Hope stood in the dining room, looking through to the kitchen, where in her mind's eye she saw the thin, gray-haired woman beckoning her with a cookie.

"Come here to Aunt Stell. You knew I'd have a cookie for you!" *The woman smiled and bent down to hug her. The sun hit the prism that Uncle Nate had hung in the kitchen window, sending rainbows to dance on the walls and cupboards. Stella lovingly wagged a finger at her husband. "Now, don't you let that child go into the loft. She might fall!"*

"She always lands on her feet." The old man laughed, then kissed his wife and took Hope's hand. "We'll be back for more cookies when

the milking is done, won't we, darlin'?" He smiled down at her and winked.

*****

"Hope?" Anton eyed her with concern.

Her hand trembled against her mouth. Cupboard doors hung askew on broken hinges, corners were laced with cobwebs, and long-dead flies dotted the windowsills. "It's not like I remembered," she said.

"Few things are." Anton touched a thin, rotted curtain, and it fell, rod and all, crashing to the floor. "It looks pretty bad."

Hope crouched to gather shards of glass and held them in her palm. "I lived here in the summers and during the holidays. The house always smelled like cookies. It was always sunny and bright. Uncle Nate kept the trees around the house trimmed because Aunt Stella loved the sunlight and it can get so dark in the mountains. One summer he bought her this prism. She hung it in the window. I was about six. There were rainbows everywhere, on the walls and cupboards. I told Uncle Nate it was the most beautiful thing I had ever seen. He used to say that Aunt Stell deserved rainbows without rain."

Anton smiled sadly.

"I used to look at it for hours," she continued. She turned her hand and watched the shards fall back onto the floor, raising puffs of dust. "I guess there are no rainbows without rain."

He didn't answer, but followed as she climbed the stairs to the second floor.

She stopped and looked into the doorway of a bedroom. "This was my grandparents' room."

"They lived with your aunt and uncle?"

She smiled a little. "They were them. I mean, that's what I called my grandparents—Uncle Nate and Aunt Stella."

"Why would you do that?" Anton asked.

"That's what everybody in town always called them. I was eight before I realized they were actually my grandparents." For the first time, she smiled openly. She could see his confusion, and it made her laugh.

The light of day was all but gone, but she was beautiful, Anton thought.

Indeed, light was somehow different in the mountains. No matter how dark it became, there was always something a shade darker. By the time they went back downstairs, Hope was only a form, one that he sensed more than saw. He stepped close and lightly touched the obvious sore spot below her left cheekbone.

"Are you a cop?" she asked.

"No."

"My husband's a cop. I thought maybe he sent you. That's why I got scared in the car. I saw your gun when you took off your coat."

"Well, I'm not a cop," he said. He could feel the air vibrate around her as she shivered beneath his coat. "Hope, you can't stay here. There's no heat, no food. I don't feel good about leaving you. I can't be responsible. Let me take you back to town."

Her eyes flashed with anger. "No one asked you to be. I'm a grown woman, responsible for myself, thank you. I'll never need a man or let one be responsible for me again!"

Anton flinched, but said nothing.

"I'm sorry…I appreciate the ride."

"That's quite all right." He backed away toward the front door. "Give my coat to Myrt the next time you're in town. She'll know where to find me."

"Thanks. You've been nice."

"Forget it," he said.

He went to his car and ran his hand along the passenger door, noting the dent and the scratched paint. "Damn locals," he muttered. Finally, he got in and drove away.

CHAPTER 7

Dan Philips shifted his weight and lit another cigarette, allowing the curls of smoke to glide toward the ceiling of the darkened lobby. Ice cubes clinked in glasses in the dining room as waiters hurried with trays piled high with delectable entrees. Ten minutes had passed since Anton had entered the restaurant unnoticed, and now he watched an impatient Daniel R. Philips drag on his second cigarette in as much time.

Although twelve years had passed since college, Dan still sported his letterman's jacket, looking every bit the college football star his dossier proclaimed him to be. The rest of him was nondescript. He had dark hair, not black, not brown, and although Anton couldn't see from the distance he kept, he imagined the hazel eyes were simply another way of saying no one really was sure what color they actually were. It was good in a way. It made him less recognizable, harder to describe. Being a government operative had its problems, and being recognized was one.

Finally, Anton approached. "Philips?" He extended his hand and watched the smile drain from Dan Philips's face.

"Pavlova?" It was the sound of incredulity to which Anton had grown accustomed. He smiled benevolently while Dan's eyes assessed his small stature. "I've been watching for you. When did you come in?" Dan met Anton's hand with his own.

"A few minutes ago, when that large group came in."

"Assessing me before the introduction? Well, we don't have to be *spies* here. It's just dinner."

Anton produced his ID and exchanged it for Dan's. They eyed each other, though Dan was obviously more surprised than he.

"From everything I'd heard, I was expecting…" Dan fumbled.

"Someone taller?" Anton finished. "Didn't you receive my file?"

"Sanderson gave me a brief summary of your work. No dossier. I'll be honest, I've sent in a complaint to Procedures. Sanderson said he was sending a top agent, first string."

"I am first string," Anton replied.

Dan stuffed his cigarette into an ashtray. "Well, we should join the others."

"Others?"

"I want to introduce you to a few of my buddies. They're here. They're expecting you."

The White Horse Inn was elegant, and Anton felt it was out of place in a town of 1,400 people. The low red lamps cast their warm glow on the tables as they passed, and Anton studied the occasional face that looked up as they walked to the large table in the back.

Columns of polished mahogany were strategically placed, dividing the large dining room into more manageable private areas. Each column, from its crown molding at the ceiling to its chair rail, boasted a pristine mirror, multiplying both light and patrons. At first glance, it appeared half the town had been seated at the table, the mirror beyond transforming the handful of faces into a small crowd.

But it was the startled face of Hope that caught Anton's eye.

"That's him?" said the man seated at the head of the table, obvious disappointment in his voice.

"This is Anton Pavlova," Dan said, answering his friend. "Anton, Steven Wykes." Anton shook hands with Steven, but there was an instant dislike. Anton surmised it was his manners that needed work.

"This is my brother, Clayton. He and Steven are among Three Rivers' 'finest,'" Dan said. Unlike his older brother, Clay was quite distinctive. He was blond with large green eyes. His features were crisp and well-defined where Dan's were not. Clay shook Anton's hand and, in turn, introduced his girlfriend, Nicki.

"Pleased to meet you," Anton said, shaking her hand as well. She was pretty and Rubenesque and tall for a woman, he thought, with brown hair streaked from the California sun. She smiled, and he smiled back at her before moving his eyes to the far end of the table.

"This is Clay's partner on the force, Jeff Lansing," Dan continued, and Anton nodded in Jeff's direction.

"If your partner is a brother of my partner, I guess that makes us partners-in-law!" Jeff said, amused by his own joke.

"Yes, I suppose." Anton chuckled at Jeff's infectious grin. He had a mass of curly dark hair and eyes that sparkled even in the dim light. He wore a black T-shirt, covered by a worn brown leather jacket and faded jeans. He looked more like a rock star than a cop.

By this time, Anton had sought out Hope's face in the mirror. She had turned away, but watched him in the glass. The once plum-colored bruises had faded in the past week to a sickening yellow-brown. Her eyes were intense, pleading.

"So, you're the 'Great Pavlova' we've heard so much about?" Steven said in a robust, but disappointed, voice. "From what Dan said, I expected James Bond, not the Little Prince."

Anton could feel the others look at him expectantly. Finally, he forced a smile.

"Your reputation has preceded you," Dan said apologetically.

Anton was anxious to get the introductions over with and looked directly at Hope. He could see the terror on her face.

"This is Steven's wife, Hope," Dan said.

"I'm pleased to meet you," he said, and relief flooded Hope's face. Anton wondered if the others could see it too or if he was simply more aware of her.

The others seemed hardly aware of her at all. Her diminutive stature got lost among her much-taller friends, if friends they were. It was obvious she did not want them to know they had previously met.

Dan turned as a giant of a man approached. "You're late," he said. "Anton Pavlova, this is Noah Cavalier."

"Nice to meet you," Anton said, shaking Noah's hand. He stood six five or more and had to be at least three hundred pounds of solid muscle. His face, too, was bruised, and he wore tape over the bridge of his nose, indicating a break. Anton discovered later he was a boxer—*a man of the ring*, Noah laughingly called himself. But large as he was, Noah was the only one who had not scrutinized his size.

They sat and Dan ordered drinks around, skipping Hope entirely as he almost had done on the introductions. Anton declined the offer but looked across the table at Hope once again. She seemed to be both a young girl and an old woman. *No, tired more than old,* he thought. He had seen it before, the pallor that made her appear weary beyond her years.

Noah took the seat beside her, gently adjusting the collar of her dress and smiling benignly when she looked up. Anton watched them curiously.

"Where are you staying?" Dan asked.

"The motel for the time being," he answered, forcing his eyes away.

"Nicki is in real estate. Maybe she can help you find an apartment."

"Thank you, I appreciate it. But I've found a place. I'm just waiting for it to be ready."

"Really?" Dan asked. "Where?"

Anton sipped his water. "An apartment above a garage. I believe Myrt owns the local diner."

"*Myrt!*" Steven made her name sound profane.

Dan turned to Anton. "So, when was the last time you spoke with Sanderson?" he asked, changing the subject as the waiter arrived with the drinks.

Anton directed his attention to Hope. "Did you want something? I don't think the waiter got your order."

"White Zinfandel," she said quietly to the waiter.

"When's the last you spoke to Sanderson?" Dan asked again. "I didn't get your dossier, as I said. I had no idea what you looked like. You walked in here right under my nose."

Steven snickered.

Anton hesitated, glancing around the table at the others. "Perhaps we could discuss business another time."

Steven laughed. "Dan's going to tell us everything anyway."

"Oh?" Anton looked at Steven. "My circumstances are unique. I guess headquarters was afraid it would put you off." He finally turned to look at Dan. "I'm good at what I do, Philips. Ask anyone who's worked with me."

Dan didn't reply.

"So…Steven, have you and Dan known each other long?"

"We were kids together. Went through school. Played football at COS."

"COS?" Anton asked.

"College of the Sequoias," Dan answered, tugging at the patch on his jacket, showing it to Anton: a large, orange 'S' with a sequoia tree emblazoned over it. "I was quarterback and he was tackle," Dan said, motioning toward Steven. He grinned and shook his head. "He's a brute. Broke *more* bones…"

"Pavlova. Is that German?" Nicki interrupted.

"Russian." Anton looked at Nicki and Clay, reaching for his water once again. "My grandparents brought me here as a child."

"I wonder why I thought it was German."

Anton motioned. "Blond hair, blue eyes, perhaps." He sipped his water and looked at Hope from over the rim of his glass, then addressed Steven. "Power and strength don't come with size, Mr. Wykes, but from a quick mind."

"I see," Steven said, noting the direction of Anton's gaze. He reached over, took a piece of bread from Hope's plate, and stuck it in his mouth.

He's pissing on her, Anton thought—marking his territory so Anton would know she belonged to him. She seemed to shrink before his eyes.

"What happened to your face?" Anton asked. The silence was palpable.

"She fell," Steven answered.

"Do you fall often?" Anton asked, still looking at Hope.

"You don't believe me?" Steven growled.

"Quite the contrary." Anton finally looked at him. "I'm sure her friends would never sit back and pretend like she wasn't getting hit. You know, if she was."

"Well, she's not."

Anton smiled and leaned back in his chair in mock relief. "Glad to hear it," he said. "All I know is, if I were a woman and a man did that to me, I'd cut off his balls while he slept."

"And if frogs had wings, they wouldn't bump their asses," Jeff said from the far end of the table.

Nicki again came to the rescue. "Hope, would you go to the ladies' room with me?" She gathered her purse and rose from the table. Hope pushed back her chair and followed.

When they were out of view, Anton looked at Jeff. "Oh?"

"You're thinking from a man's point of view, one of *vengeance*. But if you were a woman, you would think differently. You would think *survival*," Jeff said. "I volunteer at the woman's shelter, and I see these women every week. You don't know what you would do if you were a woman."

Across the table, Noah appeared intense, and Anton realized why he'd been so curious when Hope had spoken to him: she had only mouthed the words, just as Clay was doing now. Clay was speaking silently, and Noah read his lips.

The boxer was deaf.

Anton rapped the table twice with his knuckles, and when Noah looked up, he mouthed the words, "Does Steven hit his wife?"

Noah gave an almost-imperceptible nod.

"I don't need this crap!" Steven rose and tossed his napkin on the table. He shoved Noah's shoulder hard. "Don't mess with me," he growled, and left without waiting for a reply.

"What happens between Steven and his wife is none of your business," Dan hissed at Anton.

"Just as what I am in my professional life is none of *his*," Anton said. "I'll not have an assignment go sour because you're busy playing 'double-oh-seven' to impress your friends."

"You don't buy into that 'secret agent' crap, do you?"

"I buy into whatever keeps me alive. And from now on, you're buying into it too."

"Is that an order from above?"

"I can make it so," Anton said, remaining calm.

"I forgot, you have a private line to Sanderson. You always get what you want?"

"When it's important. You and I are supposed to be a team, remember?"

Dan rose from the table. "Yeah, I'll try to remember that."

He walked away, and when he was out of sight, Jeff Lansing chuckled. "*That* certainly went well."

*****

Hope sat on the tufted bench in front of a gilded mirror and rested her face in her hands.

"What's going on out there?" Nicki asked, but Hope didn't answer. She sat beside her and pulled Hope's hair out from her collar. "Oh, honey, what happened to your hair?"

"Steven cut it," Hope said.

"With what, pruning shears?" Nicki dug through her purse and found manicure scissors, then stood behind Hope and looked at her in the mirror. Her hair had been chopped, shoulder length, in great uneven hacks.

"Nicki, that's the guy. Remember I told you someone gave me a ride to Uncle Nate's last week? Well, that's the guy."

"Dan's new partner? That's just great." Nicki combed her fingers through Hope's hair and trimmed it as they talked, checking it for evenness in the mirror.

"How was I supposed to know who he was?" Hope said. "I'm sure he's wondering why I'm back with Steven."

"We're *all* wondering," Nicki said.

"You don't know what it was like. It was cold and dark, and there were animals running around in the middle of the night." She shuddered. "I started a fire in the fireplace, but the flue was blocked. By the time I got it opened, I was black from the smoke. There wasn't any water to wash with. I didn't even have a broom to clean the cobwebs. The roof leaks, and there isn't any electric—"

"I would have stayed," Nicki said.

"That's what you *think*! It's easy for you to know what you would do when you have a guy like Clay! He's the nicest guy in the world." Hope collapsed into tears. "Why did Clay leave me, Nicki? He loved me once. Why did he stop?"

Nicki stroked her hair. "He still loves you, Hope. Just in a different way," she said quietly.

Hope struggled to regain control. "Look at me. I look hideous," she said, wiping her face with her hand. "I'm sorry, Nicki. You've been my best friend since third grade. I'm glad you and Clay are together, really. How can you be so nice to me when I say such things?"

"Because you've been *my* best friend since third grade." Looking at Hope in the mirror, Nicki tugged the ends of Hope's hair to see if they matched, then snipped a little more off one side. "That guy Anton has Steven's number for sure. Anyone that isn't afraid to stand up to Steven Wykes is okay in my book." She put her scissors back in her purse, then sat facing Hope. "I guess we're all afraid to stand up to Steven, and then we wonder why you can't." She found a tissue in her purse and handed it to Hope. "I'll make you a deal. Come home with me tonight. I'll talk to the guys and see if we can get a work crew together, fix up the old house enough for you to live. You know, that guy out there is right—we haven't been very good friends."

"You've always been there when I needed you," Hope said.

"No, we haven't. But I promise, if you come home with me tonight, we will be from now on."

CHAPTER 8

Myrt had outdone herself, Anton thought as he carried the last of his meager belongings up the outside stairs to the apartment. It was larger than he had expected. It was the second story over a two-car garage, which extended over a patio, where Myrt had placed a garden table and chairs. Lattice ran the perimeter on two of the open sides, and wisteria climbed to the windowsills.

Inside, the walls had been freshly painted a pleasant taupe, the trim a crisp white. The pine floor had been polished and waxed. The living room was a nice size, and the kitchen even larger. Through the living room, he found a small bedroom and bath. It was all he really needed.

Leslie had sent his belongings, which had been in storage for several years: his books, his grandmother's journals, the portrait of his grandparents. There were other things, too, nothing of real value except to him. He sat on the edge of the freshly made bed and emptied a box.

And then there was the cup.

He unraveled the newspaper that surrounded it. It was the last remaining piece of Royal Albert bone china from Staffordshire. The lone survivor of the set he had bought Catherine.

Anton lay back on the bed, remembering that evening like yesterday...

*****

Scott and Faye Bauer had arrived at seven o'clock sharp, and Anton greeted them at the door.

"If there's one thing to be said for socializing with USIB operatives, it's that they're always on time," he had said. "How are you, Faye?" He kissed her cheek and helped her remove her coat, then shook Scott's hand.

The small San Francisco apartment was modern, with white sofas and glass-topped tables and accent lighting in the corners.

"Wow. Look at this place!" Faye said.

"Catherine wanted all new things. She wanted a designer to come and 'do the place.' We didn't bring anything from New York," Anton said.

"You brought *nothing*?"

"Well, we brought a few personal items, like the portrait of my grandparents. But it's old-fashioned and doesn't really go with anything, so it's in storage."

"Where is your bride, Anton? I'm anxious to meet her," Faye said, and Anton grinned excitedly.

"She's in her room, putting on final touches. She's nervous about meeting you. Please, sit down and make yourself comfortable."

Faye sat on the sofa, while Anton went to hang her coat. Scott followed him to the closet with his own.

"Scott, did you say anything?" Anton hesitated. "About, you know…"

"Don't worry," Scott said quietly. "Faye is a kindhearted woman. She married me, didn't she?"

Anton smiled.

Scott knew Anton was nervous. News of his child bride had rendered him the object of cruel jokes and nasty rumors. The agents in the USIB were a tight, closed community and showed no mercy to those who breached its unwritten rules. Marriage was bad enough— but to a sixteen-year-old!

"How's married life?" Faye asked Anton when the men joined her in the living room.

"It's good," Anton said, but Scott knew things were far from good.

"How are the girls?" Anton asked. He had visited the Bauers many times. Their four daughters, aged three, six, eight, and ten, had won him over. They were beautiful children, he thought. He had wound up on the floor playing board games with them during his last visit.

"Fine," Faye laughed. "You really have a way with kids."

Just then, Catherine appeared in the room. She wore almost every piece of jewelry Anton had ever given her, and a sequined dress that she swore she simply couldn't live without.

Anton stood. "Catherine, you've met Scott. This is his wife, Faye."

Faye Bauer stood and reached out to take Catherine's hand. "I'm very glad to meet you, Catherine," she said, smiling.

Scott had been right. Faye was a kindhearted woman. Seeing the two of them together, Faye in her tasteful attire while Catherine stood in her garish costume, Anton was embarrassed. Catherine had applied makeup, poorly at that, making herself appear even younger than she was, as though she had been playing dress-up.

But if Faye was startled or appalled or disgusted, one could not tell by her face. Gracious—that's what Faye Bauer was.

Anton stood nervously while Faye continued to talk with Catherine until Scott tapped him on the shoulder. "Did you say you had wine in the kitchen?" he asked, barely able to drag Anton from Catherine's side. "Don't worry, they'll be fine. Faye is good with…" Scott trailed off as the kitchen door closed behind them.

"Children?" Anton croaked.

"Listen, buddy. I'm your friend, remember?"

Anton acquiesced. "I'm sorry, Scott. You don't know the kind of hell I've put up with from the Branch. Someone left child pornography on my desk last week."

"I heard."

"Even Paul has given me hell. He says that agents should never marry because it gives them—"

"Weaknesses. I know. I got the same speech when I got married."

"Is that what a wife is, a weakness?"

"Honestly? Yes," Scott said. "But Faye and the girls are also my greatest strength. They're what keep me alive. Don't listen to Sanderson. I hear he has a lady friend himself, a psychologist, here in San Francisco." Scott opened the cabinet and chose a bottle of wine while Anton dug through a drawer for the corkscrew.

Finding it, he took the bottle from Scott and began to open it. "I couldn't leave Catherine with her family. Marrying her took care of a lot of legalities."

"You haven't slept with her." It was a statement.

Anton stopped short.

"Want my advice? Stop treating her like she's your daughter and start treating her like she's your wife, or she will never come to your bed."

"But that's exactly what everyone is sayi—"

"Let them." Scott scowled. "Let them say what they will. You married her. That makes her your wife. If you continue to sleep in separate rooms, will they stop talking? No."

Anton looked away. "I'm not a pedophile, Scott."

"If I thought you were, I wouldn't let you near my children." Scott took the bottle from Anton's hand and worked the cork. "You've simply found yourself in a delicious situation, my friend. You obviously love this girl. Just take it slow. Enjoy the dance! Romance her, for God's sake—she's your wife! Stop feeling guilty. There's no room for guilt in a marital bed." Just then, the stubborn cork popped, and Scott smiled. "Easy as pie."

Anton got three wineglasses from the cupboard. "It's not as easy as you think. We have problems."

"All newlyweds have problems."

"She doesn't want children. You know me, I love kids."

"She's young. Don't worry, she'll come around. You have plenty of time for children."

Anton thought for a moment, then reached up and took a fourth glass from the cupboard.

"Give her just a little."

*****

Dinner was delicious. Their landlady, Mrs. Donovan, had outdone herself with a juicy London broil trimmed with colorful vegetables, individual home-baked loaves of wheat bread, and crisp salad. Anton also knew there was a fresh pecan pie waiting in the warm oven.

"Dinner is wonderful," Faye said.

"Thank you," Catherine said. "I made it all myself."

Anton nearly choked. Scott and Faye both knew that their landlady did their cooking.

"Well, it's delicious," Faye said without skipping a beat and changed the subject. "Isn't the china beautiful?" She held up a bread plate, examining it. "Scott gave me the same set. I just love the pattern."

"Oh? Just like this?" Catherine said.

"Yes, the same pattern. Isn't it elegant?" Faye said.

"Who would like dessert?" Catherine got to her feet and started gathering dishes. Anton, too, rose to his feet. "No, Anton, let me do it."

It was the first time Catherine had taken the initiative, and Anton sat back down, feeling a sense of pride. He knew how capable she could be.

She hurried back and forth from the kitchen a few times, the smell of coffee wafting through the air.

"Anton, she's very sweet..." Faye was saying when there came a loud crash.

Anton jumped to his feet, followed by Scott. He pushed open the kitchen door, and there stood Catherine, surrounded by broken china.

"Oh, my beautiful dishes," she said, waiting for his response.

"Let's have dessert. I'll help you clean it up later," he said. He opened the cupboard to get more plates, but none were there.

"They're all broken," she said. "We'll have to use the old ones."

She took four 'everyday' plates from a lower cabinet and carried them and the pie to the dining room, leaving Scott and Anton in the kitchen.

"It was an eight-place setting, and there are only four of us," Anton said. "How could they *all* get broken?"

Scott crouched and picked up the single cup that had miraculously survived. "You're right, Anton. You have a problem."

*****

Anton shifted the delicate cup in his hands. He rose and placed it on the dresser below the portrait of his grandparents. *Another memory,* he thought, suddenly wishing himself back in Iran. At least there, he could rely on his training, focus on a goal.

CHAPTER 9

The bell over the door rang behind Anton as he entered the Noisy Water Café. It was raining as before, but this time each of the blue-checkered tables was full. It was warm inside, and the smell of french fries and coffee filled the air. If he hadn't been hungry before, he definitely was now.

He found a single stool at the counter.

"Hello, Anton, be right with you," Myrt said as she hurried past. Her arms were stacked to the elbows with plates. He swiveled and watched as she expertly unloaded five plates full of roast chicken and potatoes. She hurriedly filled several coffee cups, then returned to Anton.

"You need help," he said. "What's good?" He gave the menu a cursory glance.

"I have help. And it's all good!" She stood, poised with her pencil and pad.

"I'll have the chicken," he said and placed the menu back in its rack on the counter. She scribbled and went into the back, where Manny labored over the grill.

When she returned, she took a deep breath. "We're busy tonight. That's good. It means the summer is coming, and the tourists." She stood, silently surveying her domain.

At length, she turned to him. "I heard what happened last week at the White Horse. Just so you know, Hope's been staying with Nicki since then. Nicki and the boys are helping her fix up Nate's place."

"That doesn't concern me," Anton said.

"Well, Hope was afraid you knew she came to the White Horse with Steven. She didn't want you to think that ride you gave her was a waste."

"It got me an apartment, didn't it?" he smiled.

Myrt was off again to refill coffees and check on her tables. Anton could tell she loved her work. Her patrons became her children, and she was the mother hen, clucking and seeing to their needs.

She went to the kitchen and returned with his food. "Well, I asked Hope to help me fix up the apartment. She painted and cleaned. It gave me an opportunity to give her a little cash to live on for a while."

"It turned out real nice," he said. "Tell me something, Myrt. Dan grew up here in Three Rivers. What was he like as a kid?"

She laughed. "He's still a kid. He's thirty-three and still wears his letterman's jacket."

"I noticed," Anton said.

"He was one of the *worst*! He and Steven Wykes used to go through town with baseball bats and bash mailboxes, that sort of thing. The fact Steven became a cop here in this little town and Dan works for the government..." Her words trailed off as she shook her head.

Myrt left him again to run the cash register. She returned after several minutes. "That was one of Hope's problems. Where do you go if you're getting hit by your husband, the cop? Anyway, she said you were nice to her the other day, and I appreciate it."

To that, Anton didn't reply.

"Between Dan and Steven, they think they own the town," Myrt continued. "I wouldn't give a nickel for either one." Myrt poured Anton more water from a pitcher. "Now, Clayton, Dan's brother, he's a sweet boy. He's always been real quiet and thoughtful about others. You know the type, hates to see anyone left out. He and Hope dated for some time, but that was way back. They were high school sweethearts. Everyone fully expected them to get married. But Clay enlisted right out of high school, and just a few months before he got back, Dan told Hope his brother had married a little Vietnamese girl. By the time Clay got home, she had married Steven."

"Why would Dan tell her that?"

"It was a joke, a prank. Like when he dropped a dead grasshopper down the back of her dress when she was in fourth grade. It's just the kind of kid he was. And Steven had always wanted to date her, so when Hope was all heartbroken over Clay, he was there to comfort her."

"That explains a lot," Anton said. Then, deciding he might as well learn about the others while Myrt was in the mood, he asked, "What about Noah and Jeff?"

"I don't know much about Jeff. I know he was at the VA hospital in Fresno after the service. Clay used to visit him there, so they must have met in Vietnam. And Noah, his people came out in the fifties from somewhere in Texas. I think he still has a sister there."

Myrt was off again, and Anton finished eating.

"Myrt, the bill, when you get a chance," he said the next time she passed.

"I'll put it on the account. Pay me whenever you think of it."

"Can you do that?" he asked.

"I own this place. I can do what I damn well please," she said, and he smiled.

"Well, I need to go out of town for a few days," he said.

"Can you do that?" she asked, giving him a look.

He chuckled. "You're a pistol."

"Honey, I'm the powder!"

CHAPTER 10

The door swung open, and Anton stood silhouetted against the dimly lit room behind him. He wore heavy leggings from his knees to his ankles, baggy gray pants, and a black tank top.

He was decidedly drenched in sweat, his eyes wild and frenzied, yet vacant, his hair dark and matted. A single drop of sweat fell from his hair and dripped off the tip of his nose.

"Hello," Hope managed, startled by the sight. Even in the warm August night, steam rose from his skin. It had a sheen as if he had carefully rubbed it with oil. "I'm sorry. I'm disturbing you. I…I saw your light." The words stumbled past her lips.

"You came to visit?" he panted.

"Maybe it isn't a good time," she said awkwardly, perplexed by the sight of him.

"It's as good as any," he said. He pushed the door wide but didn't move from his spot.

Hope looked inside, then hesitantly went in. The room was empty except for a couch and chair, a table and lamp, all of which had been pushed into a corner.

Anton closed the door and watched her curiously as she looked around.

Finally, she turned to him. "What were you doing?" she asked.

"Make yourself comfortable. I'll be ten minutes." With that, he walked out, leaving Hope alone in the room.

Her first inclination was to run. Anton Pavlova was curious and cold, she thought, and more than a little frightening. From the other room, she heard the shower start as she tried to pull the couch and chair out of the corner. She pulled the chair around to face the couch but decided not to do more.

Anton emerged, his hair still damp but neatly combed, wearing beige trousers and a light-blue shirt. He rolled his cuffs up his forearms, then sat on the couch and began putting on socks. He looked up and realized she was staring.

"Dancers have ugly feet," he said.

"Is that what you were doing? Dancing?"

"Just working out," he said. He watched her look uncomfortably around the room. "I'm sorry. Would you like something to drink?"

"That would be nice. Whatever you have," she said.

He went to the kitchen, remembering he had picked up a bottle of White Zinfandel, and briefly wondered why. He had given up drinking after his "accident." Perhaps, he realized, he had anticipated seeing her again. He returned moments later with a glass of wine for her and a tumbler of water for himself. "I understand Clay is having a birthday bash tonight."

"Yes. That's where I've been," she said.

"Weren't you having fun?"

"I went there with Nicki, but then Steven showed up. I decided not to stay."

He nodded.

"Thank you for not saying anything back in March about taking me to Uncle Nate's," she said. "It would have been a disaster."

"That's what I figured. Don't worry about it. I'm glad to hear you're doing all right."

"Where'd you hear that?"

He smiled. "Myrt."

"She's a character, isn't she?"

Anton nodded. "She told me a little bit about your situation," he said gently. "Can you tell me more?"

Something in his voice made her feel more at ease.

"My mother died giving birth," Hope said. "I think that's why Daddy had such a hard time. He drank a lot. I think he wanted to love me, but..." She took a deep breath and looked down at her flowered cotton dress, wishing it weren't so faded. At least it no longer hung on her like a gunnysack. "He sent me to stay with Uncle Nate and Aunt Stella every chance he got, and Uncle Nate would fetch Clay to come and play with me. I guess I've known Clay longer than anyone. We were toddlers together. We were born only six days apart."

Uncle Nate had made a sandbox, she continued, and roofed it with timbers from the woods and cedar shakes to protect their tender skin from the California sun. She had been a solitary child, but when Clay came to play, they'd built sandcastles, and windmills with blades made of waxed paper and toothpicks.

"Those were simpler times," she said.

But it had ended with their teenage years, she explained. Out near the barn stood a stack of hay almost as tall as the barn itself. Uncle Nate had covered it with a large tarp. One fall boredom had set in, and she and Clay had gone outside, climbed up the bales, and nestled under the tarp. It was there they had first kissed, and by the time they'd turned seventeen, they were an item. She loved him with all her heart, and everything about her was his, held in trust, understood with gentleness and compassion. Her heart had broken when it was over.

Anton went to the kitchen and brought back the bottle of wine to refill her glass. He wasn't sure if it was the wine or her apparent loneliness, but she talked. Not incessantly, but comfortably. He watched as she removed her shoes and curled her legs beneath her, and hugging one of the couch pillows, she described a lifetime of rejection. Even the way she dressed was designed not to draw attention. Her earrings were the $1.98 dime-store variety that gave her delicate lobes just a hint of sparkle without saying, *Look at me. Do you think I'm pretty?*

But she is, he thought. The bruises were gone, and she had gained just enough weight to soften the edges of her form, to round her hips and her breasts. Her cheeks were soft and pink, and he realized for the first time that she had the most sensational jade eyes.

"I must be boring you," she said after a while.

"If you knew how long it's been since I had the pleasure of watching a beautiful woman talk, you would know...no, Mrs. Wykes, you do not bore me."

"Clay enlisted without even telling me," she went on. "He never wrote. All the time he was in the service—not one letter. Then Dan told me that Clay got married. I guess he simply stopped loving me," she said.

Anton rose to his feet and pulled her up to him. With music still playing in the background, he held her close and they danced, slowly and silently. "I can't imagine anyone not loving you," he whispered.

A decade of unspent tears rolled down her face onto the shoulder of Anton's blue shirt. He stroked the fullness of her hair and pressed his mouth against her cheek, tasting them. They stood still, his arms around her.

"He married Nicki?" he asked after a while.

"No. Turns out, he didn't marry anybody. By the time he got home and I found out that Dan lied, it was too late. Steven and I were already married."

Why would Dan do that? he wondered, but didn't ask. He stepped away and motioned for her to sit. He indicated her wine, and she picked it up to sip.

"Do you like living alone?" she asked.

He leaned back in the chair and looked at her thoughtfully as she wiped away the remaining tears, embarrassed.

"When I'm called away, I never know if it's for a week or a year. It's a lot easier not to get involved," he said. "I'll tell you what—it's 4:00 a.m. Stay the night. I'll sack out on the couch and you can use the bedroom. I'll drive you home in the morning."

"Oh my gosh! I didn't realize it was that late!"

"If you'd rather not—"

"No, it's fine, if you're sure you don't mind."

*****

It was morning, and Anton stood in the living room of the farmhouse while Hope quickly showered and changed. He couldn't believe the house's transformation. She had stripped away the old linoleum and refinished the Douglas fir floors beneath, repapered, painted, and cleaned. Even the plaster had been carefully patched. The arch between the dining room and living room had been painstakingly stripped and refinished to match the other ornate trim. It was beautiful, the kind of place that so often during the holidays he had stood outside looking in, wishing it were the other way around. Now he understood why she had insisted on staying.

"I hope I wasn't too long," she said as she bounded down the stairs. She found him gazing out the French doors of the dining room.

"This place turned out beautiful," he said, turning to her. "I can't believe it's the same house."

"After that dinner at the White Horse, Nicki, Clay, Jeff, and Noah came to help me. They come every weekend now. There's not so much work to do anymore, but they still come. You know, to play cards or watch old movies, that kind of thing." She tugged on his arm. "Come on, I'll show you my own little paradise!"

The sun shone bright overhead as they walked through the small orchard, now heavy with fruit. They followed the river at the lower end, past the grape arbor and the overgrown raspberry bushes Hope's grandmother had planted many years before. Soon they came to the woods and found a narrow path that led them into what seemed like another world.

They sat silently on a fallen log, breathing in the atmosphere. The air itself appeared green as the sunshine filtered through the thick ceiling of leaves. The sound of the branches rubbing and clashing in the wind reached Anton's ears.

"Uncle Nate calls them the old men of the woods," she whispered, watching his eyes search the treetops. "When I was little, I used to sit on this log and listen. It's like invisible swordsmen up in the trees, fighting a duel."

Anton gazed at her. She possessed a quality he had never known before. He wished he could pluck it from her and examine it.

In a nearby tree, a woodpecker knocked loudly while the multitude of other birds sang. He could hear small creatures rustle the dry leaves on the forest floor. It was so unlike the bustling city where he'd grown up. "You must have loved coming to see your Uncle Nate."

"I did. He was a veterinarian and always had animals around," she said. "He became so well-known that horse breeders all the way from Kentucky sent for him. He loved everybody, and everybody loved him. He used to keep dog biscuits in one pocket and candy in the other. 'Kids and critters,' he used to say."

"He's in a home now?"

"Yes, in Monterey. I drive up at least once a month to take him to Colma, to visit Aunt Stell's grave. I'd like to take you up to meet him."

Colma, Anton thought, envisioning the sea of tombstones.

"I'd like that," he said finally.

They fell silent for a while, the sounds of the dueling swordsmen filling the air, until Hope finally spoke. "You feel out of place with us, don't you? I mean, you're more cultured and refined."

His eyes darted to anything that moved around them, and he smiled a little. "What makes you think I'm cultured?"

"Oh, season tickets to the ballet, Tolstoy, Somerset Maugham…" Suddenly, she turned scarlet. "I wasn't snooping, I swear. The ticket and books were just lying there."

He grinned. "There is nothing in my room that I would mind you seeing."

"Tell me a secret," she said.

"What kind of secret?"

"You know, the kind that friends tell. I kept you up half the night telling you mine. Now you tell me one." She smiled at him playfully.

He looked at her, "I was a danseur. When I was younger, of course," he said hesitantly.

"A what?"

"A *danseur.* I studied ballet for many years. A *danseur* is the male dancer."

A look of astonishment crossed her face.

"Do you think that's odd?"

"No. I think it's fascinating. Last night you said you were a dancer, but I never dreamed 'ballet.' Why did you quit?"

"The USIB. One can't be a dancer all his life, and when my grandparents became ill, I needed to support them. Anyway, I'll take you to the ballet sometime. Would you like that?"

"I would love it! Do you still dance?"

Anton quickly put his finger to his lips. "Shhh, I don't even want the old men of the woods to know," he whispered, then nodded affirmatively and laughed. "No one knows but you."

She giggled delightfully.

A rabbit jumped out from behind a rock, crunching the leaves as it hopped down the trail, and Anton was immediately on his feet, reaching for his gun.

"Oh my gosh!" She giggled behind her hand, and when he saw the humor in it, he laughed too.

"I have to go. I'll be out of town for a while. I'll see you when I get back," he said.

Moments later, he was gone.

CHAPTER 11

Hope leaned back in the boat and closed her eyes. Letting the warm sun bathe her skin, she hung her hand over the side and played in the cool water. It had been months since she had moved, and now she enjoyed these days spent with her friends. She smiled to herself when Jeff began to sing "Row, Row, Row Your Boat" as the oars splashed noisily in the water.

He was funny and nice and handsome. She opened her eyes a little to peek at him. He was Clay's best friend and partner, and understandably so. He was truly one of the most loyal friends anyone could ask for. She felt lucky that he and Clay had adopted her. They had really stepped up to the plate, helping her with the farmhouse. The fact that she and Nicki were such good friends made it an automatic foursome, and it was understandable people assumed that she and Jeff were an item. They had actually spent a couple of months trying to fall in love, even tried to get romantic once, with low lights, a fire in the fireplace, and a bottle of wine. But the evening had ended with them both getting drunk and laughing hysterically at each other's ghost stories. It was then he had started calling her his 'drinking buddy,' which he'd later shortened to 'Bud.'

But on this hot summer afternoon, the four of them had come to the reservoir to relax and have a picnic. Clay had given Jeff the high sign that he and Nicki wanted to be alone, and now Hope found herself drifting along on the smooth water with Jeff manning the oars.

"Hey!" Jeff shouted, and Hope sat up and looked toward the shore, where two figures waved at them. "It's Dan and 'what's-his-name!'"

*****

Anton lowered his hand and watched the little boat glide across the water. He could hear Jeff's voice faintly in the distance as he started singing like a gondolier. When Hope splashed water at him to shut him up, they began to laugh. Anton continued to watch them as he and Dan walked along the shoreline to meet them at the landing.

Once onshore, Jeff went with Dan to find Clay, leaving Hope and Anton near the water's edge.

"How are you?" he asked.

"I'm great, thanks to you. You saw how great the house looks, and now I do fun things with my friends."

Anton shook his head. "I didn't do anything."

"You started it. You woke them up," she said quietly.

"They've always been there for you. They just felt helpless until you made the decision, that's all," he said in their defense.

"Well, Clay gave me some money for a used car until I can get on my feet," she said, "and I got a job at the lodge."

"That's great!"

When Nicki beckoned her to the picnic area, she went to help start the barbecue, and Jeff joined Anton at the water's edge.

"So, what do you think of Bud?" he asked with a mischievous grin.

"Well, she certainly has changed," Anton said guardedly, and Jeff chuckled.

"Come on, you can do better than that. She's turned back into a beauty!"

Anton smiled a little. "I try to watch what I say about other men's women."

Jeff laughed outright. "Hey, Bud, whose woman are you?" he shouted toward the women.

"My own, you jackass!" she shouted back, and Jeff doubled over with laughter.

But again, Anton only smiled. "You two seemed rather affectionate," he remarked, casting his eyes toward the boat.

"Yeah, well, that's the way it is with us. Everyone assumes the wrong thing about me and Bud. It's killing my love life! It's chemistry, my friend. I go for tall redheads with lots of leg! You know what I mean?" He wiggled his brows and tapped an imaginary cigar.

"That certainly leaves Hope out, doesn't it?" Anton said, looking in her direction.

"She treats us all like brothers," Jeff continued in a low voice. "I just thought you might want to know, in case you're interested."

"I'm not looking for a relationship," Anton said.

"I'm not selling any," Jeff said pointedly.

*****

As the afternoon wore on, it was apparent that everyone was glad to have Dan back in the fold. After all, he was one of their own. Anton quietly watched while he laughed and told exaggerated stories.

Hope stood nearby, looking past Dan's shoulder at the brooding Russian, who sat on the grass away from the others.

"Ask," she said as she came and sat beside him.

"Ask what?"

"I don't know. You keep looking at me like you want to ask me something."

"I didn't realize I was so transparent." He smiled a little. "I was wondering about your husband. I assume you still have one."

He couldn't help but wonder if Steven had seen her lately, seen how beautiful she had become. He had actually begun to fear for her—fear that Steven might try to win her back, only to begin her nightmare again.

"The divorce will be final soon. Steven didn't contest it because I gave up all claim to the property." She paused. "Have you ever been married?"

"Once." It came out in a hoarse whisper, and she knew she'd struck a nerve.

"I'm sorry. I shouldn't have asked."

"It's all right," he said, looking in Dan's direction.

"You don't like him talking about work, do you?" It was a statement.

Anton shook his head. "He's not even accurate."

"We know that," she said, and he looked at her. "He said his new partner was bigger than life, that you were an assassin on a secret mission."

"Why would he tell you that?"

"To impress us. He built you up like you were the biggest, meanest person alive, as though it made him tougher just to be associated with you. I have to say, you were a bit of a disappointment." She laughed, causing him to smile.

"I suppose I was."

*****

Dan finished his storytelling and walked down the incline to the water, with Clay following behind. "So how do you like your new partner?" Clay asked as he stooped for a small stone.

"He's moody. Good at what he does, but Jesus!" Dan stuck his hands in his pockets as Clay tossed the stone into the water. "How was it with Jeff in the beginning?"

"Jeff's different," Clay said. "I've known him since we were in 'Nam. Besides, you know Jeff—he fits in wherever he goes. Give Anton time, Dan. He's different than Jeff. It's just a matter of personalities."

"I don't think so. This guy is too connected. Sanderson still won't give me his dossier." Dan walked down the shoreline, farther from the others. Clay followed and listened intently when Dan lowered his voice. "He was sent here supposedly to take a rest, but good ol' fuckin' Sanderson seems to have a hard time sitting on jobs that 'only Pavlova' can do! And good ol' fuckin' Pavlova can't say no. We've been gone on and off for nearly four stinking months, doing three separate jobs!"

Clay watched his brother's eyes flash with that old, familiar rage. "Have you told Sanderson how you feel? It's your territory. Tell him you should have senior status."

Dan assumed a smug smile. "Anton's 'his boy,' 'his pride.' Sanderson trained him himself. Grapevine has it that it's Sanderson who's holding on to his files. I heard Pavlova's crazy and Sanderson's protecting him."

Clay sighed. Dan was in his usual form. Even when they were kids, he always had an excuse, a reason to get out of situations where someone else might have the upper hand. Clay loved his brother but knew his faults. He couldn't stand the threat of someone having more power, more control.

Clay was three years younger than Dan, and Dan had always been jealous, always vied for their father's affection. Clay grew to be more quiet and reserved, allowing Dan to fill the void that came with knowing he wasn't really McClain Philips's son. In a way, Clay pitied him. Their father made no secret that Clay was the favorite; Dan was just part of the package when he'd married their mother.

The smell of bratwurst beckoned them back to the others. "Jesus, would you look at that!" Dan said.

"What?"

"Him looking at Hope like that! Just like the night at the White Horse. And she's not even divorced yet." Dan shook his head. "I know you don't like Steven, but he's still my friend."

"They're just talking, Dan. Anyway, Steven's a jerk. Hope didn't get those bruises falling down the stairs."

"Yeah? Well, I never saw any bruises. She's just a good makeup artist. She's been feeding you a line of crap, and you always fall for it. Ever since you found out she's your bastard sister, she's been able to lead you by the nose."

"She doesn't know, so how could that motivate her to do anything?"

"I don't want to hear about it!" Dan glared at his brother. "Just see to it she doesn't get involved with my partner. Having to deal with him is bad enough. I don't want her as a complication!" He walked away with his hands clenched at his sides.

"What was that about?" Jeff joined Clay, watching Dan stomp out of sight.

"Same old thing. This business with Hope will be the death of one of us yet."

"Are you going to tell her?"

"Not unless she needs to know. I promised Dad."

Jeff nudged him and said in his best John Wayne voice, "C'mon, partner, let me buy you a beer."

*****

The next two months passed uneventfully into fall, except Noah had come home, again with a broken nose and another win under his belt. He was slowly climbing the ladder of contenders in the heavyweight division.

Hope was glad to have him back. He had always been kind to her when Steven was not, and he always seemed to silently grieve over any bruises that peeked out from her clothes. But Noah no longer had reason to grieve: the friends gathered at Hope's each weekend, where there was laughter and food and games. Even Anton managed to show up most weekends. The two men rarely spoke but had developed a mutual respect. Both worked hard to keep their bodies finely tuned, and once Noah had even complimented the smaller man on his good shape.

"I work out" was Anton's reply, giving Hope a quick glance to see if she was going to tell his secret. She had given him a knowing smile in return.

Jeff's sense of humor was in top form as well. He claimed he was giving the Russian smiling lessons, and Nicki and Clay seemed to do nothing but gaze into each other's eyes, which gave Jeff an endless supply of material.

Dan was the only one who didn't hang around much, and they all quietly wondered if it was because Steven was no longer one of the crowd.

CHAPTER 12

"Can I get you something? A little cabernet?" Hope called from the kitchen.

"No. I'd better be going," Anton said as he leaned into the doorway. "Everyone else has already left."

"It's only nine. Where's it written that you have to leave just because they did? It's cooling off—would you put another log on the fire?" She looked up at him and smiled.

"Okay, maybe for a while. But don't pour me anything." He went back to the living room and stoked the fire, putting a heavy log on top.

When Hope came in, the fire was blazing, with him sitting in front of it. She sat beside him and sipped her wine. "It was fun tonight, even though Jeff's becoming a pain in the ass," she said, smiling.

"Jeff's a good guy," Anton replied. "But Noah...I think he has a major crush on you."

They sat in silence and watched the flames lick up into the chimney. Hope started to giggle, growing louder, until she was laughing outright.

"What's so funny?" he asked.

She waved him off and fought to regain control, only to burst into laughter again.

"Okay," he said, laughing, "you've got me doing it. So, what are we laughing about?"

"I'm sorry. I was just sitting here and all of a sudden got this mental picture of me and Noah...you know, together."

"What's so funny about that?"

"He's so much bigger than me."

"Don't you know everyone is the same size when they're horizontal? Steven's a big man."

"Noah's bigger."

He watched as she sipped her wine, remembering how small she had looked sitting between the two at the White Horse Inn.

She stared at the flames and eventually began telling him about the first night, when he had brought her to the house—the smells, the strange sounds, the shadows that had seemed to move in the dark, and the silence—the incredible silence that had made her realize how very alone she was. She described the emptiness, the pain of not having anyone to talk to, or laugh with, or even sit quietly in front of the fire with.

As she spoke, Anton felt she was describing something inside him, something secret, something hidden.

He suddenly felt exposed and vulnerable and had to remind himself that she was talking about herself, not him. How strange, he thought, that she could put into words the things he felt but had been unable to name.

The light from the fire flickered in her eyes and on her skin. Slowly he reached for her face, and she turned to him as he caressed her cheek. Her eyes were moist and captivating. He moved his face closer until she could feel his quiet breathing, and he gently touched her lips. He pressed his mouth to hers, tasting the sweet wine. He felt her tremble and backed away for a moment to look into her eyes, then kissed her again.

For years, his only encounters had been with strangers, women of the night. In his desperate attempts to avoid entanglements, he had forgotten the extra sweetness of knowing the woman in his arms. There was no hurry now, no rush, just the quiet breathing and the sound of his own heartbeat.

This woman was special, he thought. She had been able to describe his own emotions, his own carefully guarded loneliness, and she made it sound like poetry. It made him feel not quite as alone, not quite as empty.

Hope's arm moved over his shoulders, and her body felt warm against his chest. Her mouth was sweet and warm. He held her hand gently as he began to kiss the softness of her neck, smelling her sweet perfume. Her hair was like silk against his face. He thought of how she had laughed about Noah earlier. *We would fit,* he thought. *We would fit perfectly.*

The sound of his own breath brought Anton back to reality.

"I've got to go," he whispered, then stood and walked to the fireplace. Only glowing embers remained, and he wondered how the time had passed so quickly. "I'm sorry. I never should have let that happen," he said when he saw the hurt in her eyes.

"What's wrong?"

He sat back down beside her. "I can't get involved. My job..." He shook his head, frustrated that he didn't have the right words. "It makes involvement impossible." He closed his eyes, angry with himself. "Hope, forgive me. You're a special person, and I really enjoy our friendship. I hope that doesn't change."

He rose once again and went to the door, where he hesitated. He turned to look at her still sitting on the far end of the couch. "Hope..."

"Good night, Anton," she said quietly.

He nodded in understanding. "Good night."

*****

His apartment was like a cage as he paced back and forth, sure he would explode if he tried to be still. Years had elapsed since he had felt like this, his body aching in a way he'd long forgotten. It longed for the touching, the tenderness. He was glad he had to go to San Francisco and suddenly thought of Leslie.

He remembered the first time they had met. She was about his height, wearing a gray wool suit, looking so straight and proper. But it was the soft round face and kind eyes that had gotten to him after months of staring at her, unable to speak. He remembered how moved she'd been the day the words had finally come. He'd caught a glimpse of her wiping a tear with her handkerchief, and it had seemed easy to trust her after that. Now she was really the only friend he had.

He picked up the phone and dialed.

"Hi, Les, it's me. Did I get you up?" he asked.

"No. Actually, I just got in. Is anything wrong?" She always asked him that, no matter what time of day it was. She had a soft spot for Anton, and he knew it. He had been her first patient after she started with the USIB.

"No, Les. Nothing's wrong."

"You didn't call me at half past midnight to breathe into the phone, did you?"

"I met somebody," he said.

"That's wonderful!"

"No, it's not, damn it! We've talked about this."

"Have you been with her tonight?" she asked.

"Been with her? What kind of 'been with her' do you mean?"

"If you had *been* with her in that way, you wouldn't be calling me, now, would you?" she said. "Why don't you go back and *be* with her instead of pestering me?"

"Shit, Leslie. You're not worth a damn anymore!"

She laughed into the phone.

"She's not the type," he said. "She's wholesome, disgustingly so. She's taking me to meet her grandfather, for chrissake, and I've promised to take her to the ballet."

"When? Maybe I can meet her."

"After her divorce is final. We thought that would be best. Listen, I'm coming up early this week. I need to talk to you."

"Call when you get into town. Good night, Anton." And Leslie hung up.

CHAPTER 13

Anton arrived in San Francisco by noon the following day. He looked forward to it with mixed feelings. Leslie wanted him to talk about himself, which he hated, but at the same time, he would be happy to see her. She'd been the rock to which he had clung after his "accident" so many years ago. Sanderson had asked her once if he was "beyond salvage," and Leslie had lit into him with a ferocity no one had ever seen before.

He strolled down the San Francisco sidewalk and breathed in the aromas of the open markets, took in the sounds of the distant street musicians, cable cars, and gulls overhead. Of all the places he'd been in his life, only San Francisco had this feel, this easy pulse.

This was the city where he had brought Catherine. They had lived here during their brief marriage, although, as he scanned the buildings now, the exact location eluded him. They had overlooked Ghirardelli Square, just blocks from Fisherman's Wharf. Catherine used to stand at the window of their apartment and watch the conductors and passengers turn the old cable cars on the turntables, giggling with delight. She had loved the city too. For fifty cents, she could go all the way to Market Street and back.

Anton remembered the tiniest details of their lives, but the large, sweeping memories were gone. He felt cheated, left with nothing. All that remained was the grief of having lost someone he had loved. Catherine had become a precious cameo in his mind, and Paul had worried he would become an emotional cripple. Anton had countered it by ceasing to have any emotions at all. He'd buried himself deep within himself, embracing the loneliness that came with being a sequestered man.

*****

The reunion with Leslie was bittersweet. She hugged him as an old friend, but it didn't take her long to get to the point.

"How are you, Anton?" she asked as they settled down into comfortable chairs in her office.

"I'm fine," he said.

She picked up a nearby book and pretended to read. "Yep. Here it is." She pointed. "'I'm fine.'" She laid the book back on the table. "Textbook answer," she said, tilting her head. "You *know* what I mean."

"I'm bored, Leslie. I'm stuck in this quaint little town twiddling my thumbs with my new partner, who, by the way, is a real joke."

"You've had assignments."

"Boring ones! Why is Paul wasting my time? I'm a first-string agent."

"You'll have to talk to Paul about that, Anton. That's not why you called me in the middle of the night," she said.

He sat back, lost for words.

"I'm lonely in Three Rivers, Les," he said after a while. "It never used to bother me. I used to enjoy being alone. But some of these people who are just friends act more like lovers. It makes me feel empty just being around them."

"Sounds like you don't have to be lonely, Anton."

"Damn it, Leslie! I don't want…"

"What? You don't want a decent woman in your life because you might fall in love?"

"The only woman I ever loved is dead, goddamn it!" His eyes blazed, but Leslie sat unaffected.

"Catherine killed herself because she was weak, Anton. She was a child, for heaven's sake. Your love didn't kill her," she said quietly. "You did the best you could."

He put his face in his hands.

"I'd like you back in therapy for a while," she said. "You have a lot of unfinished business."

He was obviously troubled.

Leslie had spent years saying those same words to him. She'd watched him wrap his emotions into nice, neat packages, storing them in the attic of his mind. That he was in a quandary over this new woman gave her hope.

In a sense, Leslie felt she had failed him. He had never really dealt with the pain or the anger he felt toward Catherine for killing their unborn child. He had locked it so deep inside he didn't even remember she had been pregnant at all. And although he could not consciously remember what she had done, Leslie saw the bitterness slowly eating him away.

"Well, are you staying up here all week?" she finally asked. "What are your plans?"

"I'll stay the night. You know, find someone."

"That's not the answer, my friend."

"It's answer enough for me." He rubbed his face with both hands. "Whores don't ask questions. They don't dig themselves into your soul…"

She watched him until her gaze made him squirm. "Does this new woman know what a degenerate you are?"

"You know, I don't have to tell you anything," he said angrily.

"Why do you, then? Are you hoping for my approval?" she asked, and he got up to leave. "You don't need my approval, Anton. What you need is to find whatever it is you're looking for. Just make sure you know what that is before you waste your time looking for it in meaningless sex."

"I'll see you around, Les," he said.

"You'll see me next week." Leslie reached for her calendar and began to write. "I'm not letting you go this time, Anton. If you want to work, I want you back in therapy. I'm arranging it with Paul. I was against you going back to work the last time. This time will be different." She looked up at him hanging on to the doorknob. "If you want to get out of Three Rivers, you have to go through me."

"You're a bitch!"

"I love you too."

He started to slam the door.

"Anton," she quickly called, and the door stopped short. "Is she pretty?"

He glanced back, disarmed. "Yeah, Les. Real pretty." He finally gave her a little smile before gently closing the door behind him.

*****

Anton took pride in his work, but just as dancers' muscles grew lax without training, he didn't want the reflexes Sanderson had instilled in him to grow dull. He busied himself by watching people, learning about them, studying them. The San Francisco sidewalks were ideal for finding subjects. As the prostitutes trickled into the night, he stood leaning against the brick storefront and watched the exchange of money between the hands of strangers.

He was tense and edgy, and had promised himself he would find just the right woman in whom to bury himself, his mind, his body. It seemed he had watched for hours before he approached a woman with honey-blond hair, and soon he followed her up a flight of stairs.

He looked around the room as the prostitute closed the door behind them and she started to undress.

"No." He stopped her and ignored the look she gave. Drawing her near, he kissed her and gently ran his fingers through her hair, caressing her face and neck. Her heady perfume seemed to fill the room as he kissed her face and shoulders.

She was small like Hope, with small features and beautiful jade eyes. He smiled at her and kissed her again as his hands ran down her back, and closing his eyes, he crushed her against him, feeling her hair against his face. How sweet, he thought, wanting her, savoring her touch.

"Come on, lover boy, this is my busy hour."

He stepped away from her quickly, as though someone had buried a foot in his stomach. He watched as she hurriedly undressed and lay across the bed.

"This is what you're here for, right?"

He stared at her, sickened at the way she spread herself.

"Hey, this ain't your first time, is it?" She climbed off the bed and came to him. She stroked his face, then, smiling, placed his hand on her breast.

Anton quickly removed it.

"Look, you've already spent my time," she said. "If you think you're getting your money back—"

"Keep it," he said, moving to the door.

"Hey." She stepped closer and gently kissed him on the mouth. "You're the kinda guy I don't mind hooking up with in my off hours."

He searched her face again. *You're nothing like Hope,* he thought. *You just have the same color eyes.*

CHAPTER 14

"How's it coming?" Anton stepped up behind Hope and put his hands on her shoulders while she shook the pan over the burner. There was a pop, then another, until the kitchen filled with the sound of popping corn.

"Almost ready."

It was the first time he felt comfortable touching her. He'd often watched Jeff and Clay touch her affectionately, and she them. He had envied them the casual contact. "Hope…" he whispered so the others wouldn't hear. She'd been so moody all afternoon, and he now chided himself for overstepping the bounds of their friendship the weekend before. "Are we okay?"

"What are you two whispering about? You're going to burn the popcorn," Jeff said as he walked up and threw his arm over Anton's shoulder. Hope could feel him tense.

"It's done, Jeff. You want to get the butter?" When Jeff stepped away, she reached up and patted Anton's hand, as if to reassure him.

He had just gotten back from San Francisco that morning and had joined the others at Hope's by midafternoon. It was rainy and dreary, so they had spent the day in the house, playing cards and listening to music. He had engaged Clay in a game of chess, in which he'd shown off his amazing strategic talents, leaving Clay thoroughly frustrated.

Nicki came into the kitchen and started getting glasses out of the cupboard. "Anton, what do you want to drink?"

"Is there milk?" he asked.

"Yeah. Are you sure that's what you want?"

"He's a growing boy, Nick. Give it to him," Jeff said as he poured hot butter over the popcorn. He handed the bowl to Hope. "There you go, Bud," he said, then caught Anton's eye and signaled him into the study at the end of the hall, closing the door behind them.

"What's up?" Anton put his hands on his hips and waited for Jeff to speak.

"I heard you ask Bud if everything was okay. I take it you haven't heard."

"Heard what?"

"She's down in the dumps. She had a run-in with Steven yesterday."

"What kind of run-in?" Anton tried to keep the urgency out of his voice, but Jeff searched his face.

"He roughed her up a bit."

"What the hell does that mean?"

"She had a flat out on Black Oak Road, and Steven stopped. He pushed her up against the car and held a gun on her while…"

"While what!"

"He ripped her blouse, felt her up, that kind of thing. Mostly just scared the crap out of her. She came to the station in tears, so Clay and I spent the night here with her last night."

"Son of a bitch!" *Last night. Oh, God, where was I last night?*

"Steven knows damn well that it's his word against hers. He's a cop. There's really nothing Hope could do. Trying to prosecute something like this is nearly impossible." Jeff could see Anton was upset, and was secretly surprised. "Don't say anything to Bud, huh? She doesn't want you to know, but I thought you should."

"Why?" He ran his fingers through his hair, pushing it away from his eyes.

"Hell, I don't know. But get that look off your face before you go back in there. There's nothing you can do, and to make a big deal out of it would only upset her more."

With that, Jeff joined the others in the living room, and Anton followed.

"What's the movie?" Jeff asked as he sat on the floor next to Hope.

"*Jane Eyre.*"

"Oh, wow. A real tearjerker!"

The local station broadcast the old classics on Saturday nights, and the friends tried not to miss them. Hope sat on the floor, and Anton on the couch behind her. He occasionally reached over her shoulder for a handful of popcorn, while Jeff spent the first five minutes of the movie trying to get Noah to rearrange his big body so everyone could see.

Anton quietly looked at the friends in the darkened room, so comfortable together, so easy. He wondered if he would ever be one of them. He'd hated being sent to Three Rivers in the beginning, but looking around him now, he realized it didn't seem so bad. Even if he was different from them, these people had at least tolerated his presence.

He looked down and saw Jeff mindlessly playing with Hope's hair. "Are you okay, Bud?" Anton heard him whisper.

"Thanks for being there. I was so scared."

Jeff pulled her head onto his shoulder and put his arm around her.

"I don't know what I'd do without you guys," she said.

"Shhh," came from somewhere in the darkness.

"Damn it, Bud doesn't get divorced every day of the week!" Jeff said loudly.

Anton reached over her for more popcorn. "So it's final?" he whispered to Hope, but Jeff leaned forward to answer.

"She's free!" he said with a grin.

Anton waited until commercial, when the others scattered to the kitchen and bathroom, to lean over Hope's shoulder once again. "Why didn't you tell me the divorce was final?" He wanted to know about the other thing, too, but didn't ask.

"I don't know. It's hard to talk about, I guess."

He wanted to accept that answer but couldn't. "Is it because of last weekend?"

"Oh, no!" She turned to look up at him from between his knees, smiling. The upsets of the court date to dissolve her marriage and then the incident with Steven had overwhelmed her. Now the gentle reminder of the weekend before felt like a breath of fresh air. She wanted to reach up and kiss him, but the others were already coming back into the room.

The movie resumed, and everyone took their places. It wasn't long before Nicki began to sniffle, with Hope soon to follow. The sad movie only primed Hope's tears. She had held back all week, but once they started, she couldn't control the flood. Anton seemed to be the only one who noticed when Jeff put his arms around her and held her tight while she wept. Jeff kissed the top of her head, whispering and cooing as he wiped her tears.

Anton chided himself for staying in San Francisco that extra day. *What a waste,* he thought. He should have been in Three Rivers to lend his support. Instead, he'd been on Eddy Street.

He looked at Jeff, whose face bent down toward Hope, whispering, while sobs rose from where she cried into his chest. Anton realized the others knew full well what was going on but sat silent, politely pretending they didn't, yet in their own way, letting Hope know they were there for her.

He felt awkward, like an intruder in an intimate scene, yet warmed by the loving friends who cared enough to endure part of her pain. But mostly, he was full of self-reproach. Where had he been yesterday? He'd spent the entire day looking for a substitute, a surrogate for Hope, someone to fulfill the fantasies born the weekend before without having to pay the price. He'd put himself on the outside by his selfish whoring, and now realized a fulfillment of a different kind happening in the room around him. Nicki, Clay, Noah, and Jeff were all being fulfilled by their unselfish affection for Hope.

He nervously put his hand on Jeff's shoulder and leaned over him to stroke Hope's hair. "She's all right," Jeff whispered to him. "She'll be fine."

*****

Anton glanced at Hope, who watched the scenery go by. Two weeks had passed since the incident with Steven, and she had yet to tell him about it. He thought perhaps the long drive to Monterey would provide them enough quiet time for her to open up, but instead she seemed engrossed in her own thoughts.

As promised, he was going to meet the legendary grandfather of Hope's stories, feeling somewhat like the proverbial young man on his way to dinner to meet his girlfriend's parents. But what he expected to find in Monterey was a crippled old man whose mind and energy lived on only in the heart of the little girl who loved him, an empty man whose entire life was reduced to Hope's fond memories.

He thought of his own grandparents now, having only thought of them in passing for the last few years. He knew the heartbreak of watching the vitality of those you loved slowly drain away until there was nothing left, and all there was to do in the end was to love them and remember how they used to be. He knew how hard it was to let go.

"What are you thinking about?" He glanced away from the road, wishing she would tell him about Steven.

"About you."

He looked surprised.

"Not too many people would spend an entire weekend visiting an old man."

"I know he means a lot to you," he said.

"So does this. You're a special kind of man, Anton."

"What should I call him?"

She smiled. "He'll let you know."

When they arrived, Anton dropped her off at the door, parked the car, and rejoined her in the lobby. He felt an odd nervousness and found himself checking to make sure his shirt was tucked in and his hair combed.

"Hi, Lisa. Where's Uncle Nate?" she asked a familiar aide, who directed them to a large sunny room where many of the residents spent their time. She walked up behind a wheelchair and kissed the top of an old man's head.

"Hope, you brat! Where the hell have you been?" The old man turned the chair around quickly and grinned. Hope had been right—he was no bigger than she was. He was frail, and his skin draped over his bony frame. His hair was almost gone, but what remained of it was snow-white. Nathan's face was thin, and one could almost see the skull beneath the nearly transparent skin. But his eyes were bright and mischievous, and they carried the same amused look about them that Jeff wore.

"You look good, Uncle Nate. How are you?" she asked.

"Oh, you know me. The spirit is willing, but bones don't fly!" He laughed a great laugh, then stopped abruptly, catching sight of Anton standing nearby.

"Who's that?" Nathan asked, pointing a crooked finger.

Anton smiled politely and stepped forward.

"Uncle Nate, this is my friend Anton Pavlova," she said. "Anton, Nathan Landrum."

The old man mustered a gentlemanly posture and met Anton's extended hand. "I'm pleased to meet you, sir," Anton said, and Nathan's eyes lit up. *Sir,* he thought, unable to remember the last time anyone had called him sir.

He eyed Anton for a moment. "What do you do for a living, son?" he asked, folding his hands in his lap and cocking his head.

"I work for the government."

Nathan's eyes narrowed. "Whose?"

Anton glanced at Hope, who looked aghast. "I beg your pardon?"

The old man's eyes surveyed him, and Hope quickly spoke. "Anton's grandparents brought him here as a chil—"

"I'll answer for myself, Hope." Anton could feel the pounding in his chest as he pulled a chair in front of Nathan, bringing them eye to eye. "I am Russian born, sir, but have been with the USIB for twenty years. I have dedicated myself to the work I do for my country, the United States. I am of sound stock and character, if that is what you question." His voice remained respectful, but firm.

Hope stared at them both, crushed to the bone, until Nathan started to laugh.

"Young man, I doubt neither your loyalty, character, nor eloquence. Hope," he said, looking up, "it looks like you pick better friends than husbands. How is the son of a bitch? Are you divorced yet?"

She pulled up a chair, shocked at what had just transpired between the two men. "Yes, it's final, Uncle Nate. I've taken back the Landrum name. How do you feel about that?"

He pressed his hand to her cheek. "I only ask that you wear it well, child, just like you did before."

"Hope has told me a lot about you, sir," Anton said, trying to be social.

"You can cut the 'sir' crap. It's like new boots: you like the way they make your feet look, but they give you blisters. I'm Nathan, but next time I'll let you call me Uncle Nate."

Anton leaned back in the chair and grinned, realizing he had successfully been thrown on his well-trained ass by an old man in a wheelchair. They began to chat, and after a while, he was more comfortable in Nathan's company than he'd been with anyone in years. They discussed everything from economics to motorcycles. Anton learned about animal behavior and Nathan learned about the latest governmental policies while Hope provided them with cold drinks from the cafeteria. Other than that, they hardly noticed her at all.

"I bet they give you hell in Three Rivers with that accent," Nathan was saying more than three hours later.

Anton chuckled. "Yeah, they do. But I've made a few friends. Hope being one." He reached over and squeezed her hand.

A sly smile crossed Nathan's face. "Are you taking the room over at Rupert's?" he asked Hope.

"Yes. I called last week and told him I was bringing a friend. We've got to go, Uncle Nate," she finally said, then hugged him goodbye. She stopped at the door and turned around to see the men shaking hands before she and Anton went out to the car.

"Why didn't you warn me?" Anton asked after they got in.

"About what?"

"You let me walk in there thinking he was a crippled old man!" he said, his voice full of laughter.

"He is. He's eighty-three, and he can't walk," she teased.

Anton grinned. "He's one sharp man, Hope. I like him. I like him a lot."

He went on grinning as he drove, looking relaxed and happy. Nathan had stripped away his guard, leaving him exposed for Hope to see a part of him that few had ever seen.

*****

The sun hung low over the ocean, and the beach was almost deserted. Anton took off his shoes and socks, rolled up his pant legs, and followed Hope into the cold water. He loved watching her dance ahead of him, stopping occasionally for a small shell or a pretty stone, which were slipped into her pockets and, when they were full, into his. She looked so carefree as she twirled and danced at the water's edge, her hair blowing in the wind and floating around her face. He stood still just to watch her laugh and run, her arms spread wide to the wind as if she could really fly.

The soft pink of the sunset gave Hope's face radiance as she returned to him with another shell. She teased him as she stuck it in his pocket, his arms helplessly full of shoes. She reached up and brushed the hair away from his eyes.

He gazed at her, her hair whipping around her face and shoulders. *You're the real thing,* he thought. *No whore on Eddy Street could ever come close.* He let the shoes drop from his arms and gently touched her face as they stood in silence, afraid that words would break the spell. She reached up once more and touched the soft underside of his neck, sending a shiver throughout his entire being. He was breathless.

"Hope, don't do that, sweetheart." Barely able to speak, he took her hand and held it. "'Just friends' don't do that." He paused, not wanting it to end yet wanting to be released from her spell. "Let's get something to eat. I saw a little place up the beach."

*****

They walked in silence until they reached the café. It had a porch with peeling white paint. The building itself appeared to have once been a fishing cabin.

They dusted off their feet and slipped on their shoes on the porch steps before entering the tiny café. Looking at the menu, they realized the place only served hamburgers. Fried, broiled, grilled, with onion or without, fries on the side, unless one preferred coleslaw. But that was all.

Anton peeked over the menu at Hope and said in his best British accent, "What shall we have tonight, my dear?"

"Oh, dahling," she said, giggling, "I just can't make up my mind. Perhaps you would be so kind as to order for me?"

"Well, my sweet, would you care for a…hamburger? Or perhaps a hamburger would be more to your liking. You may have either, regardless of price," he said with a frivolous wave of his hand.

The waitress came and he ordered for the both of them in a very serious tone. When she left, they broke out in hysterical laughter, drawing frowns from the other patrons.

"Shhh!" he said, laughing, and put a finger to his lips.

"You really know how to take a girl out on the town," she teased.

"What more could you want?" he said. "Hey, how about going with me to New York in February for a couple of days?"

"Only if you take me to nicer restaurants!" She laughed again.

"I have an assignment there. Security. It's a big party, a tie-and-tails affair, ambassadors, heads of state…"

She eyed him. "You look serious."

"I am."

"Anton, I can't go to New York with you."

"Why? I'll buy you candy." He grinned. "You'll have your own room. You wouldn't have to worry about a thing: meals, hotel…I'll even buy you a dress for the ball. Just think, you could go to New York for nothing just to mingle with a bunch of international snobs! What do you say?"

Anton's eyes were full of boyish excitement. How could she say no to that? She put him off with a simple "I'll think about it."

The waitress came and set the plates in front of them. As soon as she was gone, they broke into another fit of laughter.

*****

Anton unlocked the room and checked around quickly as he entered, a habit formed over many years of training. The floor was covered with linoleum, undoubtedly because Rupert's was so close to the beach. It was practical, but ruled out a comfortable night's sleep. The room was almost bare, having only the bed, a chair, and a second-hand dresser. Hope had insisted on paying for the room because it was her grandfather they'd come to visit, though Anton would have gladly found better accommodations had she let him.

She looked at the room. It had always been adequate for her, but seeing it through his eyes, she was embarrassed. "It's not exactly the Hilton. Rupert gives me a break because he knows Uncle Nate," she said apologetically. "When I called and said I was bringing a friend, I thought he'd know I wanted two rooms. I had no idea a dumpy little motel like this would be so busy."

"It's fine," he said. "We'll make do." He wanted to take her someplace nice but didn't want to offend her.

Hope disappeared into the bathroom, and once again he scanned the room for possible sleeping arrangements. The one chair appeared to be left over from a dining room set. It was fine for dining, but hardly for sleeping.

Finally, after half an hour, Hope emerged with wet hair, wearing a threadbare terry robe and a broad smile. "You won't believe how good it feels to get the sand out from between your toes!"

She plugged in the hair dryer and sat in front of the mirror, where she became aware of Anton's reflection. She watched as he unstrapped the holster his jacket had concealed, laying it carefully on the dresser. Along with it went his wallet, comb, and watch, as well as an unnumbered amount of seashells. When he pulled his shirttails out of his pants and began to unbutton, she realized the intimacies they were sharing. It had been years since she had watched a man go through his nightly rituals, and even though she felt she should look away, she didn't.

He removed his shirt, exposing his chest and shoulders. He was lean and muscular, with the narrow hips of a dancer.

He laid his shirt across the dresser, carefully concealing the weapon. It wasn't until he removed his belt that the hair dryer fell to the floor with a crash. Anton quickly turned to her, then walked over to pick it up.

"It…slipped," she said feebly as he put it back in her trembling hand. She couldn't believe what a perfectly beautiful man he was.

"Hope, are you all right?"

"Yes," she choked.

His mind had been on Hope's untold secret all day, and now he wondered if the incident with Steven was why she looked so flustered. He'd been aware that she watched his every move, having felt her intense gaze pierce right through him. Kneeling in front of her, he looked into her eyes. "Hope, are you uncomfortable sharing a room?"

"No." *I just want to touch you,* she wanted to say. "It's just been a long day."

"Why don't you go to bed while I'm in the shower? Where do you want me to sleep?" *Might as well tackle that head-on,* he thought.

Her face turned scarlet. "Well, there's really only one place. We could put a pillow between us."

After kissing her forehead, he disappeared into the bathroom, and she got into bed, listening to the water run. When it stopped, a surge of expectation coursed through her. Anton emerged into the dark room a few minutes later, and she heard him hang his towel over the back of the chair just before the bed moved slightly. She lay on her side, staring into the darkness, the bed seeming small, her muscles aching with tension.

"Hope," he whispered in the dark, able to feel her tremble through the pillow between them.

"What?"

"Hamburgers."

*****

The full moon cast sinister shadows as the tide crashed against the rocks. Anton pulled up his collar and stared from the pier out into the night. The pier swayed slightly beneath his feet. Almost ten years had passed since the tide had carried him out into that vast sea and deposited him, barely alive, on a craggy rock.

Earlier, he and Hope had played on the beach. *Play*—a new word for him, or rather an old one resurrected. He walked back toward shore and went along the beach, thinking of Hope's hair floating on the wind, the sound of her laughter still singing in his ears.

"I'm lonely in Three Rivers, Les..."

"Sounds like you don't have to be..."

He shook the words from his mind. *Yes, I do.*

He had long embraced his loneliness as a kind of punishment to appease his guilt for Catherine's blood. It was a self-inflicted exile from humanity.

But even though his mind felt tormented, his body yearned for the warmth he had found lying beside him. Pillows. They never made good barriers. Just the touch of Hope's small foot against his drove him crazy. Just the smell of her freshly washed skin, her soft breathing, had driven him out onto this beach at night. He thought of the whore with green eyes. She wasn't the first, only one in a long line of whores, of one-room encounters that satisfied the body but not the soul. He thought about Hope's beautiful hair and the way she'd looked crumpled in Jeff's arms, the way she had felt in his own.

No more love! He shouted it in his mind as the waves crashed against the shore. But two weeks ago had been the first time he'd walked away from Eddy Street feeling dirty and cheap, and he wondered if Hope's sweetness had spoiled his vile lovemaking with the women of the streets.

It was beginning to get light, and he sat on a rock and watched as the shore birds began to stir, studying the thin line held captive between the sea and the sky. The sand turned a golden pink as the sun rose higher over his shoulder, and he looked back toward the motel. Within lay a sleeping woman he couldn't get out of his mind. He wondered what she had done to make him feel this way. But as the sun grew brighter, the answer became clear. She had touched him and made him shiver. She had watched as he undressed. She had dared to want him.

*****

"Anton." Hope's voice came from somewhere in the distance, and he felt a warm hand on his bare skin. "Anton." The warmth caressed his shoulders. Even in his sleep, the touch fed him, nourished him. *Rescued him.* "Anton, it's almost time to check out."

He turned over, fully awake. "What time is it?"

"Ten thirty. We have to be out by eleven." Hope stood beside the bed, fully dressed.

"Give me five minutes," he said.

She waited in the car until he emerged. He stood for a moment, looking down the embankment toward the sea, then got in.

"Why didn't you wake me sooner? The day is half over."

"I wanted to let you sleep. You were gone almost all night."

He wondered if she knew why, and how she would feel about it if she did. But Hope didn't ask questions and he offered no explanation.

They went for breakfast before heading home.

CHAPTER 15

In the weeks that followed, Anton's mood relaxed and he actually laughed aloud at Jeff's antics instead of only smiling inwardly. The others commented to Hope that he seemed easier to be around. He even started talking about Three Rivers as if it weren't such a bad place after all. Hope had spent a Sunday afternoon taking him for a drive higher into the mountains. They visited the Sequoias, Kings and Mineral Canyons, and by the time they returned, he saw Three Rivers as a gateway to the Sierra Nevada's instead of a dead end after coming through the hot, dry valley.

That Thanksgiving, everyone went home to be with their families. Even Noah went to his aunt Camille's in Texas to visit his kid sister, who lived with her. Dan and Clay drove their mother to Modesto, where they spent the holiday with her brother and his family. Only Anton and Hope remained in Three Rivers after Jeff left for Fresno.

Their friendship was comfortable these days. Anton enjoyed the casual touching that he had envied Jeff in the beginning, and he found himself wondering how Jeff could be so affectionate without crossing the line with Hope.

"Is Jeff gay?" he asked while they finished their Thanksgiving dishes. Hope had fixed a feast for the two of them.

"Is that why you jump every time he touches you?" she laughed, then smiled when he didn't answer. "No, he's not."

"Then why don't the two of you click? He appears to be everything a woman would want. He's funny, charming, and good-looking—don't you think so?"

"Yes, very. Not as attractive as you, of course. But then, I've never seen him without his shirt," she teased, putting a dab of suds on his chin that he immediately wiped off.

"Then what is it?"

"I've known him since he became Clay's partner, but we only really got close after I left Steven. I don't know. I guess at the time, I needed a friend more than a lover." She dried her hands on the towel Anton held.

"And now?"

"When I start taking applications, you'll be the first to know." She smiled wickedly, then went into the living room and turned on the TV.

Anton followed and settled on the couch, but he found himself watching Hope more than the movie, remembering bits of conversations from the summer, especially the night of Clay's party. She had grown since then, matured in a lot of ways. He could feel the time drawing near when she would be ready to say yes to a man, and he feared it. He feared that some man, maybe Jeff, would take her away from the comfortable relationship they'd formed.

"What were you and Nicki talking about last week?"

She looked at him, realizing he wasn't watching the movie. "When?"

"You and Nicki spent an hour powdering your pretty noses. Everyone knows the bathroom becomes a conference room anytime there's more than one woman in it."

"Girl talk." She turned once more toward the television.

"And just what is it girls talk about?" he pressed.

"Boys."

"Whose, yours or Nicki's?" he asked, and watched her get up and go to the kitchen for another glass of wine.

"You want some?" She held the bottle up, and he shook his head.

"Whose?" he asked again when she returned.

"Mine."

"Anyone I know?"

"Anton, why do you want to know?"

"I just want to know who you talked about, that's all."

"You. I told Nicki how nice you look without your shirt and how I made a fool of myself lusting after you."

"And what did Nicki have to say about that?" he asked, amused.

"She said I'm in my prime at thirty and there's nothing more natural than a good, healthy lust now and then!" Hope roared and went back into the kitchen.

This time, he followed. "Hope, don't drink so much." He gently took the bottle out of her hand and set it down.

"I've only had two glasses."

"I'm not worried about how much you've had. I worry when you use alcohol to help you talk. Which words scare you, Hope? That you're thirty? That you lust?"

He had pinned her between his arms at the counter. He was right about the wine, and she wondered how he knew. "What are you smiling about?" she finally asked.

"You're blushing," he laughed. Normally, she wouldn't even say the word *lust*, much less admit being capable of it. "Do you lust after Jeff?"

"Really, Anton, you're becoming a bore. Of course not, he's just a friend."

"I thought *I* was just a friend."

She didn't answer, and he realized he'd pushed them both onto unstable ground. The night he'd spent on the beach only reaffirmed that friendship was all he could afford. He adored her, but right or wrong, he feared loving her. Going back to Monterey had only reminded him of the pain from the last woman he'd loved. He wished he hadn't started the conversation.

Hope reached up and kissed him gently, and he could feel the walls come crashing down around him. He felt her arms encircle his shoulders, and in his mind, he heard a voice cry out for help. But her mouth was moist and sweet, and just feeling her breath on his face triggered his arms to enfold her.

"I'm sorry," he said. "It can't be like this between us. I've told you that." Breathless and a bit angry, he finally pushed himself away.

"Forget this ever happened." He quickly left the house, with Hope still standing beside the kitchen counter.

*****

Anton had just dozed off, after having spent most of the night wrestling with himself, when the phone rang. It was Sanderson. Scott Bauer had been killed in Iran, and Anton was to take over the assignment there. The whole world knew that hostages had been taken only weeks before. What they didn't know was that some documents thought to have been shredded had, in fact, not. It was up to Anton to smuggle them out of Iran.

As he hung up, he felt sick. Scott was one of the few good men left in the USIB, and the only one who'd successfully balanced the life of an international spy with that of a good family man. They had been partners. Anton knew his wife, Faye, had known their four eldest daughters from the time they were small. Their angelic faces stuck in his mind now as he packed and left Three Rivers in the night.

Upon his arrival in New York, Anton was given the files he needed to study. The case was explained to him in great detail, and he blocked out of his mind anything that would distract him from the job he had to do. After all, it was now his job to do that which Scott Bauer had died trying to do.

He could feel the adrenaline pumping into his blood, readying his body and mind, awakening his senses as he prepared himself mentally. It was like old times, he thought, the excitement of a known danger coming face-to-face with the skill and bravery of one man. He realized how sleepy he'd been in Three Rivers with the milder, quieter jobs. They never gave him the rush of excitement that he felt now as Sanderson walked briskly beside him, filling him in on vital details.

They hurried along the darkened corridors, whispering names and places. He was stopped and cleared, then went to be examined quickly before being put on another flight, this time out of the country. In less than eight hours, he was on a jet to Tel Aviv. From there, he would be smuggled into Iran. He took a moment to look in his hand. "I pray you never need this, my friend," Sanderson had said as he pressed the small packet of cyanide into his palm.

*****

It was the day after Christmas when Anton arrived back in New York, his head held high as he turned over the documents for which he had risked his life. Sanderson was pleased. He hadn't lost the touch, he thought, and offered hardy congratulations on a job well done. Unfortunately, that was all the pomp he could afford Anton; after all, this wasn't the sort of business the US government liked to broadcast. But Anton understood. It wasn't the recognition he sought, but the honor.

As always, after such heavy assignments, he wanted to spend a few hours with Leslie to clear his mind. She always helped him become just a man again after the calculating spy he had to become on assignments, and now he looked forward to it. He was exhausted and felt a few days in San Francisco would do him good. On the flight back to the West Coast, he found his mind turning to Eddy Street. Full of tension and anxiety, he was anxious to bury himself.

After seeing Leslie, he did just that. He put on the face of a stranger, a man without a name, and stalked the San Francisco night.

But the next morning, he felt empty and couldn't explain the wretchedness he felt. As in October, he felt dirty and cheap. Somehow the sex seemed empty and crude, leaving him wanting something more than the women there could provide. There was no longer the release, the relaxation afterward. Perhaps there was still too much tension from the job, he thought, allowing his mind to drift to Hope.

What a dilemma she had created in his well-ordered life. She had made him care, bringing him both joy and pain. Her friendship had come to mean too much. If only he could find a way to contain it. These last few months, it had grown impossible to be with her and not want her. She was such a mixture of experience and innocence, having survived her marriage, and now she seemed to wrestle with her own sexuality.

He became aware that just the thought of her relaxed him, fulfilled him, gave him what he couldn't find with the whore the night before. He now realized there was nothing left for him on Eddy Street.

CHAPTER 16

"Here, my friend!" Hope handed Anton a large glass of milk. "Are you sure you wouldn't like something more festive for New Year's Eve?" She was obviously happy he was back.

"No, thanks. How many of those have you had?" He tapped the side of her glass.

"I don't remember," she giggled. "Maybe a few more than I should. Do you mind?"

"Not if your head doesn't." He shook his head, chuckling. There had been several conferences in the bathroom between her and Nicki, and he laughed quietly when Jeff threatened to lock them in if they did it again.

He remained quieter than usual, as he'd been in the beginning. There was always a period of withdrawal that followed a difficult assignment. For now, he was content to lean against the doorjamb, drinking his milk. He felt a need for stillness in the New Year's Eve commotion that flowed around him, the laughing, the dancing, the loud music. He hadn't moved from the doorway in over an hour, and the others were beginning to step around him like an oversized piece of furniture.

He laughed to himself when Hope grabbed Nicki for another conference and Jeff wouldn't let them in the bathroom. He wondered what it was about this time, recalling the conversation from over a month before. He was a little concerned about Hope's drinking, knowing she'd had at least four glasses of whatever it was. She couldn't weigh more than a hundred pounds, and he knew it was too much.

Nicki came back into the living room and switched the record. "You'd think that among four men, we girls could find someone to dance with!" she exclaimed, pulling Jeff to his feet.

As they danced, Anton glanced at Hope. She sipped her drink, then set it down and walked toward him. "Aren't you going to ask me to dance?" Her words were slurred.

"Maybe you should sit this one out," he said.

Rejection flooded Hope's face. She went to Noah and pulled him to his feet without a word.

"Hope is drunk," Anton said to Clay, who stood in the doorway beside him.

"We're all drunk," Clay replied, "except you." He watched Anton's eyes follow Hope as she danced wildly around the room. Noah sat back down, but she hardly seemed to notice. "She's okay. She doesn't get to blow off steam very often. You worry too much."

"Why didn't she ask you? She knows you would have danced with her."

Clay smiled uncomfortably. "Don't pry into things you don't understand."

"There used to be something between you..."

"Something," Clay said quietly.

Anton opened his mouth to pursue it but was interrupted by a loud whoop. Hope was doing the bump and grind, twisting unabashedly. She'd discarded her shirt, revealing the thin camisole beneath. She turned to Anton and fixed her eyes on him. She moved her hips seductively to the beat of the music, her tight jeans accentuating every move she made, every curve of her body.

Loud hoots and whistles rose from the other men, obviously feeling the same excitement that Anton now struggled to control in himself. She smiled and laughed seductively as her small breasts moved freely beneath the silk. All inhibitions had fled. Anton felt warm just watching, and now the seductress held him captive with her eyes.

He knew the alcohol was allowing her to be something she was afraid to be: sensual, lusty. He felt himself perspire, and it was hard to catch his breath. *She's beautiful,* he thought, suddenly very thirsty, unable to swallow.

Finally, the music ended and the men whistled and clapped. Hope bowed low, then stumbled into the kitchen as another song began.

Anton followed. "Let me help you. What do you need?"

"I'm thirsty," she panted. "Fix me another drink?"

"Here, I'll get you some nice, cool water." He propped her up against the counter by the sink and reached around her to fill a glass. Their legs were tangled, but he didn't dare give her more room, for fear she would fall.

"Did you like watching me dance?" She swayed slightly and grinned.

"Very much." He laughed at her. "I didn't know you had a seductress in your closet."

"Did it upset you?"

"Upset me?" He handed her the water and tried to keep her balanced enough to drink it. "No, it didn't upset me." He smiled and got a glass for himself.

"Did I excite you?" she whispered, playing with the buttons on his shirt. She unbuttoned the top three and put her hand inside, caressing his chest.

"You know damn well what you've done to me."

She reached down and cupped the hard bulge through the denim of his jeans. The warmth of her hand made him respond.

"Hope, don't do that, sweetheart. It's very difficult to be your friend right now."

"Maybe I don't want you to be my friend. I'm taking applications, Anton." She reached up and touched his mouth with her fingertips, stroking his cheek, kissing his neck. He felt a shiver race through him. He took her hand and kissed it, then held it tight to escape the feelings that imprisoned him.

"I'm drunk."

"Yes, you are."

"Are you mad at me?"

"How could I be mad at you for anything, Hope?"

She stumbled over his feet, and when he grabbed her, she flung her arms around him. "Anton, someday when I'm not drunk, I'll tell you how sexy you are." She grinned devilishly. "I'd like to kiss you for New Year's. What time is it?" She squinted at the clock.

"Three past midnight," he said.

"We're late!" Her arms wrapped around his neck, and she kissed him hungrily on the mouth.

He thought of the emptiness he had felt when he left San Francisco. Yes, this was it. This was the missing ingredient. All the whores in the world couldn't do for him what Hope did for him now. Somewhere in the back of his mind, he knew music blared. But he could not hear it. He could only hear his desperate breaths, the beautiful little moans that rose from Hope's throat.

He tried to unwrap her arms from his neck. "Hope…" he began breathlessly. "Hope. Let me take you up to bed."

"I'd like that," she said, invading his mouth.

"You've had too much to drink, sweetheart." He looked up to see Noah watching them from the doorway. "Help me get her upstairs, will you?" he said quickly to cover the awkwardness.

They coaxed Hope upstairs, where she fell into bed fully dressed. Anton stood back and watched curiously while Noah gently unbuttoned her jeans and slipped them off. He covered her with the blankets, then bent over her and kissed her face.

Anton turned and went down the stairs. He didn't stop until he was outside in the cold night air. He breathed deeply, only to discover that Noah had followed him out.

"She's pretty plastered," Noah said after a while.

"No doubt about it." Anton turned his face to the black sky and took another deep breath. "The air feels good out here."

But Noah didn't hear. He touched Anton's shoulder to remind him. "She wanted you to sleep with her," he said when Anton turned.

"She's drunk. She doesn't know what she wants."

"It's when she's drunk that she does."

Anton looked at the big man. He appeared gargantuan in the moonlight. "It's not like that between us."

"Isn't it? You better wake up and smell the coffee."

"What do you mean?"

"I'm in love with her," Noah said. "Problem is, it's you she wants. I know that now." Unable to look at Anton anymore, he turned to stare out at the night, his hands on his hips.

"I was so happy when she finally left Steven," Noah said after a while.

Anton took a few steps and touched his arm. "I thought you and Steven were friends," he said when the boxer finally looked at him.

Noah chuckled sadly. "Dan is Steven's friend. The only reason I was ever friends with that bastard was because I was in love with his wife. If I wasn't his friend, do you really think he would have ever let me near her? Let me tell you what kind of man Steven is…" He turned to face Anton fully, his eyes narrowed. "He's a selfish son of a bitch. He didn't want her, never even loved her. He just needed someone to use and possess. It made him feel like a big man to have someone to control."

Anton was in shock. "Have you told her how you feel?" he asked, realizing he was holding his breath.

"And have her pity *this* big ugly mug?" Noah pointed to his face. "I'd rather just be one of the guys, unless I really thought I had a chance."

"Do you want me to back off? Maybe not hang around so much?" Anton hated the thought, but after tonight, perhaps that was exactly what he should do. Things were getting out of control.

"No," said Noah. "I would never take anything away from her that she wanted, and right now, that appears to be you. But keep this in mind: I'm right behind you. I like you, little Russian, but if you screw this up, I won't give you a second chance."

*****

Anton lay awake that night. No matter how many times he went to his window, he couldn't get the picture of Hope out of his mind. It baffled him that she could be so timid and yet, when her inhibitions were lowered, so sensuous. It was as though while part of her tried to crawl deeper inside, another part, the one that had tried to seduce him, was screaming to get out. He smiled to himself, thinking of the

Hope in Monterey. She had trembled right through the pillow, and only a fit of laughter could relax her enough to sleep.

Had she slept? *"You were gone almost all night."* He wondered if she had been awake when he'd tiptoed out with his shoes in his hands.

But that was beside the point now. The question was what he would have done tonight had they been alone and Hope a little less drunk. She made no pretense about what she wanted. Each time he was with her, they seemed to become a little more involved, and wasn't that what he had successfully avoided for the past ten years?

It wasn't a game anymore. Anton pictured Catherine lying beside him. He'd waited months before making love to her, and then only two months later, he'd been called away on the assignment that had taken him away from her forever. He couldn't live through that again.

*****

It was Hope's company that he missed the most in the weeks of solitude that followed. *I should be used to it,* he thought as he watched the children play on the street outside his apartment. It was how he'd lived for years, but now it seemed emptier than before.

He returned to his chair and picked up the book he'd been reading, but found his mind wandering when the phone rang. He placed his hand on the receiver and took a deep breath before picking it up. "Hello," he said, but there was only silence, then the dial tone droned in his ear.

As he had over the past few weeks, he replaced the receiver and fought off the impulse to call her back. He couldn't help but wonder if she was checking to see if he was away, or if she was simply at a loss for words.

He missed her terribly. He missed the companionship, the long talks, the look of understanding in her eyes when he told her things that he'd never been able to share. He blocked it out of his mind now and retreated back into the isolation from which he'd come, feeling neither happiness nor sorrow, neither pleasure nor pain. Back he went into the world of feeling nothing. Back where it was safe.

CHAPTER 17

Anton sighed wearily as he took the Monterey exit off Highway 101. Five weeks had passed since he'd seen Hope, and he was just beginning to feel his old self again. He was cool and detached, as he had been in the beginning. His life once again revolved around his work, his books, and his weekly trips to the bay.

He patted his breast pocket and pulled out the postcard he had received from Nathan the week before, feeling a bit irritated. "See me" was all it said.

Upon arriving, he was directed by an aide to the activities room, where he found Nathan hunched over a serious game of chess.

"Hello, Nathan," Anton said in a cool voice as he sat in a chair a few feet away.

Nathan didn't look up. He moved a bishop forward, then smiled at the white-haired gentleman across from him. "Charlie, could we do this another time?" he asked, and without a word, Charlie got up and left.

"I wondered if you'd come," Nathan said when Anton took the seat across from him. Nathan set up the board for another game, then moved his queen's knight forward before he looked up again. "How are you?"

Anton moved a pawn. "I'm well. You?"

"Got a pain in my neck."

"I'm sorry to hear that."

Nathan finally looked up. "It's turning into a pain in the ass."

Anton smiled, realizing the complaints of the old man had nothing to do with physical discomfort. "What's up, Nathan?"

"How's Hope?" Nathan asked, making another play.

Anton studied him, wondering if this had been Hope's idea. "I'm not seeing her anymore," he said.

"I know. She wrote. I'd think more of you, son, if you had told her that instead of just disappearing."

Anton looked out the window for a moment, wondering why he'd come. "It's not easy," he said.

"You don't look like the type of man who expects things to come easy. Did you expect this to be? If it hurts so much, maybe it's worth fighting for."

Hurt? No, it doesn't hurt. I feel nothing. "It's complicated," Anton finally managed. He moved a pawn, exposing his king's bishop.

"You want to tell me about it, son? Uncle Nate's got open ears and a heart to match."

"What did she tell you?"

"That you don't want to be her friend anymore because she got drunk and made a royal ass of herself. Now"—Nathan leaned forward in his wheelchair—"I don't think that's true, do you?"

Anton sat silent, staring at the chessboard.

"You want to tell me what's really going on?" Nathan prodded.

"Was this her idea?"

Nathan shook his head. "She would be mad as hell if she knew I wrote you. But when you're an old man like me, you can be nosy and get away with it. Last time I saw her, I asked about you and she said you didn't want to see her anymore. She told me she'd made advances toward you. Are you going to stop being her friend because of that? If you don't want that kind of relationship, fine. But *tell* her! Let her know what the rules are instead of getting all moody because she crossed the line."

"You underestimate your granddaughter."

The old man sat back, awaiting a better answer.

"It's my work. My work dictates that I shouldn't get involved, not my body. Of course I have desires. But it wouldn't be fair to Hope to get involved."

"And you desire her? I see." Nathan nodded to himself. "You aren't in control because you want the same thing she wants. So you are willing to throw away a perfectly good friendship because desire got in the way. By the way, that's bullshit about what your work dictates. How long have you hidden behind that one?"

Anton threw him a cold glance.

"Never mind," Nathan continued, "you can tell me about it some other time. Now, listen, I don't approve of the way she acted, but hell, the girl got a little spicy. I bet *you* never did anything like that." He cocked his head, waiting for a reply.

"You don't understand," Anton said. "It's more complicated than that."

"My guess is…you've got a ghost."

Anton stared, momentarily dumbstruck. "Sorry?"

"A ghost. A ghost! You know, one of those things that should be dead and buried but keeps hanging around. You got one?"

Anton sat back.

"I really hit on something, didn't I?" Nathan threw up his hands. "God help me! Son, I understand this much: She scared you. You're afraid you'd lose control and start to really feel something. Saying *no* was too hard, so you ran away instead." He paused for a moment, then continued in a softer voice. "Now, listen, I know that all this is very real, but I want to give you food for thought, then it's up to you. I love that child." He reached out and touched Anton's hand. "And I know how much your friendship means to her. And I think her friendship means a lot to you too."

Anton looked at the thin hand covering his. "You know it does," he heard himself say.

"How much?"

"I couldn't put a price on Hope's friendship."

"You already did. You threw it all away because you're afraid you might not be able to keep your pants on."

They stared at each other.

"That's what it boils down to, is that what you think?"

"I'll tell you what I think. I think some woman kicked you in the teeth once and you're too scared to fall in love again."

Anton jerked his hand away from Nathan's and rose to his feet.

"You had to do it, didn't you, Nathan! You had to keep going until you pulled me apart. Well, she died, goddamn it! I loved her and she died!" He could feel himself shake, but Nathan remained calm, much the way Leslie did during his outbursts.

"Yeah, that's a tough one." Nathan sat back and scratched his chin. "My Stella, she died too. She was my world. Had the damndest habit of…" He looked at the trembling man standing over him. "You act like your love could have kept her from dying, but that's not how it is, Anton. People die, no matter how much we love them. I loved my Stella with all my heart. She died anyway, just over ten years ago. Funny thing, the day we buried her, there was a young man at a nearby grave. I heard him crying all through Stella's service. Tore my heart out 'cause I knew just how he felt. Looked a lot like you, son. In fact, it *was* you."

"What makes you think it was me?"

"I thought I had seen you before when we met. There was another man there too. Hope and I gave him our condolences on our way to the car."

Anton lost all color as he took the seat across from Nathan Landrum. He looked at his hands and put them in his lap when he saw they trembled.

"Now," Nathan continued, "if you value Hope's friendship, talk to her. Set rules and make her abide by them. Right now, she's embarrassed, ashamed. Don't leave her feeling like that."

Finally, Anton spoke. "Does Hope know it was me at the cemetery?"

"I wasn't even sure until she took me up to visit Stella this last time. I looked at the name on the stone where you were. It said 'Catherine Pavlova, Beloved Wife.' Don't worry, Hope didn't notice. But when I knew it was you, I knew we needed to talk."

"Are you going to tell her?" he asked.

"No. That's for you to decide."

Nathan looked at the chessboard. "Your move."

Anton took Nathan's bishop and looked up when the old man started to speak.

"Do you know why they all call me Uncle Nate?"

He shook his head.

"It's because everybody's children used to come to me for candy, cookies…free advice." He smiled warmly. "I always sort of adopted all the kids growing up in Three Rivers, kids whose parents were getting divorced, or whose dog had died. But they had one thing in common. They didn't have anywhere else to go, anyone to talk to, anyone who'd listen." He took Anton's hand back in his own. "I will listen, Anton, when you are ready to talk."

"Am I one of your strays, Uncle Nate?"

"That's up to you, son. Someday, you can tell me about the cemetery. But right now there is something you *have* to do. Talk to Hope. Poor thing thinks she's committed the sin of the century, just 'cause she thinks you're sexy, whatever the hell that is anymore." He winked. "But you've got to set her straight. There is nothing wrong with what she feels. She doesn't know that you're struggling too."

Anton took a deep breath and sighed. "I bet you were a hell of a man when you were in Three Rivers."

"I'm a hell of a man now." Nate smiled. Anton rose to leave, but Nathan held on. "Listen, son. Burying your heart won't make your wife live again. It will only make you die a slower death."

Anton reached down and moved Nathan's queen. "It's checkmate, Nathan. You won."

*****

"Haven't seen you in a while. Where ya been?" Jeff's voice filtered into the kitchen, where Hope and Nicki were putting together the usual snacks.

"Who could that be?" Nicki wiped her hands and peeked into the living room. Jeff had records scattered over the floor, and he and Anton stood in the middle of the mess. "Your friend is back," Nicki said, giving Hope a glance as she resumed putting cheese on the homemade pizza. "Why don't you just tell him to go to hell? Besides being cute as a bug, I don't know what you see in him."

Hope went to look into the other room for herself. Noah and Clay were locked in a game of poker, while Jeff and Anton stood together, talking quietly beneath the music, Anton holding a pie.

When he looked up, he smiled, but the smile faded when he saw her icy glare.

She had gotten a job at the women's shelter and had just come off an exhausting week. Two women had been terrorized by their husbands, and when the police had come, Steven was among the uniformed officers. Hope had been grateful that Jeff and Clay were also there. But the incident had left shattered windows and frightened women. Hope had had to pick up the pieces for both of them, too tired to do the same for herself.

"Hope, would you stick this in the oven?" Nicki handed her the pizza when she came back into the kitchen. Anton came to the doorway, and Nicki looked at him. "Have you been on assignment?" she asked, taking the pie from his hands. She knew he hadn't, but wondered if he would lie.

"I've been around," he said loud enough for Hope to hear. "Everybody needs a little time to themselves."

"Go for the throat," Nicki said over her shoulder to Hope. Anton frowned as she left the room.

He stood for a long time without acknowledgment. "Aren't you talking to me?" he asked after watching her move around the kitchen in silence. He couldn't understand the fury that was ready to explode inside her.

Finally, she turned. "At first, I was ashamed of how I acted on New Year's Eve," she began. "All the next week I put up with Jeff and Clay teasing me, and they didn't know the half of it. I had this nice, neat apology all worked out in my mind, and you didn't even have the decency to face me. You were so self-righteous and judgmental. You condemned me without so much as a hearing. Now you come strolling in after five weeks with a pie in your hand, like some damn peace offering!"

Anton hated to argue where everyone could hear. "Can we go somewhere we can be alone?" he asked.

"No."

"Okay, let the world hear! I'll tell you what it's been like for me these past five weeks..."

"I don't care. That was your choice!"

He stepped forward abruptly, reaching out.

"Don't!" she screamed.

It was a mortal blow. "My God, Hope…"

Instantly, Clay, Jeff, and Noah appeared in the doorway. Hope had backed herself into a corner.

Without a word, Anton pushed past them and went to his car.

"Anton!" Jeff followed him out of the house and knocked on the driver-side window until Anton rolled it down. "There's a lot you don't understand. A lot of this is not meant for you. Things happened at the shelter last week. It makes her crazy. Don't leave."

He stared straight ahead, not wanting Jeff to see his torment. "Yeah, well, there's obviously a lot about me that she doesn't understand. She thought I was going to hit her!"

"Were you?"

Anton turned to him. "How could you even ask me that?"

Jeff shuffled his feet and glanced back toward the house. "You must have scared her. She knows in her heart you wouldn't hit her, but sometimes…sometimes she regresses. You know what I mean?"

"No."

"Damn it, man! You are one hardheaded son of a bitch! Don't you know she's still scared? She didn't see *Anton*, she only saw a man. The reason she wouldn't go somewhere more private is because Steven never hit her in front of us."

"That doesn't have anything to do with me."

"If you're getting involved with her, you'll find out how much it does have to do with you by virtue of being a man. You've got a hell of a lot to learn about that woman."

"Who's going to teach me, you? You seem to know an awful lot about her. You've cried for her, argued for her…what else do you do for her?"

Jeff's face turned to stone. "I should punch you in the mouth for that. You and I need to talk. Be at Kelly's tomorrow at noon."

Anton revved his engine and sped down the driveway, leaving Jeff in his dust.

*****

The apartment was dark except for the dim lamp on the table beside the chair where Anton sat. The green silk of his kimono enfolded him as he stared into the darkness, looking much like the honored guest in a royal Japanese household: his bare feet crossed at the ankles, his chest peeking out of the exquisite garb. The stillness of the room seemed to forbid any movement he made. Even the slightest movement of an arm produced the whisper of silk on silk as the copious fabric of the sleeve found a new place to rest.

He sat motionless, hardly breathing as the image of Hope backed into the corner played over and over in his mind. At first, he tried to convince himself he didn't care, but the attempts were futile. He had gone there to work things out, only to leave things worse than ever. Now he wondered if they would ever resolve their problems or if it was over. He wondered when it had actually begun.

Thinking of how it would feel never to see her again made the recent ache in his stomach more pronounced, and his head pounded. The voluntary exile had been hard, but after seeing Nathan, he missed her all the more. He wished he could go to her. Tell her. Hold her.

He tried to remember what Jeff had said. More importantly, what had he meant? He wondered if Jeff really expected him at the local café at noon. He shouldn't have taken his hurt out on Jeff. He had only tried to help. But the others had looked threatening when they'd appeared in the doorway, so quick to jump to Hope's defense. In a way, he was grateful for their loyalty to her, but it had pitted him as the enemy, and he hated that.

When the clock struck one, the whisper of silk rose to his ears, and the dial tone blared out into the silent room. He dialed. "It's me," he began when she picked up, but beyond that, he was at a loss.

"That was an ugly thing you said to Jeff. He's been too good a friend to both of us to be treated like that. Even if there *was* something between us, what would it matter to you?"

But it would matter. It does matter! "I'm sorry. I was upset, and I took it out on him." He closed his eyes, wishing she would say something kind. The wound she'd inflicted was still open and painful. He prayed for kind words to help stop the bleeding.

"Are you there?" came her voice.

THE PEBBLE AND THE MAN

"Yes," he whispered. "Tell me you know I would never hurt you."

"What are you talking about? Of course you would never hurt me."

He looked at the receiver. It didn't make sense. Was that what Jeff had tried to tell him? She didn't seem to remember.

"Hope, are you all right?" he asked. "What do you think happened tonight?"

"When?"

"When I tried to put my arm around you."

"You hadn't been around for five weeks, so I pushed you away because I was mad."

Something was very wrong. But at least she didn't view him as a threat.

"I'm sorry, Anton," she continued. "I've been under a lot of stress lately, and after I acted like such a whore on New Year's—"

"No!" he shouted. "You didn't act like a whore. And don't you ever, *ever* say that again!" He jumped to his feet, clutching the phone.

"Anton, why are you so upset?"

"Hope, you didn't do anything wrong on New Year's. You were beautiful." The memory of her dancing took his breath away. "Saying no is the hardest thing I've ever tried to do. I've wanted you more than I've ever wanted anything. I had to stay away because I couldn't think straight when you were making me crazy like that. Don't you know what a struggle I have every time I see you? That's why I've stayed away, Hope. Not because of anything you've done."

He'd found his voice again. But there was silence at Hope's end.

"New York's only two weeks away," he continued. "Are you coming with me?"

"Maybe it's a bad idea," she said.

"Why?"

"Anton, I was upset when you stayed away. But now that I know why you did, I wonder if New York is a good idea."

"Right now, the only thing I'm sure of is that I want you with me in New York." A long silence followed, until he wondered if she'd hung up. "Hope?"

"I'm here." Her voice was faint and small. "Do you have any idea how I feel about you?"

"I have an idea."

"Don't you think it would make New York a little difficult?"

He longed to reach through the phone and caress her. "Take a chance with me." He closed his eyes and leaned his head in his hand, waiting for her answer.

"I'll have to let you know."

There wasn't much more to say, yet neither wanted to hang up. Even in the silence, the phone provided a link they hated to break.

"Let me know soon, will you?"

"I will."

*****

Jeff watched Anton as he wove his way to the back booth of Kelly's. "I wondered if you would come," Jeff said as Anton slid into the seat across from him. "I've ordered lunch."

"I owe you an apology."

Jeff nodded his acceptance and looked him in the eye. "It's hard, isn't it?" he said.

"What?"

"Being the outsider among people who know one another so well. That's how I felt when I first came to Three Rivers." Jeff paused. "I knew Clay in 'Nam. I got hurt and was laid up at the VA hospital in Fresno for a while. Clay would come and visit me there. My family was driving me crazy to become a priest, so after I got out of the hospital, I came here. Close enough to my family yet far enough away." He smiled. "At that time, the population of Three Rivers was about as big as my family. They all knew one another, knew one another's business, one another's secrets. I was the outsider. All these people were just 'faces' then."

Anton looked around the small café. Miniature jukeboxes lined the walls, one at each booth, and he let his mind be distracted for a moment. Eventually, his eyes returned to Jeff, who sat staring at him.

"I'm just curious," Jeff continued. "Why don't you hook up with Bud?"

"I could ask you the same question."

Jeff offered the same answer as before. "Chemistry, Anton. I told you last July, I'm attracted to leggy redheads!"

"Bullshit." Anton watched him stir more sugar into his iced tea.

"I'm one of ten kids," Jeff began, looking up when the waitress brought the sandwiches he had ordered. "Number seven. I survived because I'm a *nice guy*. I love everyone I meet. I always have. Yes, I love Hope." He watched to see how the admission affected Anton and smiled when he saw it had. "But being a *nice guy* has its problems. I'm caught in the role of being everybody's brother. It's a position I'm used to. It's what I do best."

"But you're in love with her?"

Jeff laughed and cut his sandwich, looking more amused than ever. "Did you hear the last part of what I said?"

"I heard everything you said. Do you love her?"

"I love her. But I'm not *in* love with her. There's a difference." Jeff took a bite and watched Anton relax. He was tempted to reach across the table and take his hand, just to see him jump; Hope had told him Anton asked if he was gay, giving him a great laugh at the time. But he decided not to. He felt a little sorry for Anton just now. "Anton, why don't you let that *nice guy* inside of you come out and play, instead of being such an uptight little son of a bitch? There are a lot of nice folks just waiting to be your friends, if that damned little Russian would get out of the way."

Anton fidgeted. The USIB had trained him to keep up his guard at all times, and now this man with smiling eyes implored him to let it down. He took a bite of his sandwich so Jeff wouldn't expect an answer.

"So," Jeff said as he sipped his tea, "are you in love with her?"

Anton nearly choked. "You have the damndest habit of throwing a man off guard," he replied after drinking some water, and Jeff looked more amused than ever. His eyes always looked like he knew something no one else did. *Like Nathan.* Anton suddenly drew the parallel: Jeff was like a young Uncle Nate. "Of course not," he answered.

"'I don't know' would be a bit more honest, don't you think?"

"Okay. I don't know."

"Well"—Jeff took up his fork again—"maybe you'll find out in New York."

"What do you know about New York?"

"Talked to Bud this morning. She asked me if I'd help out at the shelter for a few days so she could go to New York with you." He wiped his mouth with a napkin. "Finish your lunch, old man. There's a great ice-cream place around the corner."

Anton smiled and finished his lunch. It was hard not to like Jeff, despite his high capacity to irritate. He had a disarming quality that was hard to ignore and the irrepressible candor of Nathan Landrum. *If only he could keep his hands to himself,* Anton thought, finding a long arm draped over his shoulder as he paid for their lunch.

But even that didn't bother him today. Hope was going to New York.

CHAPTER 18

Anton sat at the gate where Hope should have arrived two hours before, while a procession of weary passengers moved through La Guardia. The disembodied voice cursed to haunt bus stations and airports alike shouted garbled announcements from above. He hadn't seen Hope since their argument but had called every day. He found himself a little nervous, realizing he had admitted his feelings, and wondered if she would act differently toward him. Thanksgiving was the last time they'd been comfortable with each other, and here it was, February in New York. A lot had changed.

Things had become so complex—not only between him and Hope, but he also had serious questions about his partnership with Dan.

Dan was a disappointment. He often complained about assignments, hating anything that required any degree of risk or skill, leaving Anton to wonder why he'd joined the USIB in the first place. *Why did he go through the training, the trouble, if all he wanted to do was sit on his butt in Three River*s? Anton wondered. But even aside from their work, there had risen a cool hostility between them.

He looked at his watch and decided to find a water fountain. He still couldn't shake from his mind the information that Clay had given him on Saturday. He'd had dinner with the two brothers at their mother's house, where it turned out Dan still lived.

*****

Clay had complimented his mother on the meal, and Anton agreed.

"An excellent dinner, Mrs. Phillips. Thank you for inviting me," he had said.

"You're welcome, Anthony," she answered.

Anton smiled to himself. She had called him that all evening, even after Dan and Clay had corrected her several times.

Helen Philips was a soft round woman with brown hair and twinkling eyes. Her navy-and-white flowered dress, coupled with the bibbed apron, definitely gave her a maternal appearance as she gathered the dishes from the table. "I meant to have you over sooner, but Dan says you're gone most of the time," she said.

Anton looked at Dan curiously but said nothing. Dan knew that when they weren't on assignment, the only thing Anton did was spend Saturday afternoon and evening at Hope's. Except for the brief encounter the weekend before, he hadn't even done that in over a month. Clay looked at him oddly, too, but Dan shook their gaze by helping his mother carry dishes into the kitchen.

"Dan tells me you're going to New York on Wednesday," she continued upon emerging from the kitchen with a large platter of gooey chocolate chip cookies and Dan in tow, carrying glasses and a carton of milk.

As soon as the platter was on the table, the men's hands went for the cookies like vultures on fallen prey, which delighted her.

"Yes," Anton said. "A security job."

"Why isn't Dan going? Why are you going alone?"

"Dan has a different gig here locally. And I'm not going alone. Actually, I'm bringing a date."

That was when he should have known something was amiss. He would later chide himself for ignoring the sudden alertness he had seen in both the brothers' eyes. "Maybe you know her. I understand she and Clay went to school together. Hope Landrum."

He glanced at her for signs of recognition, not expecting the shattered look on her face. It matched the glass that had slipped from her hand. Dan jumped to his feet and mumbled something nasty as he whisked his mother off to the kitchen, leaving Anton bewildered.

"What did I say?"

Clay had sat back in his chair defeatedly. "I'll tell you about it later."

Once his mother recovered, Dan spent the rest of the afternoon staring holes through Anton while she chattered nervously into the evening.

*****

Anton and Clay walked slowly down the sidewalk in the cool night air, crossed the street, and turned toward the library. There was a drizzle, not a fog, not quite rain, and the flashing neon light of Kelly's split the night.

"Hope is my sister," Clay said after a long while.

Anton stopped in his tracks.

"It's complicated. Living in a small town makes it worse." Clay looked like a kid trying to explain a broken window.

"Dan's dossier said nothing about a sister," Anton said.

"She's not Dan's," Clay said as they began to walk again. "He was a product of Mom's first marriage."

"And Hope?"

"She and I have the same father. Even *I* didn't know any of this until we started dating in high school. We were born a week apart. We always felt an attachment, something. I don't know. Anyway, Dad found out I was dating her and told me not to see her anymore. We had a big fight about it, and Mom came into the room just when Dad told me that Hope was his 'bastard.'"

They walked in silence a while longer before Clay stopped again and hesitantly finished. "Mom had a nervous breakdown after that. Dad left town for parts unknown, and Dan sits here in Three Rivers telling everybody how I destroyed the family."

Anton shook his head. "You did nothing wrong, just dated a pretty girl. Does Hope know?"

"No," Clay said quickly, "and don't tell her!"

"Why?"

"She doesn't need to know that she had sex with her brother." He fidgeted. "When I found out, I picked a fight and broke up with her. The next week, I joined the Army, wound up in Vietnam. Learned from Nicki that Hope was real torn up about it, and that's why she married that jerk Steven. I think she did it to get back at me. By the time I found out, it was too late.

"I guess I should've stopped seeing her altogether. That's the rift between me and Dan. But I just couldn't bear to make a clean break. Our moms were best friends—pregnant at the same time, for chrissake. The attachment I feel is like being twins, but from separate wombs. It's a bond. We both look just like Dad. I'm surprised you haven't noticed the resemblance."

As they walked, he continued to explain the devotion he'd come to feel toward Hope, which had only widened the gap between him and Dan. Dan's total devotion to their mother had polarized them all the more.

"Dan blames Hope," Clay said, "as if it was her fault our family fell apart. But it was Dad's. He was screwing Mom and her best friend at the same time. Dan didn't mind her so much while she and Steven were married, but now that they're divorced, it's started all over again."

Anton looked at him. "What has?"

"Dan's always been jealous of her because she was Dad's child and he wasn't. Says he doesn't believe Steven ever hit her, but I know he really just doesn't care. In fact, he and Steven were always friends and became even closer while they were married. Sometimes I think Dan enjoyed it."

"What about Hope's parents?" Anton asked.

"That's what's really sad. At least I got a happy home for the first sixteen years of my life." Clay looked off into the damp night. "Her mama died when she was born, and JC, the man who raised her, treated her like an animal all her life. Thank God for Uncle Nate. He was always good to her, and she stayed with him as often as possible."

Anton nodded, thinking of Nathan adopting strays and misfits like himself.

As they continued walking in the mist, Anton remained silent, realizing that Clay needed to say more but struggled.

Finally, it came. "I still love her, Anton. Finding out she was my sister made that love feel wrong. I've spent my adult life feeling dirty about it, and there's nothing I can do but wish her the best."

"Nicki's been a real champ," he continued. "She knows everything. But sometimes, when Hope is lonely, I have the urge to tell her, to shout out that I'm her brother and she's not alone. She feels that way a lot, you know. That's why she keeps inviting us to her place on the weekends. But I would have to lose my brother to acknowledge my sister. It's hard, being in the middle." He shook his head and stepped off the curb.

"I can't even imagine," Anton said.

Clay finally turned to him. "Do you have any siblings?"

"I don't know. I've read my grandmother's journals, and there's a name that keeps popping up, *Alexis*. But there's never a last name or context. He could be a neighbor, a cousin, a friend—for all I know, a brother. Whoever he is, he's probably still in Russia."

"Are you really taking Hope to New York?" Clay asked, changing the subject. They stopped once more to face each other.

"I'm leaving on Monday. She's coming out Thursday." Anton watched the man before him for a reaction. "How do you feel about that?"

"Does it matter?"

"It does. I'm not saying it would change anything, but yeah, Clay, it matters." He felt an unexpected kinship to Clay, touched that he'd opened up a part of himself that was so obviously painful.

"Just be good to her, Anton. That's all that matters to me."

*****

It had been a rare peek into the life of the normally shy man, Anton thought as he looked at his watch once again. The unseen voice announced that Hope's plane had arrived. He hurried back to the gate, aware for the first time of his growing concern over the delays, the icy runways. His mouth felt dry, and he could feel his heart pounding in his chest as he fought the current of people.

"Hope!" He waved and pushed against the crowd until finally grabbing her up in his arms. "Oh, Hope! I was so worried!" He kissed her desperately, standing like a stone in the rampant river of people. It seemed like an eternity had passed since they'd been together, and he realized how empty he'd been without her. He took a deep breath before opening his eyes, only to find her looking at him, surprised by his greeting.

He kissed her again, more gently, more passionately. "You must be tired," he said.

"I'm exhausted."

He cupped her face in his hands, studying her eyes. Yes, he thought, she was indeed the exact female version of Clay; not only the honey-colored hair and jade eyes, but even her features, though more petite and subtle, were those of her brother. "I'll take you to your room, where you can rest before dinner. It's a little different from Rupert's," he said, smiling.

"I kind of like Rupert's!" They laughed, and Hope leaned on his arm as they walked out.

*****

Hope had fallen asleep on Anton's shoulder as the limo wove through the snowy streets of New York. He gently shook her. "We're here, sweetheart," he said softly, laughing at her sleepy eyes as she woke. He paid the driver and signaled the porter for her baggage before leading her into the huge lobby of the Grand Hyatt Hotel. Her eyes grew wide with amazement as she looked at the women laden with sparkling jewelry and men who sat around in their finely tailored suits, sipping cocktails. Looking down at her own simple dress, she felt like the country mouse that went to town.

"You look fine," Anton whispered as they got on the elevator. But even with his reassurance, she found herself clasping his hand for comfort as a tall brunette stared down at her all the way to the twelfth floor.

Anton smiled at the woman and nodded politely, seemingly quite comfortable in his surroundings, but Hope felt terribly out of place. These were the people she had mocked at the hamburger place in Monterey. Now she'd been thrown into a nest of *dahlings* and *dearies*, of people whom she suspected never quite touched one another, even when they kissed.

"Anton, I don't belong here," she said when they stepped off the elevator.

He produced a key from his pocket. "Nonsense. You belong here as much as anyone." He pointed to another door with his eyes. "I'm right next door," he said, then opened her room and stepped inside.

She looked around the room in awe. It was absolutely beautiful, done in pale pinks and silver-gray. The furniture was oak with ornate wrought iron inserts; high-back chairs surrounded a table of oak and glass, and several large bouquets of fresh roses filled the room with the sweet smell of spring.

Anton tipped the porter, who closed the door behind him as she gazed around the room. She stooped to smell the roses and then looked at him. He looked different somehow, lacking his usual cool reserve. "Oh, Anton, this is beautiful! I *never* expected anything like this. It's lovely!"

He smiled. "I'm just glad you're here. There are a few things I picked up for you," he said, indicating the boxes on the bed. "Why don't you rest? I'll call for you at six." With that, he disappeared through the door.

Hope sat on the edge of the bed, totally overwhelmed, unable to get the comparison with Rupert's out of her mind. Anton hadn't complained, but it was obvious to her now that this was what he was accustomed to.

She opened the boxes. The larger one contained a beautiful silk kimono, forest green, to match the one she knew he owned. She smiled to herself, thinking of the worn terry robe that lay in her suitcase. The second and much smaller box contained exquisite perfume, which she dabbed on her wrists and sniffed with delight.

She lay back on the bed, thinking of the man in the next room, remembering the way he had kissed her at the airport. The last time they had kissed like that, he'd been angry afterward, instructing her to forget it had ever happened. But this time, it was he who had kissed her, and she prayed for six o'clock to hurry.

*****

One last glance in the mirror did not quell Hope's nervousness as they left her room to join Leslie and Paul Sanderson for dinner. She had never met anyone that Anton knew and had only heard their names rarely, and then only in passing. When they reached the restaurant, she was impressed by the casual air with which Anton spoke to the maître d', who in turn led them to a private table. Paul Sanderson stood upon seeing them approach. Anton shook his hand, then gave Leslie a peck on the cheek.

"This must be Hope," Paul said, and Anton smiled with pride as he made the introductions. Hope was glad the older man had ordered a bottle of wine for himself and the ladies. It helped her relax, and soon she and Leslie chatted with ease; actually found several things in common. Leslie was especially interested in the shelter where Hope worked, and the men seemed to only half-listen while they discussed women's issues.

*****

Sanderson studied the woman from the corner of his eye, still the secret agent at heart, gleaning all he could about her. "Are you aware, Hope, that the ball on Saturday is a job for Anton?" He wanted to make it perfectly clear so she wouldn't expect his undivided attention. "It means he has to do more watching than dancing. And if anything happens, leave his side immediately. I don't want him worrying about you being in the line of fire. Do you understand?"

"Paul, you're scaring her," Leslie interrupted.

"I'm sorry, but these are things she needs to know," he said.

"Mr. Sanderson, Anton has already discussed these things with me. I understand," Hope said, then added, "Have we met before?"

She was quicker than he'd thought. He knew they had, and where. He was known for never forgetting a face, but saw no reason to mention the cemetery nearly eleven years before. "I don't believe so," he said.

"Well," Leslie began after a moment, "tomorrow while you men hammer out last-minute details, Hope and I are going shopping."

Anton put his hand over Hope's. "I hope you don't mind, but Leslie knows her way around the city and said she'd help you find a dress for the ball. I never welsh on a promise!"

On cue, the maître d' approached and informed them the chauffeur had returned for the ladies. Sanderson watched Anton's eyes, which followed the women until they were out of sight. "I don't suppose you're in the mood to talk business," he said in a low voice.

Anton looked back at him. "What's up?"

"Another job on the horizon. A big one. I need you to infiltrate a suspected Soviet ring forming around NORAD."

Anton knew the North American Aerospace Defense Command was charged with ensuring defense of the airspace. He looked down while Paul continued, and already Sanderson felt his influence slipping away.

"After this job, the USIB will be defunct. All remaining agents will be disbursed. Of course, you have enough years to retire, but I *know* you. And the CIA wants you real bad."

"What's the timing for this job? I need to know."

"A year, by the time we get everyone in place. You're the kingpin, Pavlova. I know you won't let me down." He leaned on his elbows and stuck a toothpick in his mouth. Anton kept watching in the direction Hope had gone, and it worried him. "After that, you can pick up your toys and go home, if that's what you want. What do you think?"

"Sure, Paul. Have I ever said no to you?"

Paul breathed a sigh of relief. *I haven't lost him yet,* he thought, but was discouraged when Anton turned to him and asked, "Whom did you have in mind if I refused?"

"Not a living soul. I counted on you, as always. Do you think your partner is willing?"

"I'm the senior partner. I choose the jobs. I don't ask if he is willing, only if he is capable. And in my opinion, he is." His annoyance was apparent. "I don't ask anything of Philips that I wouldn't expect of myself."

Sanderson removed the toothpick and took a sip of wine. "You underestimate your own capabilities, forgetting that what may just be a job to you could be suicide for someone else. You're not just first-string, Anton. You're the *best*."

"He'll do it, Paul. Philips isn't stupid, he's just lazy."

Sanderson put up his hands and backed off the subject. Anton had cemented his commitment. That was all he needed. "They're bugging me down at CIA headquarters. They want you after this. What can I tell them?"

"I don't know," Anton said. "No,—tell them no!" He felt both surprised and relieved when the word came out.

Sanderson sat back in his chair and stared. "Frankly, your answer surprises me. What would you do, then?"

"I don't know. Settle down somewhere."

"Like Three Rivers? She got to you, didn't she?" Paul frowned. "She seems rather simple."

"She's uncomplicated."

"No woman is uncomplicated. Are you two serious?"

"I don't know," Anton said again. "It's not just her, Paul." He leaned in confidentially, and Sanderson knew that whatever he was about to say weighed heavily on his mind. "Between Hope, her grandfather, and this weird person named Jeff…they've almost made me want to be a human being again. They keep trying to breathe life into me. It makes me realize how long I've been dead." He took a deep breath and sighed. "I'm tired, Paul. Tired of playing cowboy, tired of riding shotgun for the government. When I take a shower, I only feel naked because I'm not wearing my gun. I'm losing sight of who the good guys are anymore. Let someone else do it after this. I want to do a few things for myself before it's too late. Buy a dance studio and teach, have my own home and a family. I'm almost forty-one."

Sanderson laughed. "That's hardly over the hill."

"Not for an agent. For a dancer, it's frightening. The USIB has paid me well. I just want time to enjoy it."

"Well, you've earned it. I can't take that away from you. I just can't picture you as a family man."

"Scott Bauer did it."

"Scott Bauer is dead," Sanderson snapped. "He left a widow and five little girls. Is that what you want? A lot can happen in a year. Why don't you hold off on your decision?"

"No. Now *is* the time for decisions. There's a woman in my life, whether I want it or not. And for the first time since"—the name became hooked in his throat—"since Catherine, I've met someone, and when she's not around, I feel empty inside. A woman who can make a man feel like that doesn't come along every day. I'm afraid if I ignore what I feel, I might not get another chance." He looked to his mentor, his friend, for understanding.

Sanderson sipped his wine. "There was a woman once who made me feel that way," he finally said. "It was a long time ago. But I knew where to draw the line."

The air seemed to thicken in the silence that followed. "Did you ever regret it?"

"I would have regretted throwing away my career. I've always said that a married man has no place in this business. There's a price to pay for what we want, Pavlova. Don't answer now. It's still a year away. The CIA can wait."

"This has nothing to do with the CIA or the USIB. Years ago, you still had your whole career in front of you. I've already had a full career! You know damn well the CIA would take me anytime, so don't give me that 'make a decision' crap."

Sanderson paused before speaking. "Just make sure that 'love' doesn't get in the way of your job," he said. "Have you talked to Leslie about Hope?"

Anton chuckled. "Yeah." He rubbed his face with his hand the way he often did when he was tired or frustrated. "That woman would sell me to the Gypsies if she thought they had a woman for me."

Sanderson smiled a little, and Anton continued, "I'm sorry, Paul. It's not your problem."

He drank the last of his Perrier, and they said good night.

CHAPTER 19

After breakfast with Anton, Hope joined Leslie to shop for a dress. New York City, even with its slushy sidewalks, was exciting, making her feel like a little girl again. The crisp air on her face made her want to run in the streets, the same way the ocean breezes made her want to dance on the California beaches. She learned Leslie was based in San Francisco, though she came to New York often, and also that she saw Anton frequently when he went to the Bay Area.

"How well do you know him?" Hope asked when they stopped for lunch, more to rest their feet than to eat.

"Very well, but we're just friends. I don't know him the way you do," Leslie added to quell any question Hope might have.

"Neither do I." Hope looked pensively into her coffee and then started to giggle when she realized what she had said. She looked at Leslie, and they both laughed.

"Would you if you had the chance?" Leslie asked, still smiling.

"At the drop of a hat," Hope said. "I don't know if it's me or him. I've known him exactly one year, and we can't seem to get our act together."

Leslie leaned back in the booth and listened while Hope told her how things were between them. It was interesting to hear the problems from the other side, and when Hope told her about the way he'd kissed her at the airport, she raised her brows. *Perhaps all is not lost*, she thought, but said nothing.

"Does he see you professionally?" Hope finally asked.

"You're not supposed to ask me that," Leslie said, studying Hope for a moment before reminding her that she had just talked for almost an hour about some of *her* problems, though not professionally. "I've known Anton for eleven years, and we've had a lot of these little chats because we're friends. Friends are often the best psychologists."

"You avoided that very well."

Leslie smiled from behind her tea. "Anton is a good man, Hope. Everyone has tragedies in their lives. He's had his share." The statement interested Hope, but Leslie continued before she could pursue it.

"Well"—she put down her cup—"what shall we do about your dress? I thought the red one in the last shop was gorgeous on you."

"I loved it too, but did you see the price tag?"

"Is that why you haven't decided yet?" Leslie leaned forward and smiled. "You really *don't* know Anton, do you?"

"I guess I don't. Actually, I don't really know him at all. It's like he doesn't want me to, and I wonder why I keep beating my head against the wall."

Leslie reached over and touched her arm. "Hope, don't give up on him. Please. You're the best thing that has ever happened to him." She stood briskly to cover her tracks. "Now, let's go get that dress."

*****

That evening at dinner, Anton listened with interest as Hope told him about her day. She described the dress and all the things she'd seen. Her eyes were bright, her hands animated. She was like a child, he thought, just getting home from camp. Finally, when she was done, her hand came to rest upon his, but she quickly removed it.

"Why did you do that?"

"I'm sorry. It was—"

"No. Why did you take it away? I liked it." He took her hand in his. She'd been so careful since New Year's Eve not to be forward with him, and as he caressed her delicate hand, he regretted making it so difficult for her. "Let's go," he whispered.

"You haven't eaten," she said, glancing at his plate. She'd noticed his plate at breakfast too. He hadn't eaten then either. "You look a little funny, Anton. Are you feeling all right?"

"Let's go," he said again. He signed the check, and they left.

"Anton, what's wrong?" She felt his forehead in the elevator, frowning like a doting mother.

"I'm fine," he said, preoccupied with his own thoughts. They reached the twelfth floor and stepped out. "I probably won't see you until evening at the ball. Les said she'll come by and take you to lunch." They reached her door, and he stood looking at her, his heartbeat filling the silence. "I have to get up very early…"

"I understand."

His mouth covered hers almost before she got the words out. His arms enfolded her, crushing her tight against him. He kissed her with a hunger that took her breath away. His hands wandered down her back, and he kissed her again with an abandon she had never seen in him.

"Anton." She pulled away just enough to see the fire in his eyes. His face was flush with color. "We should get out of the hall." She indicated her room, but her voice sounded a million miles away, barely audible over his own breath.

"No," he finally said. "I have to be alert on the job tomorrow. If I go in there, I won't be worth a damn." He entwined his fingers in her hair and kissed her long and hard, then backed away, turned, and disappeared into his room.

Hope stood breathless against her door, her heart pounding. She'd relished his touch, the way his body had pressed against hers.

She took a deep breath and opened her eyes just in time to see Paul Sanderson disappear at the end of the hall.

*****

That night, the door that connected their rooms loomed large. Nothing seemed to relieve the frustration Anton felt. He could still feel her against him, smell her perfume. The clothes between them had failed to disguise the supple body that had pressed against his. He sat on the bed and closed his eyes, ignoring the door that screamed to be opened, and thought of how hard he had tried to repress his feelings. Looking back over the past year, he realized being with Hope in New York was the end to which it had brought him, and he knew he'd unconsciously set himself up. There was no more denying what he felt. There was no other name for it that would lessen its degree.

He needed her in his life.

*****

The little girl sat at the window and sighed. Uncle Nate and Aunt Stell had promised a picnic in the orchard, but instead, huge drops of rain created puddles and streams. Even the crackling fire and the smell of cookies lacked their usual enticement, and Hope had long since tired of playing with the shoebox filled with pretty shells. Her sad green eyes scolded the nasty weather, then looked up at the old woman who approached.

"How you doin', sugar?" Aunt Stell smiled.

"Ain't got nothing to do, Aunt Stell" came the pitiful five-year-old voice.

"Ahhh, there's always something to do. I know! You can be Cinderella, and I'll be your fairy godmother. How's that sound?" She smiled when the little girl clapped her hands and giggled. The two climbed the stairs and didn't come down for over an hour.

Finally, Hope stood in front of the mirror, turning from side to side, grinning. The puffy green sleeves of the worn satin dress hung down to her wrists, and the high-heeled shoes clomped as she strutted back and forth, the green dress trailing behind. She wore a green velvet hat with one marvelously long feather cocked smartly to the side, and the bright-red rouge and lipstick made her feel quite the dame.

Aunt Stell went down and called to Uncle Nate, then they both stood at the foot of the stairs, awaiting Cinderella's appearance.

"Why, Stella, where did that beautiful princess come from?" Nathan said aloud as he looked up at Hope, the dress flowing behind her. "Oh, my goodness, it's Hope!" He swept her off the bottom step and held her high above him, smiling up at her as she giggled merrily. "Look, Stella! It's the most beautiful girl in the world!"

*****

"Hope, we need to go soon. Anton and Paul will worry if we're late." Leslie's voice sounded far away.

Hope stared at the beautiful woman in the full-length mirror who stared back. *Is it me?*

For years, her eyes had carefully avoided her image in the mirror while she brushed her hair, avoiding the ugliness, the bruises that Steven had inflicted. "Is it me?"

"Who did you expect?" Leslie answered, stepping behind her to fuss with the hair that lay in golden waves over her shoulders. "You look lovely, Hope. I can't wait until Anton sees you!"

Anton. She wondered how she would look in his eyes. He had called her beautiful before, but she'd thought he was just being kind. Now, almost a year after she had left Steven, her skin was as creamy and clear as the day she'd been born. For the first time, she saw herself, Hope Landrum, of Three Rivers. *If only Uncle Nate could see me now!*

"I'm ready," she said. Picking up her wrap, she followed Leslie out to the limo.

*****

Hope could feel her heart pounding as she and Leslie entered the huge Baroque ballroom with ornately painted ceilings and marble columns. It all made her think of palaces and fairy-tale kingdoms as the orchestra blended with the clinking of champagne glasses and quiet chatter. All were dressed in exquisite attire, and expensive jewelry glittered from women's necks and earlobes.

"Stay here a minute." Leslie patted her arm and disappeared into the crowd before she could answer, returning shortly with a tuxedoed Anton beside her. He stopped in his tracks the moment he laid eyes on her.

"What do you think?" Leslie asked.

But he could only stare. He finally glanced back at Leslie, as if coming up for air, before he approached the beautiful woman before him.

Anton bowed deeply and kissed the palm of Hope's hand, sending shivers throughout her being. *Is it me?* She caught her breath as

THE PEBBLE AND THE MAN

she watched the handsome Russian bow so properly, totally unaware that the people nearby had stopped talking to watch the drama unfold.

"Les, tell Paul I'll be there in a minute," he said quietly, not taking his eyes off Hope. "I've got to have at least one dance."

He led her through the crowd and pulled her gently into his arms. As they began to waltz, his blue eyes silently adored her. "You don't know what you do to me," he whispered, thinking of the battle he had waged against himself for days. They moved around the room so gracefully, so perfectly matched, and he knew the battle was over. Something had snapped the night before, and all he could hear was his own breathing and Hope's voice thanking him for the dress. Did he like it? Yes, he liked it very much, he answered, barely hearing his own words, desperately wanting to kiss her full and hard, stopped only by the propriety the evening demanded.

"You'd better get back to work," she whispered.

The music had ended, and he found himself standing before her, until he heard Leslie's voice.

"Come on, Hope, I'll introduce you to the few people I know." Leslie pulled at her arm and winked as she led her away. Hope turned to look at Anton, who stood unmoving.

*****

Though she had been prepared, Hope missed Anton terribly. Occasionally, she caught a glimpse of him and was warmed by the way he looked at her. But then his eyes would dart away to search the crowd for unseen dangers. The woman on her right, introduced to her as Elisha, had talked nonstop since the introduction. Hope smiled and nodded at all the appropriate moments, wondering where Leslie had gone, until a dark-haired man approached and put his arm around the chattering woman.

"Jacques, darling, this is the lady I saw dancing with Anton Pavlova. Hope Landrum. Dear"—she turned, addressing Hope—"this is Jacques Racine."

His face twitched nervously into an uncomfortable smile.

"Anton Pavlova. He is here?"

Hope nodded, and he and the woman exchanged glances. "I heard he had gone to the West Coast."

"Yes, he did. But he came back for this."

"What a surprise, eh, Elisha?" Jacques laughed soberly. Turning back to Hope, he asked, "Would you care to dance?"

Secretly grateful for the escape, she let him lead her away.

He smiled and took her in his arms. "You'll have to forgive Elisha. She's really quite a dear, but she is also quite a talker." He laughed, his brown eyes sparkling and teeth glistening. "So, you are a friend of Pav—of Anton's? He's a fool not to have you on his arm!"

"Do you know him well?" she asked, but the dark stranger hesitated for a moment as he waltzed her around the room.

"We met in school, the South of France," he finally answered.

"I didn't know Anton studied in France."

Jacques glanced at Elisha as they waltzed past. "It's quite stuffy in here," he said. "Would you like to step outside for a few minutes?"

Just then, the music ended and Hope quickly excused herself, feeling like the country mouse again, unaccustomed to the attentions of charming Frenchmen, although he hadn't seemed French to her at all. His skin was the color of coffee with cream, his eyes almost black. *But then, what does a Frenchman look like?* She realized she had nothing to compare him to.

What she wanted was a familiar face, someone handsome and maybe not so tall. She waved as Anton's eyes scanned the room.

"Enjoying yourself?" he asked when she approached.

"I am," she said, feeling a little better just standing beside him, and was glad when he reached out to squeeze her hand.

"Tell the truth, you'd rather be with Jeff, Clay, Nicki, and Noah, eating popcorn and crying over *Wuthering Heights*." He smiled, but his eyes continued to scan the room, and as Hope watched, she realized he was signaling other agents with his eyes.

"Only if you were there too," she said. "But this is wonderful, a once-in-a-lifetime," she lied a little, feeling guilty for not really enjoying herself.

"Personally, I'd take the popcorn and crying over *Wuthering Heights*!" He gave another signal before taking her arm and walking toward Sanderson, who was discussing business with a stout, mustached gentleman.

"Anton," Sanderson signaled as they approached, "this is the man I've been telling you about, Jacques Racine. Jacques, this is Anton Pavlova, the best man we've got. He'd be perfect for the job."

Anton shook his hand and introduced Hope, who stared, perplexed, while the three men chatted quietly. She turned around and found the first Jacques Racine laughing with a beautiful woman who lifted her glass to her lips, her diamonds glittering with a life of their own.

Hope turned back to Anton. "The music has started. Let's dance." She tugged at his arm, and Sanderson glared. "Please?" Glancing over her shoulder just as the dark Frenchman looked her way, she tugged again, urgently.

Finally, Anton excused himself and walked with her through the crowd. "Bad timing, Hope," he gently scolded as they began to dance.

"Anton, have you ever studied in France?"

"No. Why?"

"See that man over there?" She pointed with her eyes. "He was introduced to me as Jacques Racine and said he knows you from school in France."

She watched as Anton's eyes swept the crowd and fixed on the man. "*Nezar!* Damn! He's not French, he's Iranian!" Anton could feel Hope weaken in his arms. He clutched her tight as they danced, murmuring instructions into a tiny transmitter wired into his sleeve.

Finally, he lowered his arm, his hand returning to her waist. "I can't believe I missed him. He looks different, but I should have recognized him."

"Who is he?"

"I rented a room from him and his brother when I was undercover in Iran."

"He knows you're on the West Coast now. I guess he didn't expect to see you here either."

Anton looked at her in alarm. "Does he know you're with me?"

She nodded. "He tried to get me to go outside with him."

"Oh, God." He spoke into the transmitter once more, and almost instantly, a brown-haired man stepped up as if to cut into their dance. "Samuels, take Ms. Landrum back to her room and don't leave her side until I arrive."

The man nodded and swept her out of the crowd. Anton stood motionless until he was sure they were gone. Then he gave the order. The twenty-two men he commanded began to move in on the impostor.

*****

"Please step away from the window," Hal Samuels asked again, as he had several times during the long night, making Hope all the more anxious for Anton's return. Minutes had passed likes hours, hours like days, since the tall man had swept her through the crowd at the ball, not stopping until they had reached her room.

"Miss Landrum, why don't you try to relax? I'm confident Pavlova's fine. He's the best." Samuels had been trained for the security department by Anton himself during his years in New York and had a great respect for him.

"The curtains are closed," she said.

"You might cast shadows."

Hope sat quickly on the edge of the bed and burst into tears.

"Hey..." Samuels went and knelt in front of her, offering his handkerchief. "If Anton comes back and sees you crying, he's going to think I didn't take care of you." He peered under her downcast eyes, but it didn't work. "You must really be someone special," he said gently, taking back his handkerchief and dabbing her face. "I always wondered what kind of woman it would take to turn Anton Pavlova's head. Your presence at the ball took everyone by surprise."

Hope finally looked up. "Everyone?"

"Me and the other two dozen or so agents." He dabbed the last of her tears, though he wasn't sure how long the dry spell would last. Even he was beginning to worry. But only a few more minutes passed before the sound of men's laughter in the hall caught Samuels's attention, and after checking through the peephole, he opened the door for Anton and Sanderson, who laughed at some earlier joke.

"Hope, I owe you an apology," Sanderson said as they stepped in. "I have to admit, you made me angry when you dragged Anton off. But thanks to you, we caught someone very important. I'm sure you've seen the news about the hostages taken in Iran."

She nodded.

"Well, the man we arrested tonight was one of the masterminds..."

Anton watched Hope as Sanderson elaborated. It was obvious to him that she had been crying, and he wanted desperately to take her in his arms. She looked at him in return, hardly hearing Sanderson. Tears began their slow march down her face once again.

Anton stretched out his arm to her, beckoning, and she went to him.

"Well, I guess I'll be going," Sanderson said abruptly. Anton thanked Samuels, and he and Sanderson left.

Hope clung to Anton as he stroked her hair and whispered comforting words. "Don't cry, sweetheart. Don't cry. I know you don't understand the implications, but finding this guy is big. Having him in custody might help us bring the hostages home! Tonight, you played a crucial role in something bigger than you could ever imagine."

"Anton..." She looked at him. "Don't you know a part of me died tonight?"

Her words struck a familiar chord. It was the same worry Catherine had always expressed. He quickly dug a hole and buried the thought, not wanting to think about the old wound. It was Hope who mattered now. Hope was all he cared about. "This hasn't been much of an evening for you, has it?" He rotated his shoulders and neck. It had been a terribly long day, and he ached all over. The little bit of sleep he'd had the night before had been shallow, and now he felt the tension of the day gather into a knot between his shoulders. "Tomorrow we'll spend the whole day together. We'll do whatever you like." He smiled wearily.

"You look exhausted," she said, softening a little.

"I am."

"Let me change out of my dress and I'll rub your back." It was a selfish offer. Having waited so long to see him, she wasn't about to let him crawl off to sleep. She kissed him lightly and slipped into the bathroom.

After a few minutes, she emerged, wearing the silk kimono, only to find him stretched out across the bed on his stomach. His revolver lay on the dresser with his shirt carefully placed over it, allowing him easy access yet covered enough to be concealed from intruders. It was a habit with him, like brushing his teeth.

Hope sat on the bed beside him and massaged his bare shoulders. His muscles were hard from tension as she kneaded and rubbed, trying to relax him. He hadn't been aware of just how much anxiety he had stored until he felt her tiny hands granting its release.

As she rubbed his neck with her fingertips, he felt himself sinking into the bed and closed his eyes.

CHAPTER 20

All around him was a cold darkness, an outer space of the inner mind, with nothing to indicate life except the faint pulse in his veins and a warmth that had mysteriously found its way to him. He dug in close, finding comfort there, like a light that drew him to it. Safety in the night. It seemed he couldn't get close enough and he tried to bury himself, as though it would make him safe, as though it alone could save his life.

He opened his eyes and looked around at the unfamiliar images in the dark room, no longer asleep, not quite awake. *Where am I?* he wondered, suddenly afraid of the night, afraid this long-forgotten comfort would disappear upon his awakening. He shut his eyes, unwilling to give up the comfort he'd deprived himself of for so long. *Good. It's still here,* he thought. *It didn't go away.*

What's that smell? He opened his eyes and sat up on one elbow, once again wondering where he was. He rubbed his face to awaken his senses. *Perfume.* There was movement beside him and the feel of silk on his skin.

At once he was fully awake and could hear soft breathing. He nestled close to Hope. After so many years, so many brief encounters that had never seen morning, he had awakened to find a woman, softly scented with the perfume he had given her, gently wrapped in silk like a present just waiting to be opened. His hand roamed the graceful curves of her waist, her hips, her thigh. He was breathless.

"Sweetheart," he quietly called her out of a dream. "Hope." He squinted at his watch: 5:00 a.m. He should let her sleep, he thought, but was unable to stop. He pushed his body against hers. "Hope," he called again. He breathed heavily as he kissed her face until her eyes flickered open.

It took a moment for her to realize where she was. She could hear Anton's breathing, feel his hard body wound like a tightly coiled spring as he kissed her hard. "Anton…Anton…wait!" She held his face in her hands and waited for him to pay attention. "I know how confused you've been lately. Are you sure this is what you want and not just the moment?"

"Sweetheart, for the first time in my life, I know exactly what I want," he said. "I want you and Three Rivers and all the crazy friends that go with it. It's not just the moment, Hope, it's the culmination of all the other moments. Don't you know you've had me walking around like a madman for days? Make love with me, Hope."

She could feel his breath on her face, smell his cologne mixed with the roses in the room.

"Make love with me," he whispered as he pulled the sash at her waist. The silk fell away, and he could see her white flesh in the darkness as he stroked her. "It will be so good," he cooed breathlessly, pushing the robe completely away, letting it slip off the edge of the bed, into a puddle on the floor. He removed his trousers then lay back down beside her. "Tell me what you like," he whispered, his hands gliding over her silken flesh.

Hope was embarrassed. No one had ever asked her that, or even cared, for that matter. It had been so long since she'd been with a gentle man she had almost forgotten what it was like. Just feeling his hands on her made her breathless.

He realized she was trembling and smiled inwardly as his mouth engulfed hers, his loins growing hot against her leg.

"Anton…"

"We'll go slow. There's nothing I won't do for you," he cooed, then slowly slipped over her, kissing her throat and then her breasts, sucking gently and tugging at her nipples with his lips. He thought of the hot summer days in Three Rivers. So often his eyes were riveted to the graceful curves that peeked out of the low-necked blouses she wore, her nipples looking like buttons sewn into the fabric. Now, as he slipped further down, they grew erect in the palms of his hands.

He nuzzled her ribs and abdomen. He felt the soft patch of hair against his face as he kissed her, her legs tense around him.

"Anton…" she moaned, her voice sounding small and frightened. "I want you in my arms, Anton. I want you to hold me." She was breathless and needed someone to cling to, afraid of feelings she couldn't describe, feelings she hadn't felt with a man until now. It was as though he were coaxing out of her the yearlong fantasies that had kept her awake at night, had made her feel sinful the next morning. She had been taught that pleasure was selfish, and now this man called her to take part in it, to share it with him.

She shivered as he moved up her body, leaving a trail of kisses. His arms enfolded her, and she let out a soft cry as he thrust himself into her. She became aware of the intensity he wore on his face. He was the choreographer, his body the dancer. His muscles, strong and supple, moved over her with disciplined grace. She ran her hands over his shoulders, down to his narrow hips and strong buttocks as he thrust into her. At that moment, she knew she belonged to him, the dancer, the artist.

Anton slowed himself after a while and smiled down at her, his eyes shining bright even in the darkness. He lay still for a moment, relishing a pleasure that was almost too painful to hold. His hips tried to move, but his mind forbid it as he held himself back, savoring the moment.

"Don't move, Hope…God…don't move," he whispered like a tormented man. "You don't know what you do to me. You don't know how much I've thought about this, dreamed about it. How many times I've awakened in the middle of the night…" He kissed her hungrily, his lips burning against her mouth, his hips quivering with readiness.

Slowly he began to move. He commanded his body until she, too, began to writhe, her words incoherent. She was slipping into a mystical world of sensations and smells. He fought to keep his motion steady and strong until the moment was right. Faster and faster he went until at last her body arched toward him, her head pressed into the pillow as she cried out, tensing beneath him. Anton's face was damp with perspiration. Just the sounds she uttered threw him out of control, and a moment later, he collapsed over her, gasping and spent.

He felt her muscles tugging at him as they lay together, and he smiled inwardly, marveling at this woman who seemed so frightened of her own sexuality, the same woman who had just fulfilled him; his body, his mind, his spirit.

They lay together quietly for a while, not bothering to untangle the arms and legs that held their bodies close.

Anton kissed Hope's damp face. "Hi," he said. She had never looked more radiant.

"Hi," she replied, then added, "Thank you."

"Thank you?" He cocked his head boyishly to one side and laughed. "That's a heck of a thing to say."

"For taking your time. For letting me…" She didn't finish.

He smiled at her bashfulness.

"I never…I didn't know…" She trailed off and turned her head.

The glistening track of a tear caught Anton's eye. "What is it, Hope?"

"I didn't know it could ever be like this."

"Oh, Hope." He gathered her in his arms and kissed her. "Surely, in the beginning, with your husband…"

She mutely shook her head.

"Hope, look at me," he said gently, glad that he had, indeed, taken his time. "Sweetheart, I just can't understand how a man could make love to you and not want to share." He looked at her sad face. "Don't cry, little one. It's not like that anymore. With me, you can have it all." He smiled and kissed her neck, his hands gliding over her creamy flesh. It wasn't long before he once again lost control.

*****

Anton woke alone. He thought for an instant that it had all been a dream and was relieved to hear the shower running.

As he entered, he could see movement on the other side of the curtain, and with one hand, he slowly pushed it aside.

Hope was startled at first and instinctively tried to cover herself, causing him to grin. Their lovemaking had been shrouded in darkness, then blankets, once the darkness had gone. He stood in silence as his eyes roamed every inch of her body, and after peeling her hands away, he stared at the beautiful woman before him. He stepped in with her and kissed her deeply. The spray of water felt like warm hands. She clutched him, he drew her down into the tub, and they finished their passion together.

"I don't think either of us buys that 'just friends' crap anymore. Do you? What else am I but your lover?" he said finally. His eyes were happy and smiling while she sat over him, massaging his chest beneath the rising water.

"You are my prince. You are of noble birth and have come here in exile, hiding among the commoners of Three Rivers until you can reclaim your rightful place on the throne."

He laughed and lazily splashed water on her breasts. "And what will you do if you discover that I am only a man?"

"Be happy, because that is all I want from you. And to top it off, you're a quite handsome, virile one at that."

"Do you know how old I am?" he asked.

"Eighty-nine, going on a hundred and two, if you keep up the pace you've set this morning." She kissed the tip of his nose.

"Seriously, does our age difference bother you?" he wondered. Hope wasn't that much older than Catherine would have been.

"Are you going to tell her about us?"

He blinked. "Her who?"

"Whoever you have in San Francisco."

He frowned, confused. "I don't have anyone in San Francisco."

"I thought we didn't lie to each other."

Anton turned the water off with his foot and studied her in silence, seeing the injured look on her face. "I don't have anyone in San Francisco, Hope," he repeated.

"Okay." She forced a little smile, but avoided his eyes.

"No, damn it, it's not okay. You don't believe me." He scooted her backward and sat up, bringing them eye to eye. "What makes you think I have someone in San Francisco?"

Hope hesitated, but knew she owed him an explanation.

"You wear a certain look...when you've been with someone. I've seen it on your face after you've been to the bay. And just now, a woman crossed your mind."

He wrapped his arms around her and pulled her head onto his shoulder when the tears broke free. He remembered the day at the dam and how transparent he'd been, and now wondered how many other things she had seen in him. He remembered also, for the first time, having told her once that he had been married. He wondered why she'd never asked him about it, not realizing that after seeing the pain in his eyes, she'd never had the heart.

"My...wife...she was about your age. It was a problem with us," he said, very low. "That's why I wanted to know how you felt about it."

"Does she live in San Francisco?"

"No." *She's buried there, quite close to your grandmother.*

"Then who is in San Francisco?" she persisted.

This time it was he who hesitated, thinking of the prostitutes he now knew by name, and the decadent part of his life that he wanted to spare her. "No one that matters, Hope. You've got to believe me."

"She matters enough for you to make love to her." The thought of sharing him with someone ravaged her, and she clung to his shoulders, burying her face in the crook of his neck.

He realized now that he had to tell her the truth. He pulled away gently, just enough to see her eyes. "Sweetheart"—he shook his head sadly—"the only thing that matters to any women I know in San Francisco is whether or not they've been paid." He winced at the words, waiting for Hope to react. But she said nothing. "You're the one I want, little one. I know that now. No one in San Francisco could ever take your place."

Hope closed her eyes and hugged his neck. "That's what I needed to hear," she cried, and Anton felt relief wash over him. For a moment he'd thought he had lost her, and he realized how devastated he would be.

He kissed her gently on the face and neck, and she splashed him. He splashed her in return, and within moments, they were engaged in a full-scale water fight.

*****

It was a weekend in paradise for Anton, his hunger sated by Hope, and hers by him. He stared at the beautiful, delicate woman as she dried off and slipped into her kimono.

There was a knock on the door, and Hope looked up quickly as if they had been caught doing something naughty. Already in jeans, Anton went to the door and peeked out. It was Leslie.

"What should I do?" There was panic in Hope's voice, causing him to laugh.

"You're cute, you know that?" He shook his head and grinned as he opened the door. "Hi, Les, come in."

Leslie eyed the two and battled the grin that formed at the corners of her mouth. "I'm interrupting something."

Anton grinned and kissed her cheek. "Ten minutes ago, you would have."

Hope looked as if she might crawl under the bed, so Leslie was quick to get to the nature of her visit. "I'm on my way to the airport. I wanted to pick up the book you said I could borrow for the flight home."

Hope volunteered to retrieve the book from Anton's room and disappeared through the connecting doorway.

"You look like the little kid who caught the brass ring," Leslie said when she was gone.

"I guess it was finally within reach." He slipped on his shirt and began to button it.

"It's been within reach for a long time. It's you who finally reached out to take it."

He gave her a look but said nothing as Hope returned to the room. "Leslie, we haven't eaten yet," she said. "Do you have time to join us?"

"I'm afraid not. Thank you, though." Leslie looked back at Anton. "You kids enjoy yourselves." With that, she kissed them each on the cheek and said goodbye.

Anton turned Hope around and kissed her on the forehead. "Now, get dressed. I feel extravagant today and want to buy you something."

"You already did that."

"When?"

"I call a very expensive dress that I'll only wear once a bit extravagant, don't you?"

"Why would you only wear it once?"

"It's not exactly the kind of thing one wears in Three Rivers."

"Hope, sweetheart, there's a place just outside of Three Rivers known as 'the rest of the world'," he laughed, putting his arms around her. "It would be perfect for the ballet. I'm still going to take you when I get the chance."

She reached up and kissed him full on the mouth and didn't let him go until he was breathless. "It's two in the afternoon. If you really want to buy me something, how about lunch?" she said.

*****

They had gazed silently into each other's eyes all through the meal and now held hands over coffee. Anton had mysteriously recovered his appetite and now sat convinced that he was the most sated man in the world.

"Here they come," he said from behind his cup, looking over Hope's shoulder.

"Who?"

"The two old ladies who have been talking about us for the past half hour."

"And what, pray tell, would two old ladies have to say about us? That we look like we've made love four times in the past eight hours? I mean, you *do* look a little haggard," she teased.

"Shhh," he said, sipping his coffee as the women approached. They lingered near the table, each urging the other to ask a question.

"Good day, ladies." Anton nodded and smiled, his cup still held near his mouth.

Finally, the thinner of the two approached. "I beg your pardon. My sister and I were debating. May I ask if you two are related? She says that husbands and wives just naturally start to look alike, but I say you look like brother and sister." The women waited with bated breath for him to respond. He had seen them exchange a dollar bill, and he smiled, wanting to say "Actually, we're lovers" just to see their faces. Hope saw mischief in his eyes and nudged him under the table, giving him a look of warning.

"We're sweethearts," he finally said and chuckled at their disappointment as they left.

"You almost told them, didn't you?" He didn't reply, but she could tell. "I guess we do look alike, don't we?"

"Not as much as you and Clay." He waited for a reaction, but none came. "We only look alike because we're both short and blond, but trust me, you're prettier," he said, squeezing her hand.

"Not from where I'm sitting." She looked across the table, thinking of his beautifully toned body with the grace of a dancer, the grace of a lover. She felt a rush just thinking about it. Never before had she been treated as an equal in bed. Steven had treated her as a convenience for his needs, then, when he'd insisted on separate rooms, she had been glad. It was better to be alone than used.

*****

Anton gazed at her, wanting to say so much, but couldn't. How could he tell her about the whores, the fifteen-minute bouts that allowed no time for gentleness? Or about Catherine, so fragile that he'd feared she would break if he dared to fully unleash his passion? With her, it could *only* be gentleness, which hadn't always given him the emotional release he needed. Yes, Hope had been the best, the perfect combination of gentle touching and animal lust. He sensed that she needed both, just as he did.

"What are you thinking?" he asked, seeing the faraway look in her eyes.

"Those two women. It would have been nice to have a brother or a sister, don't you think?"

He could tell it was a diversion but let it go. Obviously, she didn't want to say what was really on her mind.

"I assume you're an only child too," she said.

"I don't know. I was only three when I came here. My parents could have had more. I've read my grandmother's journals, but I still don't know very much about my family."

"So it was your grandmother's journals on the dresser," she said, and he nodded.

"What about you? You've never mentioned family."

"I've got Uncle Nate."

"Anyone else?"

"No," she answered, then said, "I thought you were going to take me shopping."

He smiled and signaled for the check.

*****

They arrived back at the hotel totally exhausted. It was past nine, and it seemed like they had been in every store in the city. Anton lay on the bed fully clothed and watched Hope open the tiny box. She held the crystal prism up to the light.

"I wanted to buy you something nice, not just a trinket."

She sat on the bed next to him, dangling the prism over his head. "Isn't it pretty? It's the first one I've seen just like the one Uncle Nate bought for Aunt Stell."

"Rainbows are nice, but I wanted to buy you something more than a piece of glass." He had tried to find out what kind of things she liked, had even asked what she would want if she could wish for something material. *"I want nothing I could get with a simple wish,"* she had replied. *"Except rainbows without rain,"* she'd added when she spotted the prism at the jewelry counter at Bloomingdale's. He had mistakenly called her simple, and she'd been quick to inform him that she was *down-to-earth*. But then, that was what he liked about her. Hope was unassuming, as well as being versed in many of the high arts, which both surprised and delighted him. During the afternoon, they had discussed at length the life of Mozart and the style of *e. e. cummings*. Yet she was, indeed, down-to-earth. There was no pretense about Hope.

He watched her now playing with the silly piece of glass, half-woman, half-child, and he smiled when she looked at him. She laid the prism on the table and lay beside him after turning off the light.

"You're tired, aren't you?" she said after a moment, pushing his hair away from his eyes.

"Uh-huh," he grunted. "Somebody kept me awake last night."

"Somebody's sorry," she said.

He grinned in the darkness. "I didn't mind." He chuckled and rolled over to face her.

"Thank you for the prism, Anton."

"I just wish—"

She put her finger on his lips. "You're forgetting your manners. When someone says 'Thank you,' you should graciously say 'You're welcome.'" She removed her finger and kissed him.

"You're welcome," he said and kissed her intensely. As tired as he was, he wanted her, wanted to feel himself inside her once more before he slept, and from the way she kissed him, it was an idea they both shared. She caressed his neck and throat, which she had discovered long ago were points of sensitivity, and he felt his pulse quicken as she unbuttoned his shirt and pants. Moving over him like a shadow, she pulled off his clothes in the darkness, then removed her own.

"You're beautiful," he whispered after watching her silhouette move against the city lights outside the window, and he closed his eyes as she climbed back into bed. Lying on his back with his hands behind his head, he smiled inwardly, thinking how glad he was that she'd come to New York with him.

She leaned over him and kissed his face, his chest. She could tell he was at peace with the world. She had made advances before but had always had a safety net in one form or another, hiding behind liquor or the company of others. She felt a little timid now. Steven had always "done it to her," as if only satisfying a physical need, like food or sleep. She shuddered at the thought and willed herself to focus on the warm skin that lay beneath her.

She moved slowly, but Anton found the very hesitance in her touch exciting and tantalizing.

She rolled over and sat up beside him, feeling inadequate for this man who was so experienced, so worldly.

He stroked her hair and whispered, "It's okay, sweetheart," and she kissed him to stop the words. She ran her fingertips over his skin, as if discovering his body for the first time, hesitating, considering. She kissed his eyes closed, afraid for him to watch as her shadowlike image moved around him, still thinking of that part of him that she'd carefully avoided with her eyes that afternoon. What would he think if she put her hands there? She'd done it on New Year's Eve, but had been drunk and hardly remembered.

She knelt between his muscular thighs, stretching over him like a cat, reaching for and caressing his shoulders and chest, then slowly gliding her hands downward until they met at that sacred place and she heard a soft moan. His body was sleek and toned beneath her hands, like that of a twenty-year-old, only more masculine, more mature.

Anton lay silent and took a deep breath as he felt her tiny fingers caress the inside of his thigh. He demanded nothing, hinted at nothing, expected nothing. Her touch alone was a gift.

His eyes opened when he felt her mouth take him in. He raised his head off the pillow to look at her.

She lazily teased him, delighting in his moans as she moved her mouth up and down over the ridge. He quaked at her touch, luxuriated in the warmth of her mouth.

"Hope," he panted, pulling at her shoulders, "you don't have to do that…"

"I want to give you something, Anton. I love you." As soon as the words came out, his body tensed. She quickly reached up and put her fingertips to his mouth. "Don't say anything. I'm not looking to hear it back."

He kissed her fingertips and leaned back into the pillow, staring up at the darkness. He could feel his heart beat as her deft tongue slid over him and flickered him into ecstasy. He tried to tell her he loved her too, but only a soft moan escaped his lips. She was too good for him, he thought. She knew now that he had money, yet never took advantage. He knew she had nothing, yet she wanted to give him something. She gave what she had. She gave him pleasure. She gave herself.

He reached down and touched her hair as he caught his breath, closing his eyes tightly. It lay soft against his abdomen, caressing him as she moved. "Hope,"—he cried her name—"come here, sweetheart." She straddled his hips, and in just a few moments, he began to shudder and cry, and finally he screamed into the night.

She lay over his body, his muscles still quaking beneath her, his eyes closed, and she wondered at the tear that caught the pale light just an instant before it slid down the side of his face. She smoothed his hair and whispered softly, unaware that he loved her too and wept because the words just wouldn't come.

CHAPTER 21

Hope went home the following afternoon after spending the entire morning making love with Anton. He knew how much he would miss her as she waved once more before boarding the plane. She had already stayed longer than planned. They had called Jeff to cover for her at the shelter for one more day, and he'd instantly agreed. He'd laughed when Anton had gotten on the phone and assured him it was for a good cause. "Shit, you must've got laid!" he'd replied, and Anton could almost hear him grin over the phone. But Hope was gone now, and as he walked through the airport toward his car, the ugly airport voice scratched his nerves. Only one more day before he could join her in Three Rivers, he thought, dreading the empty night that lay ahead.

The next morning found him in yet another meeting where the agents' reports here handed in and any holes in security were discussed. After hours of debriefing the agents individually, Paul Sanderson stepped into the room.

"There was a message from your hotel. Maybe you'll know what it means," he said quietly after pulling Anton aside.

"What was it?"

"Trouble with Wykes."

Anton felt the blood drain from his face.

"It was sent by someone named Jeff about two hours ago. What's it mean?"

"Nothing good." His voice was anxious as he quickly gathered his papers. "Do you need me for anything?"

"No, I can take over from here."

THE PEBBLE AND THE MAN

Anton thanked him and caught the first flight out of New York.

*****

When Anton stopped his car in front of the farmhouse, Clay's face was at the living room window and Jeff met him at the door.

"I got here as fast as I could. What's going on?"

"Apparently, Steven had a private investigator follow you two around New York. He was waiting for her when she got home. Anton…he beat her up pretty bad."

Anton's eyes widened. "Where is she?"

"Upstairs," Clay said over Jeff's shoulder, "but she doesn't want you to see her."

"Why not?" He could feel panic rising from the pit of his stomach.

"Anton, you've got to understand guys like Steven. They have a way of brainwashing their wives," Clay tried to explain.

"She's not his—"

"That's beside the point," Jeff interrupted. "The point is, he reminded her that men hit women. That *you* might hit her."

"She can't possibly believe that." Anton's throat went dry. He had to go to her.

Jeff took him by the shoulders and looked him squarely in the eyes. "You're not listening to me. I've told you about this before. Sometimes she can't think straight. She believes him! Now, Nicki came to stay with her, but she doesn't want us guys around right now."

Anton pushed Jeff's hands away and headed for the stairs.

"Anton, if you go up there all upset, you'll send her right over the edge."

*****

Hope stood staring out the window, silhouetted in the last rays of the evening sun. Her hair was outlined with gold as the white linen curtains billowed around her. There was an odd silence in the twilight of the room, and even though Anton closed the door gently, the sound was an intrusion.

"I'm here, sweetheart," he said quietly when she didn't turn around.

"I don't want you here." The voice hardly sounded like hers. She shrugged his hands off her shoulders when he came near. "Don't touch me!" she growled. "Go away!"

The words struck him dumb, and he could feel tears gather in the corners of his eyes. This was the last thing he'd expected to come home to. Only yesterday morning, after a good night's sleep, they had laughed and romped, their play occasionally interrupted by passion. After one such bout, he'd looked at her as they lay on the floor beside the bed and said, *"I'm too old for this,"* and she'd smiled and kissed his bare shoulders. *"It's never been like this, Hope,"* he had told her, fondling the honey-colored hair that lay around her like a sunburst. *"I've never had anything as wonderful as you in my life."*

It all seemed like a dream as he reached up to stroke her hair. "I can't go away," he whispered. "I'm here to help."

"Help?" she chuckled. "Men are nothing but fucking bastards, so keep your hands off me."

"Not all men, Hope. Only guys like Steven."

"All men!"

"You don't really believe that..."

"No? Tell me to my face what I believe." She turned to him, and he stared in horror at the swollen, bruised face. Her eyes could barely open, and small cuts were still crusted with dried blood. "Not pretty, is it?" she sneered when he said nothing. His lips tried to form words, but no sound came. She started to giggle, and soon she was consumed with laughter as tears began to tumble down Anton's face.

"Don't laugh, Hope. God, please don't laugh." He tried to take her in his arms, to calm her, but she resisted.

"I'll tell you what I believe," she said. "This is what men do to women. All the time Steven hit me, he told me he loved me, told me he wanted me back. He knows about New York, Anton. He knows I got screwed in New York. And someday—someday—it's going to be you that does this to me. Someday, you'll try this too! Beating up a woman is what turns a boy into a man. Did you know that?" The laughter had ceased. "Well, I'm not going to let it happen. I'll kill you first." She growled it, like a cornered animal whose only way out was to fight.

"Hope, you know better than that. I'd never…" He caught his breath when a trickle of blood ran down the side of her face. He took out his handkerchief and stepped toward her.

"Don't touch me!" she screamed. "You're a bastard, just like the rest. How many women have you hurt, Anton? How many women did you kill to make yourself a man?"

The words tore into him, and he thought of Catherine. Hope continued muttering to herself in low, guttural sounds, accusing him of horrendous crimes. There was rage in her voice and she lashed at him, screaming her hate and anger. When he didn't react, she charged at him with her fists, trying to tear at his face the way Steven had torn at hers. Before his eyes, he saw something snap as if something had broken inside her.

*****

Hope, too, could only watch the woman on the outside as she screamed and struck at the man's face again and again, aware of him pulling her over onto the bed, where he held her kicking and screaming. She watched it in slow motion; even her own words sounded garbled and thick. The door opened briefly, and the man shouted toward it, "Get out!" He hovered over her, his eyes temporarily distracted, his jacket hanging open, revealing the gun. *The gun!* She watched her own hand reach for it—there. It felt heavy and cold. The door closed, and the man's eyes turned back to her.

She smiled as she pointed the barrel of the gun at the man's face and chuckled at the terror she saw.

"Hope, you don't know what you're doing. Give me the gun." His words came thick and slow.

But now she felt the power that men had long possessed. It felt wonderful. "I'm going to kill you, Steven," she laughed.

Anton slowly backed away and went around the foot of the bed with his hands up. Hope got up and stood beside the bed, her arms extended, the gun pointed between his eyes.

"It's me. Anton." There was a tremor in his voice. "Look at me, the color of my hair, my eyes. Listen to my voice."

"I only hear words. You're trying to trick me. Be still!" Her hands moved, releasing the safety catch. He should have rushed her while he had the chance, but never dreamed she would find the safety. He wanted to gentle it away from her, avoid using force, but now it was too late. She waved the gun in his face, and he stopped, not daring to come closer.

Hope watched the woman, and although she knew the man was Anton, there was no way to tell the other woman who he was. Anton's eyes pleaded with her to come out, to take control, but she was afraid.

"Hope, I'm Anton. I won't hurt you," he said, and Hope sat back and watched the two argue back and forth, first looking at the trembling man, then at the woman with the ugly face. Her finger twitched.

Dear God, she's going to kill him! She wanted to scream, but the sound wouldn't come out. She pushed the gun out of the woman's hand and saw the man run toward her.

"Oh, God." Finally, she heard her own voice as Anton picked her up from where she had crumpled to the floor.

He laid her back on the bed, and she sobbed, hugging him around the waist while he sat next to her, stroking her hair, taking deep gulps of air to calm his own trembling body. "Shhh, baby," he said, his hands still shaking. "It's all right, it's all right."

"I almost killed you," she sobbed.

"But you didn't." He slipped down on the bed beside her and took her in his arms. "Don't cry, sweetheart. It's over. We're going to get you some help, I promise. Just try to rest." He dabbed her face where a cut had reopened, and he wanted to kiss her, but her face looked so sore.

"I'm so tired." She took a deep breath, and before long, sleep rescued her from her pain.

Anton lay down and cradled Hope in his arms. Tears soaked into the pillow as he held her tight against him, remembering their laughter, their sweet lovemaking just the morning before. Life had seemed so beautiful then. Steven had reduced what had been beautiful to simply "getting screwed" in New York. Anton choked at the thought. He lay with her for over an hour before finally kissing her gently good night.

*****

The others stood when he appeared at the foot of the stairs. He went to the French doors in the dining room, where he looked out at the mountains. There was strength in them, a power that Hope had come to rely on when her problems seemed too big. He'd laughed at her once when she said that the mountains could make problems smaller. Now he prayed they would for him as well.

But the mountains failed him. They only seemed to weep with him as the clouds gathered at their peaks and cast dark shadows across the moonlit sky.

Nicki came and patted his shoulder, offering him a damp cloth for the cut on his lip where Hope's tiny fist had landed a surprisingly powerful blow.

"Thanks," he said and held the cool cloth to his mouth.

"Anton, she didn't mean those things. She knows you're not like that." They had all heard Hope's screams through the walls and floors as they echoed throughout the house.

"I know," he barely managed.

Jeff came up and squeezed his shoulders. "Try not to take it so hard."

Anton turned to him in anger. "The woman I made love to yesterday doesn't even know my name. Do you have any idea how it feels to come home and find her face turned inside out?" Feeling his anger mount, he turned away again.

"Yes. It's the same face of the women at the shelter that Hope sees five days a week. The faces I've seen time and again."

"I don't give a damn about those other faces!" he shouted, facing Jeff once again. Clay stepped closer, suddenly alert as Anton continued. "I'm talking about Hope! Why in the hell aren't the two of you out there arresting that bastard?"

"Hope won't press charges. I've already tried to talk to her," Clay answered. Jeff rubbed Anton's shoulders, trying to comfort him, but he jerked away, glaring.

"I should have known!" he barked, and Clay signaled for Nicki to step away. "You're nothing but a couple of small-town cops with no balls, playing big, important men in this wading pool of a town."

"Hope is the only witness. How do you think she would hold up in court?" Clay said. "Jeff tried to tell you. She's gone around the bend this time. The defense would have a field day."

"So, he walks a free man? Well, I won't have it." He headed for the door, but Jeff grabbed him from behind, pinning his arms behind his back.

"Give us your gun, Anton. Then you can go. We can't just let you blow him away."

"If you were doing your job, I wouldn't have to." At his breaking point, Anton struggled to get away from Jeff as Hope had from him.

"Don't you think I'd like to turn you loose on him?" Jeff said. "Clay and I are cops. We've got to play by the rules. Give up your weapon, then you can go."

He struggled, but Jeff held him tighter still while Clay relieved him of his revolver.

When Jeff let him go, Anton quickly stepped away and turned, angry and breathless. He stuck his finger in Jeff's face. "You keep your fucking hands off me, you fucking queer!" With that, he stormed from the house and his tires spit gravel as he sped down the driveway.

"Well, partner, should we have let him go? Steven is twice his size and has his service revolver," Clay said.

"Anton can take care of himself. Would you want that mad little Russian after you?" Jeff chuckled, trying to hide the wound that Anton had inflicted.

*****

THE PEBBLE AND THE MAN

It surprised Anton that Steven was so easy to find, that after what he'd done the night before, he would be so bold as to eat at the Noisy Water—the table in front of the window, no less. The streetlights and the flashing of Kelly's sign aided him as he watched Steven step out onto the road and turn south, then west a few blocks down. After sizing him up, Anton patted his left side instinctively, reminding himself he had no gun. Surprise was his best weapon, he decided, knowing that all his training and expertise couldn't change his small stature in hand-to-hand combat. He had to be cunning and quick. He ran through the alley and around the building and listened for Steven's heavy tread.

This had happened once in Brussels. Someone had followed him as he transported secret documents for the consulate there. He had lain quietly against the building then as he did now, listening. But then, he'd had weapons, a gun and a stiletto. Something quick and something quiet. But after watching the man die from his stiletto wounds, Anton no longer carried the knife.

He wished he had it now.

The stucco of the building felt rough and damp in the cool night air. He took a deep breath upon hearing the footsteps of a heavy man.

Steven rounded the corner, and Anton grabbed him by the shirt, throwing him to the ground in the shadow of the building. Adrenaline pumped through Anton's veins as he struck the unsuspecting man with a vengeance. Over and over, he struck him in the face, leaving reminders for tomorrow...*for Hope*, he thought.

When Steven realized it was Anton, he quickly came to his senses. The surprise passing, he managed to get the smaller man off him, but as he rose, Anton kicked the back of his legs and they buckled, bringing Steven to his knees, his face grating against the coarse stucco.

Anton stood on Steven's calves and wrenched his arms behind him, pulling his service revolver from its holster and flinging it into the river. "I don't like guys who beat up on women," he hissed. "And I don't like guys who have me followed, then get a report on what I do."

"You mean like fucking my wife?"

Anton twisted Steven's arm until something popped and Steven screamed in pain. "She's not your wife anymore. And we have something you never did. It's..." He stopped. It was none of Steven's business. Already his personal life had made him slip up. He'd been in such bliss that he hadn't picked up on the signs that he had been followed. Looking back on it, he remembered seeing the same face on at least three different occasions. "If you touch her again, I swear to God I'll kill you."

"Your threats don't scare me," Steven grunted, and Anton leaned close to his ear, not wanting him to miss a word.

"It's not a threat. It's a promise."

"You think you're tough, don't you, little man?"

"That's right, Wykes. I'm one tough little son of a bitch. You'll do well not to forget it. Touch her again—you're dead!"

Steven moaned when Anton jerked his arms upward. "They'll know who did it," he grunted, trying to push Anton off his legs.

"Maybe. But you'll still be dead." Anton pressed his full weight against Steven.

"Look at it like this. I did you a favor. She's crazy as a loon, and if she got pregnant in New York, you won't have that to worry about anymore." Steven strained to laugh. "That's what I did once. She hid being pregnant from me for five months, but I took care of it. Jesus, what a mess!"

Whether it was true or not, Anton felt sick. "Just remember, I keep my promises." With that he was gone, leaving Steven kneeling beside the building, his face bleeding, barely able to move his left arm or his legs.

*****

"If you're looking for your gun, Clay's got it," Jeff said as he leaned against the doorjamb, dressed in his robe, his hair disheveled.

"No..." Anton could see he had awakened Jeff, and felt bad. "Actually, I'm looking for someone to talk to." The anger was gone now, spent. All that remained were softly spoken words.

"You didn't exactly catch me during my social hour. It's one in the morning. I have to get up early for work, and I've had a hell of a day." Jeff rubbed his eyes. "Did you find him?" he asked after a moment, and Anton nodded. "Well, you don't look any the worse for it. I just pray you didn't leave him in a ditch somewhere."

Anton shook his head. "Can we talk?"

Jeff sighed, raking his fingers through his hair. "Frankly, little Russian, I'm tired of messing with you. No offense, but I've got a partner whose sister got beat up and a friend who got the crap beat out of her and is very near a mental breakdown. I'm pulling two jobs, mine and hers, so they won't hire someone else to take her place. I'm tired, Anton. This 'fucking queer' has neither the time nor the inclination."

His ordinarily smiling eyes were cold now, his face set and tired. He closed the door, leaving Anton standing alone on the step.

*****

The cold night air made Anton shiver as he walked through the town, along the road, and finally out into the countryside. So many times, he'd stalked the night, searching for a few minutes of warmth. Jeff had always been willing to talk before. But now the only warmth Anton found were smudge pots in the orange groves that skirted the mountains.

He wondered about what Steven had said. The thought of her carrying his child had never occurred to him. They had made love with such abandon that the possibility certainly existed. He tried to imagine how he would feel if she was indeed pregnant, and felt jubilant. But the moment faded quickly.

"You don't have to worry about that anymore."

God in heaven, he thought.

He looked up beyond the shadows of the orange trees, at the dark mountains against the still-blacker sky. He wished desperately for someone to talk to.

For the first time in his life, he went to his knees. There in the soil of the orange grove, he cried. Only once before had he felt so alone, so isolated, as this night when he wept among the trees.

The Second Year

CHAPTER 22

1980

The phone startled him awake, and he fumbled the receiver to his ear. "Yeah…"

It was Jeff. He'd be there to pick him up at three.

Anton looked at the clock as he hung up: 6:00 a.m. He rubbed his face, realizing he'd forgotten to ask where they were going, but soon drifted back to sleep.

At three o'clock, Jeff honked the horn outside Anton's apartment, and he soon emerged and got into the van.

"You look like shit," Jeff said casually as he pulled away from the curb.

"Thanks. Where are we going?"

"I thought if you spent a day in the life of Hope Landrum, it might help clear your perspective. You're working her shift at the shelter with me."

They stopped in front of a converted two-story house in what seemed to be the very middle of nowhere. It was a state-run project, something of an experiment providing immediate shelter for battered families from as far away as Sacramento. The experimental part was that local police departments offered incentives to officers who volunteered their time and efforts toward making it work, reducing costs. That was how he'd first gotten involved, but he now found himself filling in for Hope temporarily.

There was no way Anton could have prepared himself for what he found inside. There were small children, battered and bruised, their tiny limbs often sporting casts. Yet the children ran toward them. "Officer Jeff!" they called excitedly. Jeff turned on his smiling eyes, grinning as he picked one up into his arms.

"Good afternoon, ladies!" Jeff addressed their mothers.

The women's faces looked much like Hope's, but some with cigarette burns or marks left by hot grease. One woman in particular caught Anton's eye.

"Who's this?" she asked.

The women stared at Anton, the unfamiliar man who looked as if he'd been brought here as a form of punishment, thrown into a colony of lepers for some unforgivable crime.

"Ladies, I'd like you to meet Anton, Hope's friend," Jeff answered. Anton shifted his weight and smiled awkwardly.

"We heard she got hurt again. Did he do it?" another asked.

Individually they were helpless, but as a group…terrifying. Anton felt an unfamiliar panic rise in his throat.

Finally, Jeff answered. "No. He's here to try and understand a few things. All this is quite foreign to him."

"Good," a woman said, seeing the look on Anton's face.

He stood silent, frozen. This was a six-hour shift. He wondered how he would survive six more hours after the last twelve.

*****

By nine thirty, Anton sat in the passenger seat of Jeff's van and fixed his eyes on an invisible spot on the dash. Jeff sat next to him, observing his reaction. He felt sorry for Anton and wondered if he'd gone too far, aware now that he had, indeed, used this as a kind of punishment for Anton's angry words. Still, there was a lesson to be learned, and he wanted to drive it home.

"Yesterday, you said you didn't give a damn about the 'other faces,'" Jeff said quietly. "Do you give a damn now?" He saw the empty look that Anton cast his way. "Hope comes here five days a week and helps them see their own faces, the human beings behind what they see in the mirror. She gives them love, cries with them, laughs with them, diapers their babies, mops the floors. That's what she does for a living. The state doesn't pay her worth a damn, but she does it anyway."

Jeff could see Anton was numb and almost reached over to touch him, knowing that sometimes just a warm hand could bring comfort. But he stopped himself.

"Why did you bring me here, Jeff?" Anton asked after a long silence.

"Guess I was pissed. You know, for a short man, you sure have a way of looking down your nose at people. I didn't realize it until yesterday. You keep treating us like who we are and what we do isn't important just because we're from a small town. But I've got news for you. We're important to those women and children in there.

"Those kids are always happy when they see me. I am the one man in their lives that can show them a man can be kind, and fun, and safe. I show those kids what a good man looks like. I think what I do is important."

Anton stared at the dash.

Jeff changed the subject. "Hope is stronger than most. She managed to escape the cycle of going back for more. But she paid a price for it. She has some serious emotional scars, and this last time was a real blow. I tried to warn you a long time ago."

"Is that what this is about—to explain Hope's problems? If you had any idea how I feel about her, you'd know that I don't blame *her*." He rolled the window down, suddenly in need of fresh air. "But she needs help. She took my gun—"

"Yeah, I know. It must have scared the shit out of you. Then for me and Clay to take it again…must be rough for a professional like you to lose it twice in one day."

"How did you know she took it?"

"Nicki called me about four this morning and asked me to convince Bud you were still alive. She was hysterical. I guess she dreamed she really shot you. They tried to call you, but you were out all night. Where'd you go?"

"Looking for someone to talk to," Anton said pointedly, staring straight ahead. "Why didn't you tell me you knew about the gun?" he asked after a while.

"Waited to see if you would tell me first, to see how honest we were with each other."

Both men stared out the windshield, avoiding each other's eyes. Anton ventured a quick glance after a while and saw Jeff still wore the icy look that he now realized had bothered him all afternoon. "Well, I told you, so I guess we're being honest." He was exhausted and wanted to see Hope before it got too late. He wondered why Jeff still sat.

"While we're being honest…"

Here it comes, Anton thought, *the real reason for this little chat.*

"There's something we need to get straight," Jeff said. "When I was a kid, some other kids teased me because my folks had so many of us. I picked a fight. Got knocked on my ass. Anyway, I went crying to my mom and she sat me down and told me how lucky we were to have so many people who love us." He looked at the man next to him, who still stared out the window in silence. "Damn it, Anton!" He waited for their eyes to meet. "I come from an affectionate family. We were taught that there was nothing wrong with showing it. I'm not gay, and even if I were, so what?"

Anton looked away. It seemed mundane compared to the other problems at hand, but it obviously bothered Jeff very much. He hadn't been aware that his words had hurt him. He wondered now if this was the source of the lifeless eyes, if it was why Jeff had turned him away when he'd so desperately needed a friend. "I'm not used to being touched," he finally said.

"Get used to it or stay out of my way. I'm not changing for anybody, not even a stuck-up little Russian like you."

*****

Anton went to see Hope that night, even though it was late, and was relieved when she seemed happy to see him. She couldn't remember much of the night before, though he thought he saw a hint of recognition in her eyes when she noticed his swollen lip and touched it gently with her fingertips.

He slept on the couch that night and the next. Nicki finally went home and Anton stayed with Hope. After a few nights, he found himself in her bed. Just holding her close gave him a sense that everything was going to be all right, and he understood when she refused his advances.

*****

"I have to go to Paris," Anton said as he sat down in the chair across from Dan. "Have you ordered yet?" It had only been a month since dinner at Mrs. Philips's house, but it seemed like years. He wondered if Dan knew that Clay had told him their family secret.

"Where the hell have you been? What if I needed to find you, or aren't we partners anymore?"

The question surprised Anton. "I've been at Hope's. Sanderson knows I'm there. I've been in touch."

"So, the man of iron has finally succumbed to her charms, has he?" Dan folded his arms and smiled strangely. He, too, had been in touch with Sanderson and had learned that Anton had accepted the NORAD assignment. The whole Branch was buzzing about the last big job before the USIB was to disband. Just as he'd feared, Anton had jumped at it.

"Did you hear that your friend Wykes beat her up?" He sat back when the waitress came to take their order, and waited for her to leave before looking at Dan for an answer.

"How is she?" Dan asked.

Anton took stock as he drank his water. This was the man he was supposed to trust with his life, his partner in a very dangerous business.

"Like I said, I have to go to Paris. Sanderson has a security job for me and wants me to check it out. Hope's afraid to be alone, and there are a couple of times the others can't be with her. Will you check in with her then? At least she knows you. Noah doesn't get home from Atlanta for another week or so, or I'd ask him." He avoided talking about her condition.

"Sure." Dan sipped his drink. He had wanted to discuss Anton's acceptance of the NORAD assignment, but told himself it could wait. "So how was New York?"

He was amused when Anton came to life. He described the capture of Nezar from the moment Hope had 'wonderfully' pointed him out to the actual arrest. Dan chuckled to himself over how Anton loved his work and now talked like an excited child, so different from the suicidal-maniac reputation that had floated around the Branch before he'd become known as The Best. Dan laughed. *The Best. Sanderson's Pride!* He finished his drink and ordered another.

CHAPTER 23

The beautiful spring day beckoned Hope. The sky was a deep azure, and the trees wore tiny new leaves as they dressed themselves for the coming summer. She could smell the valley's orange blossoms all the way from Horn Mountain.

She walked across the meadow, where the wind made the native grasses wave like the ocean, and as she entered the woods, the distant swordsmen clashed their wooden swords in a never-ending duel. It was wonderful. The peace she needed was here. She let the memories of the past two weeks slip away, as though they could be buried here in the woods to rot along with the decaying leaves. She dug her fingers into the moist dirt and looked at it, smelled it, rubbed it between her fingers. She loved the texture of the earth. It brought her calm. It brought her peace.

She smiled when she thought of the first time she'd brought Anton into these woods. Startled by a rabbit, he had reached for his revolver. She laughed to herself, glad he was coming home today. She stopped by a stream to wash her hands before heading back to the house.

Who's here? she wondered as she approached, knowing she hadn't left the door open. She wondered if Nicki had returned from the airport with Anton, but then realized Nicki's car wasn't there.

A face appeared in the upstairs window, then quickly disappeared again.

"No!" she screamed. She ran down the driveway as fast as she could. She was alone, and Steven was back.

Why had she let Dan leave? Why hadn't she insisted he stay until Anton got back? The door slammed behind her, and she screamed, pushing herself forward. *Faster! Don't look back!*

She tripped and slid across the rocky ground. Steven grabbed her, and she felt herself being dragged up the driveway, then up the front steps of the house, his laughter ringing in her ears.

Her head hit the corner of the metal filing cabinet when he threw her into the study, and blood poured into her eyes as she crumpled to the floor.

"Hello, gorgeous!" he crowed.

She looked up at him and saw the scabbed wounds on his face as he removed his belt.

"Why, Steven? Why?" she cried. "If you leave now, I promise I won't tell anyone you were here!"

He laughed. "Why would I leave when you were about to show me a good time?" He watched her trying to get up, leaving bloody handprints as she held on to the wall and curtains for balance. "I met your little boyfriend," he said, stepping nearer. "He says you two have something pretty special. Something I never had. Well, I want it."

"Dan!" she screamed. "Steven, Dan's on his way. He called."

Steven only grinned. He knew it was a lie, because it had been Dan who'd called to tell him when she would be alone. "Scream all you want, bitch. Ain't nobody here but you and me." He pushed her against the wall and engulfed her mouth with his. She pushed him away and wiped her mouth with disgust. He slapped her, causing blood to splatter from her wound, then wrenched both her arms behind her. He wanted to do to her what Anton had done to him, but his left arm was still weak. Pressing her tight against the wall, he fastened the belt around her neck, then pushed her to the floor, where he strapped the belt to the radiator.

"If you ever loved me, you won't hurt me," she pleaded, gasping for air.

He laughed. "Nobody ever loved you except maybe that moron Clay. The only reason I married you was because you were a good fuck!"

She tried to kick him as he unfastened his pants, but he caught her ankle and tied it to the table leg with a lamp cord, bringing the lamp crashing to the floor.

Her tears and blood formed a wretched paste in her hair, and with each move, the belt tightened around her neck. Her screams became garbled as he tore at her clothes; buttons popped and scattered, rolling across the floor. The more she struggled, the more excited he became. He pulled her toward him and pinned her arms. She could barely breathe.

"*Why?*" It was a whisper.

Sweat dripped from his face onto hers. She felt her body tearing as he forced himself into her. She couldn't breathe. Soon, she felt nothing.

A shot rang out. Hope opened her eyes just as Steven's face contorted. He twisted his neck at an odd angle and stared, speechless, into Anton's eyes. He tried to speak, but another shot rang out, and he tumbled off her.

"Nicki, get a blanket!" Anton shouted.

*****

"Shhh, Hope. It's over." Anton looked up at Nicki in desperation as Hope sobbed. Nicki held a cloth on her head to stop the bleeding, while Anton rocked her in his arms and she clung to him for life.

Jeff went to the window and peered out. "The ambulance is here." He couldn't help but wonder if Anton blamed him for this. He and Clay should have gone after Steven long ago. If they had, this never would have happened. Clay stood on the other side of the room, keeping his distance as always. Helpless. Clay always had a look about him where Hope was concerned, only now his helplessness was mixed with guilt.

Damn! Jeff thought. He felt sick as Hope's fingernails tore little holes into Anton's flesh when the ambulance driver tried to loosen her grip. Finally, it was decided that Anton should go with her. They would see him later, after they finished up business here.

*****

Anton sat in the chair beside the hospital bed, where Hope fought demons in her sleep. The medication the doctor had given her had taken a long time to take effect. Now he watched as she rolled her head back and forth, mumbling incoherent words, her hands twitching.

He had failed her. He hadn't been able to protect her from the thing that haunted her now, and the bandage on her head, the wide bruise that had formed around her neck, made him cringe. Again and again he tried to push the vision out of his mind, the vision that always began with him opening the study door to find her naked and bleeding, with Steven on top of her.

A new wave of grief washed over him, and he laid his head in his arms on the side of the bed.

He was unaware that Nicki had come into the room until she put her hands on his shoulders and spoke. "Paul Sanderson is here. They want to see you now," she whispered. "I'll sit with Hope."

He nodded, then rose and left the room.

Two uniformed officers escorted him to a small bright room for questioning. Sanderson had flown out of New York to represent the USIB in what would ordinarily be a police matter, but because Anton was a government agent, Sanderson's presence was required before any kind of questioning could be conducted.

Sanderson sat grim-faced throughout the proceedings. Jeff and Clay had already given statements about the beating prior to the rape, and they, too, watched. It was painful for Anton to describe the scene. When he did, Clay left the room, and Anton wondered if he would be back. But Jeff shook his head, indicating he wouldn't.

The questioning continued. Hours passed.

"Hasn't he been through enough?" Jeff finally said.

Sanderson and the two police detectives left the room. It took over an hour, but when they returned, Anton was told he could remain at the hospital with Hope.

*****

"Anton," Jeff called before he returned to Hope's room, "let me drive you home. You look exhausted." He'd been forced to describe in detail things that no one should ever see, and Jeff was sure he felt very much alone. "When was the last time you slept?"

"I flew back from Paris today…" Anton looked at his watch. "Yesterday. I've been up for thirty-six hours. Thanks, but I need to stay here."

"I'd argue with you, but I know it won't do any good. Here." Jeff removed his jacket and began to unbutton his shirt as he pushed Anton toward the men's room. "It'll be big on you, but you don't want her seeing that when she wakes up," he said, indicating Anton's shirt.

Anton looked at himself in the mirror, seeing the bloodstains for the first time, his eyes barely able to focus. He took off his shirt and splashed cool water on his face, then washed the blood off his chest and shoulder while Jeff dabbed a damp paper towel on the tiny moon-shaped wounds across his back.

"Hope's fingernails really did a job. Maybe someone should look at it," Jeff said.

Anton shook his head. "Is she awake?"

"No. Neither are you." Jeff looked at him in the mirror. "Want me to find you a doughnut or something?"

Anton ignored him. He put on Jeff's shirt and tucked it into his pants.

"What happens to the women, Jeff?" he finally asked.

"What do you mean?" Jeff put on his jacket and zipped it partially up.

"You're a cop. You work at the shelter. What happens to women after they've been raped?" He shut his eyes against the emotions the word triggered.

Jeff took him by the shoulders. "You listen to me. If you're going to help her at all, you've got to get some sleep. You're running on borrowed time, and what she needs is someone who can be strong. If you can be strong, then she will be all right. But it'll take time, Anton. It won't happen overnight.

"I've talked to women after they've left the shelter and gone on with their lives. They all tell me the same thing. It's like getting a tattoo. After the initial shock and trauma, time is the only thing that helps. But it never goes away. They are left with scars, some visible, some not. It becomes a part of them, their history, who they are. They never forget it, but eventually it fades. The main thing is this: right now she needs *you* to be strong."

Anton leaned against the tiled wall. The fatigue had torn down his defenses, and he could no longer hold back the tears. Jeff wanted to pull him close, to comfort him, but watched helplessly while he cried against the cold, uncaring wall.

"Anton, let me help you."

He shook his head. "Nothing will ever fix this," he said and walked out.

When he entered Hope's room, Nicki stood and joined him at her bedside. "The nurse gave her another shot," she said. "She'll probably sleep the rest of the night."

He reached down and stroked Hope's face. She was finally peaceful, no longer thrashing about in her sleep. "How is she?"

"She lost a lot of blood, took ten stitches in her head. They want to keep her overnight." Nicki, too, had been questioned, having been the only witness to the shooting, and she had a pretty fair idea of what he had just been through. "How are you?" she asked.

"Numb."

She put her arm around him and gave him a hug. "I know. But Hope's a tough lady. It's going to be all right, you'll see." She said good night and left him sitting beside Hope's bed.

Anton leaned back in the chair. *A year,* he thought. It had only taken a year in Three Rivers to recreate the pain that caring brought. After eleven years of becoming impervious to caring—becoming hard—all it took was one tiny woman with pretty green eyes. He took a deep breath and closed his own, allowing sleep to finally have its way.

*****

It wasn't until midafternoon that he awoke to find Hope looking at him from her bed, her eyes empty. She sat motionless, an eerie calm around her. "Is he dead?"

Anton nodded and sat up in the chair.

She closed her eyes and took a deep breath. "Thank you."

"Hope, what can I do for you? Is there anything you want?" he asked.

"I only want to die," she said.

He rose and pulled her up into his arms, but there was resistance. He finally let her go, realizing the unwillingness with which she was being held. He sank back into the chair with a helplessness and despair he had never known.

CHAPTER 24

Jeff climbed the stairs and headed for Hope's bedroom. Clay had told him she was going to stay with Nicki for a while and that Anton had come to pick up her clothes.

"Thought I'd find you here," he said as he entered the room, but Anton hardly looked up. He was folding the clothes he had laid out on the bed. "How come you didn't tell me you were famous?"

"I didn't know I was."

"You must be. That Sanderson guy made one phone call and all charges have been dropped. Here's your gun."

He laid the holstered weapon beside the suitcase. "I was told to give it back to you by executive order. You must have a hell of a reputation in Washington."

"They don't think of me as a stuck-up little Russian the way you do. They know I do what I have to do. And I am what I have to be." He bored holes in Jeff with his eyes. They had been engaged in a quiet resentment for weeks without either understanding the reason why. All he knew was that he'd been wounded, deeply, and that Jeff had rubbed salt in it.

"Do you blame me for what happened? If so, say it. If I hadn't taken your gun, had just let you hunt Steven down in cold blood, you wouldn't have gotten off this easily. You'd be in jail right now."

Anton remained unmoved as he packed Hope's clothes with deliberate neatness. "I'd gladly give twenty years of my life if this could be erased." Closing the suitcase, he strapped the weapon across his chest.

Jeff picked up the suitcase and followed him down the stairs in silence.

At the foot of the stairs, Anton looked toward the closed door at the end of the dark hall.

"Don't let it make you crazy, Anton. Come on, let's go," Jeff said.

"She hates having that door closed. It cuts off the light from the rest of the house."

"Yeah, I know, but she's staying with Nicki for a while. We haven't had a chance to clean…"

Before he could finish, Anton strode down the hall and swung the door open. An audible gasp escaped him. He hadn't noticed the room the day Hope was raped. He hadn't even realized that anyone was there at first. After he had returned from the airport, it had been the closed door that had drawn him. Hope hated for the door to be closed, had always fussed at her friends about it. He'd gone to open it for her so she wouldn't fuss.

But now he saw the dried blood in the shape of tiny handprints that marched up the wall. He saw the stained curtains, the broken lamp with its cord still wound around the table leg.

His breathing became quick and shallow.

"Close your eyes and walk away," Jeff said.

Anton stepped into the room, screaming with rage. "You think she's the only victim, the only one who got hurt? You can close this door and pretend it didn't happen, but when I see it closed, I remember what I found on the other side! Well, I want it open, goddammit! I want to see the sun shining down the hall so I know there's nothing here!" He reached up and ripped at the wallpaper with his bare hands, spitting angry Russian words as strip after strip of the bloodstained paper tore away. Tears burned his eyes as he flung the writing table away from the wall, sending books and papers flying.

"Where can I go with my anger?" he screamed, tearing the curtains from the window. "Who can I turn to with what I feel? When he raped her, he took away the only good thing in my life! Damn him! I hope he rots in hell!" He grabbed the chair with both hands and hurled it across the room, its leg hitting the small glass prism that hung in the window.

"Oh my God! What have I done?" he cried. He went to his knees, sobbing over the shattered prism, his hands trembling as he picked up the fragments and tried to piece them back together. "It was all she wanted," he cried. "I told her she could have anything in New York, and all she wanted was this silly piece of glass."

Jeff went and knelt beside him. "You can get her another one, Anton. I think you're overreacting."

"Am I? In New York, all she wanted was this piece of glass, but when I was with her at the hospital, all she wanted was to die. I asked her if she wanted anything. 'I only want to die,' she said." He grabbed Jeff's collar, pulling him close. "What do I buy her now?"

"People who say that don't really mean it."

"No? Catherine did. She cut herself open with a butcher knife!"

The words spilled out before he could stop them, and he quickly turned from Jeff's surprised stare as vomit rose in his throat.

"Take a deep breath," Jeff said quietly. Kneeling beside him, he held Anton's shoulders as he heaved.

"Don't look at me," Anton whispered hoarsely. "Even animals have somewhere to hide, someone to go to." *I don't,* he continued in his mind, realizing that his reaction to Catherine's death had not changed even after all these years. He wished he had a hole to crawl into, a place to lick his wounds. He realized that Hope's words had set a clock ticking inside him. His fear of losing her had become the blasting powder that had just exploded inside him, leaving him defenseless and weak. Just the thought of Hope wanting to die set in motion a new wave of sickness, and he coughed and choked.

Jeff wiped Anton's forehead with his hand. "You've got someone to go to, Russia…you can come to me."

After weeks of wearing ice, Anton saw the gentleness had returned to Jeff's eyes. He said nothing as Jeff gathered him close, his strong arms surrounding him with comfort. Their arms and legs tangled as they sat on the floor of the demolished room. Anton wept until the tears no longer came.

*****

Quiet breathing was the only sound left, except for the occasional shudder that ripped through him like a remnant of the storm just passed. Anton closed his eyes, so exhausted, so spent, like a child in need of holding when he's too tired.

Yes, surely this was what it was like to be held by the father he could not remember. He became aware of Jeff's mouth as it pressed against his forehead, aware of the arms that draped gently around him, the hand that caressed his hair.

He kept his eyes closed, afraid the comfort he found with this man would look ugly and disgusting. But he found solace here, warmth and tenderness.

Jeff began to sing a soulful Negro spiritual in a low, sad voice. He, too, closed his eyes, humming the tune when the words were lost. He threw back his head when he hit the high notes, his eyes squeezed tight when he felt moved by the song.

When it was done, he wiped the moist corners of his eyes. "Back in 'Nam, I took some shrapnel—Laid in the thicket for hours, listening to the gunfire, wondering if I'd ever see my family again." Jeff stroked Anton's hair and wiped his face again with his hand.

Anton opened his eyes. He wondered how much his dignity would pay for the comfort he had found. He retreated from Jeff's embrace and sat against the wall a few feet away. He looked at the dark-haired man, who seemed oblivious to any awkwardness between them.

"I was so scared," Jeff continued, "and God, I was in such pain, when out of nowhere came the biggest black man I ever saw in my life." Jeff met Anton's gaze as if they had just spent the afternoon exchanging war stories. "This dude pulled me up in his arms and rocked me, sang me the blues all night long. It made the hurt go away for a while, dulled the pain until my company could find me. It felt so good, like crawling back in my mama's womb." He looked Anton square in the eye. "It's okay, Russia. There's nothing queer about it, you know. It's what humanity's all about, human bondage and all. Isaac taught me that. He died in my arms before morning. I had no idea he'd been hit too. Seems he needed me as much as I needed him." He turned away, his jaw tensing.

"I'm sorry, Jeff. I don't know what to say," Anton said awkwardly.

"So," Jeff cleared his throat, "was Catherine your wife?"

Anton nodded.

"How come she did that?"

"She was very dependent. Very young, only sixteen." He leaned his pounding head in his hand and waited for Jeff's reaction.

"Were you a lot older?" Jeff said finally.

"Twenty-seven. I was on assignment, and I guess she was afraid I wouldn't get back in time. So she killed herself."

Once again, Anton paled, and Jeff got up and opened a window. The afternoon sun had begun to pour into the room, and the fresh air felt good.

"In time for what?" Jeff asked as he sat back down against the wall.

"What?"

"You said she was afraid you wouldn't get back in time. In time for what?"

"Did I say that?" Anton frowned. "I don't remember."

Jeff studied him in silence.

As if hearing his thoughts, Anton smiled sadly. "I'm as crazy as Hope is, Jeff. There are things I don't remember, things that pop out every once in a while, just often enough to tell me I'm not well yet."

"Are you seeing someone about it?" he asked.

"Yeah. She says that one of these days it's all going to come to me, but not until I'm ready to handle it. Sounds like a bunch of bullshit, doesn't it?" He finally cracked a smile.

"I've heard of that, people repressing stuff. It doesn't mean you're crazy, though I have to admit, you're one of the moodiest bastards I've ever met." Jeff grinned broadly, then said, "Bud's not crazy either. She's just got a lot of issues."

"I love her, you know," Anton said after a while. "I think I love her more than I ever loved Catherine. It breaks my heart seeing her so despondent."

"So how come you never told anyone about Catherine?"

He chuckled sadly and pointed to the spot on the floor where he had been earlier. "Didn't you see me? It happened eleven years ago, and it still makes me sick. It's incredible how long it takes to bury one's dead. I've been trying to bury my baby for eleven years." He closed his eyes and leaned his head forward.

Jeff went to get him a glass of water, wondering if '*baby*' was what he'd called his young bride. "You okay, Russia?" he asked, handing him the glass. "You know, I wish I'd known all this a long time ago. I might have been a better friend." He stretched out his hand and pulled Anton to his feet.

"Do something for me, will you, Jeff? Noah got back yesterday, and I think someone should tell him what happened. Would you handle it for me?"

"Sure. Don't worry about it." Jeff kicked aside a pile of rubbish and slapped Anton across the shoulders. "Jesus, what a mess one little Russian can make," he said and laughed as they walked out.

CHAPTER 25

Anton thought of Jeff as he drove down the coast with Nathan. In just a little over five weeks, he'd run the gamut of emotions. It was a bitter pill to think that Steven had raped Hope because of the battle of male egos in which he and Steven had engaged. That she now hid among other abused women at the shelter made his guilt all the more difficult to bear.

She never blamed him. Had no reason to. But she remained distant to everyone except Noah. *"She's used to having me around when she's been hurt,"* the boxer had explained. After Jeff told him, Noah had gone to see her right away, and she'd gone readily to his arms. They held each other and cried, leaving Anton feeling like an intruder.

Noah had taken it hard. Jeff told him later that he'd gone to Noah's apartment only to discover pictures of Hope everywhere—snapshots from vacations with Steven, but with the Steven halves missing, portraits and sketches of her he had drawn remarkably well. There was even a high school picture with Hope in Clay's embrace that God only knew how he'd gotten. Jeff had described the odd feeling of sitting on the couch, facing the boxer, with Hope's pictures staring at him from every direction.

*****

"Son, don't you think it's a lot of trouble to cart me around?" Nathan's voice broke into his reverie.

"Not at all. I enjoy your company." Anton had taken him to Colma to visit Stella's grave, as Hope had always done on the first Wednesday of the month. But it seemed she wasn't doing much of anything these days. He'd seized the opportunity to see Nathan again. When they returned to Monterey, Anton found a secluded little beach, where he spread a blanket, then carried the old man to the shore.

It was late afternoon, and the beach was deserted except for the gulls that glided overhead.

"Is there something you wanted to talk about?" Nathan asked.

He watched as Anton kept trying to say something, only to back away from the words time and again. He hadn't finished his sandwich or any of the other goodies he had packed for their outing.

"How's Hope?" Nathan coaxed.

"About the same. She's buried herself in her work...lives at the shelter, as a matter of fact."

"Has she been to the house?"

"No." Anton leaned against the warm rock. He and Nathan sat side by side, watching the waves roll in and come crashing down, only to slip away again. "I don't know what to do, Nathan," he finally volunteered. He tossed a stone toward the waves, and they lashed at it like a piece of raw meat thrown to hungry lions.

"Are you still friends? I know she went to New York with you. I got a postcard."

Anton smiled sadly. "We were more than friends in New York," he said. He glanced at the old man, who smiled. "I haven't seen her for over two weeks. I have to drive out to the shelter because she won't come to the phone. Most of the time, they say she's not there. She's hiding, Nathan. She's all skinny...won't eat." He felt empty as he tossed another stone. "It was all so different before everything changed."

Nathan laughed. "It usually is."

"I failed her, Uncle Nate."

"Don't give yourself so much credit. You're not that powerful."

"But I have. When she needed me, I wasn't there. She needs me now and I don't know how to get through to her."

"You've only failed yourself. You found out that you're just a man. No more, no less." Nathan leaned his head back against the rock and closed his eyes.

"You're not helping."

"Am I supposed to?" He lifted his head to look at him. "You're the only one who has the power to do that. You have all the answers, you know." Nathan took the younger man's hand and opened it wide. "Right here! You have all the answers right here in the palm of your hand."

Anton's face remained blank, and Nathan frowned.

"Do I have to teach you kids everything?" He dug through the sand and found a small stone to place in Anton's upturned palm. "What do you see?"

"A pebble."

"Can that pebble do the things you do? Can it think? Does it feel?" Nathan slowly shook his head. "No. It's just a pebble. So who is greater, you or it?" He waited for an answer.

"It's not hard to be greater than a rock," Anton replied.

"Really? That little pebble will be here for ten thousand years after you're dead and buried." Nathan folded Anton's hand in his own, with the pebble like a seed in the warm surrounding fist. "You are what you are, son. What is, is. No one expects you to be more than human, so stop racing against yourself—you'll only lose." Nathan's raspy voice was all-knowing. "Take it from one who's fought that battle. Take it from one who knows!"

Anton looked at the person sitting beside him. He was nothing more than a tiny, crippled old man, yet somehow it would seem more fitting if he were tall and strong, wrapped in exquisite garb and flowing robes. "I'm sorry, Uncle Nate. I still don't understand."

"Empowerment, Anton. The pebble will outlast you, but you have something it does not—the power to change things. You can sit around like a rock, wishing things were different, or you can get off your ass and *change* them!"

What a treasure he is, disguised as crippled old man, Anton thought. *What treasures, these pearls of wisdom from a man who knows.*

CHAPTER 26

The drive home from Monterey always seemed to take forever and it was nine o'clock before Anton arrived in Three Rivers. He was glad he had talked with Leslie that morning. She, too, was driving down from the bay to meet them at his apartment. Hope needed help, the kind Leslie could give, the kind she'd given to him over the years.

He had stopped to call Clay and the others to implement a plan that had formed during the long, quiet drive. He felt renewed and enthusiastic as he pulled up to the shelter and parked the car.

Anton rang the doorbell and was invited in by a woman he'd come to recognize. Her own battle scars were healing, and she wore a pleasant smile framed by locks of wavy auburn hair. Her name was Valerie, and she had been at the shelter the first time he'd come with Jeff. She still remembered the look of terror he had worn.

"How are you?" she asked after sending one of the children for Hope.

"I'm all right," he said, feeling much more at ease than that first night. "You're looking well."

"Anton, you've got to get Hope away from here," she said in a confidential tone. "Staying here makes her think that our lives are normal. Her vision is all distorted. Every woman here would give anything for a nice guy like you, and…"

They looked up and saw Hope walking toward them.

"That's why I came," he said quietly, then whispered, "My God, she looks terrible."

"I know," Valerie whispered in return and stepped away.

When Hope saw who waited beside the door, she felt the unease that she always felt when he came around or called. Often, she told the other women to say she was out, or in the bathtub, trying to discourage this man who had once been her lover. She had no need of men anymore, especially this one who always looked sad and complained about the way *she* looked.

She stopped in front of him and waited for him to speak.

Anton looked passed her, to Valerie, who signaled encouragement, but just as before, he wasn't sure what to say. "Hi…"

He waited, but Hope said nothing.

"You haven't returned my calls. I've been worried."

"It's nine fifteen, Anton. You didn't drive over here to tell me that." Her voice was cold and distant.

He closed his eyes for a brief moment to block out the thin face that stirred him. "I want to take you to dinner," he said.

"I've had dinner."

"No, you haven't, Hope," Valerie cut in from behind. "Remember, you were busy and said you'd eat later."

"I'm not hungry," she growled.

"Well, I am." Anton chuckled nervously. "I haven't eaten yet, and I'm starved. Why don't you keep me company?" He tried not to let his concern show, but his eyes pleaded with her. He could feel her slipping away and feared he would never be able to retrieve her if she went much further.

"Why should I?"

"Because it's my birthday, and I just spent the entire day with your grandfather, who's doing fine, if you care. Or don't you care about anything anymore?" He had raised his voice but was instantly sorry. The other women and children in the room sat frozen in place just by the sound of an angry man. "I'm not leaving without you," he said quietly.

"And what will you do if I say no? Drag me?"

The expression on Val's face begged him not to give up, but he only shook his head. "That would be too much trouble. It would be easier to let you stay here and starve yourself to death." He choked on the thought and closed his eyes once again, remembering her words, *"I only want to die."* He had to make her want to live. "Hope, remember New York, those two funny old ladies?" He tried to make her smile, but it was plain to see she didn't care. She no longer cared about anything, not even her beloved Uncle Nate. He hadn't heard from her since the postcard, and she'd used to be so attentive to him.

Anton sighed. "So, Steven took that, too? Not only did he take away your rights, your freedom, but your will. Don't you know that what happened to you also happened to me? When Steven raped you, he took away a part of me. Standing here now…" his voice trembled. "I feel violated, Hope. I feel…raped."

He glanced at Valerie. Tears had sprung from her eyes as he spoke, but Hope stood stone-faced before him.

"You let him do it," he said. "You let him win." His hopes had been so high on the way home. But it was all for nothing. Finally, he turned and went to his car, where he sat in silence until it seemed to penetrate his soul.

Then the passenger door opened, and Hope slid into the seat beside him.

"I guess I can keep you company, it being your birthday and all," she said quietly, avoiding his eyes.

He had to restrain himself from taking her in his arms. Instead, he started the engine and headed toward town.

*****

Kelly's was the only place still open. The little town had yet to be invaded by fast-food chains with their all-night windows. The only people who ventured out were the single men and occasional woman who lived in the apartments nearby, Anton being one of those frequent patrons.

He found a table in the back, away from the familiar faces, away from the man who was trying to sober himself before heading home to the missus. The local tavern, a country-and-Western bar, produced a lot of coffee drinkers at Kelly's.

There were a few curious looks when he and Hope threaded their way to the back of the café. Almost everyone in town had known Steven, and consequently his wife. By now they also knew about the small man with the slight accent, who, as the weekly paper reported, was licensed to carry a gun.

*****

Hope tried not to be angry when Anton ordered for both of them even after she had declined to look at the menu. He tried so hard, she thought, and he chattered incessantly, as though he feared a moment of silence would become a wall between them. She watched from across the table, studying his features, watching his mouth as he spoke, and she tried to remember how it felt to touch his mouth with hers. His lips were sensual and pouty, his teeth straight and white. She studied his jawline, and then his eyes. It had been his eyes, that first day, that had pierced her until she forgot to pretend she didn't notice him. He had held her captive with the mystery behind those azure eyes. They held mystery still.

Anton stopped talking, abruptly aware of the tiny hand that had found its way across the table to his. Afraid to move or talk, he looked at her, but she instantly turned away. *It's a start,* he told himself when she removed her hand all too quickly. He smiled a little, though it was hard to smile at Hope. Her eyes were dull and hollow, her skin pale and thin. What had happened? Where was the beautiful princess he'd played Prince Charming to? He looked into her eyes and wished he could bring back the light that Steven had extinguished, restore the laughter, the teasing that had made him crazy on more than one occasion. *Does she remember?* he wondered. *Does she want to?* She had told him she loved him, and now he silently begged to hear the words again.

"Stop it."

"What?"

"You're counting the bites I take. Stop."

"I wasn't, I swear," he said. Just the mention of it made him look at the plate of food she had barely touched.

But he said nothing. Already, he was anticipating her anger once she learned he had no intention of taking her back to the shelter. He was stalling for time so Leslie could catch up with him. She was his friend and had always been there for him; now she would be there for the woman he loved.

He regretted not having told Hope that he loved her, but that wasn't what she wanted to hear right now. There were only two things she had ever told him she wanted: rainbows without rain, and to die.

"Anton, are you all right?" There was concern in her voice for the first time. He was unaware of how broken he looked from across the table. The painful knot in his throat forbid him to speak when, once again, he found the tiny hand resting upon his.

"Don't die, Hope," he choked. He squeezed her fragile hand in his, thinking of how her features were beginning to look more and more like Catherine's, fragile and frail, as though a strong wind could cause her bones to tumble to the ground and scatter in the breeze.

Hope pulled her hand from his, and it disappeared beneath the table.

"Are you afraid of me?" he asked in a faint whisper.

She nodded slowly, as though realizing it herself for the first time.

"For the love of God, why?"

"You might expect things. Things we used to do."

"If I recall, you used to enjoy those things."

"I *never* enjoyed them."

Anton knew it wasn't true. So often it had been she who had teased him, exciting him until he couldn't wait to get back to the hotel room. The anticipation alone had made the elevator ride seem endless. Once, she had teased him even when others were in the elevator with them, had giggled while standing in front of him, her winter coat hiding where her hands were. Yes, she had enjoyed their lovemaking. There was no doubt in his mind.

"We never talked about when I took your gun," she said, changing the subject. "You never mentioned it like I thought you would."

"Do you remember taking it?"

She shook her head. "Only holding it," she said. "There's something wrong with me, isn't there?" She visibly trembled, but looked up once more when Anton's smooth hand touched beneath her chin.

There was gentleness in his eyes, and he smiled at her just a little. "I promised I'd help you, but you've got to let me. I can't help you if you won't trust me. Will you trust me?"

She looked at him and nodded ever so slightly.

Anton tossed money onto the table, but as they were leaving, he stopped to retrieve the small pebble that had somehow found its way into his pocket.

*****

For a week, he stayed at the motel while Leslie and Hope used his apartment. He waited anxiously for Leslie's phone calls. Most of them came late at night after Hope had gone to sleep. Leslie told him what she could without betraying confidences and apologized for the blanket Hope had torn apart in anger. But Hope had reached a milestone that day, and it had been worth it. Would he bring another blanket and a couple more boxes of tissue?

He learned, among other things, that before Steven, it had been her father who had abused her, and Leslie confirmed what Clay had said about her mother dying in childbirth. Hope had been raised with that guilt and then blamed herself for the cruel, alcoholic father it had produced.

Anton ached for her. Ached to hold her in his arms and tell her he loved her. But Leslie said it was too soon. "In Hope's mind, that had a disastrous ending. Start new, go slow. Just be friends and let it bloom again. All the elements are still there."

He spent his days calling back and forth between Jeff and Clay, making final arrangements for a camping trip. Leslie had agreed that what Hope needed most was to be with her friends again. "Get her away from that shelter. She's seen enough battering for a lifetime. She needs fresh air and sunshine!"

Anton called Valerie at the shelter to arrange to get Hope's bag, and she and Anton had lunch. They had a pleasant conversation, and he thanked her for the help and for caring so much. As he watched her cross her long, shapely legs, he couldn't resist asking if she knew Jeff Lansing. Not really, she said, though she'd seen him playing with the kids there on occasion. Why? Nothing, he said, but when they got up to leave, he found himself measuring her height against his. At least five ten, he guessed, looking at the auburn hair that tumbled down her shoulders. He would have to give Jeff another call.

Thankful for the diversion, he felt refreshed as he walked back to the motel with Hope's suitcase in hand. He found Leslie's car parked in front, with the two women sitting inside. His heart stopped.

"Where have you been?" Leslie said with a wink. "We thought we could get you to buy us lunch!"

"I just ate, but I'd be glad to take you anyway," he said, his eyes riveted to Hope. He tried not to stare, remembering all too well the pain of freshly opened wounds—old wounds that required poking and prodding and tearing open so they could heal properly.

"Hi, Hope," he said.

"Hi," she said, looking his way. It still shocked him to see how thin she was, and her emotions were obviously raw.

"Where would you like to go for lunch?" *...sweetheart, darling, my love?*

"Could we go to the White Horse Inn?" she asked shyly.

"Hope, we'd go to the White *House* if that's what you wanted." He grinned all the way down to his shoes, and she ventured to smile in return.

Back to the beginning, he thought, *to kill ghosts, to heal wounds. Back to the White Horse Inn!*

CHAPTER 27

The following weekend, the small band of friends packed their vehicles for the camping trip, and all that remained of the initial shock of seeing Hope at eighty-seven pounds was an occasional exchange of glances. There was an unspoken agreement that she was to carry nothing, help with nothing, and there would be frequent rests during the hike. By noon they were off, Clay and Nicki in his black pickup truck, and Jeff and the others in Jeff's van.

"Smile, sweetheart, we're going to have a good time!" Anton forced himself to smile.

Anton was not the camping type, and she knew it. He had always marveled at nature, had enjoyed the walks in the woods they had used to take so long ago, but he was still a city dweller. He smiled at her in a flirtatious way, and part of her wanted to smile back. But she was uncomfortable, smashed between Noah's huge body and Anton's shoulders, her feet on an ice chest and mounds of bedrolls around her.

She wanted to sit up front with Jeff, but Dan had grabbed the seat when Anton assumed she would sit with him. She dreaded the next few days, and the days after that even more. Anton would take her home then, back to the house she once had dearly loved, the house where her grandparents had showered her with the only affection she had ever known. But now it had been desecrated, tarnished with the vulgarity of Steven's heavy breathing, Steven's dirty hands.

"Hope, what is it, sweetheart?" Anton frowned.

"Nothing."

It was a lie. Everything had been taken from her: her freedom, her rights, her dignity. She had lost herself, even her mind for a while. There seemed to be nothing left to do but follow the whims of her friends in their desperate attempts to "fix" everything. It was like playing Simon Says, only now it was Anton Says. *Anton says go camping. Anton says go home.* She leaned tight against Noah to escape from the noble man who'd acquired the responsibility of running her life. *Just like one acquires a new pet and is responsible to feed it and put it out at night,* she thought.

Noah felt her press against him but refrained from putting his arm around her when Anton looked up.

"Pine," Anton observed, sniffing the air from Jeff's open window.

Good, Noah thought; Anton hadn't read his mind. He looked down at Hope when Anton looked away, relishing her touch, the feel of her hair on his bare arm and the warmth of her body. He could smell her scent, and it drove him crazy. But he also felt the presence of the man on her other side, the man with whom she had made love. It had slipped from Jeff during the crisis and become a constant image in Noah's mind.

He looked up to find Jeff watching him from the rearview mirror, and he realized he had almost reached down to kiss the top of her head.

"Let's stop at that souvenir shop," Jeff told Clay through the CB, but his eyes continued to glance at Noah, who understood his point exactly. "Let's stretch our legs."

Inside the store, they found rows of colorful candy sticks all standing neatly in ceramic crocks and homemade gifts that lined the shelves. There were old firearms and dusty heads of mule deer that looked down from the walls, where they seemed to have hung for a millennium. The smell of cinnamon and various teas blended with the hickory and fir burning in the stove that graced the center of the store.

There was a ribbon rack with reds, greens, yellows, and blues of all different tints and shades and textures. The sight made Hope want to wrap Christmas presents even though it was late May. The ruffle-trimmed pillows and beautiful quilts lay neatly across pine benches, reminding her of holidays spent with Uncle Nate and Aunt Stell.

Uncle Nate! Feeling terrible, Hope quickly found Anton, who was browsing through the colorful tins of tea. She touched his arm. "How was Uncle Nate when you saw him? I missed taking him to the cemetery two months in a row. It means so much to him to visit Aunt Stell."

"I took him. Don't worry, he understands." Anton knew how much she loved the old man and how much he adored her too. Now she stood before him, her brows knitted like a troubled child, and he wanted to kiss the furrow away. Overcome, he bent to kiss her, but she quickly moved away.

"Don't do that," she scolded and went to stand beside Noah, who had seen the encounter.

"Why don't you buy a postcard and write to Uncle Nate?" Noah suggested quietly. "I'm sure you can send it from here."

He bent down when she tugged at his arm to receive a peck on the cheek. It was a display of affection that Anton had witnessed many times between the two, but this time it pained him. Hope wandered off to the other side of the store, unaware that though they stood an aisle apart, the men's hearts ached as one, each envying the other, each wishing he knew what to do.

It was evening by the time they reached the point where they would camp, and the men set up while Nicki and Hope fixed sandwiches. Other than that, no one let Hope do anything, and she was becoming annoyed.

Anton laid out their bedrolls side by side, next to a huge boulder, and when he joined her beside the fire, she craned her neck to look at the sleeping arrangements.

"Who's that for?"

"You and me."

"I thought I'd sleep by Noah," she said coolly, and Anton bit his tongue. He knew she felt safe with Noah and prayed that was all it was.

"Why don't you want to be with me?" he asked quietly.

Although everyone sat around the fire, Dan was the only one who stared blatantly at them, and Anton frowned at the intrusion. Hope didn't answer, and by late evening, the others had drifted, one by one, away from the glowing embers.

"It's going to be cold tonight," Anton said. He'd watched Hope brood for over an hour, with her shoulders hunched forward, her thin arms crossed tightly in front of her. "You should get tucked in."

"You're not my keeper!" She was tired of doing what everyone else wanted, tired of being the noble cause they all rallied around.

But Anton was tired too. He was weary of walking on eggshells, and his patience was wearing thin. Leslie had warned him that Hope would vacillate radically between moods. What she hadn't warned him about was how it would make him feel. "Come on, sweetheart. Let's go to bed."

"Let's?" She picked up one of the sleeping bags and began to drag it toward where Noah lay.

"Hope, why won't you sleep by me? Is it because we've made love and you're afraid I'll force myself on you? Why don't you just castrate me and get it over with?"

A hard slap stung Anton's face, and the silence that followed was deafening. Even those already tucked safely in their sleeping bags didn't dare make a sound.

"You've been wanting to slap someone all day, haven't you, Hope?" he said quietly. "I guess it may as well be me. Who knows, I may have even deserved it. All I know is, I'm exhausted and I want to go to bed. You can do whatever you damn well please."

With that, he removed his shoes, slipped into the remaining bag, and turned away. Somewhere in the early hours of morning, he fell asleep.

*****

The next morning, the seven friends set off on the narrow but worn path. Clay had suggested this area, on the other side of Kaweah, west of Yucca Ridge. It was where Uncle Nate and Aunt Stell had often taken him and Hope during the hot days of summer when they were children. It was heavily treed, and a tributary to the Kaweah River ran briskly through the area, over boulders, where it plunged over a small cliff, creating a swimming hole.

Everyone watched Hope, keeping constant vigil as they hiked down to the stream. Clay was especially attentive, but she wondered if Jeff and Noah remained distant because of what Anton had said the night before. She had never felt close to Dan, so his coolness meant nothing. She wondered why he'd elected to come at all.

She spent the whole day avoiding Anton altogether, and when they stopped to eat, she sat as far from him as possible, careful to avoid the piercing blue eyes that constantly sought her out.

"Want to share my sandwich?" Nicki asked as she sat next to her. Hope nodded and took part of Nicki's sandwich, but was still angry from the night before.

"Hope, don't overlook the reasons behind what Anton said," Nicki said after a while.

"Anton's a bully."

"All men are sometimes, especially when they're not sure how to handle a situation. It's like an ape beating his chest because he doesn't know what else to do."

"Clay never acted like that. Even when he was mad, he never said mean things." Hope was suddenly embarrassed, remembering that her old boyfriend was now Nicki's.

"Come on, you and Clay used to fight too," Nicki said. "He told me you used to have some big ones. Fifteen years have dulled your memory!" She laughed, then nodded in Anton's direction. "That good-looking guy over there cares a lot for you, girl. Why don't you give the poor guy a break? He doesn't know how to handle the situation any more than you do."

"What do you mean?"

Nicki took a deep breath and looked pensive for a moment. "Hope," she began quietly, "I was there after Steven beat you up. I saw what Anton went through. Clay and Jeff had to literally hold him down. After you were raped, he would come and sit on my couch without saying a word for hours at a time. Just sat there, staring.

"Hope, he killed a man for you! He took the chance of spending the rest of his life in prison. Didn't you ever think of that? So come on, stop acting so selfish—"

"Nicki!" Anton shouted, and she looked up. She hadn't noticed his approach, and now he scolded her with his eyes.

Hope got up and left as he continued toward them. "I don't know what else you said, but she has enough to deal with without worrying about me going to prison."

"I think you're wrong. I think she needs to worry about someone other than herself for a change."

It was strange to see Nicki stick up for him, and he couldn't stay angry, though he wanted to. He tugged the end of her brown hair affectionately. "Thanks, Nick. But leave it alone, okay?"

*****

Hope watched them from a distance and realized how much had changed. Anton had finally become one of them, though he seemed to bark at shadows where he had never done that before. He was a stranger to her now. Leslie had said it was normal for her to feel that way and that it would pass, but she hated it just the same. Only Noah felt the same to her, although today, he avoided her without explanation.

Everything's topsy-turvy, she thought as they began once again to trudge down the mountain trail. Nicki and Anton were friends, Dan didn't seem to like anybody, Jeff kept watch on Noah, and Clay was unusually worried about her. They were all strangers to her now. She had become the outsider that Anton once had been. Sleep was her only ally, her only escape, and when they finally reached the waterfall, instead of the excitation the others felt, Hope unrolled a sleeping bag and crawled off to sleep before nightfall.

*****

"I see you've touched souls with Three Rivers' last remaining flower child," Dan smirked as Anton approached the morning campfire, looking a little ragged. There was a note of ridicule in his voice that stirred Anton's curiosity.

"What's that supposed to mean?" He poured some coffee and squatted near the fire, warming himself. The morning was cold and dreary, the overcast sky gray and dull. He wondered if it might rain.

"Jeff calls you *Russia* nowadays."

"So?" He sipped the thick black coffee and looked at Dan. "It's just a nickname." He glanced toward the fall's edge and was surprised by the serious frown on Noah's face as he spoke to Hope, who looked as if she were being scolded.

Dan's voice came again. "Jeff only gives nicknames to the people he's 'touched souls' with," he laughed, "or hasn't he told you that yet? Hope is *Bud*. Clay is *Bro*…" There was a brief but poignant silence. "He doesn't call him that around me. Seems like Clay is everybody's brother but mine." He caught Anton's eye for a moment, but Anton decided not to comment. "So, when did he touch your soul, Pavlova? When did he first call you Russia?"

Anton poked the fire with a stick. "I don't remember." It wasn't Dan's business, he thought, confident that no one knew but him and Jeff. *"You've got someone to go to, Russia. You can come to me."* Jeff's voice came to his mind as he stared into the flames and thought of the room that now lay in shambles. He shook his head and wondered how he would ever explain it to Hope.

He looked at her now. Noah still seemed to berate her about something, and when she turned and marched away, there was a slow burn in her eyes as she disappeared into the woods. Noah walked toward the campfire, shaking his head from side to side as he took a mug and poured himself some coffee.

"Run into any hardheaded women lately?" Dan had also seen the exchange, but his fresh words only drew a glance from the boxer. Dan was unpredictable these days, and Noah didn't trust him. After all, Dan had remained Steven's friend to the end—a point, Anton suspected, secretly troubled everyone. But it was an obvious sore spot with Noah. There was plainly no love lost between them. Eventually, Dan got up and left.

Anton looked up, knowing there was no need to verbalize the question.

Noah hesitated. "Talked with Hope for a long time this morning before you got up," he began. "Apparently, the reason she hasn't been eating…" There was pain in his voice, and finally he just blurted it out. "She thinks she might have gotten pregnant by Steven." He lowered himself onto the rock beside Anton, who sat speechless. Only days before the rape, *he* had been with her. If she was pregnant, it most likely was his. It was unlikely Steven would have impregnated her. He hadn't…*finished*.

Anton, pressing his stomach with his fingertips to relieve the pain that grew there, looked at Noah.

"Yeah," Noah continued, reading the look on his face. He threw the rest of his coffee into the dirt and looked off into the distance. "I thought of that too. More likely yours, isn't it? Jeff told me."

"Does she really think she's pregnant?" Anton couldn't hide the tremor in his voice.

"She doesn't know. The trauma alone could have stopped her cycle. She knows that."

"Has she ever been pregnant?"

Noah studied him, his eyes questioning.

"Steven said something once that made me wonder. I want to know if it's true," he prompted, and Noah's face became grim.

"You don't want to know, Anton."

But Anton insisted, and Noah finally broke down and told the story.

She had gotten pregnant a month before she and Steven had taken separate bedrooms, and had hidden her pregnancy for months. He had always told her he didn't want children. When he'd found out, he'd gone into a rage and beaten her, leaving her on the bathroom floor to deliver her own stillborn son. Noah had come by the next morning and found Steven watching TV while Hope lay near death on the cold tiles.

"She was about five months along," Noah said, his hand outstretched before him, palm up. "It fit right in my hand…perfect. It was so beautiful and perfect…" He covered his face with his hands and sighed.

"My God, Noah, why didn't you do something? Why didn't you take her away from him then?" Anton's face turned red with rage, his eyes set like stones in the fire.

"She was his wife. What could I do?" Noah hung his head, his hands now hanging limp between his knees. "The truth is…I'm not much of a fighter, Anton." He looked up in shame. "In a lot of ways, you're a bigger man than me."

"Cowards don't become professional boxers. You're the number three contender to the title, for chrissake. Why couldn't you have given some of that bravery to Hope? It takes guts to be where you are!"

Noah smiled and shook his head. "No, it doesn't. It just takes a big body. The fans think I'm great, but the critics—they know. I've never gone more than four rounds in my career before I knock out my opponent. I've got one good punch, and I get it in early because I know I can't last much longer than the fourth." He tapped the side of his head and winked. "Don't tell anyone…It's glass." He stood to leave, but turned momentarily. "Like I told Jeff this morning, I'll never fight you for Hope. I only know how to love her from a distance."

The boxer left, leaving Anton numb. He pitied Noah, but more, he anguished for Hope.

He watched her come out of the woods and sit alone on a rock near the thundering falls. Her features looked more and more like Catherine's, he thought. More and more like a seven-month-old fetus…dead…buried, like Catherine.

Anton suddenly felt sick and held his stomach, gasping for air. Dizzy, he closed his eyes, wondering where the thought had come from.

"Something wrong with your stomach, Pavlova?"

He jumped at the sound of Dan's voice.

"There was a time when a field mouse couldn't sneak up on you. You're losing your touch, old man!"

"I'm not in the mood, Dan," he said, gathering his wits.

"What are you in the mood for? Bouncing a baby on your knee?"

Anton reeled. "That was a private conversation. Next time, I expect to be advised of your presence."

"Don't worry," Dan laughed coldly. "I already knew about Hope losing the baby. And that Noah's got no balls," he added. "Steven knew it too. We used to laugh about the poor bastard hanging around, yearning like a lovesick cat."

At that moment, Anton decidedly hated Dan Philips.

Dan continued, "I already know all that. And I know more about you too." He chuckled and began to walk away.

"What's that supposed to mean?" Anton said from behind, and Dan turned.

"I'm getting out of the NORAD job," Dan said, "even if I have to destroy you to do it. Die if you want to, if that's what it takes to be a patriot. Problem with you is, you have such a damned inferiority complex about being Russian that you think you have to die to prove that you're American."

"I *am* an American. I don't have to prove that to anyone. I do what I do because I'm good at it. NORAD's not an impossible job, Philips. You're just afraid to take chances. You'll never be great by being afraid."

"No. But I'll be alive." Dan turned to walk away but was met by a hard fist across the jaw. He reeled backward and landed on his back in the dirt, staring up at Clay. "What the hell was that for?" he asked, wiping the trickle of blood from the corner of his mouth.

Clay reached for his collar and pulled him to his feet. He hit him again, and Dan stumbled backward, this time tripping over a rock and landing in the brush.

Dan was in shock. His brother had always kept to himself, controlled his anger, even when Dan had provoked him. Now he was more aggressive than he'd ever seen him.

"For the last month, I've been furious with Jeff because I thought he left Hope alone that day. I just confronted him and found out that you relieved him, told him not to stay because you would be with Hope. But you weren't, were you? You left and called Steven. You set her up, didn't you, you bastard! All this time, you said you didn't believe Steven was beating her, but you knew it all along. You liked it, didn't you, Daniel—having him do your dirty work so your hands stayed clean. Then you set her up to get raped! You always hated her, were always jealous. Tell me, brother, was he doing your dirty work for you then, too?"

Clay was furious, but by this time Anton was out of control. He threw himself on top of Dan and began punching him again and again in the face as he once had done to Steven. Dan tried to fight back but was surprised by the power the small man possessed. His return punches were futile as Anton poured out his vengeance, and while his own brother looked on, Dan was reduced to a state near unconsciousness.

Jeff and Noah came running and pulled Anton away. "I ought to kill you, you son of a bitch!" Anton lunged for Dan again, but Noah threw his arms around him. He bucked and strained to get away from the boxer while Jeff held Clay back.

Dazed and bleeding, Dan moaned and tried to sit up.

"Go home," Clay said at last and tossed the keys to his truck into the dust. "You don't belong here. Letting you walk away is the last thing I'll ever do for you, Daniel. As far as I'm concerned, you're dead."

"You can't push me out of your life like I don't exist," Dan said feebly as he rose to his feet. "You're my brother, whether you like it or not. You can't deny me."

"Deny? You mean like how I've denied Hope for the past fifteen years? You aren't any more related to me than she is. Now get out of my sight."

The words were daggers in Dan's heart. Dan had always been possessive of his little brother, the one who'd been the light of their father's eye, as if it were through Clay that he'd merited any love at all from McClain Philips.

"Clay..." Dan reached out his hand, but Clay turned his back. Finally, Dan gathered his belongings and headed back up the narrow path.

*****

Nicki and Hope watched the fight from the edge of the river, but the loud rush of the falls had drowned out the bitter exchange.

Once Dan was gone, Hope ran to Anton and threw her arms around his neck. "Anton, are you all right? What happened?"

But all he could think about was the arms that encircled him, her tiny body that pressed against him. He wrapped his arms around her and held her tight. "I'm all right. What happened doesn't matter," he said and buried his face in her hair. "Sweetheart, don't ever shut me out again. I can handle your anger, but not your silence. Scream at me, curse me, but don't ever stand silent against me. I'm so sorry about what happened to you. Please don't let it become a barrier between us."

Without warning, all the horror she had suffered, the pain and the terror, welled up and began to spill out. She had not been able to face her own devastation with Anton. They hadn't cried together, hadn't held each other, hadn't grieved. He drew her tight in his arms and held her while the flood of tears rolled down her face. He stroked her hair and kissed her forehead. "Go ahead, my love," he whispered. "Tomorrow I'll show you the sunshine."

The others discreetly disappeared and didn't return until evening. Anton had started another fire, and he and Hope sat together against a rock, holding each other. Hope looked exhausted as an occasional shudder ripped through her.

"Poor Hope," Nicki whispered after she had finally fallen asleep in Anton's arms.

"No," he whispered. "Now she can begin to heal."

*****

The sunrise was picture-perfect when Hope awoke. From the campsite, she could hear the roar of the water and the chatter of blue jays in the nearby trees as she opened her eyes to the beautiful sky. It was incredibly lovely, she thought—the surrounding mountains cradled her, all warm and rested, cozily tucked in the warmth of the sleeping bag. She turned toward the movement beside her and slowly became aware of where she was. Anton was still asleep, propped against a rock, his shoulder having served as her pillow. The sleeping bag had been draped around them where they cuddled in the warmth of the morning sun.

Suddenly she remembered why they were there, what had happened, but she quickly pushed the memories back, trying to recapture the moment before when she'd awakened for the first time without the ugly memories haunting her. For just a moment, she'd forgotten; for just an instant, she had been free of the stress, free to enjoy the things she hadn't even noticed for so long, like the mountains and the sky.

Anton's eyes were still closed as she snuggled beside him, studying his face. He wore a sore-looking bruise just under his cheekbone from the fight the day before, and she wondered what it had been about.

But just now, she felt the warmth of his slender body, his quiet breath on her shoulder, the arm that still clutched her in his sleep. There was something more familiar about him, she thought, more comforting. She held his hand beneath the bedding, his fingers lax. She rested her head once again on his shoulder and drifted back to sleep.

*****

After breakfast, everyone decided to go to the swimming hole at the base of the falls, where there had formed over the centuries several beautiful pools, but the first plunge into the icy water sent them scurrying onto the sun-drenched rocks, where they lay like well-fed cats on a sunny windowsill in winter.

Anton hadn't gone in; instead, he sat against a tree and watched as Jeff threw Hope off her rocky perch, back into the water. She yelled and laughed, giggling when she managed to pull Jeff into the water with her. Anton reveled in the music of her laughter. She and the others played on the rocks like children, pushing one another into the icy brink. Their laughter echoed against the mountains and blended with the constant roar of water. He prayed the play and sunshine would slowly push away Hope's world of doom and despair.

After a while, he looked up to find Jeff dripping over him. "I knew that if anyone could make her laugh, it would be you," he said to Jeff, not noticing the mischief in his eyes.

"Yeah, but don't you think it's time for you to make your contribution?"

"What contribution?" he asked warily.

Jeff smiled down at him. "It's your turn, Russia."

"No, no, no..." He shook his head, waving Jeff off. "That's snowmelt." He pointed at the pool. "I don't think it would be very dignified for a government agent to freeze his balls off in public, thank you."

"I still say you're nothing but a stuck-up little Russian," Jeff said, and with that, he grabbed him by the arms and hoisted him over his shoulders. An instant later, Anton was thrown into the icy pool.

The roar of laughter could be heard even before he surfaced, and when he did, he gave a loud whoop from the cold. Hope laughed hysterically as he climbed out, shivering.

"You enjoyed that, didn't you, you little shit!" he said as she nearly rolled with hysterics, Nicki laughing at her side. The other men seemed just as amused as Anton walked past the women, mumbling affectionate obscenities while he unbuttoned his shirt.

"Oh my," Nicki gasped, poking Hope to turn around. "You told me how beautiful he was when you got back from Monterey, but..."

Hope turned to look at Anton, oblivious of his own sensuality. His broad shoulders curved with firm, ripe muscles, accentuating his slender waist. His wet blue jeans clung to him, showing strong buttocks and calves. The fullness of his groin would have been obscene if he weren't otherwise so magnificently beautiful. Even the other men turned in frank admiration as he spread his shirt over a warm rock.

The indignity he had suffered had been worth Hope's merriment, but when he glanced in her direction, he became aware of the staring eyes. "What's wrong?" he asked.

"How old are you?" Clay asked, and he looked around at their faces. His age seemed to be a fascination with the group, and it amused him.

"I just turned forty. Why?"

"You look twenty," Nicki said. She looked at Clay and teased, "Why don't you look like that?"

"I work out," Anton explained.

"So do I," Clay said. "So do Noah and Jeff."

By now, Hope was ready to burst; Anton could see it coming. "I work out a lot," he said, hoping to keep the secret she was dying to tell. But it was to no avail.

"He's a dancer," she proclaimed. "He teaches part-time at a studio in San Francisco."

Anton visibly winced and held his breath, waiting for a reaction, but for a moment there was only shocked silence.

Jeff was the first to speak. "No shit? What kind of dancer?"

"Jazz…and," he added hesitantly, "classical ballet."

"God bless America! You're just full of surprises, aren't you?" Jeff said.

"I don't actually teach," he corrected Hope. "There's a studio beneath the room I have up in the bay. I hang out there a lot."

Jeff thought for a moment. "Hey, Russia, do you suppose that's why you're so defensive? About guys, I mean?"

"I hadn't really thought about it." He was just getting over his initial embarrassment when the women started giggling again.

"Nicki wants to see the rest of you," Hope announced loudly, and he blushed right down to his soggy shoes. At that point, the women had successfully embarrassed everybody, including themselves, and Anton was grateful to let the conversation die.

"I've never been so embarrassed in my life," he moaned when everyone began to drift apart. Hope approached, the blush still evident on his cheeks while he pulled off his shoes and socks.

She ran her hand over his back, wiping the droplets of water. "I'm proud of you, Anton. A year ago, you would have never put up with this. Just look at you. You're dripping wet and barefoot." She pointed at his feet, his toes still white from the cold. "And now everyone knows you're a dancer."

"Yeah, well, I'll never live that one down." He looked toward Jeff.

"The point is that everyone here respects and admires you." *And I love you,* she almost said, realizing that the old feelings were coming back. The numbness had begun to wear off.

"Is something wrong?" He took her by the shoulders and frowned.

"I'm starved. What do you say we go back to camp and raid the ice chest?"

He laughed and hugged her, unaware that just the touch of his bare skin reminded her of what had been. He paused for a moment, wishing he could kiss her, but appeased himself knowing how far she had come, not knowing that he had come further still.

*****

All in all, Anton felt the camping trip was a success as they trudged back up the path the following day. The van was quite full by the time they finished packing it, Dan having taken Clay's pickup two days before.

Everyone was quiet on the way home, unwinding, relaxing. But the incident with Dan had Anton disturbed. He had temporarily pushed it out of his mind, but as they drove toward Three Rivers, he made a mental note to call Sanderson. Something would have to be done.

"Go to Paris with me," he said abruptly, and everyone turned to look at him. He was afraid to leave Hope alone in Three Rivers until something could be resolved with Dan. There was no telling what he might do.

"Paris, France?" she asked, wide-eyed.

"No. Paris, Texas," he teased.

"Hey, I'll go!" Nicki volunteered, and everyone laughed.

"Do you remember Jacques Racine? I'm doing a job for him as a personal favor for Sanderson. It's security for the Bolshoi Ballet while they perform in Paris. He thought it would be helpful to have some security who could speak the language. Come with me, Hope." He squeezed her hand, but she hesitated.

"I don't know," she said nervously, remembering New York. "I don't think I'm ready."

"Separate rooms," he said, and she gave him a look. "Separate hotels?"

"Oh, go with him, Bud!" Jeff said, looking at her in the rearview mirror, and the others chimed in. Only Noah remained silent.

Anton leaned close to her ear. "Nothing will happen unless you want it to. No pressure, I promise," he whispered, and after a moment of uncertainty, she finally agreed.

CHAPTER 28

Hope looked at the farmhouse and held her breath. Anton's car was still in the driveway, where he had left it, and now he opened the van's side door and climbed out. He held out his hand. "Come on, sweetheart. We're home."

They waved goodbye to the others as the van disappeared down the drive. He unlocked his car and threw his gear in the back while Hope went into the house. *It was good to be back*, he thought. The familiar house, the surrounding orchard, and the meadows felt more like home to him than his own apartment, he thought as he bounded up the steps and went inside.

His heart sank.

Hope stood in the sunlit hall, staring into the room beyond. The destruction was more than he'd remembered, and as he looked around, he was overwhelmed by hopelessness and despair. He'd forgotten to tell her about the room.

"What happened?" Hope's voice was husky. He couldn't tell if it was shock or anger that possessed her as she walked a circle around him, looking at the mess.

"I was upset."

"Upset? Someone who was upset might rearrange the furniture. You destroyed the whole room." She glanced toward the window where the prism had once hung, then at the shards of glass below it.

"That was an accident, Hope. I feel terrible about the prism. I'll get you a new one. I'll fix the room." He closed his eyes, not wanting to see her despair, but the gentle touch of her hand on his brow opened them again.

She stood in front of him and caressed his cheek. "Do you really think I care about the room? I'm the one who should apologize. I had no idea how all this affected you, Anton. I've been so wrapped up in feeling sorry for myself that I hardly even noticed what you were going through. And the worst of it is, you've tried to tell me! Please forgive me, my love."

My love! His heart leapt at the words, and he gathered her in his arms, fighting the urge to smother her with kisses. "I'll take you shopping. We'll get new furniture and pretty curtains. And a bookcase—you need a bookcase in here." He held her small face in his hands. "It'll be so beautiful when we're done."

"Can we go tomorrow?" she asked, suddenly caught up in his enthusiasm, but Anton recovered his composure.

"After you go to the doctor. That's more important."

"I feel all right. I'm eating…"

"I know," he said, putting his hand under her chin, "but we need to know for sure whether or not you're pregnant."

Her eyes clouded with anger. "Noah told you, didn't he?"

"Only because he cares. He's worried about you."

"What if I am?" she asked tentatively, searching his face.

"It could be mine, you know. Probably is." He smiled to reassure her. "It would make a difference in the kind of wallpaper we pick out."

"And what if it's not yours?" she asked, and he hesitated.

"I don't care," he said finally. "I don't care. Just promise that if there are any decisions to be made, you'll come to me. We'll make the decisions together, okay? Promise me."

*****

Hope had promised, but after he spent most of the next morning at the doctor's office waiting for her, watching pregnant women of all sizes come and go, and reading all the birthing literature and parenthood magazines, she emerged to announce that he was boning up for nothing. To celebrate, they went to lunch at the White Horse

Inn and then began their shopping extravaganza, which lasted more than a week.

It was a week filled with laughter and lunches and ice-cream cones in the afternoon to "fatten things up." They went as far as San Francisco, and while Anton checked out dance studios, Hope spent the days either shopping alone or visiting Leslie. All in all, they had a wonderful time, showing each other the things they liked and disliked; dishes, towels—little bikes with training wheels…

"What about this?" Anton held up a big teddy bear. "It's really soft. Feel."

"It is," she said, squeezing its head.

"Want it?"

"What would I do with a teddy bear?" She laughed and made him put it back. But as he did, he was overcome with a severe depression that lasted the rest of the day.

*****

"Sounds like you two are playing newlyweds," Leslie said as Anton stretched his legs out in front of him. He had stopped to visit her before heading back to Three Rivers via Monterey to visit Nathan, and she was thrilled by the turn of events. After having seen Hope the day before, she'd been certain it was just a matter of time.

"We were shopping, for crying out loud." Anton scowled. "Stop trying to marry me off! You shrinks are always reading something out of nothing."

"Why are you so angry?"

"I'm not."

"What kind of things did you look at?" she asked, and looked smug at his answer. "From dining room tables to a teddy bear? Interesting. For her study, I presume." He gave her the finger, and she laughed. "What else?"

He wanted to tell her about the bedroom suite they had both liked, but decided not to. Not after what she had said. But when "a crib" slipped out, he froze in his chair. "I mean a bedroom suite," he tried again, but Leslie wouldn't allow the recantation.

"I'm more interested in the crib," she said, pensively.

"Damn it, Les, you're a pain in the ass! I don't know why I come here." But the diversion failed, and he found himself telling her about the depression that had overwhelmed him after returning the bear to the shelf.

"Sounds like you would like to have a baby," she said. "Were you disappointed that Hope wasn't pregnant?"

"Did she tell you she lost a baby a few years ago?" he asked, ignoring her question. When Leslie nodded, he told her about the strange effect it had had on him. Although she made no comment, she jotted a note on the table beside her. "Stop taking notes."

"It's my grocery list," she said and put down the pen. "Hope tells me she's going to Paris with you this summer."

"I'm afraid to leave her alone in Three Rivers. Have you talked to Paul about Dan Philips?"

"No. I've left a message for him. I've also sent out an order for Philips to come see me. I'm supposed to do a workup on all the agents every six months, but he hasn't kept his appointments. From what you tell me, he could be dangerous."

"He scares me, Les. With Hope, I mean. I didn't realize how jealous he was of her."

"Make an old girl happy and answer a question honestly." She looked him in the eye. "Are you in love with her?"

"Hopelessly." Telling Jeff he loved Hope was one thing; telling Leslie was quite another. Somehow, that made it official. "I love her more than I ever thought I could, Les," he confessed, and smiled as he stood to leave. He bent down and kissed her on the cheek. "I love you too, old girl."

"If you didn't, I'd charge you more." She chuckled as he went out the door.

*****

Leslie went to her desk and rewrote the notes she had made. Anton was closer to coming full circle than ever before, closer to remembering the details of Catherine's death and the baby she'd refused to have. After all her years of study, it still amazed her that some people would rather end their own life than to share it with anyone else. Catherine was a classic; nothing more than a selfish child, Leslie thought, though she would never say as much to Anton. Catherine's weakness and dependence on him had been the very source of her power, the leverage she'd needed to get anything she wanted without having to give anything in return. He had given her love, protection, and security, and she'd always wanted more.

Catherine had learned of her pregnancy a month after Anton had left for London. Upon hearing the news, he had done then what he tried to do now with Hope: go shopping. He'd shopped all over Europe, only in the finest stores, and sent a huge box filled with gifts for the baby, including a teddy bear. For Catherine, he'd bought an exquisite necklace of emeralds and diamonds, which he had kept, wanting to give it to her in person. When the box had arrived, Catherine had torn it open, thinking it was for her. When everything within was for the baby, she'd picked up the knife she had used to open the box and stabbed herself in the stomach.

Leslie had been convinced for years that Catherine's death had not been intentional. She'd simply bled out while trying to do away with their child.

After Anton's return, he had searched for Catherine for days, not believing she was dead. Finally, an office worker had shown him police photographs of her body lying in the pool of blood, her belly obvious with child, her hand still on the knife.

The rest was history. Ten days later, a man had been plucked from a rock just out of San Francisco Bay. When his identity was learned, the USIB had called their newly hired psychologist to treat him; he'd been one of her first patients.

Leslie sat back in her chair and heaved a great sigh. It had been a long, hard road for the man from Russia, the three-year-old child shipped to America in a trunk. That hurdle alone had taken months of intense therapy to overcome.

He was close to clearing this one now; she felt it in the little things he did and said. He was getting closer to dealing with his fury, his anger at Catherine for what she had done. Soon he would have to deal with the fact that Catherine couldn't bear for anyone else to need him as a child would. That would have forced her to grow up and drawn Anton's attention away from her. She'd ended the competition before it ever began.

After finishing her notes, Leslie turned in her chair and opened the filing cabinet, only to find an empty space where Anton's file should have been.

She poked her head into the outer office, where her new secretary sat. "Susan, where's Mr. Pavlova's file?"

"Mr. Sanderson told me to send it out," Susan answered. "I thought it was strange, but he insisted."

"When was this?"

"About two weeks ago," she said.

"Did he say why he wanted it?"

"I didn't send it to him," she said. "He asked me to forward it to a Mr. Philips in California."

"Get Mr. Sanderson on the phone. I don't care if he's in a meeting at the Pentagon, just get him!"

Leslie felt sick as she sat back at her desk, and her mood was evident when she answered line-one a moment later.

"Leslie, I've been meaning to call you," Paul said on the other end.

"How dare you instruct my secretary to send my files out of this office!" she said without preamble. "You don't know what you've done!"

"May I assume this is in regards to Pavlova?"

"You know it is."

"First of all, they aren't your files. They're property of the USIB, of which I am in charge. Secondly, I've done only what I had to. Apparently, Anton had threatened to kill Steven Wykes two weeks prior to the shooting, and Philips knew it. It could have reopened the case, possibly sending Anton to prison." He sighed. "Leslie, if I had allowed a more thorough investigation, he could have been charged with first-degree murder. Philips said he'd keep quiet in return for the files."

"You've never given in to blackmail before, Paul. You're only worried because you got him executive clemency and you're afraid of looking like a fool to the president. Anton has a dissociative disorder. Dan is out to destroy him, and you just handed him everything he needs to do a good job!"

"Leslie, dear…you've got to stop being a mother hen to that man. Everyone in the Branch knows he's your favorite."

"He used to be your favorite too, Paul. Or has all that changed because he won't go into the CIA with you and they won't take you without him?" Her words were vicious, but they both knew it was true. For years, Sanderson had been riding on Anton's reputation. Even the USIB wanted him to retire; they kept him only for the influence he had with Anton Pavlova.

"Let's not make this personal, Leslie," Sanderson said.

"Then let's not make anything personal. I just want my files out of Philips's hands."

"It's too late. You could ask him for them, but he'd just make copies, if he hasn't already."

"Then I won't ask." She slammed down the receiver and leaned back, not sure what to do, but positive now that she must take matters into her own hands. Anton was the one dedicated, truly honorable agent left from the USIB's heyday. Far too many agents had left in the past few years, leaving only those the CIA or the FBI didn't want, and the security department, which simply wasn't geared for espionage. The Branch seemed to be sinking from the holes, floundering in the apathy of the agents that remained. It had all happened during Sanderson's tenure, and even *he* didn't seem to care anymore. He had carelessly thrown his best agent to his enemy after years of devoted service.

Slowly she picked up the phone, remembering the fight with Dan that Anton had told her about. She had to trust someone.

"Detective Clayton Philips, please…"

CHAPTER 29

Dan leaned against the clapboard siding and lit another cigarette, thankful for the shade the awning provided. He stood outside the grocery store for fifteen minutes, going over exactly what to say when Anton stepped out. Leslie Fairchild must have thought she was smart, sending Clay after Anton's files. But it didn't matter now. He'd gotten what he wanted.

So, the Great Pavlova has a chink in his armor, Dan thought. According to the psychological report written by Leslie over eleven years ago, the act of killing his baby could have driven Anton to kill his own wife if she hadn't already done it herself. But he loved her, so he totally blocked out what she had done. It was the perfect setup.

He tossed the cigarette to the pavement and crushed it beneath his foot when Anton came out. "Haven't seen you for a while," he said and received a cold stare in reply.

"I can't imagine why you would want to," Anton said after a moment and walked past Dan to open the door of his car. He put the bag of groceries inside, then straightened to face him. "What do you want, Philips?"

Dan put another cigarette in his mouth and cupped his hands to light it. "Sanderson says you've taken some time off. I'm glad," he said, feigning concern. "Hope needs someone to take care of her, after the abortion and all."

"You don't know what you're talking about. Believe me, if she ever did anything like that, it would be because she thought it was Steven's."

Dan chuckled. "I don't think so. After all, she tried to keep the one she *knew* was his."

He walked away, heading toward the liquor store across the street. He turned to look at Anton once more, just in time to see him heaving beside his car. If Leslie's notes were correct, Anton didn't even know what it was that made him sick.

Yes, he thought, it was a useful lie. The seed had been planted.

*****

The following weeks were filled with joy as Anton and Hope repapered and decorated the study. It was Anton's first taste of domesticity, having moved from place to place during his career. Even during his short time with Catherine, they had never attempted to nest. But Hope was different from Catherine, having a strong nesting instinct that was evident to anyone who walked into her house. She loved having her things around her, loved the homey, comfortable feeling that Anton had only envied during his solitary life.

"They say that if two people can wallpaper an entire room without getting into an argument, they're compatible." Hope winked as they finished the last strip of paper and stood back to admire their work.

"Is that so? What does that say for us?" he asked, and she leaned on his arm affectionately. He loved it when she touched him, which she did more and more. They often held hands and hugged now, and he was permitted an occasional peck on the cheek. But what he longed for was the passionate embrace, the long, intense kisses that now grew vague in his memory. "Are we compatible?" he asked, nuzzling her.

"Maybe." Then without thought, she gently pressed her mouth against his.

He pulled her into his arms and kissed her hungrily, but she pulled away.

"Anton, I'm sorry. I'm just not ready."

"It's okay," he said, but there was disappointment in his eyes.

"I love you, and I'm so afraid of losing you. I'm just not ready, and I'm afraid you won't wait for me."

He reached out and drew her back into his arms. "I'll wait, sweetheart," he said gently, "for as long as it takes." He stroked her hair, trying not to let the heartache show.

*****

Hope had arranged to go to work at the lodge once they returned from Paris, but for now, she consented to do nothing while she regained her strength. Anton had become her constant companion since the camping trip, sleeping on the couch, going to his apartment in the mornings to shower and change. Eventually, she bought him a razor and a few toiletries, which she put in the downstairs bathroom, and a few items of extra clothing found their way into the bottom drawer of the filing cabinet. "Unmentionables are under *U*," she teased, just to see him blush. She loved him and reminded him of it often, but the stairs that ultimately led to her bedroom remained, unspokenly, off-limits.

By the third week of June, Anton grew restless and argumentative. Hope suggested he get away for a while, to which he reluctantly agreed. The accidental meeting with Dan had been on his mind for weeks. Each time he tried to approach Hope about it, he talked himself out of it at the last minute. He kept trying to reason with himself that the doctor had said she was not pregnant, but it had been Hope who told him the results, not the doctor. If she had had an abortion behind his back, what would keep her from lying?

But it felt odd not having her by his side as he walked alone through the Japanese Tea Garden of the Golden Gate Park. Without any forethought, he'd been drawn to San Francisco, as always when he was anxious or frustrated. Perhaps Hope was right about needing to get away for a while. Her constant presence had built up a lot of frustration—smelling her perfume, catching little glimpses of her more private moments, like running to the phone in her nightgown or brushing her hair before bed.

THE PEBBLE AND THE MAN

He had already spent two days in the city, and for two days he'd worked out relentlessly at the studio, dancing eight and ten hours a day respectively, trying to sweat out the anger at what Dan had told him, the ache it had left in his soul. Now, as he walked amid the trees, it seemed nothing would help. He followed Park Street over to Geary and headed east until he found himself in the part of town where the sounds, even the women's faces, were familiar.

"Hi, honey! I haven't seen you for a while. Figured you must'a got yourself hitched or somethin'." It was a woman everyone called Candy. He stopped to talk for a while.

"No, I've been around." He stuck his hands in his pockets. "Isn't it kind of early for you, Candy? I thought you didn't like daywork."

"Shit," she said, "either the nights aren't as long as they used to be or I'm gonna have to raise my rates. A body can't hardly make a living anymore!"

Anton chuckled, and she smiled in return. He stepped back and averted his eyes when a tall man in a brown business suit approached. Candy talked to him for a few minutes before he walked away grumbling obscenities at her.

"Damn businessmen," she slurred. "Act so high and mighty until an important client comes to town!"

Anton chuckled, watching the man turn the corner.

"What about you, honey?" She looked at him. "Could you use a little pick-me-up?"

"That's not what I came to town for, Candy." He shuffled his feet a little.

"What did you come to town for, then?" she asked.

"Hell, I don't know."

Seeing his restlessness, she looked at him with startlingly kind eyes. "You always got somethin' hurtin' inside of you, don't you, honey? It's hurtin' you right now."

"You know me pretty well, don't you?" He gave her a weak smile and patted her cheek with his hand.

"Tell you what—I'll let you have extra time. Ol' Candy can be real understanding," she said invitingly, and before he knew it, he found himself in a small green room above a sandwich shop; the tangy smell of barbecue sauce hung thick in the air.

As the door closed behind him, he began to feel anger well up inside. He didn't understand its source; he only knew it had been there from long ago. Just watching Candy now, he could feel all the buried emotions rise up into a pointed rage. He removed his holster and laid his shirt over it, then removed his pants. Once again, as he had over the years, he brought his unexpressed anger to the women of the streets.

He pushed her toward the bed and began to tear at her clothes, ravaging her flesh and spouting angry words. He held her down, ripped at her and covered her mouth. After long minutes of torment, a primal scream issued from his throat, and he collapsed.

He came to rest, breathing heavily, his jaw and eyes clenched tight.

She whimpered. "Anton, why—?"

His eyes opened, and he stared at her. He had never given his name. *Never.*

"Mary Ellen," he gasped.

She stood beside the bed and dressed slowly. "I wondered how many times it would take before you recognized me. But you've never done me this ugly before!"

He saw the marks he had left on her and felt wretched now that it was over. He'd hurt her, but just the moment before, he hadn't even cared. He had wanted to hurt her. Hurt someone.

"I'm *sorry*. I don't know what came over me!" He saw the red handprint on her face and wondered how it had gotten there. "I don't know what happened. I'm sorry!"

He took her by the shoulders and looked deep into her eyes. "What are you doing here, Mary Ellen? You're smart—you were going to nursing school. You could have done anything, but God, not this!"

"I could ask you the same thing, Anton. What are *you* doing here?"

He searched her face, trying to find the high school sweetheart that he now knew was hidden within this stranger. "But you were going to be a nurse..."

"And *you* were going to dance!" she shouted. "This is Eddy Street, Anton. It's where people go after their dreams have died."

"People don't become prostitutes just because they've lost their dreams."

"So what the fuck are you?" she asked. "We're all prostitutes in one way or another. Whatever it is you're doing for a living that requires you to carry that gun…" She motioned toward the dresser. "Do you get paid for what *you* do? Because that makes you a whore just like me."

Suddenly, he recognized his bond with the whores of Eddy Street. It was a brotherhood and sisterhood of strangers who had sold their souls.

He retrieved his wallet and took out all the money he had. "There's over eight hundred dollars. It's yours." He backed away from her with tears in his eyes. "I'm so sorry."

*****

He felt wretched as he walked back toward the park. It was a long way from Eddy Street, but he needed to get as far away as possible. It had happened like this before, and he always hated himself afterward. It was as though he had no control over this anger that had no source he could understand. He walked faster and faster along the broken sidewalk, trying to put distance between who he was and what he had done. Faster and faster he went until he finally broke into a dead run down the San Francisco streets. But there was no escape, no rhyme, no reason. He could not run fast enough to escape that ugly part of himself. Finally, he reached the park, where he collapsed, breathless, on the cool green grass.

More than an hour had passed before a car horn bleated in the distance, bringing Anton to his senses. He looked at his watch and jumped to his feet, thinking of Hope for the first time in hours. He had promised he would come back in time for the weekend gathering. *"Like old times,"* she had said, looking forward to the whole group coming back to the hill to eat popcorn and watch an old movie. The thought rolled over in his mind as he raced to the nearest pay phone and dialed her number.

"Jeff!" He was glad it was he who had answered. "Tell Hope… tell her I got hung up. I'll be late, but I'm on my way."

"Where the hell are you?" Jeff barked.

"Just tell her I'm on my way!" He quickly hung up.

*****

All the way home, Hope's small face haunted him. Somehow, he knew that what he had done had nothing to do with whether or not he loved her, yet it was Hope who would be hurt the most if she found out. She wouldn't understand. This decadent side of him had tormented him for years before he'd ever known her, and now, as he floored the pedal, he wondered if she would know.

It was late evening when Anton pulled into Hope's driveway, having stopped by his apartment for a quick shower. The lights were still on, and through the open window, he could hear music and laughter. No one had gone home yet. He tried on a smile in the darkness, but it felt stiff and unnatural, like a rented tuxedo. He rubbed his face and finally forced himself to go inside.

"You made it!" Nicki smiled, still dancing to the music as he stepped in. The movie had ended, but the party hadn't. Hope had been planning it for weeks, waiting only for the study to be finished. It was a coming-home party for herself, she said. A party to rid the house of ghosts so she could love it again.

"Where's Hope?"

"The kitchen," Nicki said as she danced away.

He went toward the kitchen, stepping over Jeff, who sat cross-legged on the floor with records scattered everywhere in his never-ending effort to organize Hope's albums. "Hi ya', Russia!" Jeff slapped Anton on the leg as he stepped over him.

Hope was busy at the counter, and he stepped beside her. Taking the cheese from her hands, he began to grate it for whatever she was preparing for the oven. "Sorry I'm late," he said without looking at her.

"I've been worried sick about you!" she scolded, turning around to look at him. But when his eyes met hers, she quickly looked away, and they continued to work in silence.

*****

From where Anton sat on the couch, through the French doors of the dining room, he could watch the full moon move slowly over the mountains. The night was hot, but the moon cast cool blue patterns on the floor. He had completely stripped himself, and now only the sheet covered the lower part of his body. He had grown accustomed to sleeping on Hope's couch, and after everyone had gone home, he automatically went to the linen closet and pulled out his bedding.

Hope had been silent all night. In a way, that was harder to take. She showed no sign of anger, no sign of grief, had in fact remained polite, not even sarcastically so. If it weren't for the silence, he would have thought she didn't know.

But she did. From the moment she'd first looked at him, she had known, and it broke his heart to watch her avoid his eyes for the rest of the evening. After everyone had left, she'd simply gone upstairs, leaving him alone in the living room to do as he pleased, to stay or to go. It didn't seem to matter.

He leaned his forehead in his hand and sighed while he stuck his bare feet and legs out of the sheet, wishing it weren't so hot. Crickets chirped loudly outside the open window, and blue patches of moonlight slowly moved across the floor. He felt numbed by what he had done. He wasn't really worried about Mary Ellen, although seeing her was a shock. He'd been with her as Candy, and knowing that side of her, he was sure she was bragging about the eight-hundred-dollar trick she'd turned.

It was Hope he had the most regrets about. He hadn't even thought about her, hadn't even remembered her, as if the man he'd become had never known Hope Landrum at all, her sweetness, her giving nature. It wasn't until he had rid himself of the burning anger he'd bottled up since seeing Dan that he'd thought of her at all.

As the blue patches of moonlight began to ascend the stairs, he spotted tiny feet that peeked out from the green silk kimono he had given Hope in New York, and when he squinted in the darkness, he realized that she was sitting at the foot of the stairs. He wondered how long she had been there.

"I wondered whether you would stay," she said in a low voice as she went into the dining room and looked out the French doors. The moonlight shone white against her hair as she turned to him and let the silk robe fall to the floor, leaving her nude body silhouetted against the moonlight.

Anton stood and wrapped the sheet around his waist, tucking it in as he approached her. His hand gently touched the soft curve of her breast, and she caught her breath. "What are you doing, Hope?" he whispered.

"I won't let her have you without a fight," she said.

"There's no contest. It would be like racing a mule against a thoroughbred."

Hope's tears glistened in the moonlight, and he anguished for her. "At least she gave you a ride."

"Oh, Hope," he breathed. "You aren't ready for this. How can you offer something you're not ready to give?"

"Because I love you and I don't want to lose you. By the time I'm ready, you might be gone." She stepped into his arms and forcibly wrapped them around her.

"How can you love me?" he said, gently pushing her away. He searched for answers, but none were there. "I don't deserve your love. My God, Hope, look what I've done to you!"

She looked so beautiful, so pitiful, and just the touch of her hand on his face felt like she had caressed his soul.

"My love is not earned," she said. "It's given."

No one had ever loved him so completely, so unselfishly. She was always the giver, the sacrifice. He picked up the robe and wrapped it around her shoulders.

"Sweetheart, I just can't."

She started to cry. "What else can I offer you? I have nothing else to give."

Anton felt a sob rip through him as he pulled her back into his arms. "Your forgiveness, Hope. That's all I want." He wept, and led her to the couch, where they entwined themselves in each other's arms until hours had passed and all the tears were spent.

*****

Anton stroked her hair and sighed. Hope lay against his chest, silently blinking at the vague grays of early light. She had finally seen the darker side of him, the ghost that followed him, degraded and tormented him, and he wondered what morning would bring. She remained silent while he tried to explain that what he had done was out of his control, yet she clung to him as though afraid of letting go. He couldn't help but wonder if her clinging was her way of saying goodbye after listening to him trying to explain his behavior. That wasn't what he meant to do, but now that it was too late, he realized it was exactly how it had sounded.

"Hope...do you want me to get my things?" He spoke low, trying to keep the tears out of his voice. But she said nothing, only clung tighter still, blinking at the gray light.

Anton could feel his heart pounding, and he was grateful for the breeze that finally found its way through the window. He looked around the room, and in the dim light he saw the pictures and small quilts that Hope had hung on the walls, the country furniture, and the Amish rocking chair that held a calico-print pillow she'd made. He looked at the fireplace, now cold and empty. An ache went through him, and as if she felt it too, she looked up, making him realize that he had cried outwardly. He clung to her and squeezed his eyes tight as he wept.

*****

Anton woke alone. Already, the sweltering heat suffocated him. He looked around quickly for Hope, but she was nowhere to be found. When he realized she wasn't in the house, he dressed quickly and checked outside for her car, relieved to find it still there. Eventually, as he had so many times before, he found the path in the woods and followed it until he spotted her in the distance. She sat on the fallen log, where she absentmindedly dug into the dirt with a stick. He went and sat beside her and looked up at the treetops, where the distant swordsmen still fought in the hot summer wind.

"Some things never change," he ventured.

No reply came, just the endless digging of little holes in the moist dirt, her hands wrapped around the stick so tight her knuckles had turned white.

"Hope..."

But there was nothing. She hadn't even looked up to acknowledge his presence. It was as though he weren't there. After a while, he left, stopping only once to look back at her before leaving.

Hope remained in the woods, which seemed to be the only cool spot in the heat of the day. Often, she had come seeking tranquility, but today the woods had nothing to offer. She watched a distant rabbit hop lazily between the trees and was reminded of the first time she'd brought Anton here. She smiled sadly to herself and looked down the empty path. They had been through so much since that day.

"Anton," she called softly, hoping he had hidden just beyond the bend, but she jumped to her feet when a cold shiver ran through her. She walked toward the edge of the woods and stopped to look across the meadow, where in the distance, Anton put a small bag in the back of his car. "No," she gasped and began running toward him. "Anton!" she cried, watching him get into the car and shut the door.

He glanced in the mirror, then turned around when she called his name once more. He got out of the car just in time for her to fly into his arms.

"Don't go! Oh, please don't go, Anton! I can't bear it! I love you!" She kissed him, crying, telling him she loved him...*just please don't go!*

CHAPTER 30

When Hope arrived home from shopping, she was greeted at the door by Anton and three dozen long-stemmed red roses, which he exchanged for the packages in her arms. "Hi, sweetheart," he said with a warm smile.

"Are these for me?" she asked.

"No. Jeff sent them to me. For goodness' sake, of course, they're for you!" he laughed. "I ordered them this morning, but you shot out of here so fast you were gone when they came." He peeked into the bag she had brought from town. "What'd you get?"

"I bought some shirts for your trip." Hope watched him curiously while she put the roses in a vase. "Why the flowers?" she asked, sniffing them with delight. He had worked steady for the past week, preparing for the Paris job, and she had begun to wonder if he'd forgotten she even existed.

Anton laid the packages down and put his arms around her. "I've been a jerk, and I don't want you to think I'm ignoring you. It's just that this job is so important." He nuzzled her neck, wishing he weren't so busy and that she were ready for him. The scent of roses reminded him of her room in New York, and he was more in the mood for a good, healthy romp in the hay than the grueling work that still lay ahead. "When this is over, I want us to take a vacation. There are things we still need to talk about that I just can't get into right now. I've still got a ton of work, and I'm mentally exhausted." He wanted to discuss the possibility of him moving in on a more permanent basis but thought that after what he had done, allowing a little more time would be wise. He still felt terrible, and the fear of losing her now made him anxious to dig in deeper, to bury himself in her life. Perhaps make commitments.

When Hope laughed, it startled him out of his thoughts, and he found himself clinging to her. "I see," she said. "After we get back from Paris, you want to take a vacation! Need I remind you that I have a job waiting for me? You've been supporting me for over a month already!" She kissed his cheek lightly before he went back to his work. "There's something I want to talk to you about too."

"Can it wait, babe? I've got all this work, and I'm pooped. I'm just so distracted right now. Maybe once we get to France. The first week will be hell, but after that, I'll have more time. Did I tell you Hal Samuels is going? He'll be your escort while I'm working. I hope you don't mind, but I figured that at least you know him and he's a man I trust."

Anton seemed to rattle out random thoughts, and Hope realized that he was, indeed, too distracted to discuss anything of importance. While shopping, she had run into Clay and learned that Dan and Anton had had an altercation three weeks before. It had dawned on her while driving home that this had happened the same time Anton had become so edgy that she suggested he get away for a while. Whatever their argument had been about, she was now certain it had something to do with his unacceptable behavior.

But for now, she was contented to watch him hover over the blueprints spread on the dining room table while eating from a plate he held in his hand. Hope wondered if he even knew what he was putting in his mouth as he peered over the edge of the plate at his work.

The blueprints had arrived in Three Rivers the week before, blueprints of the buildings to be used by Russia's Bolshoi Ballet while they toured Paris. Anton scanned each doorway, each window, and every vent a hundred times. The hotels, the Théâtre le Ranelagh, the restaurants—each was combed by Anton's trained eyes while he made little notes to himself on a pad of paper now smudged with chocolate.

A week had passed with Anton up at dawn each day, working silently until late into the evening. He was only aware of Hope when she fed him or occasionally cornered him for a hug and a kiss. The incident of three weeks before had not been forgotten but was temporarily pushed aside in favor of the security job in Paris.

Anton himself was not one of the security guards, but the master planner, the architect of the invisible net that was to surround the lives of his native countrymen over the course of several performances. It seemed odd that it would be an American, though Russian born, who would design and implement security for the Bolshoi Ballet, but Anton was perfectly suited to the job. After he negotiated the terms of his employment, it was an earnest gesture of trust between the United States and the Soviet Union. It was a first, and the entire world watched.

Hope knew the intense pressure he was under and made no demands of his time or attention. When large phone bills began to come in, Anton only smiled and said, "My uncle will pick them up," then looked back at his work, unimpressed, while Hope sat on the couch in awe at how many times he'd called Washington.

He was pleased at obtaining permission to use the security department of the USIB, even though technically it was not a USIB job. Jacques Racine had hired him privately, with the permission of both governments, of course, and Hope was in awe that the man in the middle of the entire international hubbub now stood over blueprints in her dining room, mindlessly eating cookies. She had always known what he did was important and that he was an expert in his field, but now she was seeing for the first time the preparations that had been cloaked from her during the New York job, and she was impressed by his close ties to the White House. She smiled to herself. *He probably wasn't kidding when he said we could have lunch there if that was what I wanted.*

*****

Hope felt lost and would have probably panicked if Hal Samuels hadn't stayed by her side until they reached Paris. Anton had left the week before, and she'd begun to question why she was going at all. She was aware of the magnitude of the job and the important role

Anton played in it. She wondered if she looked like a fool, following the heels of such an important man like a puppy in need of direction. Except for the day he had given her the roses, he'd hardly spoken to her in weeks, and even though intellectually she understood, the emotional part of her did not. Suddenly, halfway across the Atlantic, Hope just wanted to go home.

Samuels was kind, as always. He asked if she was all right when he realized she was on the verge of tears, but she forced a smile and only complained about being tired. He had already been apprised of Anton's schedule and kept her mind occupied by telling her about the places he planned to take her while Anton worked. "I pulled the best darn job of the whole department," he said with a grin, but she only smiled in return.

After arriving at Le Bourget Airport, Samuels made a quick call to let Anton know they had landed safely. Then they were whisked through customs, and soon Hope found herself in the back of a long, dark limousine heading out of town.

"Where are we going?" she asked. All the signs that led to Paris were pointing in the opposite direction. "Aren't we going to the hotel?" She could feel the edge of panic rising in her stomach, but he only smiled.

"Mr. Pavlova has a surprise for you" was all he said, and within minutes, they pulled into the gates of a large country estate. It was the summer villa of Jacques Racine, who had graciously opened it to Anton during his stay while he himself stayed at his flat in the city. The driver followed the long narrow drive until the huge structure came into view. It was stone, with turrets and balconies, and an unbelievable set of stairs that led up to the ornately decorated entrance. Immaculate lawns surrounded alabaster tubs overflowing with flowering hydrangeas. Through the pillared pavilion was a garden unlike anything Hope had ever seen.

In the back of the idling limo, where Hal Samuels had asked her to wait, she unrolled the dark-tinted window and stared out at the garden until someone opened the car door.

"Hi, sweetheart. Hal says you're not feeling well." The moment she stepped out, Anton swept her into his arms. "Shh...what's wrong,

Hope?" He kissed her tenderly when an unexpected tear rolled down her cheek.

"I'm all right now. Just tired." She quickly wiped the tear away as Anton looked over her shoulder at Samuels.

"Hal says you've been depressed." He lifted her face with his hand and looked into her eyes. "What is it?"

"I guess I've just been a little insecure lately," she said, forcing a smile when she saw a proper-looking couple on the steps behind him.

"I've neglected you, haven't I? Well, I'm going to start making it up to you right now. Come with me." He led her toward the steps, where she was introduced to the 'houseman,' James, and his wife, Diane. They bowed and curtsied respectively, and Hope nodded in turn, not knowing what the proper response would be, before Anton led her into the house.

Everything inside was like a romantic tale from the turn of the century, like a Gothic novel that Hope had mysteriously stepped into. The foyer was beautifully adorned with marble inlay, plaster rosettes on the ceilings, and curved stairs that led to the upper floors. The fabrics were velvets and satins, and the rooms were filled with vase after vase of fresh flowers.

"Oh, Anton, it's beautiful!" she said, awestruck, and he smiled broadly.

"I thought you would like something more than a stuffy hotel. I'll let Diane take you to your room to rest. I want to thank Samuels before he leaves." With that, he left her at the foot of the stairs.

"This way, miss," the matronly woman said, and Hope was led to the top of the stairs, where they entered a beautiful bedroom that overlooked the garden. As in New York, it had been filled with red roses.

"It's lovely," Hope said as she gently touched the veil of lace that canopied the bed. "Everything is so beautiful."

"It used to be like this all the time," Diane said wistfully, "before the missus died. It's been gloomy for so long…" Diane stopped when she saw she had evoked sympathy. "But then your Mr. Pavlova came. He told me, 'Flowers everywhere, Diane!'" She laughed. "We were so delighted, James and I. 'E's my husband, you see. We opened all the curtains and windows and let the light in, we did!"

The woman's cockney accent delighted Hope. She had worried about not speaking French. "Doesn't Mr. Racine live here?"

"Oh, 'e comes and 'e goes, stays at the flat in Paris mostly. James and me, we see to the place." She closed her eyes and sniffed the scented air. "Oh, 'ow I love to 'ave flowers in the house again!" She looked at Hope. "Now, your Mr. Pavlova, 'e's a real gentleman, 'e is. 'E knows what a lady likes." She paused and looked Hope up and down. "You're tired, dearie. And 'ere I am, chatterin' like a little bird. You rest. James will be up shortly with yer things." She curtsied and closed the door behind her.

*****

The sun was peeking between the blue satin curtains when Hope opened her eyes, awakening to the light rap at her door. "Come in," she said, sitting up with the blankets drawn to her chin.

"Good morning, miss." It was Diane with a breakfast tray. Hope had missed dinner entirely and slept through the night. She watched while Diane set down the tray and opened the curtains, inquiring if she'd slept well and chattering delightfully.

It was odd being the recipient of so much attention. Hope hardly knew what to do and squelched the urge to jump up and start making the bed.

"Shall I open a window, miss?" Diane said after a while.

"Yes. Thank you," Hope said, and when the woman opened the window, Anton's voice could be heard from the garden below.

"Good morning, Diane," he called up to her. "Can Hope come out and play?" The woman laughed merrily, and Hope bounded from her bed and went to the window. "Good morning, my love!" He beamed up at her.

"Don't move!" she called back before darting away. She quickly dressed and ran down the stairs with a piece of toast in her hand, only because Diane insisted, and soon met Anton in the garden with a passionate embrace. "If you're trying to impress me, it worked." She smiled at him, looking more radiant than she had looked in a long time. "But now can I just be little ol' me again?"

"Hope, you're you whether it's in Paris or Three Rivers." He took her hand, and they walked through the garden while he told her the schedule for the week, explaining minor changes and what she could expect. "Samuels will be here for you in about an hour," he said. She was visibly disappointed, though she had already known what the first week would be like. "We'll have two weeks after that, Hope. I'm sorry I've been so busy. We never really had a chance to talk. I don't want you to think that I've taken…what I did lightly."

The mention of the incident left Hope speechless. Her eyes searched his for a moment before she finally spoke. "I don't want us to ever talk about it again," she said. "I love you, that's all I know." She kissed him and smiled. "Do you know why I was depressed yesterday? It was because I felt like I didn't deserve you. I feel so inadequate. Even in Three Rivers, I'm a nobody, and here you are, an international hotshot who calls the White House like one would call one's Aunt Millie for tea."

"'Hotshot' is just the job title." He laughed as he pulled her into his arms and held her tight. "I'm no hotshot. My job is just a job, not the means by which I measure myself."

"What are you talking about?" She began to laugh, and he grinned, shaking his head.

"Hell, I don't know. You'll have to ask Leslie. She's the one that pointed it out." They laughed together and walked until Anton had to leave. Samuels arrived soon after, and Hope didn't see Anton again until the following morning.

*****

The week was filled with the Eiffel Tower, the Basilique du Sacré-Cœur, the Louvre, and innumerable other historical sites. But Hope mostly looked forward to the early-morning walks in the garden with Anton, when the dew still hung on the leaves as they strolled hand in hand. Often, they were silent, just enjoying the songbirds and one another's company, and they laughed quietly between themselves whenever they spotted Diane peeking at them from the upstairs window.

By Friday, most of the meetings were out of the way. The last one was scheduled for that evening, and Hope had been invited. It was a dinner meeting, and although the dinner itself was rather formal, hardly anyone in the building had dressed in evening attire. It amused her to see the beautiful ballerinas and the virile danseurs in blue jeans and cotton shirts, some with scarves or sweaters loosely tied about their shoulders. They laughed and spoke in Russian, as Anton had done on rare occasions.

He'd booked Hal Samuels as escort for the whole week so he could bury himself in the final preparations for the ballet troupe. Tonight he had gathered the entire troupe to run down the dos and don'ts pertaining to the security measures he'd taken. He had been in meeting after meeting with ambassadors, managers, the Bolshoi personnel, but he wanted to address the dancers themselves, get to know them a little, help them feel safe and comfortable in a foreign land. He was relaxed, knowing that after tonight his time was his own.

After the dinner, the dancers remained seated around tables of six, sharing carafes of wine, talking and laughing among themselves. Soon it would be time for Anton to speak to them. Hope watched him and Jacques, heads together in last-minute discussion. Jacques had been kind in allowing her to attend the less secretive meetings with Anton, recalling it was she who had spotted the impostor who'd used his name in New York. He allowed Anton to give her special security privileges, though it was Anton who hadn't allowed her into most of the meetings "for her own protection."

It was exciting and romantic to be part of the hullabaloo that surrounded the performers, and for the first time, Hope could truly appreciate Anton's attraction to his work. As he stood at the lectern and began to speak, a hush fell over the dancers. Their eyes turned to him in obvious surprise that he didn't need an interpreter.

Hope had no idea what he was saying as the Russian words flowed from his mouth. She couldn't help but wonder if it felt good for him to speak in his native tongue. After all, there weren't many opportunities to converse in Russian in Three Rivers.

As he spoke, he smiled often, occasionally getting laughter or a smattering of applause. Hope wished on several occasions that she understood the language, especially during what appeared to be a Q&A. At one point, one of the men said something and nodded toward her, and Anton's reply was followed by a round of laughter. Just when she thought they were laughing at her, Anton turned to her and smiled. "Stand up, Hope, so I can introduce you. He asked if you were my wife. I told him you were one of my best security guards." He winked and introduced her properly.

As she sat down and Anton took another question, Jacques leaned toward her. "They like him," he whispered. "That's good."

*****

Anton was enjoying himself more than ever before. Not only was he doing what he loved to do, but he could also speak in the language of his youth to people who did what he admired. He was in seventh heaven, and the performers loved him. He knew their terms, understood the pain of sore muscles, and sympathized with the rigors of their craft. Getting them to trust him was an important part of the operation, and he indulged himself a little more than usual, explaining not only who he was but that he, too, was a trained dancer.

"Where were you born?" a woman asked.

"Leningrad," he said, touched by the interest in his personal life.

"What year were you born?" asked one of the danseurs. His serious expression startled Anton. The man's face was lean and finely chiseled, his eyes a deep blue, and he wore a mane of light-brown hair.

The world seems preoccupied with my age, Anton thought. "Ah, 1941," he said.

"Mr. Pavlova," the man continued, "may I speak with you in private later?"

Anton glanced at Jacques, who nodded after the request was translated into English.

"That would be fine. What is your name, sir?" he asked for the record.

"Alexis…Vishnyakov."

Anton stood frozen at the podium.

Finally, Jacques wished to say a few words through their interpreter while Anton sat down beside Hope. He grasped her hand tightly beneath the table, and she could feel him tremble as the name drummed in his ear: *Alexis, Alexis, Alexis…* He stared out into the crowd, where, from the middle of the room, a pair of blue eyes stared back at him, curious, waiting—searching.

"Anton," Hope whispered and gave him a glass of water. He drank the entire glass. "Do you think…?"

"I don't know. But right now, my stomach is turning inside out," he whispered back. From the moment Alexis Vishnyakov spoke, Anton's world stood still.

CHAPTER 31

Jacques Racine unlocked the tall oak doors to his office and led Anton and Hope inside. The walls were covered with rich mahogany, and the bookshelves climbed to the top of the ten-foot ceilings at one end. The chairs were covered with deep-red velvet except for the large oxblood leather chair behind the ornate desk. The floor was covered with elegant Persian rugs, and the stained glass lamps gave the room a quiet, elegant glow.

"I'll leave you two here. When Mr. Vishnyakov arrives, I'll bring him to you," Jacques said after being apprised of the situation. He had graciously offered the seclusion of his private office and was eager to make everyone as comfortable as possible, even if it was just a case of mistaken identity. He liked Anton and wanted to help in whatever way he could. The auditorium simply was not the place, he insisted.

For the next ten minutes, Anton could almost feel himself age as he stood in the middle of the room, afraid to sit. Hope stood beside him, her tiny hand squeezing his, trying to give him comfort as he tried not to speculate.

He jumped a little when the door swung open and the graceful danseur stepped into the room. Jacques said a few words that nobody heard, then excused himself, closing the door behind him. Hope stepped back, melting into the wall as the drama unfolded.

The danseur finally spoke, his English broken and poor. "Do you know who I am?" His face twitched nervously as he stood a little distance away.

"I'm not sure," Anton said. "Do you know me?"

"Perhaps."

Both men visibly trembled, afraid to speak. What if they were wrong—or right—in their speculations?

"How do you think you know me?" Anton asked after a long silence.

"I am twenty-nine years old," the danseur began. "A son was born to my parents eleven years before me. He was kidnapped at the age of three by my grandparents. Until the day my mother died, she grieved the loss of her firstborn, her son...Anton." He searched Anton's face for recognition of the story he told. "Anton, you look *so* much like her."

Anton was in shock. Alexis glanced at Hope as she touched Anton's arm. "But the name?"

"It was changed," Anton said, not taking his eyes off Alexis. "I was born Anton Pavlovich Vishnyakov. Pavlova is the feminine variant of Pavlovich. It's how my grandparents kept me hidden for all those years."

"Then he must be the *Alexis* from your grandmother's journals. He's your brother, Anton! Alexis is your brother!"

Speechless, the two men fell into each other's arms, their tears of joy intermingling as they both tried to talk at once. The Russian and English were so painfully mixed it was a miracle anyone understood anything. They patted each other's back and hugged again, finally pulling away to look into each other's wet, smiling face.

Anton grabbed Hope's hand and pulled her to them, and the three of them embraced. "This is Hope," he said. "I wanted her here with us. I hope you don't mind."

Alexis smiled down at her and took her hand. "I don't mind at all," he said, then said something else in Russian that made Anton smile.

"Yes, she is lovely," Anton repeated in English, causing Hope to flush.

"Alexis, I don't want to intrude," she said. "Please feel free to speak Russian. I don't understand a word of it, and I'm sure there are a lot of things you want to talk about."

Unlike Anton, Alexis was a tall, sinewy man, as handsome as his brother, yet differently so.

"Thank you. You are kind," he said.

They finally sat and began talking, each obviously comparing notes, each telling his brother about his life, his work. Hope left sometime after midnight and found Jacques sleeping in the outer office. He awoke and helped her locate a pot of tea and a few biscuits, which she served to the brothers, unnoticed. After a while, she fell asleep on the settee with her head on Anton's lap. She was only vaguely aware as he unconsciously stroked her hair, speaking in a low voice, but around four in the morning, she awoke. Anton was crying over her, his face in his hands while Alexis whispered to him, his hands resting on Anton's shoulders.

"I always thought they gave me away," Anton cried in Russian. "I thought they didn't care that they would never see me again. I've spent my whole life thinking they sent me away."

"Anton, that isn't true. When I was nine years old, our mother cried on my birthday because she missed you. That made you twenty, and she still mourned. Anton, look at me!" He took his brother's hands and knelt down in front of him. "They loved you! Papa died when I was five, but he always spoke as if you would come home at any moment. But Mama, she knew you wouldn't be back. After Papa died, we were hungry most of the time. No one had any food. Times were bad. During those years, she was glad you were in America, yet it tore her in two, wanting to be with you but wanting you to have a good life.

"Our grandparents emigrated during the war and asked if they could take you, but Mama said no. They were gone the next morning, and so were you. They lived in the same house, you see. Our grandmother did the laundry, so it was not so unusual to see her folding your clothes or taking care of you in the middle of the night."

"But our grandmother mentioned you in her journals," Anton finally said.

"Mama wrote to them twice. Once when I was born, and then again when Papa died. I wrote to them when Mama joined him. Perhaps that is why they never referred to me as a child in the journals."

"That's right! The only reference to you was 'When Alexis wrote…'"

"Apparently, they received the letters but never replied. Perhaps that is why Grandmother kept the journals. Maybe she felt a need to write but feared writing to *us*. We must forgive them, Anton. I really believe they did what they thought best."

"Best for whom?" Anton replied. His tears had subsided when he noticed Hope. Her own face was streaked with tears, even though he knew she had no idea what they were saying. He bent down and kissed her forehead, and she caressed his cheek in return.

"Are you all right, love?" she asked.

"Yes," he said, "I'm all right."

While she'd slept, Alexis had asked about her, feeling too uncomfortable when she was awake even though she spoke no Russian. Anton had briefly told him about their relationship and the brief but passionate affair, the beating and the rape, and now the slow recovery. He ordinarily wouldn't have told anyone, but his emotions were so open he seemed to pour everything out.

"Alexis is going to come and stay with us here at the villa, if you don't mind," he said.

"You know I don't mind." She wiped the last of her tears and sat up beside him. "Alexis, you're welcome to stay with us anytime," she told him, and he smiled.

*****

It was difficult for Anton to convince Bolshoi personnel to let Alexis stay at the villa. Even though he assured them that Alexis would have his personal protection, he knew it wasn't protection they worried about but his possible defection. Anton was a little surprised when they finally agreed to it. Two days later, he found his brother on the doorstep with his bag in his hand.

"I must go into the city each day for rehearsal," Alexis told him as he stepped inside.

"And to be accounted for, no doubt!"

"No doubt!" He laughed and swung an arm around Anton's shoulders the way Jeff had often done.

The rest of the day was spent exchanging anecdotes from their lives, stories about friends, and experiences. Alexis made a special effort to speak English, broken as it was, around Hope, often pulling her into the conversation.

By evening, the three sat in the cozy parlor, where Diane served them dinner. Hope sat quietly amazed while Anton talked about their life and friends in Three Rivers. It was interesting to see them through someone else's eyes.

"Noah's not famous, Anton," she said after a while, giving him a look.

"Yes, he is," he answered. "In boxing circles, he's very famous. You just know him as one of the guys, but he has a whole entourage of people who work for him and follow him around. Where do you think he is when he's gone for weeks and months at a time? Pick up the sports section sometime. You'll be surprised."

She stared, astonished. "Really? What else don't I know about our friends?"

"You know them better than I do, Hope," he said, then said a few words in Russian, and Alexis glanced at Hope. "*One of our friends is her brother, but she doesn't know,*" he said. "*I'll tell you about it later.*" Alexis nodded slightly and took a bite of roast.

"Are you married, Alexis?" Hope asked.

"No. I'll not marry as long as I live in the Soviet Union," he said doggedly, and Anton looked up but remained silent.

"I thought that was a wedding ring," she continued, and Alexis looked at the simple band he wore.

"It was Papa's," he answered, then slipped it off his finger. "Here, Anton, I want you to have it."

Anton looked at the ring his brother held out to him. "I can't take that."

"You should have something that belonged to Papa." He smiled and pressed it into Anton's hand. "You see? Now it belongs to all the men in our family!"

"Family..." Anton whispered the word like a prayer as he slipped the ring onto his finger and smiled at his brother. "I can't tell you what this means to me. Thank you, Alexis."

"And you, Hope," Alexis asked after a moment, "what about your family?"

"I have Uncle Nate," she said. "He's my grandfather."

Anton laughed at the confused expression on his brother's face and explained about the legendary man of Three Rivers whom everyone called Uncle Nate.

"He sounds very wise." Alexis chuckled and leaned back in his chair while Diane cleared away the dishes.

"He's probably the wisest man I know." Anton looked at Hope, who smiled. "And he has the prettiest granddaughter in the world." He leaned over and kissed her, then stood and stretched. "I'll go see if your room is ready, Alexis."

"He seems quite taken with your grandfather," Alexis said to Hope when he was gone.

"Uncle Nate thinks the world of him too," she said.

"What about your parents? What do they think?"

"You look tired, Hope," Anton said.

She was relieved to see Anton standing in the doorway. "I am," she said, and retreated to her room after saying good night.

"I've said something wrong, haven't I? I'm afraid my English is not good," Alexis said apologetically.

"No, you didn't say anything wrong," Anton said, and began telling him the story of Clay and Hope, the father they shared, and the father Hope thought was her own. "It's awful to grow up thinking you weren't wanted. I thank God that I found you and learned the truth, but I'm afraid that in Hope's case, there wasn't a soul who really wanted her other than Nathan. He's the one who named her. I guess he thought she would need it."

"What about the brother?" Alexis asked.

"He loves her, I'm sure of that." Anton rubbed his face wearily. "I've got to talk to him, especially now that I've found you. I know now what it would mean to her. To tell the truth, I think she's still in love with him."

Alexis studied his brother momentarily. "Are you going to marry her?"

Anton sat, deep in thought. He and Hope had never even alluded to marriage, although Leslie claimed they had without knowing it. He thought of Catherine and the ache she had left behind, but realized now that Hope could leave the same scars, whether they were married or not. "I don't know," he finally said. "We still have a lot that needs to be worked out, but yeah, I'd like to think that we will marry someday."

"I like her. She understands people like us. We're the last of the line, you know. Our family will be gone if we have no children."

Anton looked down at the floor. "I'm not sure she wants children," he said, recalling the pain he felt when Dan had told him about her abortion. He shivered and looked up to find Alexis watching him.

"Why would you say a thing like that?" he asked, but Anton only shook his head, realizing he had found something he couldn't share, even with his brother.

"I don't know. I'm getting tired, I guess," he said, backing out of the conversation, and after a few more minutes, he showed Alexis to his room.

CHAPTER 32

The first performance of *Swan Lake* was only a week away, and the brothers spent every waking moment together, including during rehearsals, when Anton sat in the darkened auditorium, watching Alexis onstage. Alexis's part in the production was the *pas de deux* in Act II and as his brother danced, Anton's eyes were glued to his movements, his balance, his form. Occasionally, Anton's eyes would narrow, as if questioning a movement, but more often than not, his face reflected his absolute delight in what he saw.

Sometimes Hope would join him, and when an occasional burst of temper flared between the dancers, Anton explained that it was all part of the process, part of "getting it right." He remembered all too clearly the temper he'd had as a dancer at eighteen, still young and raw, desperately wanting to be great, torn between the stage and the government. Sanderson had won, had convinced his young recruit of the job he needed to do for his country, appealing to Anton's patriotism, Anton's desire to prove himself as an American.

But now the chill of the empty auditorium and the smell of the dancers' sweat rekindled those early ambitions. He was pleased when Alexis asked him to the stage to talk for a moment after rehearsal was over. "What do you think?" his brother asked, mopping his face with a towel.

"You're good, Alexis, very good. I'm proud!" Anton beamed up at the man who stood above him on the stage.

But Alexis wasn't satisfied. He motioned for Anton to come onto the stage with him, and when he did, Alexis folded his arms across his bare chest and looked his brother in the eyes.

"If you were my teacher and I your pupil, what would you tell me?"

Anton smiled and shook his head. "You're the professional. You are the one who dances with the Bolshoi."

Alexis remained adamant. "What would you tell me if I were your student?"

Anton hesitated. "You are very good, Alexis," he began, "but in your *grand jeté*, stay in the air longer, freeze yourself in space." Anton drew pictures in the air with his hands. "The audience loves that. A really high jump with a good *ballon* is the most spectacular of assets to a danseur, but it is rare." He gave Alexis a sidelong glance. "There's a technique. I developed it when I was young and not so afraid to take chances. I can show you…"

A slow smile spread across Alexis's face. "Show me!"

He grabbed Anton's arm, and before he knew it, Anton was walking out of the dressing room in the traditional tights and bare to the waist. He was relieved that Hope had gone out for a while as he bent and stretched, warming his muscles while Alexis rested from the long hours he had already put in. Finally, side by side, Anton explained the technique he had developed, stopping often to explain each movement, each transition, then finally to watch as Alexis tried the technique for himself.

"Try again. Become my shadow," Anton told him as he leapt across the stage.

"I've always been your shadow," he said, and Anton paused. "But now that I know you, I know it is a good place to be."

Alexis gave him a slow smile, and side by side, they danced.

*****

It was an hour later when Hope returned to the auditorium and quietly took a seat in the darkness beside Alexis, who watched other dancers onstage.

"Where have you been?" he whispered as he leaned toward her.

"Shopping. I wanted to find a gift for my friend Nicki," she answered and looked around at the rows of empty seats. "Where's Anton?"

"He's here," Alexis said, turning to watch the look of astonishment spread across her face as she finally realized where he was.

"Oh my God!" she gasped, recognizing Anton onstage as he gracefully lifted the prima ballerina high into the air, then lowered her into his arms. His body caressed hers as they moved together in sensual form.

"They look like they're in love," she whispered, and Alexis took her hand, squeezing it slightly.

"They're supposed to," he said. "That's the way he looks when he is with you." He pressed her hand to his lips. "Have you never seen him dance?"

She shook her head. "Never. What got him up there?"

"He was showing me a technique and said he had always dreamed of dancing with the Bolshoi. Sonia hadn't left yet, so I asked her to dance with him."

Anton flew across the stage, taking great leaps and hanging in the air with great buoyancy, as though they were simple maneuvers, and Alexis caught his breath. He squeezed her hand tight and sat at the edge of his seat, totally caught up in the excitement of the dance. "He never should have given it up. Never!"

"He told me your grandparents were ill for a while before they died and he had to find a way to take care of them," she explained, neither of them taking their eyes off the stage.

"It's a crime. After all those years of work. Damn!" Alexis looked at her. "I'm sorry," he said. "Hope, you've got to encourage him to buy the studio he told me about. He owes it to the world to teach." He looked back at Anton. "I wish I had such a teacher. He has techniques that I've never seen. Anton must teach me, Hope. I want him to show me everything he knows within the next week."

Hope looked at him. His body curved with the same musculature as Anton; even his neck and face were strong, and his eyes intense as he watched his brother onstage. It was on that stage that Anton did what now seemed natural for him to do. It was while he danced that Hope saw Anton Pavlova for who he really was, the secret behind the quiet Russian who had first come to Three Rivers.

As he moved, she almost expected him to kiss Sonia. It was as though they were making love through dance.

*****

In the week that followed, Alexis found Anton to be a hard taskmaster, demanding perfection as he watched rehearsals. The other dancers noticed frequent conferences with the man they now knew was Alexis's brother. They noticed, too, that the onetime *corps de ballet* dancer, who had once danced with frenzied intensity, was now tempered with new style and grace.

"The other dancers talk, Anton," Alexis said as they walked down the Parisian street toward the sidewalk café. "They say I'm interpreting my part too much instead of just dancing."

"Isn't that what you're supposed to do?" Hope asked from between them.

"I'm afraid the Soviet Union would consider that Westernized thinking," he said, smiling down at her.

"Interpretation is often the difference between good and great, Alexis," Anton finally said. "Perhaps the ones who are talking feel threatened." He had been distracted for the past three days, though only Hope had noticed. She'd seen him unconsciously patting the left side of his chest during their outings in Paris, feeling for his revolver, and today he seemed especially nervous.

They finally reached the café and ordered something to drink. "Is it true that interpretation is welcomed in America?" Alexis asked, instinctively lowering his voice, but Anton didn't answer.

After a moment, Hope finally answered, "Yes, it is, Alexis," then frowned at his brother. "Anton, what's the matter with you?"

He turned to her, and she saw the worried look on his face, as if he already knew what was on Alexis's mind.

"I want to defect," Alexis whispered, and Hope drew in a deep breath. Anton gave her a sobering stare.

"You can't, Alexis," he whispered back. "Not here. Not this tour!"

"Why? You can help me."

"Don't be a fool! That is exactly what they are expecting. Over my shoulder are two men. They followed us from the villa three days ago and have been with us ever since. They are plainclothesmen. Soviet police."

Hope scanned the crowd with her eyes.

"Don't look at them!"

"All the more reason for me to go with you," Alexis whispered angrily. "How do you think I feel having my own government spy on me? How would you like to be a prisoner in your own country?"

"Don't you think I want to take you with me?" Anton saw the hurt on Alexis' face. "Alexis, those men—their job is to catch you before you get into the hands of the right authorities, and if they do, you'll never see the outside of Russia again. You'll never *dance* again! I should have known it was too good to be true when they allowed you to come to the villa with me."

"You could be wrong."

"I'm not! Security jobs like this one are only part of what I do, Alexis…" He paused before breaking the cardinal rule. "I'm also an American agent. Do you understand? A government spy. I recognize one of them, and believe me, they would kill you rather than let you go."

A deafening silence followed. It was as though Alexis had been struck dumb, and he blinked at Anton as a slow panic began to seize him.

"Anton only wants you to be safe, Alexis," Hope said before Anton continued.

"Word is out that I'm your brother. If you do not try to defect this tour, they'll think you are a loyal comrade and not follow you so closely next time. Have patience. It might be a year, or even two, but wait until it is safe!"

The disappointment on Alexis's face was evident, but he knew Anton was right. He casually glanced at the two men, who quickly looked away.

"What should I do?" he finally asked, looking back down at the table.

"*Dance.* Become the great danseur that I see in you, and I swear to you, if you ever set foot on American soil, I'll find you," Anton promised. As the three of them clutched hands in the center of the table, Anton knew that helping his brother defect was the single most important thing he must accomplish with his life.

"And for now?"

"We will enjoy each other's company. Hope and I will stay until after the first performance, but then we must go."

"But that's tomorrow night!"

"My very presence here puts you in jeopardy. We must cut our stay in Paris short."

Alexis squeezed both their hands, as if afraid of letting go, and was embarrassed when a tear slipped down his face. "It's going to be hard…" *saying goodbye…* the words he could not finish.

"I know," Anton choked. "I know."

*****

After leaving the café, the three of them clung to one another for the rest of the day, and after dinner, Hope excused herself, sensing that Anton and Alexis needed time alone.

It was well past midnight when she heard a light tap on her door. "I saw your light," Anton whispered when she peeked out into the hall. "Can I come in for a few minutes?" he asked, embarrassed by the look she gave. "I just want to be with you, Hope. It seems like an eternity since we've been together."

She gave him an understanding nod, and he stepped in. He watched her slip into the green kimono, covering the lacy white nightgown she wore. When she turned to him, it took his breath away. He'd been so busy he had failed to notice that the color had returned to her cheeks, the light to her eyes. It almost startled him to see how beautiful she was once again, and as she stepped into his arms, his eyes rested on the unmade bed.

"We never had our long talk," he said, kissing her brow. "I'm afraid I've neglected you terribly. I told you we'd have time after the first week, but I've spent all my time with Alexis." As he spoke, he could feel the softness of her hair against his face, smell the fragrance of her perfume.

"I'm just glad you found each other, Anton. Don't worry, I understand. But it's been hard on you, hasn't it, love?" She looked at him and teased, "You haven't kissed me for a whole week!"

"A week? That's impossible," he smiled back. "How have I survived a whole week?" He kissed her tenderly, feeling her soft breath on his face. "Oh, Hope," he began desperately, "when will we make love again?" He was still tormented over what he had done the month before and feared the time that kept slipping past. He desperately needed reassurance, and somehow the act of making love was also the act of forgiveness that he needed. But Hope failed to understand his urgency.

"Anton, I love you. Can't that be enough for now?" She pushed his hair from his face and smiled sadly. "I love you!"

He took a deep breath. "When we get home, we need to talk." He kissed her, ready to leave, and then turned once more to glance at the unmade bed. "Good night, sweetheart," he said before closing the door behind him.

*****

The sun shone bright the next morning as Hope wandered through the garden alone, feeling melancholy about having to leave. She knew she would miss the villa and Diane, who had taken care of her as though she were a princess. She also knew that saying goodbye to Alexis would be especially hard on Anton, and that was what she dreaded most. She plucked a dewy leaf from a chestnut tree and studied it, as if the answers to life could be found there, but only sighed after a while and continued her walk.

"Hello," came a voice from behind, and she turned to see Alexis.

"Good morning," she said. "I didn't know you were in the garden."

"I came to see you," he said. "Chances are, we won't see each other alone after the performance tonight."

Hope looked away, feeling tears rushing to the corners of her eyes, and Alexis quietly pulled her to his chest. He held her there for a time in silence before speaking.

"There are things that I normally would not say, but because I may never see you again, I must," he whispered, gently lifting her chin until their eyes met. "Marry my brother, Hope. Marry him and give him children. For the both of us!"

"I don't know if it will ever come to that, Alexis," she cried.

"He told me what happened to you, and I am sorry." He pulled her tight against him once more and kissed the top of her head. "Don't be angry with him for telling me. We've told each other so many things that rarely pass between two men. But we've lost so much time, and in our eagerness to know each other, many things came out that probably shouldn't have." He took her hand and kissed it. "Come. Walk with me."

They walked in silence, hand in hand, until coming to rest on the stone bench amid the summer flowers.

"Anton says you don't want children," he finally said.

Hope gaped at him. "Why would he say that?"

"I was hoping you could tell me."

Hope said nothing, too shocked by what he had said, but reassured him it wasn't true.

"You and he would have beautiful babies!" He laughed after a while. "Marry my brother, Hope," he said. "Marry him and give him children…for the both of us. You will make some beautiful babies for the brothers Vishnyakov, yes?" He grinned, and she smiled in return.

"Does Anton really look so much like your mother?" she asked, then laughed at the expression on Alexis's face.

"When I first saw him, I thought, *Alexis, that man looks like your mother!*" He laughed loudly. "And when I heard his name, there was a lump in my throat so large I could not eat. Then"—his eyes grew wide—"he opened his mouth, and out came Russian words!" He shook his head. "I was so scared!"

"He was too." She hugged his arm affectionately. They sat together in the sunshine, listening to the birds and watching the flowers sway in the gentle morning breeze. "I envy Anton," Hope said after a while, and Alexis looked at her. "It must be wonderful to have a brother, someone who belongs to him no matter where he is. Even governments cannot change the fact that you are brothers.

You belong to each other for a lifetime, and even when you are apart, you'll be in each other's heart."

Alexis's eyes filled, and he cleared his throat. "I envy him too." He caressed her hair, pushed it behind her shoulders, and smiled. "Hope, have some beautiful children for my brother. For me!" He leaned toward her and kissed her gently on the mouth. "I shall miss you," he whispered, then quickly moved away.

They stood and began to walk again. What should have felt awkward felt comfortable. Their closeness seemed natural, and as they approached the house, they saw Anton watching them from the terrace.

"If you weren't my brother, I'd steal her away from you," Alexis said. There was no attempt to hide their clasped hands.

"I'd put up a hell of a fight!" Anton said, then they went inside for breakfast.

*****

It was opening night, and Anton sat beside Hope, he in his tuxedo and she in the beautiful evening gown he had given her in New York. Together they watched Alexis give his best performance yet, and when it was done, Anton leapt to his feet with tears streaming down his face as he applauded.

"Bravo! Bravo!" he shouted, a proud smile stretched across his face. He grabbed Hope's arm, and they made a dash backstage, where, upon seeing his brother, he threw his arms around him and they laughed excitedly. "Someday you will take the lead! Someday you will be *premier danseur étoile* and be Prince Siegfried in *Swan Lake*! And my eyes will watch your every move, Alexis!" Anton wagged a finger of warning, laughing proudly. "My brother will someday be the Prince!" he went on excitedly as a crowd of people began pressing in on them.

"I owe you so much, Anton," Alexis whispered in his ear as they hugged once more, tears falling down their faces. "I love you, my brother."

Already the Bolshoi personnel moved in to separate the brothers, as they had known they would.

"And I love you, Alexis. I will find you, I promise," Anton whispered just before they were pulled apart. The Soviet police knew he was leaving tonight and made no attempts to hide their identity, and as Alexis was pulled away, Hope grabbed his hand in the crowd but only looked into his eyes, speechless.

"Remember me!" he shouted to her as he was torn away, and she saw the tears streaming down his face just before he disappeared into the multitude.

She and Anton were quickly escorted from the building and found that it was Samuels who had come to their aid. He hurried them into the back of the limousine, where they clung to each other, crying in each other's arms.

The day had passed too swiftly, and though Anton had said his private goodbyes before the performance, he thought of a hundred things that he'd forgotten to say. But it was too late. Alexis was gone.

In only eight days, a stranger had come into his life and left a gaping hole where there once had been nothing. Anton began to wonder if *love* and *pain* were synonymous. He thought of Catherine and concluded that it wasn't she who had caused him pain but the fact that he'd loved her at all. Whether it was a wife, a lover, a brother, or a friend, loving had once again made him feel like his body and soul were being torn apart. In only eight days, he had relived his entire life, had meshed his life with that of another man, had danced with him, cried with him, bared his soul to him. Now the emptiness was as real as hunger or thirst.

After the tears were gone, there was only numbness and the warmth of Hope's small hand in his.

CHAPTER 33

By the time they arrived in New York, Anton looked haggard. He had stared silently out the window the entire flight, not eating, not sleeping. Hope took it upon herself to change their flight to the West Coast. She secured a small suite in a modest but respectable hotel, where Anton finally crawled off to bed, too exhausted to argue.

At four in the morning, Hope awoke with a start. "It's just me," came Anton's voice. "You didn't lock your door."

"I didn't know I needed to," she replied.

"You don't." There was pain in his voice. "I need to be with you. I woke up and I was alone, and God, I don't want to be alone right now." She reached up and took his hand, guiding him into her bed. "I feel like I've lost everything."

She put her arms around him and kissed his brow. "No, you haven't, love," she whispered. "You have me and Alexis."

But Anton shook his head. "I've lost Alexis." He looked at her in the darkness. "and I'm losing you." During the flight home, he had remembered the job that awaited her and realized he was frightened of her independence. For two months, he had provided for her, taken care of her. In his mind, it had kept her from slipping away completely. "Hope, don't take that job at the lodge."

"You aren't losing me," she said gently. "I have to take the job, Anton. I have to get back on my feet, support myself. I already owe you a lot of money."

He bolted up and stared at her. "Why don't you just slap me in the face!" he barked, startling her. She hadn't been aware that he actually enjoyed her dependence on him. "Don't take that job. Please."

"How would I live?" She frowned as he lay back down beside her and gathered her in his arms.

"I'll take care of you. I'll give up the apartment and move in. That's what I've wanted to talk to you about."

Hope's small fingers pressed against his lips, stopping the words. "*Peter, Peter, pumpkin eater, had a wife and couldn't keep her,*" she sadly recited. "*He put her in a pumpkin shell, and there he kept her very well.* Hope Landrum would die in a pumpkin shell, Anton. You asked me once why I was doing something that I wasn't ready to do. Well, you aren't ready for us to live together either. You would be doing it for all the wrong reasons. You aren't losing me, Anton, but you've got to set me free."

He buried his face in her hair and sighed, remembering the prideful, stubborn streak he had seen in her eyes the day he'd found her alongside the road, suitcase in hand. It seemed so long ago now. "I just want to take care of you."

"I know, love." She stroked his face. "And maybe you will someday. But right now I need to know that I am capable of taking care of myself, without any pressures, including the pressure I feel with you sleeping on my couch," she carefully added. "Wouldn't you rather I come to you when I'm ready, instead of us making love because I feel pressured? I just need time."

*****

Anton was grateful for the few stolen days in New York. By the time they reached Three Rivers, he almost felt himself again, though it was hard when Hope went back to work. In her absence, he removed his few belongings from her house, setting her free to become the woman that she'd been growing into when he'd first fallen in love with her.

In the month that followed, he began to relax. Hope was especially attentive, and even on the days they didn't see each other, there were long, affectionate phone calls and funny greeting cards in the mail. Fridays and Saturdays were often shared with Jeff, who had been abandoned after Noah left town and Nicki and Clay sought seclusion, leaving the others to speculate on their impending engagement.

*****

"I wonder where Jeff is tonight. I thought he'd be back by now," Anton said as he and Hope walked through the parking lot. The fresh air felt good after they left Mick's bar. They had fallen into the habit of going there with Jeff, but tonight he hadn't shown. After one bottle of Coke, Anton had tired of the smoke-filled room, so they'd departed, seeking the ice-cream parlor instead.

"He's helping his sister in Fresno move. You know how those things are. They always take longer than you expect." Hope stopped for a moment to lick around the cone, catching drips. "You're trying to fatten me up. You're also succeeding in starting me on a bad habit!" she teased.

"What kind did you get?" he asked as they started walking again.

"I don't know. It's purple," she answered, causing him to burst into laughter.

"Sweetheart," he laughed, "what did you ask for when you ordered it?" He shook his head and grinned, realizing the childlike quality he had always adored in her had returned.

"I just pointed and said, 'Give me the purple kind.' Here, you taste it." She stopped and held the cone toward him, and putting his hand over hers, he took a bite.

"Mmmm...it's good!"

"What is it?"

"I don't know." He licked it thoughtfully. "If I tell you how beautiful you are, will you share it with me?" His eyes sparkled with the reflection of distant lights as he laughed, and Hope became aware of his hand over hers. It was as though he were touching her for the first time and the ice-cream cone was an excuse to hold her hand. She began to tremble when they both took a bite, their faces only an inch apart.

"Let's go to your place," she whispered, and within minutes, they had crossed the three blocks to Anton's apartment.

It was neat, as always, and Hope turned on the radio while Anton went to change his shirt, complaining of the cigarette smoke that still lingered. Bare-chested, he turned to find Hope watching him from the open door.

"What is it?" he asked, seeing the look on her face.

"Wild blackberry," she said, and he began to laugh.

"What?"

"My ice cream, I think it's wild blackberry." She gave him a silly grin, and he drew her into his arms. Her hands ran over the breadth of his back, and the touch of her fingertips on his bare skin took his breath away. "Turn out the lights," she whispered.

"Oh…" He sat on the edge of the bed. "Are you sure?" She smiled down at him and unbuttoned her blouse. "Hope…" he mumbled as his hands gently pushed it from her shoulders, revealing the graceful curves of her breasts. She stroked his hair as he kissed her. "Oh, God, it's been so long…" He drew her down beside him on the bed. She kissed his neck and throat, and as she touched him, he closed his eyes. *So long,* he thought, drinking in the nourishment of her touch. "Oh, sweetheart, I thought this moment would never come." Kissing her passionately, he pressed his hips against hers. She caressed the bulge in his pants, and he moaned.

Anton was breathless and ready as he fumbled with his trousers. He had no way of understanding why a sudden migraine overcame him. He tried to focus on her face to get his bearings, but felt sick.

"Anton, what is it?"

He rolled away from her and stumbled into the bathroom, trying to catch his breath. He gasped for air, afraid he might pass out, and all he could think about was that he wanted her to leave.

He was holding onto the sink and splashing cold water on his face when Hope appeared in the doorway. "Get out!" he yelled. "I can't make love to you, not after what happened!" he snapped, his face dripping.

She stood, frozen by the shock of his angry words.

Tears streamed down her face as she quickly dressed, wishing she could think of something to say. But there was nothing. *He doesn't want me...after what happened?* She repeated it over and over in her head, trying to understand as she went out the door.

As soon as she'd gone, the pain in his head brought Anton to his knees. His stomach burned, and he gasped for air. He couldn't go after her even if he tried.

*****

It was late August, and the night breathed fire as Hope clung to the tree across the street from Jeff's apartment. Even she did not fully comprehend the wave of emotions that had brought her here, and now that the tears were gone, she waited. It was another hour before the lights went on in the corner apartment, and Hope took a deep breath to calm her trembling body. Finally, after half an hour more, she wiped the perspiration from her palms before crossing the street and knocking on Jeff's door.

"Hi ya', Bud! I was just getting ready to go out and find you two!" Jeff stood in the open door, toweling his wet hair. "Where's Russia?" He peered out, only to find Hope was alone.

"Anton's not going to Mick's tonight," she said as she entered the apartment and looked around. "Looks like it's just you and me."

Jeff gathered an armload of scattered laundry and dishes. "I wasn't expecting company," he muttered sheepishly and disappeared for a moment, coming back seconds later with empty arms. "How come he's not going?"

"He must have changed his mind," she said absently, looking through his record albums. "Do you mind if I put on some music?" she asked, avoiding his eyes.

"Go ahead. I'll go put on a shirt." He headed for the bedroom.

"You don't have to, Jeff," she said quickly, stopping him in his tracks.

"What?"

"I mean, we don't have to go to Mick's tonight. Everyone there would just ask where the 'little Russian' was." Hope forced a smile, and he laughed.

"Yeah, they would, wouldn't they?" The regular patrons had come to know them as a trio and now teased them anytime one was missing. Jeff looked at Hope sideways for a moment. "Somethin' on your mind, Bud?"

"Why do you ask?" She turned to him, jutting out her chin with false bravado. She wondered if he could see through her.

"Nothin'. It's just that you've never come to my place before. I guess it threw me." He disappeared down the hall and returned after a few minutes, pulling a black Led Zeppelin T-shirt over his head. "Well, what do you want to do?"

"We used to just sit and talk, remember?" She felt like she would cry, but forced herself to regain control. "We could order pizza. How's that?"

She sat on the floor and sorted through the records while Jeff scratched his chin and watched her. She had totally thrown him this time, but he dismissed it as his imagination. "Yeah, we could do that," he said, thinking a change of pace would be nice. "Just don't get my records all screwed up like yours. You want something to drink?" he asked, and she nodded.

"So what's Russia doing tonight?" he asked. He handed her a glass of wine, then sat on the floor and began to straighten up the albums she'd already changed her mind about. He looked at her just in time to catch the tail end of a look that could have killed.

"I didn't ask."

"O...kay." He smiled at her but knew something was definitely wrong. He decided it was better not to get involved, especially when Hope was not herself. He picked out some soothing music, hoping it would help, and after a while, they fell into comfortable conversation. It was just like old times: sitting on the floor, drinking and eating some old crackers that Jeff didn't remember buying.

For a while, Hope forgot.

"Do you remember when you first left Steven? Clay and Nicki, you and I used to hang around all the time. Everyone in town thought we were a number, remember?" Jeff laughed a little and lay back on the carpet.

"Maybe we tried too hard," she said and set her glass on the coffee table. "Maybe if we had relaxed a little…" She leaned over and kissed him on the mouth.

"What the hell was that?" he said, pushing her away.

"Didn't you learn about that in high school?" She got up and took their glasses into the kitchen, where she poured another round, leaving Jeff lying on his back, staring at the ceiling.

"Listen, Bud, what about Russia?" he asked when she returned.

Hope reached for the phone and set it between them, shoving the receiver into his hand. "It's over. Call him. He'll tell you the same thing." She dialed the number, and Jeff put the phone to his ear.

"Hello" came Anton's voice. "Hello?"

Jeff looked into Hope's eyes and hung up.

"It's over. You should have asked him," she said.

"I believe you," he answered quietly.

"So what did you feel?"

"What?"

"When I kissed you, what did you feel?"

"Shocked," he said.

She leaned over him again and kissed him full and hard, returning to the passion that had been cut short hours before. She kissed him with hunger and desire, and after a while, he drew her to him, relishing the warmth of her body. Her kisses were moist and sweet, her hands gentle against his brow.

"Jesus!" He sat up, breathless, and pushed her away. "How much have you had to drink?"

"I'm not drunk, Jeff. I know what I'm doing." She was starting to panic.

"That makes one of us!" Jeff rose to his feet, taking a deep breath, and before he knew it, Hope was headed for the door. "Hey! What's the matter with you?" he called after her.

"Forget it!" she screamed over her shoulder. "Just forget it!"

*****

The country band was singing a Willie Nelson tune when Jeff walked into Mick's. It was crowded, and the smoky haze made it nearly impossible to see. He wasn't sure what he expected to find, but he'd spotted Hope's car in the parking lot, and all he knew was that he had to find her. He'd been her friend too long. They had been through too many hard times together for him to let her go, especially when she wasn't herself.

"Tony, is Mick around?" he asked the bartender.

"Where're your little buddies?" Tony asked with a grin as he handed Jeff a beer. Everyone in town knew Jeff Lansing was a cop, and his first beer was always on the house.

"I don't know. You seen 'em?"

No, Tony hadn't seen them, but he'd just come on. He went to ask Mick while Jeff waited at the bar, sipping his beer.

"The fella's not here, but the little lady's dancing in the far corner," Mick said, coming to see Jeff himself. "Got problems, Jeff?"

"Hope not." He thanked him for the beer, then walked the crowded dance floor until he found Hope. She was in a man's arms, dancing a slow, sensuous dance. "Excuse me, cowboy." He tapped the man on the shoulder and flashed his badge. "The lady you're with is under arrest." He grabbed Hope by the wrist and dragged her out to his van, where he pushed her inside.

"What do you think you're doing!" she screamed.

"What in the hell do you think *you're* doing!" he threw back at her and unrolled the window. The heat was suffocating as they sat glaring at each other. "What the hell is going on? Talk to me, Bud!"

He waited for what seemed an eternity before she could respond. Eventually, a tear broke free and slid down her cheek, followed by another.

Jeff reached over and squeezed her hand. "Just talk to me, Bud. I'll listen," he said gently.

A long time passed before she said, "I don't think I can feel anymore."

He watched her. Her eyes shone with tears, and her chin quivered. He could hardly stand it. "What's that supposed to mean?"

She jumped at the sound of his voice. "Don't yell at me, Jeff!" she cried, and he squeezed her hand again.

"I didn't yell at you, baby. Just talk to me!"

Again, there was a long silence, but finally the words began to come. "Sometimes, I wake up in the middle of the night. I want someone to hold me, touch me. I try to remember what it's like to make love, and I can't remember. I just lie there for the rest of the night feeling dirty and untouchable…" She stopped for a minute to blow her nose, avoiding Jeff's eyes when she continued. "The only thing I remember is being raped…and feeling dirty. Sometimes I get up at three or four in the morning to take a bath, but nothing helps."

Tears flowed down her face, and he watched as she silently tried to put it all together.

"I feel so dirty," she sobbed. "I just wanted someone who's kind and gentle to help wash away what I feel." She cried into her hands while he looked on.

"Do you really think that cowboy in there gives a damn about how you feel? He's just looking to get laid, Bud! How could you go looking for someone in a bar like that?"

"That's not where I started!"

There was a silence before Jeff's eyes went wide. "Whoa." He stared at her in the darkness. "Is that why you came to my place tonight?" he asked, but she remained silent, staring out the window. "What happened between you and Russia?"

When her answer came, it was barely audible. "He thinks I'm dirty too."

"That's impossible."

"Is it?" She looked at him for the first time. "He said he couldn't make love to me because of what happened! You figure it out." Her pain was evident as she opened the door to get out.

"Bud, wait!" He reached toward her as she slid off the seat.

"I'm going home, Jeff. I just want to go home."

*****

Hope stood on the porch in her worn terry robe, watching the pair of headlights work their way up the mountain road, wondering whose they were. After a few minutes, it was the sound of Jeff's van she recognized, and she became aware that she'd been praying it was Anton. Again, the deep wound he had inflicted began to open, but she forced back the tears as Jeff pulled up and stopped.

"Hi," he said gently when he got out of the van. "How come you're standing out here in your bathrobe?"

"I saw your lights," she said. *I thought it was Anton.* "It's past two. What are you doing here?"

"Oh, I was in the neighborhood," he said and cocked his head to one side.

"I live in the mountains, Jeff. I don't *have* a neighborhood." She forced a smile that broke his heart.

"Did I wake you up?" he asked as he followed her inside. But before she could speak, he noticed that her hair was damp and realized that she had just gotten out of the bath. He ached for her.

"No, I was awake," she said, turning to him. "Why are you here, Jeff?" she asked as he stepped near.

He touched her face and looked into her sad, swollen eyes. "I was worried about you, Bud," he said softly. "I've been driving around for hours." He stroked her cheek and marveled at how soft she was. "I don't want you thinking something is wrong with you, and I don't want you going to strangers. Not for this." He kissed her tenderly on the mouth, put his arms around her, and held her for a while until it was she who reached up to him. Again, he gently kissed her, and as he did, a tear slowly found its way down her face.

"Jeff…"

"Shhh…it's okay," he whispered, wiping the tear away. "It's going to be okay…"

*****

When Jeff awoke, he found Hope standing at the open window of her bedroom, the white curtains billowing around her, her hair blowing in the breeze. The night air smelled of rain, and she seemed to be waiting for the storm. He wondered how many storms she had faced alone in her life.

Tears had marked their bittersweet lovemaking, and in the midst of her passion, she had unconsciously called for the wrong man. Now she stood, statuesque, like a sentinel guarding the rare summer storm. She turned and looked at him, then turned back toward the dark sky. "Forgive me," she said.

"There's nothing to forgive," he replied.

"I've used you. I never meant to do that."

"I have no regrets, Bud." It pained him to see that the tears had returned when she looked at him again.

"Thank you for making me whole…" She began to cry, and he stretched his arms out to her, beckoning.

"Come here." He put his arms around her and held her once again, kissing her lightly on the forehead while she cried.

CHAPTER 34

Anton's head was pounding when he awoke. He had been sick most of the night until finally falling asleep on the floor beside his bed. When the doorbell rang, he moaned to himself and rubbed his face before stumbling to the door. One glance at Jeff's stony face made him turn and plop into a chair, leaving the door open.

"You look like shit," Jeff said as he entered, closing the door behind him.

"Thanks. Where would I be if I didn't have you to tell me these things?" he moaned and peeked out of one eye. "You don't look so hot yourself."

"What happened last night?" Jeff asked.

Suddenly, he had Anton's full attention. "I don't think that's any of your business."

"Let's just say it became my business. Bud says you wouldn't make love with her because you think she's 'dirty.'" He sat on the couch across from Anton.

He said nothing. The truth was, he didn't really know what had happened the night before.

"She showed up at my door," Jeff began and continued in detail up to the point he and Hope had departed Mick's in separate cars.

Anton put his face in his hands. "Oh, God," he said, almost half an hour later.

"Then why did you say you couldn't make love to her 'after what happened'? I interpret that the same way she does."

Anton sucked in his breath and looked at Jeff. "Is that what I said?"

"Don't you know?" Jeff frowned and watched Anton stumble into the kitchen to make coffee. "What the hell is going on with you?" he demanded, following him.

"I got sick!" Anton yelled back. "I got sick…the way you've seen me. I didn't want Hope to see me. I guess I said whatever came to mind to make her go home and figured I could explain myself later. I had no idea she'd take it like that." He leaned his head into his arms on the counter, feeling like it would explode from the pain, and Jeff took over making the coffee. "I mean, it's been six months since the rape. How could I know she still felt that way?"

"Women who are raped often feel that way for the rest of their lives," Jeff said. "They always wonder in the back of their minds if there was something about *them* that made it happen. Now Hope feels like it's true because you didn't want her to see you throw up." He put his arm around Anton's shoulders and helped him back to the couch, where he lay down. "Man, you really got sick, didn't you?"

"I've never been this sick before." Anton looked at him. "I can't believe Hope went looking for someone else. I can't believe I said something to make her do that. Talk to her. Tell her that's not what I meant! God, I hope she's all right."

"She was sleeping when I left," Jeff said and glanced up to find Anton glaring at him.

"And when was that?" he asked. The chill in his voice sent a shiver up Jeff's spine. "When were you with her last? After you left Mick's? Have you left out part of the story, Jeff?" Anton sat up. "You motherfucker! I left her in the lurch, so you took it upon yourself to finish the job?"

"We're not talking about sexual frustration, Russia. Her whole ego was involved, her whole self-esteem."

"So, what did you do after you left Mick's? Show up at her front door with your cock in your hand? How fucking noble!" Anton screamed. "Tell me I'm wrong, damn it. Tell me I'm fucking wrong!"

"Don't you dare turn what happened into something sordid. It wasn't like that."

Anton jumped to his feet, his head ready to explode. "Then it's true!"

"Russia…" Jeff reached toward him, but he quickly moved out of reach.

"Just get out," he whispered hoarsely. "How dare you bring your guilt to my doorstep. Get out!"

Jeff backed away from his friend, who looked so ragged and broken, but stopped at the door before leaving. "I never meant to hurt you, Russia. I swear to God, I never meant to hurt you."

*****

Saturday was exceptionally warm for the third week in September. Everyone turned out for the ball game at Hope's. As predicted, Nicki and Clay had announced their engagement, and Hope was throwing them a party. Jeff invited Valerie from the shelter, feeling that a party at Hope's would make a safe first date. Noah had arrived back in town, along with a few of his friends that no one seemed to know: his manager, his "cut" man, and others.

One could smell the barbecue for miles as Hope flipped burgers on the grill and sliced purple onions and fat red tomatoes from her garden. With so many extra guests, she wondered if all of Three Rivers had caught wind of the food. She didn't mind the extra work; it gave her an excuse to keep busy. She didn't look at Anton, who chatted nearby. He had mysteriously shown up that afternoon, and he watched her from a distance. Occasionally, when the sound of his voice reached her ears, she had to fight back tears caused by the wound he had inflicted almost a month before. After a while, Nicki came back to the house from the meadow for a fresh supply of cold beer for the ballplayers. She took a moment to sit at the picnic table and chat with Hope but left again when the crack of a bat announced someone's home run. When Hope looked up, Anton had disappeared into the house.

*****

"Jeff, can I see you a minute?" Anton glanced at the other people in the living room, then followed Jeff into the study, closing the door behind them. His mouth was dry as he went to the window and peered out at Hope beyond the oak trees. "There are a few things I need to know," he began. His anger had been replaced by emptiness, and he hated the fact that it showed in his voice. "When the three of us used to hang out at Mick's, the regulars used to tease us about sharing Hope. Did we?"

Jeff answered gently, seeing the hurt on Anton's face. "It wasn't like you think, Russia. I can't believe you even have to ask. Of course not."

"I think you made love to her. Did you?" He forced the words, the feelings of betrayal overwhelming him.

"Yes and no," Jeff answered as he stepped closer behind Anton, who continued to watch Hope through the window. "We never shared her. It only happened once, Russia, I swear." Anton felt Jeff grip his shoulders, bracing him for what he was about to say. "Did we make love?"

Anton closed his eyes.

"All the time I made love to her, she was making love to you. It was you she wanted, Russia, not me. It was your name she called in the dark." Jeff's voice was steady but passionate. "She loves you."

"Did she tell you that?" he asked.

"She didn't have to. She thought I was you that night, and she made me wish I were," he added in a whisper. He waited a moment while Anton blinked back the tears. "Are you going to tell her you know?" Jeff asked.

"I've got to say something. I can't let her go on believing the rape was her fault. I don't know, Jeff. I don't have any answers."

Jeff backed away to leave but paused before opening the door. "Russia, it's up to you whether or not this thing destroys us. I don't care about myself, but think of Bud. She still loves you. Can you throw that away?"

"What if you got her pregnant?" The question burst forth before Anton could stop it. It had been on his mind constantly, consuming him for a month.

Jeff stepped close once again, slowly shaking his head. "That's real important to you, isn't it?" he said gently. "Don't worry, she's not." He caught Anton's gaze and continued, "Did I ever tell you where I caught that piece of shrapnel in Vietnam? Well, my gift from Uncle Sam was a free vasectomy. It's irreparable. Not that they haven't tried. I've had four surgeries. Why do you think I haven't gotten involved with anyone? Don't worry, my friend. The worst thing she can get from me is a cold." He smiled at the look of pity that crossed Anton's face and patted him on the back. "I'm going to get Bud. I want you to talk things out instead of letting it fester. But keep in mind that it was my fault. I should have gone to you first, before it got out of hand. Don't blame her. When she came to me, she was upset and confused."

He turned toward the door, but as he opened it, Anton said his name.

"Jeff, I'm to blame too. We'll share it, you and I."

Jeff nodded before closing the door behind him.

*****

Anton stood at the window, watching the hungry people swarm the picnic table now laden with food. Hope looked busy, as she had all day, helping her guests with whatever they needed. As he watched, he thought of the last time they'd been together, the way she'd touched him, caressed him, and he wondered suddenly if she had caressed Jeff the same way.

He forced the thought from his mind when he saw Jeff join her outside. Pulling her away from the other people, Jeff lowered his head in private conversation. A look of horror crossed Hope's face, and even from where he stood, Anton could see the tears well up in her eyes.

Jeff told her, he thought, saddened by the pain it obviously caused. He stepped away from the window and looked around the room he had once destroyed. It was a good room now. They had spent weeks putting up new wallpaper and shopping for furniture. He sat at the beautiful desk he'd bought to replace the broken writing table, looking at it the way she did each time she used it. He rubbed the oak with his fingertips, feeling the fine grain.

Hope had fussed about the money he spent, insisting that what he had destroyed was junk anyway. But he saw it as an opportunity to give her something nice, something of quality. She deserved quality, not the pain he had caused her. He put his face in his hands and sighed from the weight of it all.

"Jeff said you wanted to see me."

Hope's voice sounded small and distant, and when he turned, he found her standing against the closed door. Her eyes were red and puffy, and she wore a look that seemed to make her disappear.

For a long time, they looked at each other, neither knowing what to say.

"You look tired," Anton said finally, but again the silence prevailed.

"Talk to me, Hope! A man could die in your silence!"

She began to cry, and he realized he was seeing her as Steven had a hundred times.

"Good God, Hope, I'm not going to hit you!"

"Isn't that what you want?" She quivered like a frightened bird. Steven had struck her so often for a moment she fell back on old patterns. It made his heart bleed.

"I'd rather put my arms around you."

"Aren't you afraid you'll get dirty?"

Anton felt a sharp pain rip through him. "Oh, Hope! I wish to God that you hadn't gotten raped, for your sake. But it could never change the way I feel about you! That's not what I meant. I swear!"

Hope broke down and sobbed openly, her eyes glassy as she struggled to speak. "Jeff told me that you know…" she cried, "and changing the words now can't fix what's been done!"

There was a crash in the other room, and Hope, quickly wiping her face, ran out to see what was going on, only to find the house full of people. She fought her way through the crowd and gasped when she found herself face-to-face with her father.

"Well, well!" he said. "I told your friends that I wanted to see you, but Lansing here said you were busy."

Anton could see the look of positive terror on Hope's face when he caught up with her. When he asked her who the man was, he answered for himself.

"JC Landrum," he said with his hands on his hips. "And who are you?"

"Anton Pavlova."

"Well, I'll be a son of a bitch. The kid got herself a Russkie!" he said, hearing the accent that no one else seemed to notice anymore. "I wonder what Pop would say to that!"

"Who are you?" Anton asked.

Hope trembled beside him. "He's my father."

"Why don't you crawl back in your hole, JC," Jeff said, and within moments, a scuffle ensued. It was obvious to Anton that Jeff and Clay had dealt with JC before. Noah pushed his way to the front of the crowd and broke them up.

"What are you doing here, Daddy?" Hope screamed. Her nerves were ready to shatter.

JC stepped up and looked her in the face. "Don't ever call me that again, little girl," he snarled. "I found out that Pop changed his will, leaving this place to you! I came here to tell you I'll contest it in court." He pulled a piece of paper from his shirt pocket and waved it in her face. "I'll win too. You aren't a legal heir, and I can prove it. I wound up having to raise another man's bastard, and I'll be damned if I'll lose my inheritance to her!"

"What's that?" Hope could only whisper.

"Don't do this, JC," Clay begged. "Don't."

"A letter," JC answered. "I intercepted it years ago. It's addressed to your *real* daddy. Your mama wanted him to know you were his. But he already knew. He knew it the day you were born, then had the balls to go to her funeral three days later."

Hope's face was white, the crowd silent. Her small voice carried in that silence. "I don't understand. What are you saying?"

"Honestly Hope, are you really that stupid? Why do you think McClain—"

"JC, please don't tell her like this," Clay pleaded, but JC continued.

"Why do you think McClain Philips made Clayton break up with you? You were fucking your own brother!"

Hope's knees buckled, and she sank to the floor.

Anton threw a fist and caught the man on the jaw, landing him against the radiator. "Son of a bitch!" Anton jumped on top of him and hit him twice more before Noah could pull him off. Jeff quickly cleared the room while Clay took Hope to the couch. Within minutes, JC was gone and all that remained inside were the close friends.

Noah sat Anton down at the dining table and took his hand, gently turning it over in his own. "Jesus! Why'd you hit him so hard?" Noah muttered. "Can you do this?" He wiggled his hand, and Anton copied him. "Try this…"

Anton watched Jeff and Clay surround Hope, speaking in soft whispers, occasionally stroking her hair and wiping her tears. Clay put his arms around her while Jeff went to get her a glass of water.

"Anton, your slip is showing," Noah said, and he looked up. "Wiggle your little finger."

"I can't. Is it broken?"

"Don't know. You're lucky my man Carl is here. He can fix anything." He patted Anton's shoulder and left, returning after a moment with his friend.

"You really cut loose on him. What happened?" Noah asked as Carl began to bandage Anton's hand. Following Anton's gaze, he continued, "You look like you've been under some kind of strain lately. You two have a fight? Well, she's sorry."

"How do you know?"

"Hell, I've been watching that woman for years. I know every look she's got, and believe me, she's sorry. I can tell by the way she looks at you when you aren't busy staring at her." Noah chuckled when Anton turned, hoping to catch her eyes, but Clay was blocking his view. When Carl finished, Anton thanked him and got up to leave.

Hope jumped to her feet and stopped him at the door. "Anton, don't go."

"You and Clay have a lot to talk about," he said quietly.

"You and *I* have a lot to talk about."

"I'll come back another time…"

"I'm scared that you won't!" she cried, and he forced a smile.

"I will. I promise." He glanced into the room, where Clay sat waiting for her. "Go. Be with your brother," he said. "At least you get to keep yours."

He slipped away feeling that he'd been right. He had lost both, Alexis and Hope.

CHAPTER 35

Nathan sat quietly and watched Anton mindlessly scoot the food around on his plate. It was the first Wednesday of October, and on the way home from the cemetery, they had stopped for lunch. Anton had learned that Hope had canceled her trip to see her grandfather and decided to take Nathan to Colma himself. But today, the casual conversation was missing. In its place was Anton's preoccupied silence.

"What happened to your hand?"

Anton looked up, suddenly aware he hadn't spoken for a while. "I'm sorry, Nathan," he said, "I've had things on my mind."

"I can tell," Nathan said, tapping his fingers impatiently on the table. "So who'd you hit?"

"Your son." Anton watched for a reaction, but there was none.

"He probably deserved it."

"He did." Anton fell silent again.

"It's hard to sit here and watch you not talk."

"I'm sorry, Nate. Would you like to go?"

"You haven't eaten," Nathan pointed out.

"I'm not really hungry."

"What if I told you I know about what happened?" The old man trod lightly.

Anton sat back in his chair. "My God, she must tell you everything."

Nathan nodded with a gentle smile. "She knows I don't judge my children. I listen, and then I try to guide them." It had been his hallmark, his specialty, the thing that made all the children of Three Rivers love him. "Have you tried to talk about it?"

Finally, Anton gave his version of what had happened. "You know what kind of man I am, Nathan. How could she think that I felt she was dirty?"

Nathan sat back in his wheelchair and pressed a bony finger to his lips. "You sound like the little boy who went to play hide-and-seek then cried because no one came to find him," he said. "How was she supposed to know what was going on if you didn't tell her? You bring on a lot of your own misery, son. Tell her! Tell her about Catherine and that sometimes you get headaches so bad they make you sick."

"I can't. I can't talk about it."

"Then tell her you can't talk about it! It's not that hard…"

As Nathan continued, Anton surveyed the old man, wondering why he had changed his will. He was thinner than before, paler, but there was still a sparkle in his eyes. There was still light. His quick humor, his sharp tongue, had not diminished. *How could JC be this man's son?* he wondered.

"Anton!" Nathan snapped. "Help me to the john and see if you can pay attention long enough not to drop me!"

*****

"You missed the turnoff," Nathan said matter-of-factly. "You're about as useful as tits on a boar."

"Let's go see Hope," Anton said, glancing at the old man in the passenger seat.

"What's the matter? Afraid to go see her by yourself?"

"I don't know what to say to her."

"Then don't say anything. That's a lesson I learned in my youth." He laughed and looked out the window. "You were all three stupid, you know—you, her, and that young cop. What's his name?"

"Jeff," Anton said. "I thought you knew everyone in town."

"That's the young man Clay met in Vietnam, isn't it?"

Anton nodded.

"I met him once after he and Clay hooked up. Seemed like a nice young man, a loyal friend. Were you and he friends?"

Anton could see Nathan looking at him from the corner of his eye. Nate was toying with him. "We were friends."

Nathan said nothing. He resumed watching the landscape rush by. He had a knack for that: starting a conversation, then going silent so you had to finish it in your head.

"So are we going to Hope's or what? She won't be expecting me, and she certainly won't be expecting you. Let's drive down and surprise her. What do you say?" Anton looked away from the road long enough to watch a slow, mischievous smile spread across Nathan's face.

*****

It was almost dark when they pulled into the driveway. Nathan's face was glued to the window. *Home,* he thought. He had finally come home to his mountain. He wished he could walk so he could fly into the house as he had done so many times before. How clearly he remembered the day he had bounded up the steps and thrown open the door. There by the fireplace stood Stella, wide-eyed and smiling, her rich brown hair tumbling down her back.

"Well?" he asked, breathless.

"We're having a baby!" Stella ran into his outstretched arms, and he kissed her face, her neck, feeling the warmth of her skin as happy tears rolled down his face. So long…so long they had prayed, and now they would finally have a child of their own. He had loved everybody else's children, pretending they were his. But now, from his own seed, from their own love, a child had been conceived! He kissed her joyously as he laid her down by the fireplace, and they celebrated their joy with passion.

"Nathan?" came Anton's voice.

He rubbed his eyes with his knuckles, embarrassed. "I'm just a sentimental old fool," he said, staring at the house.

"Come on. Don't do this. Hope will think I've upset you." Anton put his handkerchief in Nathan's hand. "Let me go in and tell her we're here. I'll be right back." He patted his knee before disappearing into the house.

Anton returned moments later with Hope by his side. The first week of October had already brought a few cool nights, and as Nathan held tight, Anton carried him into the house, where a cozy fire crackled in the fireplace. The house smelled of fresh-baked bread; two warm loaves lay on the kitchen counter to cool. It was as though the house itself had known he was coming home and opened its arms to welcome him.

Hope carried in the wheelchair, and Anton gently placed Uncle Nate in the seat. Nathan wheeled himself around, looking at the various changes she had made. He couldn't stop the flood of memories that raced through his mind. He had a story to tell in each room, and Anton and Hope stopped to listen to every one, caught up in his excitement. It was so precious, so contagious, that they laughed and cried along with him.

After a while, Nathan was taken upstairs, and again he flew from room to room, finally stopping at Hope's bedroom. He fell silent, staring at the bed. The mattress was new, and the bed had been stripped and refinished, but it was in that bed that he and Stella had made love for over fifty years. He pushed himself forward and touched the post. So many nights her cold feet had crept over to his. So many times he had awakened with desire for the woman he loved. In this bed, they had played and giggled, argued, pouted, cried. Then he thought of the first time he had awakened in this bed alone. How big it was. How empty. He had been lost without her; the one person in the world who could bring him comfort was gone.

Nathan turned his chair to face Anton and Hope. "You listen to me!" he scolded. "Whatever has come between the two of you, let it go! One of these days, I'm not going to be around to bandage the wounds you've inflicted on each other! Someday, you're going to reach out and there won't be anyone there. Then it will be too late!"

Anton and Hope stood frozen in place, neither knowing what to say.

"I'm sorry," Nathan said at length, seeing the shock on their faces. "I'm tired."

Anton carried him down the stairs to the cot he'd set up in the study. It had been a long day for Nathan, and Anton could tell the excitement had been too much for him.

"I meant what I said, you know," Nathan said quietly as Anton helped him get ready for bed. "I was thinking about how much I miss Stella."

Anton laid him back and pulled the blankets up around him. "I know, Uncle Nate. We're trying to work things out. You know we both love you."

Nathan reached up and patted Anton's cheek with his thin gray hand. "Just love each other," he whispered.

*****

"I love having him here, but I wish I had known he was coming," Hope said when Anton joined her in front of the fire. "I can't take off from work right now. Besides, I can't lift him. How am I supposed to take care of him?"

"I missed the Monterey turnoff, and we decided to just keep going. It's only for a day or two."

"But how can I take care of him if I can't lift him?" she repeated.

"I'll stay."

She looked at him.

"I'll sleep on the couch. It'll work out. You'll see. But call in tomorrow and spend the day with us."

"I can't," she said.

"Why not?"

"The well pump had to be replaced last week. I'm barely making it as it is. I can't afford to take off work."

"Don't worry about it."

"If I don't, who will?"

"I will! Would you stop arguing with me?" Anton rubbed his face, weary from the hours of driving. "I'm sorry, Hope. It seemed like a good idea at the time. How much was the pump?"

"I don't want your money, Anton." She sounded angry.

"Let me help you out. You don't have to pay me back," he said and started to reach for his wallet, but she stopped him. "I just want to give you a little freedom from that crummy job."

"My crummy job gives me everything I need," she said defiantly. "It gives me pride and independence. Don't take those away from me." She paused for a moment, softening her voice. "Anton, I appreciate what you're trying to do, but I have to make it on my own."

"Why? Why won't you let me help you?"

"Don't you see? This is the same trap I fell into with Steven. What was really gratitude, I mistook for love, and you know the price I paid. I don't ever want to *need* you."

She stared at the fire, unaware that her words had struck a mortal blow. Catherine had needed him, he thought. She had needed him for everything. Without him, she couldn't have survived. *Didn't survive.*

He stood, wanting desperately to leave, but then remembered the old man in the next room and felt trapped.

"What's the matter?" she asked, and when he didn't respond, she reached up and squeezed his hand. "Please, let's not fight."

He sat numbly, staring into the flames. Minutes passed in silence before he could look at her, but when he did, the hurt of the past month gathered itself into one big knot.

"Anton, what's wrong?"

"I feel very alone," he said and closed his eyes.

"You're not alone."

He opened them and saw her leaning toward him, but the inches between them seemed insurmountable. She hadn't kissed him since that night in his apartment, before he had caused her so much pain. How could she possibly want to kiss him now?

Finally, it was she who found his mouth, hungry for her acceptance, her affection. He felt himself tremble as she kissed him, and he thought his emotions would explode. He kissed her desperately, clinging to her as if he were drowning.

"I love you," she murmured between his kisses, and he clung to her, swearing to himself he would never lose her again.

*****

Nathan stayed on the mountain until the following Monday, which was longer than anyone expected, but it gave Hope the weekend to be with him, allowing her to work the rest of the week without guilt. It also provided him and Anton time alone to discuss the problem of JC and Nathan's will. Nathan was very upset when he learned of the incident, though he had known the truth about Hope's birth all along. The fact that she was so unwanted had made him only love her more, and hearing the cruel way she'd learned about her brother made his blood boil.

"I don't want JC to have this place," Nathan said, looking up at the treetops, listening to the whispers of the wind. "He doesn't appreciate the woods or the river. He doesn't understand they have a life of their own the way Hope does. She always understood." He dug into the dirt and rubbed it between his fingers the way Anton had seen Hope do on many occasions. When Anton told him, the old man smiled. "You see what I mean?" He sniffed the dirt, then held it to Anton's nostrils and smiled when he inhaled. "It's Mother Earth, son. Like crawling up in your mama's lap and smelling her perfume. Hope, she knows. Just like she knows the swordsmen and the mountain.

"JC doesn't understand those things. Never has. I can't let him have this place, son. Why, you've come to mean more to me than he does." Nathan patted Anton's leg. "Why don't you buy it from me?"

"What?"

"I'd rather you have it than him. I know you'd appreciate it more."

Anton declined. Like Nathan, he thought it should belong to Hope. But as the days passed, he began to formulate an idea that Nathan loved. He made Nathan promise not to tell Hope, and the final the plan was made. Anton was to purchase the ranch and draw up a will of his own to be held by Clay. Hope would have the place one way or another, and this way, JC couldn't do anything about it.

CHAPTER 36

In the weeks that followed, Anton and Hope stepped gently with each other, allowing time to heal their wounds. Only once did Hope mention Jeff's name, expressing her grief that she had ruined the friendship between the two men.

"We're still friends," Anton said, secretly realizing that Jeff's betrayal had hurt almost as much as Hope's. It was his caring for Jeff that made it all the more unbearable. But Hope didn't believe him, and finally, as a gesture, he made a point of calling Jeff to invite him to Mick's with them.

It was awkward at first, but then, they had known it would be. Jeff and Hope got a little more drunk than usual, but by the end of the evening, the two men, Jeff with his bottle of beer and Anton with his Coca-Cola, were laughing about the fact that Anton had indeed broken his little finger on JC's face. It was strained frivolity, but they all knew the next time would be a little easier, and the time after that easier still.

*****

"Why the hell do you want to rake all these leaves?" Jeff stood with the rake in his hand, looking at them. "You live in the wilderness, for chrissake."

"Not all of them," she answered. "Just the ones around the house where the grass is."

"But we've been working for two hours and aren't even close to being finished. The wind keeps blowin' the piles around." Jeff looked at Anton, who stood nearby. "I think Bud just keeps us around to do these dumb jobs. What do you think?"

Anton grinned, and the two laid down their rakes simultaneously and slowly walked toward her.

"Let's get her!"

They bolted toward Hope, and she let out a squeal as she dodged between the trees. The brisk air was invigorating as the three laughed and played among the dry leaves, scattering the piles they had so painstakingly assembled.

"It's not fair, two against one!" Hope shouted breathlessly as they stood for a moment to catch their breath.

"Jeff, you go around that way and head her off." Anton leaned on his knees and waited for just the right moment to pounce.

"Come on, you guys, leave me alone!" she laughed.

"What are we going to do when we catch her?" Jeff shouted back as he took his position.

"Tickle her," Anton said.

"No tickling!" She started running, and Anton chased after her, finally tackling her into a big pile of leaves.

"I got her!" he yelled triumphantly. He held her down and began to tickle her, and she squealed and pushed against his chest, finally grabbing his hands to make him stop.

"Anton...I can't breathe!"

He lay over her and laughed a villainous laugh.

She grabbed him under the ribs, and they tumbled in the leaves, laughing until they were both out of breath and lay panting. Hope threw an unexpected handful of leaves into Anton's face.

"You little....Come help me, Jeff!" he shouted before wrestling her down again and lying over her so she couldn't get up.

"Looks like you've got things pretty well under control," Jeff called. "I'm thirsty...going back to the house," he added and discreetly disappeared.

Anton pinned Hope's arms to the ground and smiled at her. "Now, what are you going to do?"

"Depends on what *you're* going to do," she said.

"I ought to lay you right here."

THE PEBBLE AND THE MAN

"I'd like that!"

"You would, wouldn't you!"

"It's so wonderful to hear you laugh again, Anton."

He engulfed her mouth with his. Hope felt like the big pile of leaves was a giant brown bed made just for them. She loved the way his body felt on hers, the warmth of his breath against her cold skin as he kissed her face and neck. The wind came up and blew his hair, making him look wild and free, and its howling in the trees made his embrace seem like a fortress where she could hide.

This was the part of him that she had known was hidden somewhere, the playful part of him that even he hadn't dared to explore because it made him forget to be the staid agent who had become the pride of the USIB. For this brief moment, he forgot who he was, remembering only what he felt.

Hope held tight around his shoulders as he kissed her, the smell of him mingling with the dry leaves. She opened her eyes to the sky and watched as the wind shook the remaining leaves until they rained down around them. She looked at him. His face was flush with excitement, his mouth hot and moist as he snuggled close to her ear. She closed her eyes and took a deep breath.

Anton tensed. "I can't…"

She opened her eyes again. "What?"

"Hope…"

"Is it me?" She began to cry, unable to believe what was happening. He tried to get up, but she held him tight. "Tell me! I have a right to know."

He finally released himself from her embrace and took a deep breath, turning his back to her as she sat crying in the big pile of leaves.

"What terrible thing would happen if we dared to make love?" she shouted at him, the anger in her voice cutting him until he couldn't stand it anymore.

"I'll call you," he said and walked away.

"Damn you!" she shouted, but he didn't turn around. He disappeared around the corner of the house, and soon she heard the sound of his car fade into the distance.

When she entered the house, she found Jeff standing in front of the open refrigerator, drinking from the bottle of cold water. He quickly put it away when he saw her. "Why are you crying, Bud?"

"Go home, Jeff, before I make another mistake."

She lay on the couch and cried into the pillow as Jeff closed the front door quietly behind him.

*****

At 4:15 in the afternoon, Mick's was a different place. The smoke was almost nonexistent and one could actually see the rough-hewn timbers overhead. There was no loud band, and only an occasional tune followed the sound of a coin dropping into the jukebox. After the tune, all that was left was the quiet conversations of the handful of patrons, including Anton and Jeff, who spoke in whispers and answered in nods.

"Why didn't you tell her? There's no shame in just telling the truth." Jeff sipped his beer and watched while Anton played with the paperclip he'd found on the table.

"No shame? Would you want to be involved with a guy whose bride found it necessary to kill herself with a butcher knife?" He laid his head in his arms and, after a moment, felt Jeff's comforting hand rub across his shoulders. "Besides," Anton continued, "it doesn't explain why it happens when I'm with Hope. First, I get sick and suddenly I'm unable…I've never been unable."

"What do Hope and Catherine have in common?" Jeff asked.

"Not a damn thing. I've been racking my brain, but I can't think of a thing."

"Maybe you should go see your friend—what's her name?"

"Leslie."

"Bourbon, straight up. Right?" The sound of Dan's voice made them both jump as he set a glass on the table in front of Anton.

"I see you've read my files," Anton said coolly.

"Yes, as a matter of fact," Dan replied. "I was supposed to see them a long time ago, but Sanderson must have accidentally misplaced them at the time. I found them to be *very* interesting reading."

"Sanderson does nothing by accident," Anton said, glaring. "I thought you were sent to New York for debriefing."

"I'm back," he said. "Drink up, Pavlova!"

Anton stared at him, hardly able to speak. "Why do you hate me so much—because of NORAD? You know I had to accept that job. I'm the only one who could pull it off."

"Yeah, but it's gone sour. Everyone in the Branch has a bad feeling about it, and I don't want to die!" Dan hissed at him and swallowed his own drink in one gulp. He slammed his glass down on the table and leaned into Anton's face. "I've lost everything on account of you. My best friend, my brother, and now *my job*. You deserve what Hope did," he snarled, then stalked off, leaving Anton to stare at the drink in front of him.

"Are you all right?" Jeff asked as he watched Anton stare at the glass in front of him. He touched it gently, rotating it to watch the amber liquor touch the rim all the way around. "Put it down, Russia. You've come too far to take a drink now."

"How do you know I have a problem?"

"I've spent too many hours in this bar watching you suck on a Coke. I'm not stupid," Jeff said as Anton continued to toy with the drink. "What did Dan mean 'what Hope did'?"

Anton picked up the glass and rubbed the bottom with the palm of his hand, stroking the side with his fingers. It was like foreplay, teasing, tantalizing... He ran his fingertip around the rim and eventually dipped it into the glass, then put it in his mouth. It tasted sweet. "She had an abortion. She murdered my child," he said, almost catatonic.

Jeff reached over and touched Anton's wrist to remind him of what he was doing.

Again, he dipped his finger and put it into his mouth. "It kills the pain, Jeff."

"It kills more than pain, my friend," Jeff said. "You've had to fight this battle before, Russia. You want to tell me about the last time?" He wanted to ask more about Hope, but it was Anton who needed him right now.

Anton stared into the glass as though it were a mirror. He remembered walking for what seemed like an eternity. He looked at his hands and thought of the bleeding cuts that had stung from the salt of the sea as he'd clung to the jagged rock, the waves leaping up all around him like hungry tigers.

"I woke up in the hospital with my hands tied down," he said. "All I wanted to do was touch my face—you know, like you do in the morning to help you wake up." He looked at Jeff and waited to see if he understood. "I just wanted to touch my face to know it was really me."

Finally, Jeff nodded. "When was this?"

"Right after Catherine died. I guess I went off the deep end." He looked up and, seeing the look on Jeff's face, gave him a little smile. "Don't look so worried. I'm not going off the deep end again."

"No?"

Anton realized he had lifted the glass to his mouth and was a breath away from taking a drink. "Why don't you take it away from me?" he whispered.

But they both knew the answer. It was a battle that only he could fight. Deprivation was not the cure. After a long moment of silence, he set the glass on the table and pushed it away.

Someone dropped a coin in the jukebox, and a tune began to play.

"You want to tell me about Hope?" Jeff finally asked, sipping his beer.

"Nothing to tell. She had an abortion."

"Where'd you hear that?"

"Dan."

"You heard that from Dan, and you believed it?" Jeff was beside himself. "The guy who told Hope that Clay got married in 'Nam? He's a liar! He tells convenient lies to control people. I wouldn't trust Dan to shine my shoes!"

Once again, Anton laid his head in his arms. His headaches came much more frequently and for almost no reason at all.

"Look at yourself," Jeff said. "Talking about Hope having an abortion makes you react the same way you do with Catherine." He got up from the table, taking the bourbon with him, and returned seconds later with a glass of water. "You want to know what I think? I think your getting sick had nothing to do with Catherine. I think that when you started to…you know, make love…you subconsciously thought about her having an abortion and it made you sick, just like what's happening right now."

Anton drank the water. "Playing psychologist, are you?"

"Just go see Leslie."

CHAPTER 37

When Anton answered his door, he was surprised to find Hope, who entered his apartment in silence after he stood to one side. She handed him a slip of paper when he politely asked how she had been.

"Where did you get this?" he asked after a quick glance.

"Dan."

"You're talking to Dan these days?"

"He put it on my doorstep and knocked. When I answered the door, I saw him driving away."

"Do you know what it is?"

Hope nodded, biting her lower lip to fight back the tears he could see in her eyes. "It's your wife's address." She paused when he turned his back to her to look at the paper once more. "You weren't faithful to her, and you weren't very fair to me. You lied to me, Anton." She began to cry. "I asked if you had someone up in the bay. You said no!" She had wanted to go and meet the woman face-to-face, but Jeff had insisted that she face Anton first. Just seeing him tore her apart. She stepped behind him and gently touched his arm. "Anton, how could you let me fall in love with you?"

"Well, don't." He turned. "Don't love me. I don't want you to!" He went to the closet and put on his jacket, then signaled for her to follow him.

"Where are we going?" she asked as he opened the car door.

"To see my wife."

*****

The drive to the Bay Area was spent in silence. They were like two strangers on a bus who avoided looking at each other, as though even a glance would be an intrusion. When Hope occasionally broke into tears and hid her face against the glass, Anton stared straight ahead and swallowed his emotions like bile.

"Anton, let's go back. I'm sorry. I have no right to interfere in your life." She looked at him again. It was as though he hadn't heard a word. "Anton, I don't want to hurt her. I can't imagine how I would feel! Please, let's turn around." She touched his arm, but he stared straight ahead, silent.

He took the Colma exit out of habit, she thought, knowing he had taken Nathan there several times. But Anton pulled into the cemetery. He stopped the car and got out.

"Anton?" She followed him.

He went and stood beside Stella's grave.

"Hope, do you remember when you went to New York with me and you asked Paul Sanderson if you had ever met? He said no, but he lied. He didn't see any reason to bring it up. But he was here the day you buried your grandmother. He was here…with me."

"What are you saying?"

"Catherine is here, Hope. She's dead."

Hope gasped, suddenly aching for him—the lifeless face, the eyes that no longer sparkled. He stood and looked across the lawn at Catherine's stone for the first time since that day. He had brought Uncle Nate several times, but had made it a point not to even glance in the direction of Catherine's grave. Finally, he crossed what seemed like miles to the stone.

He knelt and caressed the letters of Catherine's name with his fingertips. *Odd*, he thought, unable to feel the pain he had expected.

After a moment, he turned to Hope. "Does this answer your questions?" There was something distant and a little frightening about him.

"When I thought you had a wife, I was upset, but at least it explained why you kept pushing me away. I guess I'm asking myself the same question again."

"Take a good look, Hope! The answer is right here in front of you!" He stood, pointing at the grave. "She killed herself, damn it! She picked up a fucking butcher knife and stuck it in her gut!"

"I don't know why Catherine did that, Anton. I only know that I love you. Please, help me work out whatever it is between us!"

"I don't want to love anyone. I don't give a damn about anyone!" he screamed. He grabbed her by the wrist and wrestled her to the ground.

"This is what happens to women who love me! Why don't you and Catherine have a little chat? Let her tell you that she's nothing but bones because her flesh has been eaten away! Ask her if she still loves me now! Ask her!"

"Stop it, Anton, you're hurting me," she cried.

He pressed her body flat over the grave and held her down. "How's it feel to know that just six feet away are the remains of someone I loved, someone I made love to!"

"What do you want, Anton!"

"Say you hate me. Say the words, 'I hate you, Anton.' Say it!"

"I love you," she cried.

"Damn you!" He lay over her, sinking her deeper into the damp grass. "*I hate you, Anton!* Say it!"

"I love you!"

"Yeah? How much?" he growled. "How much do you love me, Hope? Enough to let the bugs eat you away and the earth consume you? Do you love me as much as Catherine did? Enough to die for me?"

"I love you more!" she screamed. "I love you enough to *live* for you!"

Suddenly, he felt he was suffocating. "Oh, God," he cried, unable to breathe. He released her and sat, hugging his knees. From deep within, something surged upward, and he thought he would explode. Something primal and excruciating issued from his throat. A deafening scream that would have torn a hole in him if he hadn't let it out. He collapsed.

*****

When Anton opened his eyes, the fog was rolling in. Hope held him in her arms, crying softly as she stroked his hair. Finally, his breath was calm and he lay quiet. He looked to the side, where Catherine's stone stood like a monolith over him. He wondered if in death she, too, had stood over him, bigger than life itself. For the first time, he felt free of her. Free from the guilt he had carried like a precious cargo.

He had finally said goodbye.

He looked at Hope. Grass stains and mud smeared her cheek, and her eyes were swollen and red. "Anton, are you all right? I've been so worried."

He sat up and cradled her in his arms, gently rocking back and forth. "Shhh, sweetheart, I'm so sorry," he whispered. "Forgive me." He told her about the breakdown he had suffered after Catherine's death and the long hospital stay that had followed. He wanted her to understand everything about him, things only Leslie knew.

Even as they drove home, he continued, but by the time they reached his apartment, he told her the bottom line: for reasons that even he could not understand, he doubted he could ever make love with her again. Could they just be friends?

Hope rejected the idea. They parted, tearfully agreeing not to call.

CHAPTER 38

Anton rubbed his face and leaned back in the chair. He had often come to see Leslie; after all, she was his friend. But today he felt a vague nervousness as she silently reread parts of his old file to refresh her memory. A long time had passed since he had seen her strictly on a professional level, and now even the whispers of turning pages made him all the more apprehensive.

He had promised Jeff he would come, and anyone who knew Anton Pavlova knew he kept his promises. Even Hope had begged him to come.

That had been a week ago, but it felt like an eternity since he'd said goodbye to Hope. *I'm no longer her prince,* he thought, hearing the pages turn. *No longer her lover.* He closed his eyes and thought of when they had laughed and played in the bathtub in New York. *"I don't think either of us would buy that 'just friends' crap anymore, do you?"* he had said. And the sad truth was, she didn't. Not prince, not lover, not friend—he wondered what his title was now.

Finally, the folder was laid aside and Leslie smiled. "You look tired," she said quietly while straightening her skirt across her knee.

"I haven't slept well," he answered, then hesitantly added, "Les, I think I'm having another breakdown."

Leslie saw that the possibility frightened him. She leaned over and patted his hand. "Let me be the judge of that. Why haven't you slept well?" she asked, but was met with silence. "Just tell it to an old friend. We'll get a lot more accomplished that way." Her face was round and sweet, her gray eyes kind. He had always loved her face.

Not that she was especially pretty, but she had an elegance that few women had these days.

"I have dreams," he finally began with a deep breath. "They always start out wonderful. I'm happy and content. I know that no one can hurt me." He felt stilted and watched her take off her shoe and rub her ankle. He smiled inwardly. That was her way of trying to make him feel more relaxed. He had watched her do it over the years, and oddly enough, if often worked.

"What are you doing in your dream?" she asked, slipping the shoe back on.

"Nothing. I mean, I can't see anything, but I'm aware of my body and my thoughts."

"Then what?" she asked. It was déjà vu for Leslie, watching Anton struggle for words. They had been friends for a long time, and a smart-ass quip had become his way of showing affection. But now he searched for a place to fix his eyes, and his hands twitched like restless children.

"I'm not sure I can explain it," he said. "It's like someone cuts off my oxygen, my nourishment. My body begins to feel like…the blood has ceased to flow, and I start to suffocate." He looked at her to see if she understood.

So, he's finally come, she thought, *finally come to finish the journey he started so long ago.* It was bittersweet to watch him now, to see the fear in his eyes as he looked to her for guidance. She prayed that she could finally bring him home. "What's that like, Anton? Can you tell me?"

"It feels like I'm dying." He nodded to himself in sudden recognition of how it felt.

"Where do you suppose you are? Why can't you see anything?" She pressed a finger to her lips, thoughtful. "Somewhere you thought was safe and warm…"

"I don't know." He rubbed his face like a tired child.

He had always done that, from the day he'd been rescued from the sea with a tangle of kelp wound around his head, and she could read him by the manner in which he did it. He knew the answer but was reluctant to say the word. "Sounds kind of like a mother's womb, doesn't it?"

He agreed, though he couldn't make sense of the dying feeling that had always awakened him in a cold sweat. "What am I remembering, Les?"

"Maybe it's not a memory but a projection. Maybe you're projecting yourself into someone else's place."

"Whose?"

"Well, if you are indeed in a womb, my guess would be a baby's place." She leaned back and crossed her legs, watching him carefully while his eyes searched the room. "Anton, do you know any babies who died?"

"Hope's," he whispered, jolted by grief from the story Noah had told. He found himself holding his hand out in front of him as if to cradle a tiny head in his palm. *"Perfect,"* Noah had called it. *"She was five months along, and it was perfect."* He held out his hand to Leslie as if to show her what he saw in his mind's eye.

She smiled, but that wasn't what she needed him to remember. "Any more?" she asked, and saw anger begin to seethe behind his silence. She softly called his name twice before he would respond.

"She had an abortion." He spat the word. "Hope had an abortion! Dan told me! She killed my baby, Les!"

She said nothing, only waited to see where it would lead.

"Why do the women I love keep killing my children?" he screamed. Tears of anger slipped down his face.

Almost home. "You said 'women.' Hope and who else? Who else killed your child?"

Anton's face went white as he gasped Catherine's name. He turned quickly and held on to the chair, feeling dizzy.

Leslie stood and put her arms around him. "You don't have to get sick anymore, Anton. You know the truth, and you can deal with it."

He swallowed hard. "What are you saying?"

"That maybe you were in such grief over Catherine's death that you couldn't express your *anger* at what she had done." He kept trying to turn from her, but she wouldn't let go. "Anton, don't get sick this time. Get *angry!*"

Anton dropped back in the chair and buried his face in his hands. Agonized wails rose from deep within.

Leslie knelt in front of him and whispered, "The whole reason your grandparents kidnapped you was so you and your children and *their* children could live in freedom forever. Without children, the separation from your parents would have been for nothing." She smiled softly. "It was losing the baby that made you sick all this time, not losing Catherine."

He sat trembling. "That's hard to believe…"

"Why? Look at your friend Nathan," she continued. "From what you've told me, children were the most important thing in his life. Anton, you grew up with no sense of belonging, of family. You place a high value on your offspring."

Anton's tears began to subside, and he sat quietly for a while, picking at the arm of the chair.

"What are you thinking, my friend?" Leslie asked after several minutes.

"I think I hate her," he said, then glanced up. "That's awful, isn't it?" He looked at her, expecting disapproval, but she smiled and returned to her chair.

"Anton, Catherine took from you everything you could give. You jumped through hoops to keep her happy. She exhausted you both financially and emotionally, and what did she give you in return? Nothing. She wouldn't even give you a child."

"She was weak…"

"She was selfish. That beautiful little cup that you've held on to for all these years—why do you keep it?"

"It reminds me of Catherine."

"I disagree. I think you *want* it to remind you of her, but it doesn't. It reminds you of your baby."

"I don't understand."

"She destroyed your child, just like she destroyed the dishes. She couldn't stand to share *anything*. Not even a pattern on a plate! She played on your pity so she could have it all, including an excuse to give you nothing in return." Leslie looked into his eyes. "Isn't that why you love Hope? Because she gives yet asks for nothing?"

Anton turned his head at the mention of Hope's name. "She killed my baby too," he said. "And if I do love her, then why can't I…"

Leslie smiled. "You just answered your own question, my dear! If you thought she had an abortion—killed your child—why would you give her a second chance?" She leaned into his face and made him look at her. "Hope wasn't pregnant."

"Dan told me she had an abortion."

"Of course he told you that, but it was a lie. He got your files, Anton, all my notes. He knew exactly what to say."

"How do you know it was a lie, Les? What if it wasn't?"

"When did she have time? You were with her twenty-four hours a day from the time you went camping until the time Dan told you that. Did she slip out while you were in the shower? When?"

Anton was aghast. He sat back in his chair, ashen. Pushing Hope away, her night with Jeff—it had all been based on the lie Dan had told. A lie he had believed! "Oh, God, Leslie, you don't know what I've done!"

"I know things that *you* don't know you've done. Like the prostitutes, Anton, where you've taken all your anger over the years. Did you ever enjoy one of them?" She shook her head knowingly.

Anton thought of Mary Ellen and winced, only to find his friend chuckling softly. He closed his eyes and groaned. "God, I wish I had known all this," he said. "Les, why didn't you tell me long ago? Why did you wait until I was falling apart?"

"You aren't having a breakdown, Anton. What you are experiencing is a break*through*. If I had told you, would you have believed me? Anyway, you weren't ready. The trauma of dealing with what happened to Hope shook loose memories, and you had to come to terms with them in your own time."

Anton pushed his hair back and sighed as he rose to his feet. "Yeah, but I've hurt so many people in the process. The last time I saw Hope, I hurt her, Les. I scared her real bad."

"I know she loves you. Go to her. Talk to her." Leslie stood and straightened his collar.

"What if it's too late?"

She kissed his cheek and smiled. "It's never too late."

CHAPTER 39

Anton sat in the front seat of Jeff's van, looking at the house on the hill. Snow had fallen low on the mountain three days before, and now the Christmas lights seemed to wear colorful little halos. They sat quietly for a while, and Anton couldn't help but recall Christmases that had gone before. With no family or friends to share the holiday, he had often accepted assignments that got him through the mad rush of holiday cheer relatively unscathed. But the NORAD job wasn't for a few more months, and that was all there was left for the USIB, leaving him to deal with being alone at Christmas until Jeff had come to his rescue.

He missed Hope terribly. After the incident in the cemetery, he had only seen her once. They had run into each other while shopping, and he'd somehow talked her into having a cup of coffee at Kelly's. For an instant, he'd been hopeful as they'd sat at the table and were served.

"You're looking well," he'd said. She'd been breathtakingly beautiful, with the blush of cold on her cheeks.

She'd smiled hesitantly and sipped her coffee, but then there'd been an awkward silence. "Anton…" He'd reached over and touched her hand, but it had only opened the floodgates. "I'm sorry, Anton. I can't do this," she'd said, and fled from Kelly's crying.

"We're here," Jeff said after a long time, and Anton looked at him with apprehension.

"Yeah." He looked back at the house, so cheerful and Christmassy. "I'm not sure I should have come, Jeff. Just seeing me a few weeks ago made her cry. She couldn't even talk."

THE PEBBLE AND THE MAN

"It's Christmas Eve, Russia. Bud said I could bring someone if I wanted, so I did." He laughed a little when Anton gave him a look. They both knew this wasn't what she'd had in mind. Actually, he hadn't wanted to come. The pain he had seen in Hope's eyes at Kelly's was almost more than he could bear. But Jeff had persisted, vowing he wouldn't leave Anton alone during the holidays even if it meant missing Hope's gathering himself.

Finally, Jeff got out and Anton followed. When the two walked into the house, the chatter came to a halt. Everyone turned their head toward Anton, obviously surprised that he had come. Most of all Hope, who stood in shock in the kitchen doorway.

"Merry Christmas, Bud!" Jeff said in his usual irrepressible manner, striding across the living room to plop a big, wet kiss on Hope's cheek. But she only looked at him with dismay and walked down the hall toward the study. Jeff glanced over his shoulder at Anton and followed.

"How could you bring him here?" she cried when they were alone. "How could you do this to me?"

"Bud..." He shook his head and stepped close to her. "It's Christmas Eve, for chrissake!"

He was pulling at her heartstrings, and she knew it. "Yes, and I wanted to have a happy one. Now you've ruined it!" she snapped, but stopped when she realized Anton stood at the door.

"No, he hasn't, Hope."

"Anton, it's not that I want you to be alone. It's just that I...I just can't..." She choked on the words, and he pitied her.

"It's okay, sweetheart. I'll go." He reached out and stroked her honey-colored hair, and just the feel of it in his hand tore his heart in two. "I'll go," he whispered. He produced a small box from his pocket and handed it to her, looking embarrassed. "I brought you something," he said, forcing a smile.

"You shouldn't have bought me anything, Anton..." She looked at the box and tried to give it back.

"It's nothing," he said, "just a dumb piece of glass."

Hope let out a sob, then ran past him, through the door, and up the stairs, where she threw herself on the bed in tears.

"Smooth move, Sandpaper," Jeff gently scolded, but it wasn't necessary. Anton was already full of self-reproach. He had promised her long ago to replace the prism, but it had taken months to find one that was the same shape as the last. When he'd found it, he'd thought it would make a perfect Christmas gift. Now he realized the sentiment that Hope had attached to it.

"Jesus." He raked his fingers through his hair and sighed. "Take me home, Jeff. I think I've done enough damage for one night."

"No. You're the one that made her cry. You go fix it!" he said and pushed him toward the stairs. "Clean up your own mess this time, Russia. When she's done crying, I'll drive you home."

Anton took a deep breath and slowly climbed the stairs.

Hope lay sprawled across the big four-poster bed, crying into her pillow. Just the sight of her heaving shoulders, the muffled sounds of her sobs, made Anton hate himself for coming.

He crept quietly into the room and rested beside her. Finally, he dared to reach out and stroke her hair. "Sweetheart," he said gently, "I'll go. But I just can't leave while you're crying. I just can't. Please, little one…" Another sob ripped through her, and he took a deep breath, feeling helpless. "Sweetheart, please don't…God, you're killing me, Hope!"

He put his face close to her ear and begged her not to cry, and when she turned to face him, what he saw wrenched his heart. Even in the pale moonlight, he could see her look of absolute despair. She looked like a child whose life had crumbled in around her.

"Oh, Hope, I'm sorry." He kissed her forehead, and when she reached up, he became aware that his own face was wet with tears. He took her hand and kissed it, then kissed her forehead, and her sobs began to quiet. "Shhh…" he whispered, and kissed the moist corners of her eyes.

Hope could feel Anton's breath on her face, the warmth of his body lying beside her as he tried to ease the pain that just seeing him had brought. She wiped his face as his gentle mouth swept over her, kissing her eyes, her cheek…

He brushed ever so gently over her mouth and lingered there when he felt a slight movement, a slight pressing of her lips against his. Afraid to speak, or even to think, he pressed his lips gently against hers. Again her mouth sought his until they were locked in a tender embrace.

It was bittersweet, this unexpected tenderness before having to say goodbye. Anton closed his eyes tight, wondering if he would survive it again, and as the panic rose in his throat, he kissed her hard and passionately, trying to imprint it on his mind, never wanting to forget.

"Oh, Hope, I love you," he whispered miserably. "I love you! I can't stand being without you. It's tearing me apart," he cried and continued telling her over and over the words that had gotten lost in a hotel room in New York. He had finally found them, and within moments they lay naked together, their clothes peeled away by passion. There was nothing left between them but warm skin and gentle hands.

*****

The others were becoming restless, wondering when Anton and Hope would return so they could open the presents. They elected Jeff to quietly go up the stairs, hoping he could discreetly ascertain when they would be down.

When he reached the open door of Hope's bedroom, he found them locked in each other's embrace, their naked bodies moving with a slow, powerful rhythm in the moonlight. For an instant he looked away, but there was something magnetic about them, and his eyes were drawn again to the bed.

They hadn't noticed him, too consumed by their passion while he stood silent, marveling at how utterly beautiful they were, how perfectly matched. Their skin looked like silk in the moonlight, and the only sound was Hope's soft moaning as Anton moved over her, her leg gracefully curled over the back of his thigh, her hand roaming the valley of his back toward his strong buttocks. The gentle curve of her breast peeked out from beneath him as he raised himself off her, allowing the moonlight to shine between them for a moment while his narrow hips rocked back and forth.

Jeff stood breathless, mesmerized by the scene, in awe of the power and the grace that he saw in the man he called Russia. He felt humbled by his sensitivity and his strength, and suddenly he loved them, Anton and Hope, as one.

As Hope arched toward her lover, her hands grasping for him, leaving small marks across his back, Jeff trembled, hearing her cry out. Soon Anton, too, writhed in ecstasy, crying Hope's name, collapsing in her arms.

Jeff quietly closed the door and leaned against the wall outside the room, breathless and trembling. They belonged to him, he thought, Anton and Hope, and he knew that something deep inside him had changed forever.

*****

After the passion was the quiet. Time halted somewhere between ecstasy and reality. As Hope lay against Anton's chest, she wondered if he still planned to go, not knowing that he wondered if she would allow him to stay. Each silently wondered if the bittersweet passion of their goodbye had reversed the damage, but for now remained content, quiet, and warm. They had crawled beneath the blankets and fluffed the pillows just so, had entwined their arms and legs to hold on to whatever might be left between them.

"Do you want me to go?" Anton whispered after a long while. The thought devastated him, but he knew the longer he stayed, the harder leaving her would become.

"If you go, I'll cry. Then you would have to come back and make love to me all over again." She smiled up at him, and he melted.

"Oh, sweetheart, I love you!"

"You've never told me that before," she said quietly.

"That's because I've been a fool. Oh, Hope, I feel terrible about so many things." He kissed her and proceeded to tell her about the things he had just learned about himself: that he'd thought she had aborted his child, and about Catherine, and his own burning anger at them both. He turned over to face her. "Hope, that's why I acted the way I did at the cemetery. I was so angry at Catherine…at you…

and the worst of it was, I didn't even know why. Just like I didn't understand why I couldn't make love with you." He looked into her eyes and melted at the compassion he saw.

"I'm sorry you had to go through it alone, Anton."

"I had to do it alone. Thinking I had lost you forever was the worst of it."

She snuggled close to his body and purred contentedly. "Well, you don't have to worry about that anymore."

"Marry me."

"What?"

"Marry me, Hope, just as soon as I get back from this last assignment. I'll be retiring then. We can buy the dance studio in San Francisco…" He paused, looking pensive, "…have a couple of kids." He looked at her and was relieved to see her grinning. "Does that mean yes?"

"Oh, yes! To everything! Alexis would be so happy if he knew you bought the studio. He wanted that for you so much!" She looked around the room and grew quiet. "I never thought I'd leave this house, but I know it's inevitable. San Francisco will be fine, as long as I'm with you."

Anton felt a warmth surge through him when he remembered for the first time that the house belonged to him. He had never thought of it as his house. It was always Hope's in his mind. He smiled inwardly, knowing he already owned the house she so dearly loved, but he said nothing about it, saving it as a surprise for their wedding day. Yes, he thought, it would be his gift to her and she would never have to give it up! "You said you'll marry me and we can buy the studio…"

"And yes, I'll have your baby!" She laughed and threw her arms around him. He laughed and embraced her, and soon they were lost in passion. *Alexis would be happy about babies too*, she thought, smiling to herself.

They made love and planned their future together until falling asleep, deliciously happy, in the early hours of morning.

*****

Christmas morning, the sky was cloudy and the mountain had received another light dusting of snow. Anton and Hope awoke simultaneously, having stayed in each other's arms all night.

"I smell bacon," Hope said, sniffing the air, "and coffee."

Anton sniffed the air, too, and broke out in a grin. "Those little shits didn't go home!" he laughed. They dressed and went downstairs.

Nicki had just set a platter of bacon and eggs in the middle of the table, where Jeff, Noah, and Clay sat drinking coffee. They stifled grins when the two arrived, but said nothing.

"Guess what I got for Christmas," Hope said, resting her hands on Jeff's shoulders.

"Laid," Jeff smirked, grinning from ear to ear. They all laughed when she playfully slapped the top of his head.

"I got engaged!"

"No shit?" He turned to Anton. "No shit?"

Anton grinned. "No shit."

*****

"I'm happy for you. Really, I am." Noah extended a congratulatory hand to Anton later in the privacy of the study. But then there was a moment of silence in which Anton pitied the man. "I'm going to Texas, closer to my Aunt Camille and kid sister, Elizabeth. I've stayed in Three Rivers too long," he said and started to leave. At the door, he turned. "Do me a favor. If something happens, if something goes wrong…write me and let me know. I pray it doesn't, because I know Hope loves you, but just in case, I'll give you my new address."

Anton could only nod. Moments later, Noah got in his car and left.

Jeff was ecstatic at the news and floated around the house in a daze, causing Anton and Hope to wonder if he'd ever go home. Clay and Nicki had left soon after Noah, but it was as though Jeff had a stake in the marriage and wanted to wait around for the wedding. Finally, after being reminded that his own family in Fresno was probably eagerly awaiting his arrival, he left. At last Anton and Hope were alone.

They hung the prism in the window, called Leslie and Uncle Nate to give them the good news, then dressed warmly and took a walk on the snow-covered mountain.

The air was fresh and crisp; the naked trees seemed to hold the snow on their branches for cover. The pines and spruce bent with the weight.

By evening, the fireplace crackled bright and warm, and they cuddled on the couch with an endless supply of smiles and caresses.

"I love you, Anton," she said, stroking the arm that rested over her.

"I love you too, sweetheart. Merry Christmas."

The Third Year

CHAPTER 40

Anton opened his eyes to find Hope grinning at him, her legs curled around his torso, his pulse racing. She had been teasing him in his sleep, and he pounced on her, reveling in the laughter that filled the room until, at last, they lay exhausted in each other's arms. It had been that way for over three months, and for three months, he'd fallen in love with her over and over again. He felt happy and carefree, unlike any other time in his life, and each time he looked at her, she was more beautiful.

"I'm glad I don't have to work today," she said as she caressed his strong chest.

"When are you going to quit that crummy job?" he asked and received a lighthearted frown.

"I thought I'd wait until after you got back from your assignment. It'll give me something to do to pass the time—unless, of course, you'd rather I sit around and mope!"

"But you don't have to work. I've put your name on the accounts." He began to laugh when she tickled him, refusing to be serious. They had argued about money continuously, Hope insisting that she didn't want to be a *kept* woman until after the wedding, to which Anton could do nothing but moan in frustration. It had almost become a joke with them, her stubborn independence against his stubborn pride. *"How would it look for the wife of an international hotshot to be scrubbing floors in a lodge?"* he had asked her once, to which she'd insisted that she only did it to keep him humble.

"Stop tickling me!" He grabbed her wrists and rolled over her when she wouldn't stop.

The bedroom door burst open, and Anton grabbed the sheets, covering them quickly. "What the hell…?"

"I thought you guys were done." Jeff looked only slightly embarrassed and smiled when Anton began to berate him from the sanctity of the warm bed. "I brought you breakfast." He held out a large tray.

"How the hell did you get in here?"

"With the key."

"What key?"

"The one under the mailbox." Jeff's face remained absolutely innocent, and Anton's obvious frustration started Hope giggling.

"There isn't a key under the mailbox!"

"Sure there is. I put it there myself after Bud asked me to have a few extras made for her. Figured I might have use for it sometime." He set the tray on the ruffled blankets and, after slipping off his shoes, proceeded to climb onto the foot of the bed, where he sat Indian-style, the tray of food between himself and the angry Russian.

By this time, Hope was exploding with laughter, and the angrier Anton became, the more she laughed. Jeff uncovered the tray, revealing sausage and eggs, hash browns, blueberry muffins from the bakery, and coffee.

"What the hell are you doing, Jeff!" Anton demanded, and again he was met with innocent eyes.

"Ever since you two got engaged, you don't play with me anymore!" Jeff answered, and Hope roared. Anton only slapped one hand across his forehead and groaned in frustration, falling back into the pillows.

Jeff was like a pet, he told Hope later. When you stopped petting him, he got lonely and pushed his head up under your hand to remind you he was still around. There was nothing left to do but eat, so Anton and Hope sat naked on the bed, the sheets tucked carefully around them, while Jeff sat at the foot of the bed, chattering as though it were all perfectly normal, until finally, almost an hour later, he carried the dishes downstairs.

*****

THE PEBBLE AND THE MAN

Jeff was waiting at the foot of the stairs when Anton finally came down. "That Sanderson guy is here," he said quietly.

"What's he doing here?" Anton paused for a moment. "Jeff, could you excuse us for a bit?"

"Yeah. Sure. Where's Bud? I have to clean up the kitchen before she sees it," he added, and Anton laughed when he peeked in at the mess.

"You're lucky she takes long showers." He could only shake his head as he went into the living room, where Paul Sanderson stood with his hands in his pockets, looking at the picture of Anton's grandparents, which now hung over the mantel. Anton had dreaded this day, knowing that sooner or later, he would be called away.

The North American Air Defense Command was a joint agency of the United States and Canada, and for the past two years, secret meetings between the two countries had been held in Seattle, Washington, but had been infiltrated by what were believed to be Soviet spies. Anton's job was that of a counterspy, to ascertain what information had been gathered and what information had been sent. It was a big job, a dangerous job—too much for one man alone. A year ago, Sanderson had promised him a full network of people to ensure his safety, but what Sanderson told him now was a nightmare. He was to go it alone. No network, no outside contacts. It was all his. The USIB had just let all its people go, the security department, everyone. Even Leslie was turning to private practice after the debriefing period, and in a month, Sanderson himself would retire. Only Anton remained, the sole heir of the last remaining job of the USIB.

"You're sending me to my death, Paul. You know that, don't you?" He leaned back into the couch. "Why wasn't I told about the changes months ago?"

Sanderson avoided his eyes as if contact would demand a reply.

"Damn it, Paul! How could you do this to me?"

"You're prepared," Sanderson finally said.

"Not to die, I'm not! I was prepared when I thought I had a backup, had contacts! If you had told me months ago, then maybe!" He shook his head and moaned. "How much time do I have?"

"Tomorrow."

Anton looked aghast.

"You can do it. You're the best."

"I'm a man!" he shouted. "Nothing more! When are you people going to realize that?"

"You can do it, Pavlova. I know you can."

Anton watched his superior walk slowly around the room, picking up small objects, looking at them, then putting them down again, totally unaware of his anger. How many years had he given to this man? How many hoops had he jumped through for Paul, just as he had for Catherine? Only Hope demanded nothing of him.

"Isn't that your grandparents?" Sanderson looked up at the picture once more. "What's it doing in Hope's house?"

"It's my house. I bought it."

Sanderson looked at him sharply, remembering the young man of twenty-seven, confused, injured, lacking direction after Catherine had died. But now Anton knew what he wanted, and Sanderson could feel his influence slipping away. "So…you two are serious?"

"I told you that a year ago in New York."

"No, you didn't. You asked my advice, and I told you to leave her." Sanderson waved his hand in a sweeping motion, indicating the room and the things it contained. "Anton, all this…it's not for you. You could never be happy with this kind of life. Neither could I. That's why I left the woman I loved."

"Did you? Or did you give her a good job with the USIB and air fare to New York whenever you wanted a piece of ass? What you did, Paul, was refuse to marry her, to give her a home and a family. I've watched you use Leslie just like you've used me!"

"Is that what she told you?"

"I'm not stupid, Paul. I figured the two of you out a long time ago. Using me is one thing. I allowed it to happen. But Leslie…" Anton shook his head.

"She's a big girl, Pavlova. She could have called it quits anytime." He was shocked that Anton would question anything he did. The Russian had finally come of age, he thought. He turned away for a moment, trying to get back to business. "I know you're upset, but if you'd remained connected with Dan Philips, you wouldn't be alone in all this," he said at last.

Anton only shook his head and reminded Sanderson that it wasn't true. Dan had mysteriously disappeared two months earlier.

"You've never balked on an assignment before," Sanderson said.

"I've never had anything to lose before." He stood and faced Sanderson. "I have a woman who loves me. I have a home and friends for the first time. I don't want to die, Paul."

"Then don't." He pressed Anton's hand. "Do the honorable thing. I pray you never need this." With no further adieu, Sanderson went through the door, having once again pressed a packet of cyanide into Anton's palm.

Anton turned around and found Jeff staring at him. "You heard?" he asked, and Jeff slowly nodded.

"Take care of Hope," he whispered, hearing her footsteps on the stairs.

"I will."

*****

"No!" Hope screamed when Anton told her. "Why now? Why does it have to be now?" she cried, unconsciously touching her still-flat abdomen. She had learned only the day before that Anton's seed had begun to grow. "Anton, can't you put it off? Can't it wait?"

"I'm sorry, sweetheart, I can't. I told you it would be around the middle of April. It's only a week earlier. Look at it like this: the sooner I get it over with, the sooner we can be married." He glanced at Jeff, who knew it wasn't as simple as he was making it out to be. "The brat here is going to watch after you for me."

As always, Hope read the worry in his eyes, just as she read his efforts to make their parting easier, leaving her with the dilemma of the news she had saved for today. But after remembering the torment that Catherine had put him through, she didn't have the heart to tell him about the baby. "Anton, hurry home. I'll miss you terribly," she finally managed.

"You'd better." He laughed a little, and within twenty-four hours, he was gone, leaving behind him Hope and the tiny child within her that he would never know.

CHAPTER 41

The ensuing months were lonely for Hope, and time seemed to stand still except for the increasing difficulty with which she concealed her pregnancy. It was near the end of June, and until now, each time the phone rang, each trip to the mailbox, was accompanied with a silent prayer that Anton was on his way home. But there were no letters, no phone calls, only Sanderson, who now sat grim-faced in her living room. Life had played a cruel joke. Anton had been taken prisoner by the Soviets, and then somehow lost between the two continents.

Dan's legacy of misdeeds continued. In his efforts to foil the NORAD job, he had fingered Anton as a counterintelligence agent; they had been waiting for him.

"Hope," Sanderson continued, "if you love him, pray he's dead. I can't begin to tell you the horror stories if he's still alive. The Soviets won't even admit they have him, but we know he was taken out of the country," his voice droned on, leaving Hope numb.

"Mr. Sanderson, I think you should leave," she finally managed.

"I'll be in touch if there's any news," he said stiffly before going out the door. But he knew there wouldn't be any news. The Soviet prison system had swallowed several of his men over the years. There was never any news.

That night, Hope lay awake in her room, wondering why she couldn't cry. There were no tears, and even the following day, when she told the others, there was only the numbness that she couldn't shake. Clay and Nicki stayed close to her in the weeks that followed, and Noah mysteriously showed up.

It was Jeff who grieved the most. He buried himself in his new relationship with Valerie, almost as if trying to replace the part of him that felt "broken off." When Clay insisted that Hope continue having the weekend gatherings, Jeff stayed home more often than not, unable to watch Hope, who looked more beautiful, more radiant than ever. She wore a new glow just under her skin, a warmth, and instead of becoming thinner as she had in the past, she looked healthier and fuller.

*****

"I thought you were supposed to take care of me," she said to him one day, standing on his doorstep, but he had to force a smile. He felt oddly separated from her now.

"Seems you've got Noah to do that," he said, spotting the boxer who waited in the car. They had invited him to dinner, but he'd declined the invitation. "Has there been any word about Russia?" he asked, and wondered about the blank eyes that stared back at him. "Have you heard from that Sanderson guy?" he tried again. It was as though Hope had been frozen in place, just before she went pale and collapsed on the stoop.

"Noah!" Jeff yelled to the boxer and quickly knelt beside her, finding blood on the pavement. "My God, call an ambulance!"

*****

Jeff sat in the waiting room, staring at his hands, barely aware that Clay had finally arrived and stopped to talk with Noah, who stood a few feet away. Three hours had passed, and there was still no word. He put his head in his hands and sighed. He'd promised Anton he would take care of her, watch over her, but instead resented her healthy glow. He loved Anton like a brother, though he had never quite put it into words before, and it hurt him that Hope displayed almost no grief at all, had only become more beautiful. "Holy Mary, Mother of God..." The prayers of his childhood tumbled out.

"Jeff," Clay's voice came from nowhere, and he felt an arm lie across his shoulders while he shook, realizing he was crying. "The doctor is here," Clay said quietly, and Jeff looked up at a young man wearing green surgical scrubs.

"I understand one of you is related to Hope Landrum," he said as he approached.

"I'm her brother," Clay answered. "Clay Philips."

The doctor shook Clay's hand. "Dr. Wilson," he introduced himself. "Your sister is out of danger."

"What happened to her?" Jeff asked urgently.

The doctor turned to Jeff. "Are you the father? I'm sorry. The baby only lived about forty minutes. We tried everything, but it just came too early."

"She was pregnant?" Jeff gasped.

The doctor looked at Noah, then Clay. "I know this is hard, but he needs to sign some forms."

"He's not the father. The father is…" *an international spy, currently captured by the Soviets.* Clay stopped, realizing the truth sounded ridiculous. "…his brother," he lied and silenced Noah with his eyes.

"I see. Well, one of you needs to sign some forms," he persisted, and Clay assured him they would before they left.

Eventually, Clay and Noah went home, but Jeff remained. Every time he asked to see Hope, the nurse on duty had an excuse why he couldn't. Finally, after twelve hours had gone by, he dragged a chair from the waiting room and parked it in front of Hope's door to make his presence known. After becoming a total nuisance, he was finally permitted to sit beside her bed.

*****

When Hope awoke, depression crept over her as she slowly became aware of where she was and why. She put her hand on her abdomen. The precious bulge was gone, and she was overwhelmed by the emptiness left in its wake. Slow, desperate tears rolled down her face, and it wasn't until a while later that she became aware of the strong hand that lay over hers. It, too, trembled, grasping at the empty spot where she had once carried Anton's child.

Jeff's face reflected everything she felt. He was unshaven and pathetic, and she could tell he had been crying.

"They won't let me see my baby, Jeff," she whispered. "Every time I ask, they dope me up."

She watched as he stood and put the side rail down, then, sitting on the bed next to her, gathered her up in his arms. "The baby's gone, Bud," he choked. "I would give my life if I thought I could bring it back."

"I still want to see my baby," she cried. "Jeff, it was all I had! As long as I had Anton's baby, I had Anton. Don't you see? As long as I carried his baby, I knew in my heart that he'd come home." Tears rolled down her face. "Now the baby is gone…Anton is gone…" She began to sob, and Jeff pulled her closer into his arms.

He realized now that she hadn't grieved because she hadn't accepted the reality of it. After all, how could she believe he was gone when a part of him was still growing inside her?

"Oh, Jeff, I need to hold my child just once. Don't I have a right to hold my baby? They won't even tell me what it was. They said it's better not to know, like not knowing would help me forget. But I'll never forget, Jeff. You've got to help me!"

She gasped from the sobs that racked her tiny frame, and it broke his heart. The guilt for what he thought about her could never be forgiven. He started to get up, but she grabbed at his clothes.

"Don't leave me! They keep doping me up so I won't think about it. Jeff, please don't let them do that to me anymore!"

"I won't, Bud. I won't." He kissed her forehead and stroked her until she finally began to calm down. After a while, he rang the button and waited for the nurse to appear, and moments later, a heavy middle-aged woman entered the room.

"Visitors aren't allowed on the beds," she snapped, looking sternly at Jeff.

"It's hard to comfort someone through bars." He didn't move, only held Hope tighter. "Bud wants to see her baby."

"Can I see you outside in the hall, mister....who are you?" she asked, and Jeff gave his name. "Well, Mr. Lansing, could I speak to you in private?"

"Jeff, it's a trick. They'll separate us and won't let you come back! Then I'll never get to hold my baby." Hope began to cry again, clutching at Jeff's clothes.

"I won't leave you. I promise," he assured her, then looked back at the woman. "Bring the baby," he demanded.

The nurse disappeared, but returned moments later with an orderly who carried a small tray, upon which was a hypodermic needle. "Miss Landrum is upset, Mr. Lansing. I think you should leave and let her rest." The nurse picked up the syringe and stepped toward Hope, who began to tremble violently.

Jeff pulled out his service revolver and leveled it at the woman's head. "Touch her and I'll blow you away, lady. Bring the child!"

The orderly dropped the tray and ran out as the woman stepped back, finally disappearing through the door.

*****

An hour passed before the door opened again, and when it did, Jeff glimpsed security guards on each side of the door. He drew his weapon before he realized it was Clay who had entered.

"What the hell do you think you're doing?" Clay stood before them with his hands on his hips. "They called me and said my partner had flipped out!" He abruptly smiled, half-angry, half-amused at the two all cuddled and comfortable on the hospital bed.

"Hope wants to see her baby, and they keep doping her up against her will," Jeff said. "She has a right not to be doped up, bro. She has a right to hold her baby. I'm just trying to protect her rights. That's all." Jeff's uncombed hair fell in bunches of curls, and he had spent the night in his clothes. He looked like a radical from the sixties.

"Jesus, Jeff. You're a pain in the ass, you know that? Let me see what I can do. Meanwhile, try not to shoot anybody, would you? It would look bad for the department." Clay paused and looked at

Hope. "You all right? Do you want him to stay?" he asked, and she nodded. He wearily scratched his head, then left.

He returned half an hour later, accompanied by Dr. Wilson and a young nurse, who carried a tiny bundle in her arms. The doctor went to the side of the bed and smiled down at Hope while listening to her heart with the stethoscope. "How are you doing, Hope? Are you all right?" he asked gently, glancing at Jeff, who frowned at him in return. "Mr. Lansing, I understand what you're trying to do. Really. But the baby is dead. You do understand that, don't you?" He peered under his brows until they both nodded. "It's cold," he warned, and again they nodded. Dr. Wilson took the small bundle from the nurse and laid it in Hope's arms.

A hush fell over the five people in the room as Hope's hand moved slowly over the bundle. "You can change your mind, Bud." Jeff gave her an out if she wanted it, but she didn't. Her small hands carefully, calmly peeled back the blanket until at last the tiny child was revealed.

"She's pretty, isn't she?" Hope's eyes found Jeff's.

"Yeah. Real pretty," he answered in a gummy voice. "I didn't realize you were that far along."

"You didn't even know I was pregnant, silly." She giggled nervously, and bitter tears flowed down her face. "I was almost six months along. I must have gotten pregnant at Christmas."

"Christmas?" Jeff looked at the baby, wondering if he had watched this child being conceived. "Can I touch her?"

"Uh-huh. Feel her hair."

Jeff's fingers joined Hope's in the soft, downy fuzz on the baby's head. It felt cold and strange, so still.

"I'm going to name her Rose." Hope blinked back the tears. "Anton always gave me roses." She smiled weakly at the others in the room. "I want her buried proper. Near my grandmother," she said with resolve, her voice suddenly strong and clear.

"I'll make arrangements," Clay said, and stepped closer to look at the infant.

"Thank you, Clay."

Seeing that everything was fine, Dr. Wilson called the nurse out of the room and sent the security guards away. Sometimes, allowing one to grieve was the best medicine, he thought; sometimes tears, the best cure.

Eventually, Clay left the room, leaving only Jeff and the nurse behind. "Do you want to be alone, Bud?" he asked quietly.

"No. Stay." She folded the blanket around the child, leaving only her little face to peek out of the cover, then cradled Rose in her arms and quietly sang a lullaby while Jeff wept at her side.

Valerie went to see Jeff that night, having heard from Clay what had happened, and he went readily to her arms. They made love for the first time, in silence. There were no words, only Jeff's tragic expression that needed comforting, and when they were done, his silent tears fell into her soft auburn hair.

*****

Rose Pavlova was buried a week later. Hope looked tired, and Jeff wished he could restore the color to her cheeks, the fullness he had resented only the week before. But that fullness had been Rose, and now Hope sat on the folding chair beside the tiny opening in the earth, looking empty and hollow, as if she were burying the last thread of hope for Anton along with their tiny infant daughter. She had grieved terribly all week, and after the brief ceremony, she insisted on staying until the grave was filled. Only Jeff and Valerie stayed behind, watching over her.

She laid two dozen white roses on the sod after it had finally been replaced, but bent down again after a moment and took a single rose. She carried it to a distant grave and laid it there. "At least she's with her baby," she said quietly, and Jeff took her by the shoulders from behind. "She died with her baby…"

"I know. Russia told me," he whispered, kissing her hair as she stared at the stone.

"How much do you love me, Hope?" Anton had screamed. *"Do you love me as much as Catherine did? Enough to die for me?"*

"I love you more!" she had cried back. *"I love you enough to* live *for you!"*

The words rolled over in her mind, and she heaved a sigh. "Take me home, Jeff," she said, leaning back against him, suddenly exhausted. "It's been a long day."

CHAPTER 42

When Hope opened the door, Noah stood before her with a big bouquet of flowers. It had been weeks since she had seen him—not since the day they had rushed her to the hospital, to be precise. He wore a new jacket, shirt, and tie, his hair neatly combed, and she smelled cologne.

He looked quite handsome, really, except for the obvious ridge of his nose, which had been repeatedly broken. Hope had affectionately called it his score card once, back when life was simple; with each win in the ring, his nose had first suffered another terrible break. But just now, he looked surprisingly handsome.

"I haven't seen you in a long time. Where have you been?" She opened the door wide, inviting him inside, and he handed her the flowers.

"I'm sorry. I should have been with you..."

"Can I get you something to drink?" she asked when he struggled for words. He seemed uncomfortable with her for the first time, fidgeting while she poured them each a glass of wine. She put the flowers in water and fussed with them for a moment, then carried the wine into the living room, where they sat on the couch. She thanked him for the flowers and was warmed by the look of embarrassment that crossed his face, but afterward, there followed an uneasy silence.

"Hope..." Noah looked down at his hands and frowned. "Why didn't you tell me you were expecting?"

"I don't know. I guess I kept thinking Anton would come home and that he should be the first to know."

He had looked up to catch her words. "I would have married you, baby and all. You know that, don't you?"

Hope reached over and took his hand, smiling at him affectionately. "I know you would have," she said gently, "but I wasn't looking for a husband, Noah. Besides, how would you feel about having a child that only grew to be half your size and had blond hair and blue eyes?"

"I would have loved it and thought it looked like the man its mother loved," he said earnestly. "How do you feel?"

"I'm well."

"What did the doctor say?"

"Stress. I've been under too much stress," she said.

Noah nodded and looked at the tiny hand in his own. It was so delicate, so beautiful. She had always been beautiful to him. "Marry me, Hope," he said.

She was stunned, but he continued, afraid that if he didn't, he would never be able to say all the things he'd already told her in his mind.

"I love you. I always have, even when you were married to Steven. I hate myself for not taking you away from him. Anton was right, I could have made your life different, easier."

"Oh, Noah!" she gasped. "I just can't. I have to wait for Anton!"

Noah slowly withdrew an envelope from his pocket and handed it to her.

"What's this?"

"A letter from Anton."

She withdrew her hand from his and caressed the words, as if touching Anton's handwriting brought them a little closer.

"He wants you to marry me, Hope. I told him I was in love with you almost two years ago. Then, when you announced your engagement last Christmas, he promised to let me know if, for some reason, things changed. If he's still alive, he knows I'm here. He knows I'm asking you to marry me."

Hope turned the envelope over in her hand and read the postmark. It had been sent the day before he was seized.

"I want you to marry me. Anton wants it too, or he wouldn't have sent the letter. He knows I'll take care of you and that I can give you a good life."

Hope sat, numbed by what she had heard, wanting desperately to run up the stairs and cry into her pillow. But Noah's eyes begged her to answer.

"I can't," she choked.

He flinched from the words. "Am I so bad?"

She put her hand on his cheek and looked into his eyes. "Oh, Noah, my dear, sweet friend. You've been kind and gentle and loving. You've always come to me when I needed you. You've always been there. But I love Anton."

He looked away. "I know you do," he finally said. "But Anton's not here and he's not coming back, or else he wouldn't have sent this." He tapped the letter in her hand. "Don't you think you could learn to love a guy like me?" He forced a pathetic smile that broke her heart. "Is it because I'm a boxer? I have a chance at the title in October, but I'll quit after that. I promise." He was begging.

"Oh, Noah!"

"If you'll marry me, I won't fight anymore. I'll quit right now if that's what you want!"

"Noah, stop. You love the game. If you quit because of me, you'd always regret it, resent me! Please, can't we just stay as we are?"

"No! I love you!" he shouted. "I've always loved you. I want to make love with you, have children with you!" Tears sprang from his eyes, and he lowered his voice. "Marry me, Hope. Please!"

"I can't," she whispered. "I just can't."

Noah took a deep breath and wiped his eyes, not knowing what to say, but knowing he had to leave.

"Hope, can I kiss you, just this once?" She nodded, and he drew her up in his arms. She could taste the tears as his moist lips pressed hers, full of passion and pain. "Oh, God, I love you," he cried, pressing her against him once more before finally letting her go. He stood and quickly disappeared through the door.

*****

Noah had sat in his car for a few minutes, trying to collect himself, wondering if he'd approached her too soon, when he saw her bolt out of the back door and run across the meadow toward the woods.

Out of breath, Hope found herself surrounded by the woods, where she had often taken her grief. It had been over a month since she'd come, since she had visited the old men of the woods. High above her they whispered, clashing their barked swords in the breeze. She stopped for a moment, smelling the sweet, damp earth, and closed her eyes to soak in all the sensations that her soul hungered for.

There was a movement, and a rabbit bolted across the path in front of her, causing her to stumble and fall against a tree, and from somewhere deep inside she felt her own primal voice screaming into the treetops. "Anton! Where are you!" she cried, and slumped to the ground.

Where was he? The weight in her heart held her against the musty earth. How could he send a letter relinquishing her love? God, how she missed him! How she missed the joy she had found growing inside her, her little Rose. But both were gone now, and she cried alone in the woods.

Noah stood silent and still on the meadow as Hope's painful pleas echoed against the treetops, finding their way out into the sky. They were cries he could not hear, but he knew them just the same. Just as he knew now that she would never be his.

*****

Hope stood with Clay and Nicki, Valerie and Jeff, watching Noah's young sister cry into her Aunt Camille's arms. It was the end of October, and Noah's fight was done.

They had gathered at Hope's to watch the big moment he'd been waiting for, his shot at the title. As they readied their popcorn and beer, the camera swept the Las Vegas lights. Everyone jumped to their feet and cheered upon seeing their friend enter the ring. It was all so exciting!

"Four rounds," Jeff had shouted, "always before the fifth!" And they watched and waited for the punch that never came. Noah had the chance to deliver it perfectly several times, but he only backed away and danced around the ring.

"You'll wear yourself out, damn it!" Clay grumbled as Noah moved back and forth, already into round six. The crowd began to boo in the stadium, but Noah only danced and took the punishment from his opponent.

His nose was broken in round seven, and Clay and Jeff collectively groaned, shaking their heads. Noah was exhausted, the punch still undelivered. Round eight: "Stop the fight, damn it! Stop the fight!" Clay and Jeff both yelled at the television screen. There was silence in the room as the stadium crowd leapt to their feet. The TV camera panned to the broken man lying on the canvas. Valerie stared in shock, and Nicki cried. The camera zoomed to focus on Noah's lifeless form, his eyes open but devoid of vision. A hand motioned the camera away.

*****

"Are you all right, Bud?" Jeff's arm went around Hope as the casket was lowered into the ground. Her face was white, as it had been since the doctor had given her a sedative; she had gone into shock, had stayed overnight at the hospital, the night Noah died.

"Yes," she whispered, nodding to Jeff. He had begged her not to come, but she had to, she'd said. She took her turn gently tossing a single rose down onto the casket.

"We're dwindling," she whispered. "We're all dwindling away…"

CHAPTER 43

The blindfold didn't keep Anton from knowing he was almost back to his cell. He listened to the boots of the soldiers echo behind him as he was marched blindly down the corridor, counting the number of times the stench of concentrated urine struck his nostrils. It helped him count the cells of the other prisoners: three on the left, two on the right. It was close. He braced himself mentally and waited for the guard to make him stumble and fall. He was near, almost to the cell. "Ugh!" His face hit the floor, followed by laughter that came with equal predictability.

Each day was the same. After being interrogated for hours, he had to take the walk back to his cell and suffer this last humiliation. Always the guards wanted this one last laugh, and watching him fall with his hands tied behind him seemed to amuse them. Again, he found himself facedown on the cold concrete floor. The guard pulled him to his feet and removed the handcuffs and blindfold before shoving him into the cell.

Anton wondered what day it was, wishing he could keep track. Sometimes he was awakened in the middle of the night, blindfolded and then kept awake for long periods. When he was returned to his cell, he had no way of knowing if it was the same night, the following night, or what often felt like the night after that. By doing that, the Soviet general had ensured he lost track of time long ago, confusing him and rendering him more vulnerable. He touched his face with his fingertips, glad his beard had grown out. It helped protect his skin from the grating concrete floor when the guards tripped him. But there, just above his right brow, he was sure the lump was increasing in size. He had to try to turn his head the other way, let this side heal. He touched his cheeks and his nose, feeling his face, trying to remember what he looked like. It was important to remember who he was, what he was; important to remember because if he ever forgot, his spirit would die. Then he would die.

Finally, through the barred door, he was handed a small tin cup containing an insipid liquid, which he drank fervently. Awful as it was, it was nourishment, all he would get for the rest of the day. Protecting his health, both physical and mental, was the game.

After drinking the cold broth, he huddled in the corner of his cell, cold and tired, hugging himself for warmth. As he drifted off to sleep, he found his mind, as always, floating back to the mountain that stood above Three Rivers.

When he awoke, only two hours had passed, and his eyes opened to a pair of black boots near his face. He followed the gray woolen trousers upward until he came to the face that looked down at him. When he sat up, the black boot caught him under the chin, sending him tumbling against the concrete wall with a thud. And so began more hours of intense interrogation.

He endured his pain in silence. The two soldiers who had been his guards stood by while his interrogator, his tormenter, became increasingly violent. This had become the norm, going from the milder cigarette burns to the electric shocks until finally, out of frustration, he was sent back to his cell. There, he was savagely beaten by the older guard.

Anton wondered about the younger man. He had caught his eye once and thought he'd seen a hint of remorse just before the older man had yelled. "Mikhail, don't look at him!" he had growled, and the young man's gaze had dropped away from Anton's face. "That's how they get to you," the older guard had warned as he'd stepped over Anton's broken body and left the cell.

"That's how I remind you I am human," Anton had whispered as Mikhail went through the door, closing it hesitantly behind him.

*****

Anton lay crumpled in the corner of the dark cell, choking and spitting blood. For days, he had been awakened each time sleep tried to rescue him. His bruised face was badly swollen, and his head felt large and heavy.

It went on interminably. Each time his eyes closed, a black boot kicked him. At last, his eyes closed and he was unable to feel the boot that buried itself between his ribs, although he knew it had. *I'm dying,* he thought, sorry that he had thrown away the packet of cyanide that Sanderson had given him, wishing he had a simpler way. But it was near. Soon, he wouldn't have to hurt anymore.

*****

Darkness surrounded him, and he felt weightless as he moved through the void. Voices became louder and louder as he moved toward a small light in the distance. The closer he got, the clearer the voices became.

Mama! Papa! he cried. He tried to run to them but soon realized it wasn't by his own power that he moved. *Do you know me? I am Anton. I'm your son!* he called. Tears ran down his face as they waved, and he struggled to reach out to them. They knew him! They recognized him! It was the greatest joy he had ever known.

He had come, finally, through the dark passage when he realized they were not beckoning him but motioning him away.

"No!" he screamed. "I want to come with you! Don't leave me here!" But slowly they receded into the distance, and once again it was dark.

Are you afraid to die? came a voice.

Yes.

Then don't.

Anton opened his eyes and watched the young soldier dab his bruised face with a cool, damp cloth. Mikhail's eyes were intense, and Anton didn't dare move, afraid that the rare act of kindness would stop.

"I'm glad you are finally awake, Pavlova. I need to speak to you, and I'm running out of time," he said in a whisper. "Do you remember what I told you before you passed out?" Anton painfully shook his head, wondering if this was a new tactic to get him to talk.

"Chulpenyev has been transferred away from your cell, but I can't help what happens to you on the other shifts. I will do what I can. There's food wrapped in a blanket…" The guard looked up and listened. "Someone is coming. Try to hang on until I come again."

"Chulpenyev?" Anton whispered the unfamiliar name.

"The other guard. I must go." He stood and hurried from the cell.

Anton groped in the darkness from where he lay and pulled the blanket over him and, in doing so, found the small package Mikhail had left. For just an instant he hesitated, wondering if it might be tainted. Then, realizing the absurdity, he devoured the piece of cheese and the roll. There was also a bit of butter, which he laid directly on his tongue. It was sweet and creamy, and for almost a minute, he was euphoric.

It seemed like forever before Anton saw the young man again. He found himself wishing he would come, anxious to find out why he had been kind after all the months of cruelty. Just having the thin blanket was a luxury, and he was surprised the other guards hadn't noticed and taken it away.

He heard footsteps and moved to the corner of the cell. Keys rattled and the door opened. It was Mikhail, but he was not alone. The man with him wasn't in uniform. Anton realized he had become so accustomed to uniforms that this outsider, this civilian, frightened him even more than the guard who had beaten him.

"Mr. Pavlova."

Anton felt himself crawling, backing deeper into the corner as the man reached toward him. *I'm an animal!* he thought. "Please don't touch me. I'm sick. I'm all broken up inside," he whispered.

Mikhail knelt near him. "This man is a doctor, Pavlova. Let him look at you."

The old man touched him gently on the side of his face. His eyes were kind, and Anton hugged his hand and cried as Mikhail went to the door and stood watch. The doctor spread the blanket on the floor of the cell, where he helped Anton to lie down. Removing Anton's clothes, he examined him.

"Burn these garments, Mikhail. His whole body is infected. He must be washed and given clean clothes, and I need to bandage his ribs."

Anton lay naked on the blanket, shivering, barely able to hear the whispers.

"Will he be all right?"

"He will die from infection in days unless he gets help now. It may already be too late."

The stench of the open sores on his skin reached his nostrils, and he began to vomit. Quickly Mikhail knelt and wrapped the edges of the blanket over him. He picked up the near-weightless man and carried him out.

Anton fought to stay awake but kept blacking out, and before he knew it, he could feel warm water coming up all around him. He had been put in a tub, and Mikhail held his head above the water as the doctor held his arm.

Anton panicked when he saw the syringe in the doctor's hand, tried to wiggle free, but he soon realized that the water itself was too heavy. There was nothing he could do but watch the needle pierce his skin and slide beneath. The doctor pushed the plunger. It was too late.

*****

When Anton awoke, the light blinded him, but he soon became aware of the fresh breeze that swept in from the open window. When his eyes began to adjust, he saw the man in the corner wearing a crisp white coat reading a book. From outside the window came street sounds—automobiles and people's voices. It was music. *I'm back! I'm home!* He pushed his legs over the side of the bed, but in his weakened state, he crumpled to the floor.

"Guard!" the man yelled in Russian, and the door swung open. The young guard ran toward him and lifted him back onto the bed.

"You mustn't try to escape, Pavlova," he whispered sternly and signaled the orderly out of the room.

"I thought I was home. I thought…" Anton stopped. For the briefest moment, he'd thought his nightmare was over, that his torment had finally come to an end. "Why didn't you let me die?" he mumbled angrily.

"Pavlova…Anton. It won't be so bad after this. After what you have gone through, the commander knows that you know nothing. You would have talked by now. I've convinced him it's a waste of his time." Mikhail held a glass of cold water to Anton's lips. "I hope you can forgive me for the things I've done," he whispered.

Anton sipped the water, trying to calm himself. "Why are you helping me now?"

"I know who you are. I kept thinking I knew you from somewhere, then I remembered. Paris."

"Paris?"

"The KGB followed you. They had been warned by one of your own men about the job you were to do, but they hesitated arresting you in Paris because you were too visible, too much in the public eye. I was there. I was one of the…" He stopped when the look of suspicion flooded Anton's face. "You're wondering why I'm telling you this."

Anton tried to take a deep breath, but the tight bandages around his ribs prevented it.

"Are you in pain?" Mikhail asked when he moaned softly, but he didn't answer, his suspicion growing deeper by the minute. "I am telling you this because your brother…"

Anton's eyes grew wide.

"Yes. We knew about that too. The KGB decided not to act in Paris because it had hit the Western papers. Even TASS had picked it up. Like I said, if the whole world weren't watching you, the KGB would have taken you a year ago."

Anton couldn't believe that the soldier had told him so much. "You're putting yourself in a dangerous position," he said.

"Tell me, why didn't you help your brother defect? I know he asked you."

"What makes you think that?" Anton asked guardedly. Mikhail knew too much, helped too much.

"Sonia, the ballerina. She is KGB. But she's also in love with your brother, and as a favor, she asked me to show you kindness. She said you danced with her, and she admires you."

"What's the connection?" Anton asked.

Mikhail smiled ironically. "She is my sister."

The orderly returned with a tray of food. It was regular hospital food, but to Anton, it was a feast. Mikhail helped him sit up, and he began to eat. "My uncle is the commander," Mikhail said, and Anton looked up from his food, checking the door that the orderly had just closed behind him. "I convinced him that you would be worth more alive than dead and that you were much too professional to divulge any information. He knows that beating you is useless."

"Thank you for that." He still wasn't sure he could trust this man, who apparently played both sides, but it didn't matter. He'd saved his life.

"He's sending you to a prison camp."

"Siberia? The gulag system was shut down more than twenty years ago!"

Mikhail glanced over his shoulder. "Not completely..." he whispered.

Anton's eyes grew wide. "If I'm sent there, my people won't even know where to look for me!"

"Did you think that we could just let you go? If you follow orders, at least you'll stay alive!"

Anton sighed and took a bite. Yes, perhaps he should be grateful.

And so, it was. Anton stayed at the hospital for over a month, healing and trying to gain weight. But before he knew it, he was on a train headed for the frozen wasteland of the north.

CHAPTER 44

After days of tiresome travel, Anton, along with eight other prisoners, stepped off the train onto the crunchy white snow. He was thankful for the worn coat he had been given and wrapped its generous size tightly around his body as the blast of the freezing air hit his face.

February in Siberia. The thought was sobering.

It seemed like an eternity had passed since he'd left Three Rivers, and Hope. All he did was think about her now. Picturing her face was his only joy, the only thing that kept him alive. Often, in the prison in Moscow, he had returned to his cell anxious for time alone just to think about her, his only escape from the hours of torment.

He stood shivering, watching the soldiers talk among themselves, while keeping a watchful eye on the nine ragged men. Anton looked at the other prisoners. All wore the same expression, one of exhaustion, loneliness, and fear. He wondered if his own expression matched theirs. He looked at the prison compound, the high wire fencing on three sides, the fourth side a high wooden wall, where guards perched themselves as lookouts. Eventually, the nine men were divided into two groups. Anton and two others were held back, while the other six were escorted to the other side of the wall, apparently to another compound.

"Keep your eyes straight ahead, Pavlova, or you'll be joining them," the guard warned as Anton watched them disappear from sight. He quickly looked away and followed the other two men in the direction the guard had indicated. They were taken to a small cabin, the walls lined with bunks, and in the middle of the room stood a small black stove fueled by coal. The other prisoners gathered near the stove as the guard stood at the open door, pointing the new arrivals toward vacant bunks, and after a few minutes, he was gone.

"Welcome to Palm Springs." A tall man smiled at him.

"American?" Anton asked.

"As George Washington and Babe Ruth!" he replied with a laugh. "Sterns." He extended a hand toward Anton as the others looked on.

"Pavlova." Anton reached toward his hand, but it was abruptly withdrawn. "I'm American too," he said, frustrated. But nobody spoke; they only looked at him, except for the heavy man in the corner, whose eyes were fixed on the needle and thread that he weaved through small bits of cloth.

Anton turned away and stretched himself across a bunk in silence, and after a while, the quiet chatter of the prisoners resumed. From where he lay, he watched the big man take long, exacting stitches as he pieced together the brown and gray bits of cloth. To Anton's right, a man lay across his bunk, reading a tattered paperback of *Jane Eyre*. Anton closed his eyes and thought of Saturday nights spent on the mountain above Three Rivers. It was while watching *Jane Eyre* that Hope had cried in Jeff's arms. How long ago? Anton allowed his mind to wander, to remember, to feel Hope's warm body next to his, her warm hands gliding across his brow, pushing the hair away from his face. *I love you*, he heard her whisper, and he smiled in the darkness.

Shots were fired and Hope's warmth disappeared as Anton sat up quickly, confused about where he was, suddenly aware he had fallen asleep. It was dark, and his back ached from being curled up in a ball in an effort to stay warm.

"Get used to it, mate," came an English accent in the darkness. "It happens nearly every night. The other side of the wall. Go back to sleep."

"What goes on over there?" Anton asked.

"It's bloody awful, I've heard," the Englishman answered quietly. "They work you 'til you drop, then they do away with you, if you see what I mean. Only a few have made it back over to this side, and they say we've got it like summer camp. So keep yer nose clean."

"I'll remember that."

"Are you really an American?" he asked after a long while.

"As George and the Babe," Anton mimicked softly and gave a brief explanation for his accent. "It'll be my doom, I'm afraid," he finally said.

"Hang around me, mate. I'll teach you the Queen's English. Confuse the hell out of them all." He chuckled. "I'm John Baskerville. Everyone calls me Bask."

"Glad to meet you, Bask."

"What do your friends call you—Pavlova?"

"No." Anton thought of the name Jeff had given him, but it didn't seem wise to go by *Russia* at the moment. "Just Anton."

"Anton it is, mate." Bask fell silent and, after a few minutes, was snoring softly.

The following day, Anton was guided through the daily routines by Bask, the tall, lanky Englishman from the night before. He found him charming and funny, as much as was possible under the circumstances. It was a relief to have a companion after the long months of isolation, and eventually even Sterns came around.

The days were boring and tedious, but Anton constantly reminded himself of the alternative and continued stitching gloves or making leather goods during work hours, from five until five. At noon, they were allowed an hour of exercise, to walk around the compound.

As Bask had warned, shots were fired nearly every night, and for the first two weeks, Anton awoke each time silently mourning the poor soul whose time had come. Only rarely did the guards fire shots on the side he was on, though one man had been killed a few days before when he'd attacked one of the guards, and as always, the man they called Patch had been beckoned outside and hadn't returned for the rest of the day.

*****

He was a curious man, Patch. Large and quiet, he sat night after night in the cabin, sewing, while the others played cards or chatted among themselves.

"What are you making?" Anton asked him, picking up the edge of what he worked on so fervently.

"A blanket," he said without looking up.

"This piece has a hole in it." Anton stuck a finger through it and recognized a large letter *S* with only the top of what looked like a pine tree, the trunk of the tree now completed by his finger. *College of the Sequoias!* "Where'd you get this?"

"Where do you think?" said Patch.

Anton looked up and saw Bask and Sterns frowning at him. They went to the door and signaled him to follow.

"Where does he get the material?" Anton asked once outside, but was met with a long pause as the two men exchanged glances.

"Haven't you noticed that he leaves the cabin each time a gun is fired?"

Anton thought about it a moment, then nodded.

"He takes the clothes off the dead bodies, sometimes while they're still twitching."

Anton stood numbed, realizing that Dan had, indeed, preceded him. He had set him up, just as he had done to Hope.

After a while, he felt Bask's hand on his shoulder. "Sorry, mate. That's how old Patch stays so nice and fat. He trades the blankets for extra food. His blankets are some kind of souvenir to the soldiers who have duty here, and if they get a blanket with an embroidered bullet hole in it, it's considered all the more valuable."

"Where's the human heart in all this?" Anton asked rhetorically.

"There is no human heart in this place, mate. We all have something. With me, it's that book I read. I've read it forty-seven times, and when I reach a hundred, my time is up."

"What do you mean, your time is up?"

Bask smiled a little, catching Sterns's eyes. Sterns smiled back before walking away. "I mean, when it comes my time, I'll go jump on a guard. You know, donate my clothes to the souvenir trade!"

"You can't be serious."

"Bloody serious. It's common, you know. When a fellow just can't take it anymore, he jumps a guard and bang, it's over. Simple suicide."

Anton gave him a disgusted look.

"You surprise me, you know," Bask continued. "I always thought you spies were a cold, heartless lot. But you almost make me think you could really give a damn."

They began walking the perimeter of the compound, and Anton pulled up his collar. "I've killed. I didn't like it, but I did it. But it always had purpose."

"For Mother Russia?"

"For Miss Liberty!" Anton said nastily.

"Sorry."

"Being heartless was what made me good at what I did, but that was before I met a woman with pretty green eyes." He smiled a little. "Shot my insensitivity all to hell."

Bask laughed out loud, and before he knew it, Anton was telling him about Three Rivers, Hope, Jeff, and the others.

The two became inseparable. As they walked each day, Bask listened and laughed at the stories Anton told. He was a good listener, and was particularly interested in Jeff.

"Why are you so interested in Jeff?" Anton asked one night while they played cards.

"Just curious, I guess." Bask trumped Anton's queen of hearts with a five of spades, and Anton grimaced.

"About what?"

"Your relationship." It took a moment, but Bask smiled when Anton finally realized what it was that he was asking.

"No, no, no." Anton laughed and shook his head. "He's been father, brother, and son…and sometimes pet…but never, never that!" He threw down his ace of spades and smiled. "You have to understand. Jeff is…well, he's Jeff."

Bask watched him, but said nothing.

*****

It had been a short but curious conversation, and as the days passed, it slipped completely out of Anton's mind while he worked at the menial tasks assigned to him.

Bask often looked up from his work at Anton, who worked across the table. They had become friends, but as the weeks rolled into months, Bask seemed edgy.

"What would you do?" he asked quietly one day.

"What?" Anton looked up from his work.

"Say, if your friend Jeff made a pass at you. What would you do?" he asked nervously, and was relieved when Anton smiled.

"I used to think he had." Anton chuckled but resumed stitching leather when he looked up and saw the guard watching him. "Scared the hell out of me until I realized it was just his way," he whispered.

"What is his *way*? What does he do?"

"He touches. He likes to touch people. He's very philosophical about it. He says that touching people physically makes it easier to touch them emotionally, so he touches. Purely benign. It drove me crazy at first." He pulled the leather thong through the hole and looked at Bask. "Why do you ask?"

Bask felt his face turn red and quickly returned to his work. "No reason," he mumbled, relieved when the guard announced that it was time to quit. The scooting of chairs and shuffling of feet temporarily got him off the hook.

Once outside, they began to walk as they did each day. The bitter cold bit at their exposed skin, and they tried to burrow deep into the necks of their ill-fitting coats.

"What's up, Bask? Something's been eating at you all week," Anton said quietly as they trudged through the frozen snow.

Bask didn't reply.

"What is it?" He turned and stood in front of him, forcing him to stop.

Bask looked down at Anton, whose sapphire eyes seemed to be the only bit of color in the lifeless, dormant land. His hair was white at the temples now, blending into the blond. He was small and handsome and kind, and John Baskerville knew he loved him.

"What is it, John?" Anton's uncharacteristic use of his Christian name touched a vital nerve.

"I don't feel like walking today," he finally said. "I think I'll go back to the cabin."

THE PEBBLE AND THE MAN

Anton saw the look on his face as he turned away and watched him disappear across the compound. It was the first time Bask hadn't been with him during this hour. It was the hour they had always savored, the only time they were alone enough to really talk, and after a moment, he, too, crossed the distance to the cabin.

"I thought we were good enough friends that we could tell each other anything," he said from the door, seeing they were alone. He went and stood at the window beside his friend and looked up at the tall man. "John…"

Bask looked at him briefly, then focused his gaze outside the window. "Are you really so blind? So naive?" He turned to study Anton's face.

"I don't know what you're talking about, so let's forget it, okay?" Anton said brusquely, his body stiffened unconsciously into a defensive stance.

"I'm in love with you."

"You don't know what you're saying."

"I'm gay."

"Don't tell me that!"

Bask looked out the window once more. "It's easy for you. You have your friend Jeff, who is allowed to touch you. Even the other prisoners touch one another, pat one another's backs. They have the simple human contact that lets them know they're still alive, that they can still feel. You think you've been accepted by this group because I'm your friend, but don't you see? I'm just an outsider too." Bask turned to face him. "I was very lonely, Anton, before you came. You were accepting and friendly…"

Anton stared at him while the sounds of the other prisoners came from behind. They filed in, warming themselves by the stove, barely noticing the two. It was as though Anton had been planted where he stood as Bask crawled onto his bunk.

The following day, the menial work was done in silence and Anton walked alone during the noon hour. The next day was the same, and soon a week had gone by, then two. Finally, nearly three weeks had passed in silence.

"You want to walk with me today?" Anton had wanted to ask him for weeks but had always found it too difficult, and even now, he kept his eyes on his work.

It was a long time before Bask could reply. "I still am what I am," he whispered.

"My friend?" Anton forced himself to look up.

There was silence when their eyes met, and Bask pressed his lips into a tight line. "Yeah, mate. Still your friend," he finally replied.

At noon they walked side by side, their coats pulled up around their ears; even their mouths were covered. "Why the hell do you need so much exercise?" Bask shouted over the squalling wind, his eyes squinting from the cold. "The cabin is more comfortable even at its worst!"

"I used to be a dancer," he called back. "I want to get back into shape!"

"Yeah, you'll look real good when they bury you," Bask grumbled, then stopped to look off into the distance. "Well, I'll be damned. You don't often see that."

Anton paused to look in the same direction, where he saw a guard bringing a prisoner from the other side of the wall. After a moment, Bask began to walk, but turned around when he realized Anton wasn't with him. "What is it, mate?"

"Bauer!"

"What?"

Anton turned toward the cabin, and Bask had to run to catch up.

"Scott Bauer," Anton mumbled in disbelief. He stood aside as the prisoner was led up the steps and taken inside. He waited until the guard was gone, then hurried inside, where he found a thin, pathetic man lying on a bunk.

"Scott...Scotty!" Anton knelt over him and caught his breath when Scott Bauer turned to him, looking ancient and worn.

It took a moment before the light of recognition came to his eyes. "Pavlova?" he asked, still unsure.

"Yes, it's me, Scotty! It's Anton!"

Bauer sat up and threw his arms around Anton's neck, laughing and crying all at once.

"I thought you were dead!" Anton said. "Sanderson told me himself that you died in Iran."

"That doesn't surprise me," Bauer frowned. "Anton, we need to talk about Sanderson. Don't trust him. He sent that Philips guy ahead of you. Philips is here! He set you up!"

"He's dead." *He got what he deserved,* Anton thought.

"How do you know?"

"Let's just say I know a patch when I see one. Leave it at that."

Scott eyed him curiously but nodded assent. "How are Faye and the girls? Have you seen my family? I need to know…"

"The girls are fine, Scott. Prettier than ever," he said, and Bauer grinned.

"And Faye?" he asked excitedly, and Anton winced. "What? What's the matter? Is she okay?"

"Yes, she's well, Scotty. But Sanderson told her you were dead. She's remarried."

Bauer sat back on the bed in horror.

"Scott, she thought she was alone, and having five little girls, she felt overwhelmed. Faye and Catherine had one thing in common, you know: neither liked to be alone."

Bauer took a minute to catch his breath. "It's ironic, isn't it, Pavlova? We both married needy women, thinking it was forever. But it backfired. You lost Catherine, and now I've lost Faye, because they didn't want to be alone." Bauer winced at the irony, and Anton nodded.

"I suppose you're right."

Bauer sniffed and quickly changed the subject, obviously holding back tears. "What about you? Did you ever remarry? I heard from Dan that you were seeing someone."

"Engaged. To an independent little cuss this time." He chuckled softly. "But she's not waiting. I sent a letter to a fellow who's also in love with her. I assume they're married by now." It was the first time he had acknowledged the letter; he'd blocked it from his mind. His throat dried up, and for the first time, he realized it was over.

"My God, how could you do that?" Bauer whispered.

"I love her," he croaked. "I didn't want her to be alone. She was special." Anton shook his head and wiped his eyes. He saw the look of sympathy on Bask's face. "Scotty, this is John Baskerville, just about the only friend I have in this godforsaken place. Bask, this is Scott Bauer."

They nodded to each other. "What's wrong, Pavlova?" Bauer asked. "No one wants to be your friend? That accent giving you hell again?" They laughed a little as he looked at Bask. "I always told him he should see a speech therapist and get that damn thing fixed." He stood beside the bunk and stretched, then headed for the door.

"Where are you going?"

"Out for some air."

"Wait, I'll go with you."

"No, Anton. I need to be alone," he said, and Anton sat back down as Bauer turned and went out. He wore an odd expression, and it took a moment to register before Anton jumped to his feet.

"Scotty, don't!" he screamed, running to the door.

A single shot rang out, and he stood helpless as Scott fell to the ground. It was too late. The guard knelt in the snow, pushing Bauer's body aside as he holstered his gun.

"Oh, Scott…" Anton began to cry and felt Bask's hands on his shoulders as he wept.

Patch pushed passed them, and Anton gasped as the man headed toward his onetime friend and colleague.

"No!" he screamed. "You son of a bitch!" He darted toward Patch, and another shot rang out. The weight of Bask's body pushed him into the snow, and it took several seconds to finally wiggle free.

"John!" he cried, watching the snow turn red around him. He gathered him in his arms. "Oh, John, why the hell did you do that? It was meant for me!"

"I couldn't let them have you, mate. Besides, I'm awful tired of reading that damn book." He gave Anton a pained smile.

"Don't die, John," Anton choked, rocking him in his arms.

"I love you, mate," Bask whispered. "Can you ever forgive me for that?" He smiled, then faded in Anton's arms.

"Oh, God." Anton looked up at the two guards, who stood idly by while Patch stripped Bauer of his clothes. "Damn you all to hell!" Jumping to his feet, Anton lurched at one of them, but the guard caught him and wrenched his arms behind his back. He closed his eyes as the cold barrel of a gun pressed against his temple. He heard the hammer cock, could feel himself sweat in the cold. "Goodbye, my love," he whispered.

"Stop!" came a shout in the distance.

Anton opened his eyes.

"Don't shoot that one." A guard approached breathlessly, seemingly unaware Anton spoke Russian. "They want him back in Moscow. He's dying anyway, and they want to trade him while he's still worth something. They say the Americans have agreed to give back one of ours in exchange for him," he added, glancing at Anton, then the bodies. "That was close," he grumbled to the other guards. "You guys certainly made a mess here. Did you have to ruin their clothes?"

CHAPTER 45

When the train jolted, Anton awoke to find the guard who sat across from him staring. There was no telling how long he'd slept, only the dull ache in the back of his neck and the grogginess that took a while to shake. Outside, the land was still covered with snow, though an occasional village could be seen in the distance, indicating that they were nearing civilization. He was being returned to Moscow under special security, instead of the cattle car in which he had left, and he watched the guards relieving one another or sitting in pairs. They all stared at him curiously as they spoke among themselves about their prisoner, unaware that their language was not a barrier to him. It was a stupid blunder in security, Anton thought to himself, his training still a vital part of him. But he said nothing.

"I've never seen a dying man before," one guard had said that morning, causing Anton to wonder how many prisoners he'd shot and killed. Weren't they all dying men? He was amazed at the pitiful expressions he had earned by dying slowly, and yet there had been no pity for Bauer, or for John. He turned his face toward the window to escape the staring eyes, the ones who were trying to imagine how he felt, to make their own lives seem more valuable. Often during the trip, he had wanted to scream at them to stop staring, but suddenly, it didn't seem to matter anymore.

The frozen landscape rolled past, and he thought about Hope and the walk in the snow on Christmas the year before. The snow had been beautiful then, he had been warm and happy, but now there was only the cold, the emptiness that he prayed he had spared her by sending Noah to her.

A tear rolled down his face, and he quickly glanced at the guard, who still stared.

"Poor bastard," said the soldier who had come to relieve him, and the other man nodded.

Anton leaned his head back and closed his eyes, hoping to go back to sleep.

In time, the train screeched to a slow halt, and Anton was led under heavy guard to a car, which then sped him through the streets of Moscow. It was the middle of the night, but he was fully awake. "Where are you taking me?" he asked in English. But the soldiers remained silent until at last they came to a large building, where Anton was led inside. His handcuffs were removed, and he was given a razor and towel.

"Shave," the soldier said, then scraped his own cheek with his finger in case his English was misunderstood. He accompanied Anton into the bathroom, and Anton had to smile. The guard had been given strict instructions not to leave him alone with a razor.

But it was the first glance in the mirror that shocked him. He was thin and pale, his hair almost completely white, and as he finally scraped off the last of his whiskers, he stood staring for a moment at the unfamiliar face.

"Take off your clothes," the soldier said, pulling at his garments, and he stripped to the skin while the man started the shower. Anton could only stare in horror at the unfamiliar body riddled with scars.

After his shower, he quickly dressed in the freshly laundered clothes that were brought to him. He was then led to an office, where he was left alone for the first time. It was a full twenty minutes that he sat alone, and when the door opened, it was Mikhail Golikov.

"Mikhail!" He almost jumped with excitement. "It was a brainstorm! What a way to get me back to the States!"

"It wasn't a brainstorm, Pavlova. The hospital tests confirm..."

Anton looked at him in disbelief. "I'm not really dying." He shook his head, smiling in defiance. "It's all a hoax. You really had me going there for a while." His smile slowly faded when Mikhail didn't answer. "No..."

"I'm sorry, Pavlova." Mikhail watched him sink into the chair while he explained about the tests, but Anton barely heard the words. *Sepsis…liver…twelve to fourteen months…Alexis…*

He looked up. "What?"

"Your brother, Alexis. We've arranged for you to see him. He flew in last night."

"He's here?"

"Yes. It's almost dawn, and your government is sending a plane to fly you to Frankfurt in the morning. You only have a few hours," Mikhail continued, then went to open the door. Before Anton's eyes, his brother walked into the room.

"Anton!" Alexis threw his arms around his brother, and they cried in each other's embrace. "Anton, what have they done to you?" His eyes swept over him in shock, and after Mikhail slipped into a quiet corner and lit a cigarette, they fell into quiet conversation.

"I'm not sure I should go home, Alexis," Anton was saying more than two hours later.

Alexis frowned. "I don't believe Hope would have married Noah," he said, trying to console him.

"They've told her I'm dead. She would have no reason to wait for me."

"How do you know what they told her?" he argued.

"They give us cyanide, Alexis. If things go wrong and there is no evidence that we're alive, they assume we used it." Anton rubbed his face wearily. "If they told Bauer's wife he was dead, what do you think they told Hope? The government likes to bury things quickly. They don't like loose ends like wives and girlfriends hanging around, asking questions."

In the long silence that followed, Anton felt sorry that Alexis had been told about him. It would have been easier if he didn't know. "How's your dance?' he asked, trying to change the subject.

"How can I ever dance for my country again after what they've done to you?" Alexis hissed, glancing at Mikhail, who tried to look disinterested.

Anton looked at his brother and was frightened by what he saw. "Alexis. You *must* dance, and dance harder and better than ever. I'm running out of time, and I made you a promise I intend to keep."

Alexis shook his head. "Do you really think they will let me tour America as long as you are alive?"

The door opened, and a man in a gray suit signaled Mikhail.

"I'm sorry, Pavlova," Mikhail said. "Your plane is here. It's time."

Anton and Alexis stood, facing each other. "I'm never going to see you again, am I?" Alexis said.

"You listen to me. I swear to God, if I have to come back from my grave, I will find you! Watch for me, Alexis. Watch for me!" They stood staring at each other, words no longer necessary.

"Remember me," Alexis whispered.

"How can I forget?"

CHAPTER 46

It all seemed like a dream to Anton as he settled into the hospital room in New York. The flight had taken him to Frankfurt, to London, then home. He could just barely remember the air travel, though the hordes of reporters stuck in his mind. He was glad that Samuels had met him in London to help with the press. They had asked cruel questions, and he was exhausted, leaving him unable to speak for himself. In a matter of hours, his emotions had bounced from the highest highs to the lowest depths, and all he'd wanted to do was sleep. "Is it true that you're dying?" one brash young reporter had asked. "Why do you suppose the United States would deal with the Soviets for a dying man?"

"Ignore him," Samuels had whispered and helped Anton into the awaiting car. Without words, they had sped through the crowded streets of New York to the team of doctors who awaited him.

*****

But in the weeks that followed, the test results were the same, and Leslie Fairchild was called upon to help with the debriefing. Anton's depression made it almost impossible for the CIA to extract information, but with Leslie's help, they finally got what they wanted.

As bad as the assignment had been, as poorly planned, Anton had managed to accomplish the impossible: he had actually gotten the information the government wanted without spilling to the Soviets what he knew. But the debriefing had left him depleted, and when there was nothing more that the doctors could do, he was finally released from the hospital.

"Where will you go now?" Sanderson asked as he watched Anton pack a small bag. "The CIA still wants you, even if you can't work for very long."

Anton looked up at his onetime teacher and friend but now only saw the man who had used him. "Go to hell." He glanced at Leslie sitting quietly in the corner, then continued to pack.

"Are you going back to that woman?" Sanderson asked.

"What does it matter to you, Paul? You got what you wanted. You got your recognition." He picked up the bag and headed for the door but turned momentarily. "I feel like a gum wrapper that you used then threw in the gutter. How could you even ask me about the CIA? When I was eighteen, all I wanted to do was dance. Now I don't even have that. I'm just the guy who made you famous. What was in it for me, Paul? What was in it for me?"

Again, he glanced at Leslie and closed the door behind him. He looked down the corridor one way, then the other, realizing he had nowhere to go.

*****

Anton walked the city streets for hours, free to come and go as he pleased for the first time. With his bag thrown over one shoulder, he simply wanted to lose himself in the city.

As evening approached, he watched the prostitutes come out like relics from another time, and from the corner of his eye, he watched his own reflection following him in the glass of the storefronts. He stopped in front of a bakery, pretending to look at the cream-filled delights, the cakes and strudels. In reality, it was the unfamiliar face reflected back at him that caught his eye. After a while, he walked on, past furniture stores, ice-cream shops, until again he found the unfamiliar face staring back.

"Are you a fight fan?" a voice came from beside him, and he realized he had stopped in front of an appliance store, where the television in the window had drawn a small crowd as a boxing match drew toward its final round.

"Not much," he replied. "I only kept up with a boxer named Cavalier." He looked at the man beside him, whose eyes were glued to the set. "I've been out of the country. Did Noah Cavalier go up for the title yet?" he asked, and the man turned.

"You *really* must have been out of the country. It was in all the papers. Noah Cavalier died in the ring."

"When?" he asked urgently.

"October. They should have stopped that fight. He didn't even fight back. Christ, I lost a bundle." His attention wandered back to the set in the window, hardly noticing that Anton had bolted down the sidewalk toward the drugstore on the corner.

"Phone!" Anton demanded breathlessly at the counter, then charged in the direction the clerk had pointed. He threw some coins into the machine and dialed.

"Hello…"

Anton closed his eyes, savoring the familiar voice. "Jeff…"

"Russia? Is that you?"

"Yes. Yes, it's me!" He almost cried the words.

"We've been worried sick about you! Tried to call a hundred times, but that son of a bitch Sanderson wouldn't put me through!"

"Jeff, how's Hope?" He nervously wound the phone cord into knots around his fingers.

"She's all right, I guess. She heard about you on the news a month ago, for chrissake. First that you were coming home, then that you were dy—really sick. It was a hell of a blow to hear it on the news, Russia. Why haven't you called? She's been sitting by the phone day and night since you got home."

"I thought she was married. But I just heard on the street that Noah was killed. Is it true?" Anton felt a twinge of guilt when he prayed Jeff would confirm what he'd heard.

"Then Hope's not married?"

"Engaged," Jeff said, and Anton's heart went into his mouth. "To you, you jackass," he laughed, hearing Anton's panic in the silence, and Anton exhaled. "When are you coming home?"

"I don't know. How can I go home, Jeff? I'm dying." The words made his mouth go dry, and he closed his eyes against the silence at the other end.

"Yeah, we know," Jeff said quietly. "Come home to us, Russia. Come back where you belong."

Anton heard the tears in Jeff's voice and fought back his own as they both fell silent. He realized that he had to decide where he wanted to die, and the prospect of leaning on strangers was one he abhorred.

The operator cut in. His three minutes were up.

"Tomorrow. San Francisco." There was a click, and Anton looked at the receiver in his hand. Jeff was gone, but he had made his decision. He was going home.

*****

The moments before debarking the plane played havoc with Anton's stomach as he inched his way forward behind an old woman who carried a shopping bag. When they reached the gangway, he hurried passed the other passengers. Finally, he found himself corralled by small gates and bars designed to keep traffic moving smoothly, but beyond the crowd and the bars stood the familiar dark-haired man, whose eyes searched the weary passengers as they moved slowly through the gate.

"Jeff!" Anton shouted, waving his hand.

Jeff's gaze pivoted in his direction. "Russia!" he called back, and leapt effortlessly over the stiles to pull Anton out of the crowd. "Russia! My God!" He threw his arms around his friend, crying and laughing at once, and in his enthusiasm plopped a big kiss on Anton's cheek, which was immediately wiped off.

"God, Jeff," he laughed, "you're like a big dog!"

Jeff grinned and hugged him tight. But behind Anton's back, he grimaced with the pain of seeing his friend looking so thin. After a while, Jeff forced himself to smile. "Brought the snow with you, I see!" He ruffled Anton's white hair.

"Yeah. It happened almost overnight," he said, a little embarrassed. "First time I saw it, I thought I was looking at someone else." Anton furrowed his brow. "How do I look, Jeff, really?"

"Shocking! Absolutely shocking!" Jeff shook his head and made little clucking sounds, then laughed. "Put on another twenty pounds and a tan, you'll be fine." He threw an arm around Anton's shoulders and led him through the crowd.

The ugly airport voice sounded like music when it reached Anton's ears, but then he realized it was his name that had been announced: "Anton Pavlova, please pick up the customer courtesy line."

He frowned when the thought occurred to him that it might be Sanderson. He was tired after the long years and the demands that had gone with his job, and the anxiety that throttled him now blinded him to Jeff's knowing smile. Reluctantly he picked up the white customer phone in the lobby. "Pavlova…"

"Hi, Hotshot," came the sweet, melancholy voice, and Anton spun on his heels, scanning the crowd.

"Over here!" the voice laughed, and there, in the distant booth, he saw Hope.

The receiver fell from his hand, and he darted through the crowd until she was in his arms. He folded them around her, his lips devouring her sweetness, until finally he looked into her eyes.

"Hi, sweetheart. I'm home."

The Fourth Year

CHAPTER 47

1982

Alexis Vishnyakov stormed off the stage in a fury, his clothes clinging tight with the profuse sweat produced by the hours-long rehearsal. "It's not fair! It just isn't fair!" he screamed.

"Here, drink some water." Sonia offered him a glass, and he poured it down his throat, then threw the glass, shattering it against the wall.

"It makes me so angry! They're so stupid!" he shouted at her. Again, she tried to calm him, but he wouldn't listen. Since the Paris tour, Alexis had constantly been reprimanded for his new style, and again the director had criticized his form. "Interpretation is the difference between good and great," he fumed.

Sonia sunk into a chair in the corner. "Alexis, you're quoting your brother again. You are Russian; he is American."

"We are both dancers!" Alexis knelt in front of her. "You saw him," he whispered. "You danced with him. You know he was great! Anton was greater than I will ever be, and I am now the *premier danseur étoile*!"

His urgency alarmed her. She and Alexis had become partners, he having finally reached the highest rank for a danseur, and she already the prima ballerina. But she feared for him. Again, she asked to be allowed to reason with him while the others waited out his anger.

"Sonia," Alexis continued, "when he danced, he brought new light, new imagery, new excitement to the stage. Tell me if you think I'm wrong."

"It's not for me to say if you are right or wrong, Alexis." She frowned in grief at his behavior. He was following the same pattern as the other greats: Nureyev, Baryshnikov… "You're leaving us, aren't you?" she asked in a low voice, feeling the corners of her eyes grow moist. She put her hands on either side of his face and forced him to look at her. "Tell me."

"I don't know." He pulled away from her a little and buried his face in the towel that hung around his shoulders, fighting off the images of Anton's thin face. His problem with the Bolshoi director and what had happened to his brother, although separate incidents, kept getting muddled in his mind until he could hardly separate the two.

"Alexis, look at me," she said as she touched his hand. "You will never get to America if you continue to act like a spoiled child. If you don't want to be left behind again when we tour, I suggest you play along. Dance how they want you to dance. And smile! Perhaps your brother is already dead, or perhaps he will be by the time you make it to America. But if you don't try, you'll never make it, and for as long as he lives, he will be looking for you to come. Is that what you want—Anton searching for you for the rest of his life?"

The silence between them was unapproachable as her words dug into his heart.

"Why are you trying to help me, Sonia?"

"I am content in the Soviet Union. Russia is my home. I have my family. But for you, my love, there is no contentment. I see that now. There is so much more out there for one such as you, and I want you to be happy."

He looked into her soft brown eyes and longed for the contentment he saw, just as he wished he could have fallen in love with her as she had with him. *Poor Sonia,* he thought, *torn between wanting me and wanting to set me free.*

"When your time comes, Alexis, I'll grieve the loss. But I'll help you if I can. For now, you must dance. And dance as they want you to. And smile as they want you to smile. Only you can know what is in your heart."

Alexis heaved a sigh. She was right, and he knew it. But to play the contented dancer when his heart burned with rage was almost more than he could bear. Already he found dancing a mockery of what he felt.

He finished the rehearsal, but as he did, he wondered if the others saw the invisible strings that had been affixed to his arms and legs. *Like the puppet Petrouchka.* He wondered, too, if they could see him tear at them with his mind.

CHAPTER 48

Leslie got out of the car and stared at the farmhouse, laughing aloud. Anton, Jeff, and Clay were all up on ladders, attaching a giant red streamer around the house and a huge bow atop the porch roof. "What are you doing?" she called. "You're supposed to be getting ready for the wedding!"

Anton glanced at his watch. "The wedding!" He jumped down from the ladder and hurried past Leslie but turned momentarily to kiss her on the cheek and say hello to Nathan, who sat in her car. "Clay, could you help with Uncle Nate?" he called behind him and disappeared, leaving a trail of laughter.

"He looks good," Leslie said as Clay approached.

"Between my sister and my wife, you'd think he's being fattened for slaughter!"

"I understand you've gotten married since we met," she said.

"And I'm almost a papa!" he answered, spreading his arms wide to indicate Nicki's girth.

"That's wonderful," she said, then looked back at the adorned house. "What are you guys doing?"

Clay looked at Nathan and smiled. "This, Dr. Fairchild, is what happens when a Russian asks you to help wrap his wedding gift for his bride." He waved his hand toward the house, and they laughed.

"Where's Hope?" Nathan asked.

"She stayed the night with me and Nicki," Clay said. "We're meeting them at the church later."

Sixteen years before, it had been Nathan that Clay had gone to when he'd learned the details of Hope's birth. It was everyone's beloved Uncle Nate who'd comforted and advised him, and now he stooped beside the car and looked into the old man's eyes.

"Ironic, isn't it? Seeing each other on Hope's wedding day," he said quietly, and Nathan gave him a benevolent smile.

"I told you it would all work out someday, didn't I, son? Now help me out, Clayton. My chair is in back."

Clay did as he was told.

*****

Three hours later, the men piled out of the car, all looking quite handsome, including Nathan, who sported a rather large bow tie. They went into the church, where Hope waited nervously. They had decided on a church wedding. "It would make me feel more married," she'd said, and Anton had laughed, shaking his head. "Well, I certainly want you to feel as married as possible!" And so, Hope had made arrangements with the little church at the end of town, where she had attended with her grandparents as a child.

She found herself standing at the altar, listening to the pastor read Bible passages, and she turned to look at Anton. He was still a handsome man, she thought, only differently so. His beautiful blue eyes and white hair, along with his new gray suit, gave him a cool, refreshed look.

Jeff leaned forward slightly and winked at her from Anton's other side, and she smiled.

She said her vows and listened as Anton said his with passion and meaning. Anton leaned forward and kissed her gently. "I love you, Mrs. Pavlova," he whispered as they turned. After being smothered with hugs and kisses, Hope knew it was the happiest day of her life.

*****

"Why are we stopping here?" she asked Clay, who parked the car on the gravel road at the foot of the driveway. She turned around and saw that the cars behind them were doing the same. Jeff got out of one and helped Nathan into his wheelchair while everyone piled out. "What's going on?" she asked.

Anton handed her a piece of paper. "It's your wedding present. You'll have to get out to see."

From the look on Clay's face, she knew they were in cahoots. She slowly got out of the car and was led to the top of the drive.

"Anton!" The farmhouse wore a giant red bow, and all around the porch hung baskets of beautiful flowers. "I don't understand."

Anton and Nathan grinned at each other, and he tapped the paper she held in her hand. "It's the deed. The ranch is paid in full: all legal." He withdrew a pen from his breast pocket and pointed to a line. "Sign here, sweetheart. Hope Pavlova." The name tasted sweet in his mouth, and he smiled as she looked at him in astonishment. He took her in his arms and kissed her until someone coughed, reminding him they were not alone. Laughing a little, he led her inside.

*****

It was an open-house affair. A lot of Jeff's and Clay's friends came, as well as several of Nathan's "children." Among the eventual crowd were a number of curiosity seekers who realized that the famous American spy from the newspapers was none other than the man who'd shot Steven Wykes. But those were few and eventually were politely culled out by Jeff and Clay.

"Smile!" a voice came, and when Anton turned, there was a flash in his face. "Don't you think getting married when you only have a year to live is a waste of time?" the voice said as he tried to clear his vision. When the bright spots faded, he was looking at the brash young reporter from New York.

"What are you doing here?" he demanded.

"Press." The man flashed an identification card in his face.

"Let me introduce you to my best man," Anton said, reaching through the crowd and tugging at Jeff's sleeve. "He'll be glad to show you *his* ID!" Anton glared as he watched Jeff escort the man off the property.

"Thanks," he said when Jeff returned, and he smiled when his friend switched glasses with him, his empty one for Anton's full. "You're a good man, Lansing," Anton said in a low voice.

"I'm the *best* man, Pavlova!" Jeff said, and joined Valerie in the corner of the room.

The food and champagne flowed, the guests elbow to elbow. Occasionally Anton and Hope spotted each other and smiled, longing to be together. But when Anton turned back around after one such contact, his eyes fell on the man who stood by the door.

It was JC Landrum.

"What the hell do *you* want?" Anton growled, hoping to take care of the matter before Hope spotted him. But JC stood, his ill-fitting suit in dire need of brushing. Then Anton realized that he had, indeed, come in a suit and tie. It threw him for a moment.

"I heard my little girl was getting married," JC answered nervously. "I had hoped for an invitation, but I guess that was expecting a little too much."

"If I recall, you made a point to tell her in front of all her friends that she *wasn't* your little girl."

JC's gaze dropped away from Anton's. "I'm sorry. Tell her…tell her I've stopped drinking and I'm sorry. For everything." He turned to leave.

Anton stopped him. At first, he wasn't sure why, but something stirred in him that he finally recognized as compassion—compassion for a man who'd suffered with the same disease that he had always struggled with, had always hidden. "How long have you been dry, Landrum?" he asked beneath the music.

"A year, almost. Eleven months."

"Rough?"

"Yeah, sometimes it's been real rough." JC stood awkwardly, unsure whether or not he was being kicked out. He glanced in Hope's direction, where she was laughing and talking with Nicki and Clay. "She sure looks like Clayton. Like McClain…" he said, and Anton saw pain in the man's eyes as though he realized he had robbed himself. "Well, I won't trouble you anymore. Go back to your party," he said, then turned to leave.

"Would you like to talk to her?" Anton asked, but he shook his head.

"Just tell her what I said."

"Daddy?" Hope's voice came from behind him, and when he turned, he found her standing beside her new husband. Their eyes locked for a moment until finally he had to look away. "Would you like to come in and have something to eat? Uncle Nate is here. When's the last time you saw him?"

JC's eyes filled, and he shifted his weight nervously.

From a distance, Anton caught Leslie's eye, and she smiled, nodding her approval. He realized she was right. *Healing begins here,* he thought. It was time.

"There's iced tea in the kitchen. I'm sure Hope would be glad to help you." Anton extended a welcoming hand to JC, who hesitated at first, then accepted it gratefully.

*****

Anton was weary by the time most of the guests had left. Only a handful remained. JC had volunteered to drive Nathan back to Monterey, allowing Leslie to stay a little longer. The caterers were cleaning up, and Hope danced with Jeff while the rest of them sat around, talking and laughing.

"Isn't the groom going to dance with the matron of honor?" Nicki teased. "Or is a seven-months-pregnant woman repulsive to you?"

Anton smiled wearily. He didn't have the heart to tell her how tired he was. The two months at home had not replenished the energy that the year before had stolen. "Sure, I'd like to dance with you." He rose from his seat and put his arms around her, laughing at the big belly that was in the way. "Being tall and pregnant sure makes it difficult for us short guys, Nick," he said, but suddenly frowned and stepped back.

"It's all right. It just kicked," Nicki said.

Leslie immediately rose to her feet.

"Are you going to dance with me or what?"

"Of course, I am. You look especially beautiful these days," he said. He offered his hand, and they began dancing once again.

Leslie let out a sigh of relief. *Yes,* she thought. *Healing begins here.*

CHAPTER 49

Thomas McClain Philips was four days old, and the beam on Clay's face was unmistakably one of pride. He clumsily passed the infant into Anton's nervous hands. Hope and Nicki giggled from the kitchen as Anton's eyes widened with awe.

"My, is he supposed to be this little?" he asked.

"He was over nine pounds. Trust me, he's big enough," Clay laughed, hovering over his son. "Feel that grip!"

Anton offered the child his little finger as Clay had done. Little Thomas wrapped his tiny fingers around Anton's. "Good heavens!" he exclaimed, then looked at Clay. "How's it feel to be a daddy?"

"Like nothing I've ever felt before." Clay shook his head, proclaiming the question unanswerable. "How's it feel to be an uncle?" he asked, and laughed at the shock on Anton's face.

"I am! I'm an uncle! I never thought of that." Anton felt an odd sensation settle in the pit of his stomach, one of anxiety and responsibility, but it was countered with sudden attachment and love. "*Family,*" he whispered to himself, feeling a twinge of grief for Alexis. His eyes filled as he smiled nervously at Thomas, pressing his lips together to stop the rush of emotions. He hardly even noticed when Clay was beckoned out of the room and Hope took his place on the couch.

"What do you think?" she teased, carefully watching his eyes.

"This is incredible," he said. "I've seen pictures, but I've never actually held a newborn before." He cooed and clucked at the baby on his lap.

"Pick him up," she suggested, but Anton was reticent. "Oh, come on. He won't bite," she teased, until he finally lifted the child to his shoulder.

Anton was overwhelmed by the soft, warm body that lay against him, and the fuzzy little head that bobbed and bumped against his neck. He chuckled quietly. "I like being an uncle," he proclaimed, and Hope smiled.

"How would you like to be a daddy?" she asked.

He looked at her, speechless.

Her face wrenched into a pathetic look of abandonment.

"Hope, are you telling me..." he began in a hoarse voice.

Hope's mouth gaped for a moment, as if to speak, but then she bit her bottom lip.

"My God, Hope, I thought we agreed! You said you'd take care of that!"

"Please don't be angry," she cried. "I want it. I *need* it!" Rivulets of tears flowed down her face as she begged him to understand. "Don't you want our baby?"

"I'm dying, Hope!" He stood quickly, and little Thomas began to wail as Hope tensed backward into the couch. The jolt of Anton's words was the first time she had faced the reality of his impending death, and when he turned and saw the expression on her face, he ached for her. "Hope, sweetheart. There's nothing like holding a baby to make a man realize his responsibilities. I won't *be* here!"

"I've held your baby, Anton," she said. "I know what the weight of the world feels like." The gentle reminder was painful, but she just had to make him understand. He had lamented for Rose for months after she'd told him. She couldn't believe he didn't want this baby now.

Thomas finally stopped crying and attached himself firmly to his uncle by two fistfuls of hair. Anton held out his free arm, and Hope went to him. They hugged in silence.

What was there to say? he wondered, kissing the top of her head.

"Oh, little one," he cooed as the baby gurgled in his arms. "You finally found it, didn't you? I offered you anything in New York, but there was nothing you really wanted. Now you've found it." He backed away just enough to see Hope's face. "You finally found something you wanted so badly you felt you had to take it." He smiled slightly. "You're a tricky lady," he continued. "You bring me to Nicki and Clay's and put a baby in my arms to get me all primed. I should call foul."

She looked up and caught the tail end of a smile. "Are you angry?"

"Yes, irrevocably," he said.

"Do you forgive me?"

"No," he said, and Hope buried her face against his chest. "Ask me if I understand."

"Do you understand?" she asked, looking up with hope in her eyes.

"Yes, my love. I understand," he whispered. He pulled the baby's hand away from his face and kissed her tenderly. "I'm not happy. Raising a child by yourself will be hard. I'm so sorry I won't be here to help you. But yes, Hope, I understand."

He understood other things, too. Her pregnancy imprisoned them in Three Rivers, where their friends could help take care of them, and the question of going to San Francisco was out. He ached with the need to search for Alexis, his desire to buy the studio, to browse the bookstores and museums. But one fact remained. Because of her difficulty in carrying a child, she would need care—the kind of care that he'd counted on her to give him during the final stages of his illness. Unfortunately, they were both due at the same time, just when they would need each other the most.

*****

Jeff watched the gloomy face as Anton picked at his food. They had fallen into the comfortable habit of having lunch together twice a week at the Noisy Water Café, and for two weeks now, Anton hadn't been much company.

"Atlas," Jeff interrupted Anton's thoughts. "Wasn't that his name?"

"What?"

"Atlas, you know, that Greek guy who carried the world on his shoulders." He sipped his coffee and watched Anton smile. "It was something like that. Atlas…Anton…I can't remember."

Anton chuckled quietly. "I'm a dying man with a pregnant wife. It's not the world, but it's enough."

"Let me carry some."

"Which half do you want, the dying half or the pregnant half?" he joked, but the seriousness on Jeff's face sent a shiver down his spine.

"I want you both, Russia. I know you want to go to the bay. I'll come and take care of you. If I didn't have to pay rent, I could live comfortably on my VA disability." Jeff continued to expound on his well-laid plan while Anton listened in disbelief.

"Jeff, I couldn't let you do that. You've been Clay's partner for years, and if you take that kind of leave, he'll have to find someone else."

"We've already discussed it. He wants what's best for his sister. Everyone knows you're itchy to go to the bay, and if I go with you, there won't be a need for you to stick around here." Jeff smiled at the look on Anton's face. "You're still not used to everyone knowing your business, are you? Well, it has its good points."

Anton moistened his lips and looked at the man who sat across from him. What had once been amusement in his eyes was now gentleness and compassion, and for that moment, he felt a bond that he had never felt before. "Why, Jeff? Why would you disrupt your whole life for such a crummy job? Do you even know what you're offering to do? I need someone to help me die."

Jeff looked thoughtful for a moment, then finally leaned forward and spoke in a calm, clear voice. "Bud came to me once. She needed me, and right or wrong, I was there for her. And now you need me too, and I'll tell you the same thing I told her. I can't have you going to strangers, Russia. Not for this."

The Christmas Eve he had walked in on them, he'd known his life was changed. It had been a forewarning of the duty that lay ahead, and the experience with Rose had been a test of his courage.

"I told you a long time ago, I'll be there for you, Russia. You can come to me."

The Russian quickly wiped his face, moved by the passion in Jeff's voice, and was relieved when he sat back and grinned.

"Finish your coffee, old man. I'll buy you an ice cream."

CHAPTER 50

Jeff felt an ache in the pit of his stomach as he watched Anton sitting in the chair beside him. In front of them was an ornate oak desk, behind which sat a solemn-faced man with an overly pleasant smile. He watched while Anton spoke quietly and couldn't help but think that under normal circumstances, his friend would never have allowed such pretense. He felt numb, except for the cold knot in his stomach, and wondered what to do with his hands. He felt immobilized while Anton made his own funeral arrangements, his voice remaining soft and calm, showing no sign of sadness or regret.

Anton had asked Jeff to accompany him, not wanting to be alone and not wanting to leave the burden to Hope, who had burdens enough of her own. Jeff was his friend, always had been. Even during the brief encounter with Hope, he'd known Jeff had never meant to hurt him.

The funeral director stepped out to find brochures, and Anton turned to the man beside him, but Jeff looked away.

"Jeff, it's all right," he said, reaching for his hand. He squeezed it and didn't let go, remembering how frightened he once had been of Jeff's touch, only now finding solace there.

"Jesus Christ, Russia. How can you do this?" Jeff's face contorted, and tears broke through his tightly closed lids.

"This part is easy. It's the dying that's hard." Anton swallowed and looked up as the director came in and sat across from them. He glanced at their tightly clasped hands and gave a disapproving look that made Jeff uncomfortable.

"Jeff..." Anton looked at his friend. "That's all right too."

*****

"Let me buy you a drink. You could probably use one," Anton said as they walked slowly down the San Francisco sidewalk. The bells of distant cable cars brought them comfort.

"No, no thanks," Jeff said after a moment's hesitation, and Anton smiled.

"Don't worry, Jeff. I'm still just a Coca-Cola cowboy," he said.

It was late afternoon, and the bar was just beginning to fill. The two sat quietly in the back, watching the comings and goings of the barkeeps as they prepared for the evening rush. There was a song on the jukebox, and a loud-voiced woman sat at the end of the bar, trying all too hard to find someone to help fill the empty night ahead. Anton thought of all the empty nights he had tried to fill in just the same way. He wished he could tell her it would only make her lonelier in the end. But then, that was what Leslie had tried to tell him, to no avail. It had taken Hope's sweet love to save him from dying a bitter man.

He thought of her now and looked at Jeff, who stared blindly into his beer. "I hate for Hope to be alone."

The words made Jeff look up. "She won't be alone, Russia. Clay and I will see to that."

"I don't mean like that." He felt his face twitch nervously. "She needs someone who can hold her, kiss her, someone who can make love to her." He swallowed hard. "I can't even do that anymore."

Jeff looked at him sadly. When they had first come to the bay five months ago, Anton had been full of energy. He'd spent hours upon hours dancing, teaching, and had energy to go out afterward to dinner or the ballet.

"You know," he continued, "there were five of us guys in the beginning and only two women. I sure thought there would be better odds for Hope." He took a sip of his cola. "I sure wish Noah was around. He was in love with her. But he's gone. Clay is her brother, and Dan is dead. *I'm* dead. You, Jeff, you're the only one left. What do you say?" Anton looked at him intensely, but Jeff continued to stare into his beer.

"You know that Val and I are talking about getting married."

"Do you love her?"

"She doesn't mind that I can't have kids, Russia. How many Irish Catholic girls am I going to find that don't want kids?"

"Shit!" Anton said. "What the hell is this, the bruised-and-reduced sale? You're twice as good a man as she's ever had, and you know it! If you're in love with her, marry her, but if it's kids you want, take my wife. I've already got one started for you!"

Jeff looked at the angry Russian and tried unsuccessfully not to laugh. "Last time I took her, you got pissed!"

Anton exploded with laughter, and together they laughed until they cried.

Finally, when they settled down to a chuckle, Anton signaled for another round. He reached into his pocket for money, his vision still blurred from tears. "I can hardly see," he laughed and wiped his face, pouring the contents of his pocket onto the table. He scooted it around, looking for the right change.

"Shit, no wonder you're short, you've got rocks in your pockets," Jeff said, spotting the smooth gray stone among the change. "Didn't anyone ever tell you that'll stunt your growth?" He grinned as the barmaid set another beer in front of him.

But instead of laughing, Anton only slipped the stone back into the pocket from which it had come. "I'm sorry, Jeff. I had no right to ask you about Hope."

"Forget it," he answered, wondering why Anton hadn't laughed.

Another coin dropped into the jukebox, and soon Willie Nelson's voice filled the room.

"You've always known who you were, haven't you, Jeff," Anton began after a while. "I accused you of being gay once, and instead of backing off to prove me wrong, you simply told me to stay out of your way."

"I don't know what you're getting at."

"I envy you," Anton continued, pulling the stone from his pocket again. He placed it in the middle of the table. "I've carried this pebble around with me to remind me of who I am. But you… you know who you are and you're comfortable with it." Jeff glanced at him curiously, and he smiled, explaining how the pebble had come to him. "You are who you are, Nathan said. Stop racing against yourself, you'll only lose." Anton turned the pebble between his fingers, studying it. "You've always known who you were, and you like yourself. That's nice. There must be great peace in that. John Baskerville knew who he was too. He had just begun the struggle to accept it when he died."

"What do you think I am now?" Jeff asked quietly.

"That's the joke, isn't it? The joke was on me. The point is this, Lansing: It doesn't matter what you are. You *are* my friend. You *are* sensitive, giving, and free." Anton narrowed his eyes. "You are what you are, gay or straight. I tried to pigeonhole you, and the joke was on me because now I'm dying and the only one I trust to help me go down easy is you, Jeff Lansing, no matter *what* you *are*."

"I'm straight…"

"I don't give a damn!" Anton said. "Didn't you hear what I just said?" His face contorted, as though he would cry, and Jeff realized he was struggling against the inevitable.

Jeff stood, went around the table, and sat beside his friend, putting his arm around Anton's shoulders.

"I'm just learning," Anton said angrily. "I'm just now finding out who I am and who the people are around me."

Jeff said nothing, only waited while Anton regained control.

"I'm sorry," he said after a while. "I'm usually not given to self-pity."

"You're entitled," Jeff said, and Anton leaned back in his chair, exhausted.

"I want you to have this," he said after a long while. He slipped the ring off his middle finger. "It's large on me, so it might fit you."

"But that belonged to Alexis and your father…"

"And now to you, from one brother to another." Anton rubbed his face and sighed. "I'm all right. Let's go."

"Good thing *you're* all right. I'm afraid you've gotten me a bit drunk." He flashed a grin as he tossed Anton the keys. They wove through the crowd with Jeff's hand still on Anton's shoulder. "I'm telling you, Russia, you'll never grow with rocks in your pockets," he said as they strolled to the car.

It was so much like Jeff, Anton thought, to joke when he was afraid to cry. He looked at the long hand draped over his shoulder and smiled as Jeff fingered the simple gold band.

CHAPTER 51

Hope's pregnancy was in full bloom, and she fidgeted in the seat beside Anton, trying to get comfortable. The ballet was wonderful tonight, and as always, Anton searched the dancers' faces, hoping and praying to find his brother. He was out of time, and he prayed that Alexis would make his appearance tonight. The pain was almost impossible to conceal. He hoped that Hope's fidgeting would overshadow his own.

From the corner of his eye he saw Jeff looking at him. Hope handed Jeff the opera glasses and pointed toward the stage. He humored her and looked where she had pointed, then handed them back, only to look at him again. *He knows,* Anton thought. *He knows it's my last ballet.*

He touched Hope's hand, then patted her belly and smiled. "I want my child to know the ballet, sweetheart. Bring her here. I don't ask that she dance unless she wants to, only that she is exposed to it."

"How do you know it's a 'she,' Hotshot?" Hope teased. She looked absolutely radiant in the new dress he had bought her.

"I can feel it in my bones," he grinned, but gritted his teeth with pain when she turned away. He glanced at Jeff, who still watched him. "I need a little water," he whispered in Hope's ear and kissed her cheek.

Jeff watched him leave the darkened auditorium and longed to follow, but knew it would alarm Hope. He kept an eye on his watch. Five minutes passed, then ten.

After fifteen, he leaned toward her and whispered, "I'll be right back," then quickly disappeared.

He walked out into the lobby and checked around, then looked in the washroom, but Anton was nowhere to be found. "Excuse me." He approached two men who chatted quietly over cigarettes. "I'm looking for a short fellow with white hair. Have you seen him? About fifteen minutes ago."

"There was a guy staggering around here a while ago," the taller man said. "I think he's drunk."

"Where'd he go?"

"Outside. It's pouring rain, but I figured it would help him sober up."

"Oh, God," Jeff mumbled and headed for the door.

Outside, the rain quickly soaked his evening jacket, and the rain-drenched streets shone with the bright lights of passing automobiles, hampering his vision. "Russia!" he called. "Russia, where are you?" He strained to see through the pouring rain, and as a bolt of lightning split the night, he spotted a dark mass on the sidewalk. "Russia! Oh, my God!" he cried, and ran down the street.

He knelt beside the man who lay crumpled on the wet pavement, gathering him up in his arms. "Russia, it's me. I'm here," he said, holding Anton's face close to his own.

Anton opened his eyes for a brief moment. "Jeff," he whispered. His voice was almost gone as the storm beat down on them. "Take me home, Jeff. Don't let me die in the rain."

*****

"We almost made it, didn't we, my love?" Anton's eyes didn't open for a while, and Hope looked up at Jeff in panic. "I'm here." Anton looked at her and smiled. "You looked beautiful tonight, all pretty and round."

"The baby's going to be here any day, Hotshot," she said, as if a bribe could keep him from dying.

"Jeff..." He turned his head and took his friend's hand, feeling the ring he had given him. "Kiss the baby for me. Tell her it's from Daddy." The words were sweet on his lips, like sweet cherry wine. *Daddy.* He closed his eyes and savored the sound of it.

"Stick around and kiss her yourself," Jeff said to be funny, but failed.

Anton squeezed his hand for the effort. He loved Jeff more than he'd thought he could ever love a man. "My friend, I won't be here to see the sun rise."

Hope sobbed and laid her head on Anton's chest. The pain of watching him die was more than she could bear. She was grateful for Jeff's presence. His strong hand held her shoulder while Anton feebly stroked her hair.

"I'm not scared anymore. Don't cry. Don't waste the time we have left," he said. "Hope, you must do something. Someday you must have my grandmother's journals translated, so my little girl will know her heritage. I always meant to read them to you, but we had so little time…and so much of that, we wasted." He tensed as a bolt of pain shot through him, and he squeezed his eyes tight until it lessened.

"I'll get your medicine," Jeff said as he started to stand.

"No," Anton said, waiting for the pain to subside. "I want to be awake. I want to feel Hope beside me. Help her, Jeff."

Jeff rose and walked around the bed. He helped her slip out of her beautiful maternity dress, and he laid it on the chair while she crawled beneath the covers beside Anton, who smiled as her big belly wiggled and churned.

"I love my baby," he said, laughing a little. "I know I was upset at first, but I'm glad you have her. Tell her that Daddy loves her and he's sorry he missed her birthday…"

Both Hope and Jeff wept silently. Jeff lay down beside Anton and stretched his long arms around the couple and their unborn child. "Do you want to be alone?" he asked with difficulty.

"Stay, Jeff. I don't want Hope to be alone."

"Anton, please don't die!" she cried, but he only smiled gently.

"I must, my love. I've seen Mama and Papa again, and this time, they beckon."

"Tell them to wait!"

"My daughter must see the ballet. Promise me, both of you. I'm making you both accountable," he said anxiously, and after they both promised, he seemed content. They lay together in silence, with only a gentle, bittersweet laugh from the small man, whose baby rolled and tumbled within its warm fluid nest beside him. There was no more pain, no more time, only the people he loved most in the world. "I love you, dear Hope, more than all of creation. Thank you for making me whole," he whispered, and a moment later, he was gone.

*****

Anton had been right, Jeff thought as he stood at the front door, watching fingers of sunlight shoot up in the east. He hadn't lived to see the sun rise. Jeff took a deep breath of the damp morning air, but it came out jagged and broken. They had taken Anton away, and somehow he couldn't bring himself to close the door behind them. He stood against the doorframe, watching in the direction the coroner had gone.

"Jeff!" Hope's voice echoed throughout the house. "The baby!"

He raced to her room, where he found her gripping the blankets around her. Her eyes were on fire, and tiny beads of sweat had already formed on her brow. "I'll call the doctor," he said, grabbing some towels and packing them around her.

"It's too late! It's coming!" She gulped another breath of air and pushed.

"Bud, don't push. Stop it!" he yelled, but again she bore down with a vengeance.

"I need you, Jeff," she cried. "Help me."

"I can't. I don't know how."

"You're a cop!"

"What the hell does that mean?"

"Cops deliver babies!" Again, she took a deep breath and bore down.

"Only on TV. Stop that, Bud!" He started for the phone, but she grabbed his arm and pulled him between her knees. "Holy Mary, Mother of God." Jeff crossed himself. She was right. There was no time. The baby was out to its ears.

For an eternity, Hope's sobs were only background noises as he coaxed and pleaded, sometimes in frustrated shouts, other times in gentle whispers.

"It hurts," she cried.

"I know, Bud. Try again," he cooed, and with the next push, the head was out.

"What is it?"

"We haven't got that far yet. You just pay attention to your end," he teased, and she tried to smile, but another pain shot through her. *Poor Hope,* he thought, looking into her frightened, ravaged face. Nothing had ever come easy. "Push, Bud." He eased the left shoulder out, and with only one more push, the slippery infant glided into his arms.

"Why isn't it crying?" she said in a panic. For an eternal moment, her world came to an end.

But Jeff quickly wiped the baby's face and gave it a pinch, bringing forth a healthy, lusty squall. "Oh my gosh," he said, laughing. "Would you look at this? It's Russia with a dirty face!" He took off his shirt and wrapped it around the baby.

Hope watched the dark-haired man as he sank into a world of his own, the baby as much a part of him as he would ever know. "It's Russia, Bud. It looks just like Russia!" Laughing through his tears, he checked the baby again. "Well, not all over. It's a girl, just like he said it would be." He pressed his mouth against the baby's soft wet cheek and kissed her. "That's from Daddy, little one," he whispered. "He's sorry he missed your birthday."

After a few minutes, Jeff handed the baby to Hope, who immediately took her to her breast. She closed her eyes to rest while Jeff called the doctor. Mother Earth had given her back a piece of Anton before taking him to her own bosom forever.

The Years After

CHAPTER 52

Jeff sat on the park bench and watched the drops of rain plop heavily into the puddle, only to look up and see a tall strawberry-blond woman heavy with child.

"I said, you're getting wet," she repeated. She looked at him a moment longer and continued when he didn't speak. "I'm going past the parking lot if you want to share my umbrella."

"Didn't your mother ever tell you it's dangerous to talk to strangers?" he said.

"Didn't your mother ever tell you to come in from the rain?" she retorted.

"Look lady, three days ago I delivered a baby on the same bed where my best friend died just the hour before. Yesterday I buried him, and today my girlfriend left me because I wasn't giving her enough attention. I've got nothing left to give. Leave me alone. I'm tired." Jeff blinked rain from his eyes as thunder rolled in the distance.

"Aren't you charming? I suppose catching your death out here will fix all that."

He looked up at her again.

"I live nearby. Come on, I'll fix you some tea."

"I suppose you'll tell your husband I followed you home, and he'll let you keep me as long as I sleep under the porch."

She stifled a laugh. "I don't have a husband."

"Boyfriend…"

"I don't have one of those either."

He looked at her protruding stomach but dropped the subject. "Aren't you afraid I might try something?"

"Are you?"

"No."

"Well, I don't have anything to steal, and I'm already pregnant. I figure that anyone who doesn't know when to come in from the rain and looks as pathetic as you do can't be all that dangerous."

"You don't know that." Jeff's dark curly hair hung heavy, matted around his face by the rain. "I could be a bum who just lives in the park."

"No. You're not a bum," she said. "Nice watch, nice shoes… your shirt is tucked into your pants. A bum would have figured out how to get a blanket or a coat. You have neither. You just look like some poor, lost soul."

She smiled beautifully as Jeff found himself rising to his feet.

"My name is Linda Walker."

"Jeff Lansing."

Before he knew it, he sat in a grungy little second-floor apartment and she was handing him a cup of hot tea. The tiny kitchen was gray and depressing, made even more so by the naked forty-watt bulb that hung over the table. "Been here long?"

"Six months." She sat across from him with her cup poised in front of her, sipping it quietly. They studied each other for a few minutes until she finally broke the silence. "I have three uncles and a brother, all of whom are priests. They're paying the rent on this place so my mother's wealthy friends won't know I'm pregnant."

Jeff nodded and sipped his tea. "Won't they get a little suspicious when you bring home a baby?"

"I'm not bringing it home. That was the deal. I have to give it up for adoption, or my family will disown me."

The thunder roared outside, and Jeff watched Linda as she stood to get more hot water, which she offered him. He nodded and thanked her. "What about the father? Or is that too personal?"

She smiled, dipping her tea bag into her cup. "That's funny. I saved my virginity until I was twenty-one. My friends threw me a party and I drank too much. I woke up pregnant."

"That's a kick in the pants."

"Yeah, I don't even know if I had fun. I have no idea who the father is. So what about you? I saw you sitting on the bench. When it started raining, you didn't even seem to notice."

"I already told you."

Linda put down her cup and looked at him seriously. "You mean that was the truth? My, aren't we a pathetic pair!" She appeared pleased when he finally smiled. "You're very handsome when you smile. You have nice eyes."

"I haven't shaved for three days, and I'm soaked to the bone. If Russia were here, he'd tell me I look like shit." He winced. "Sorry."

"Russia. That's a funny name," she said.

Jeff elaborated a little, but stopped midsentence. He turned his head to wipe his eyes, and she looked the other way to give him privacy.

"You must have loved him very much," she said after a while.

"Yes...very much." He looked down for a moment. "I bet you think I'm gay," he said, not sure why.

"Does it matter?"

"No. It doesn't matter. Even Russia didn't care what people thought anymore." Jeff turned away again. The only sounds were those of traffic outside the sheet-draped window and the slow, methodical drip of the kitchen faucet.

"I'll tell you what I think. I think you should go into the bathroom and change out of your wet clothes. I'll hang them by the stove. There's a razor in the drawer. Feel free to use whatever you need."

Jeff hesitated, but the alternative was to go back out in the rain and walk home. Finally, he nodded and disappeared into the bath.

After he was shaven and dry, exhaustion took over. With Hope in the hospital and Anton gone, he desperately needed a good night's sleep. But his clothes were taking forever to dry. After Linda offered him a simple but warm dinner, the warmth of the blanket wrapped around him lulled him into a peaceful rest on the couch.

*****

"Jeff?" Linda nudged him a little.

He sat up. "What time is it? Are my clothes dry?" He realized he had fallen asleep. It was dark, except for the dim light in the kitchen.

"It's ten thirty, and no, they're still damp. But it's still pouring outside. Why don't you stay the night?" she suggested.

"No. I shouldn't have stayed this late. I don't want to cause you any problems." He stood quickly and momentarily lost his bearings.

"That's very noble. But it's too late for me to worry about my reputation. Stay. It's all right."

He sat back down, finally agreeing that it made no sense to go back out.

"You're sitting on my bed," she said.

Jeff jumped up again, realizing it was a fold-out couch. "Now that you mention it, I didn't see a bedroom."

"No. This is it."

He helped her get it ready, then stood dumbly while she slipped between the covers. "We'll have to share," she said dryly. "This is all I have." She turned over on her side while he dropped the blanket and slid in beside her.

Tired as he was, he found it difficult to get back to sleep. Pictures of Anton raced through his mind, along with Hope and the baby. Hope had named her Anna, after the famous ballerina from the turn of the century. It was what Russia had wanted, Hope told him.

Anton had fathered three children and never had the pleasure of holding even one. The thought made Jeff sad beyond belief. Tears came all too easy now. *And poor Bud,* Jeff thought, *giving birth only an hour after the death of her husband...*

But then, for the first time in months, Jeff's thoughts turned to himself. "Be strong for Hope," Anton had drilled into him. "She's going to need you. I'm going to need you. I hope you can be strong enough for the both of us."

He closed his eyes and stifled a sob. Russia had needed him, Bud had needed him, and even Valerie had approached him at Anton's funeral with, "*When are you coming home, Jeff? I need you...*" He shuddered, remembering the argument that had ensued.

What about my needs? he wanted to scream. He rolled over and cried into the pillow, feeling forsaken, destitute, and alone.

"Jeff?" Linda's soft hand ran across the breadth of his shoulders, and he turned to her. "Come here," she whispered. Like a child in need, he went to her arms and cried. "Shhh…" Her hand swept gently over his brow, and she kissed his forehead.

"There's nothing left for me to give," he said. "I'm empty…"

"It's okay," she whispered and held him tenderly in her arms until all that remained were jagged breaths that seemed to tear through him unexpectedly. "Shhh…" She kissed him gently on the mouth.

The warmth of her lips comforted his soul. He kissed her again, and then again, until finally they embraced. He kissed her throat and the gentle curve of her breasts.

An involuntary moan escaped her lips.

"I need you," he whispered desperately, and his hands pulled urgently at her nightgown. "Linda," he cried, suddenly aware of her swollen stomach. "Linda! I can't take a chance with your baby. Oh, God!" He took her hand and wrapped her arm tightly around him. "Hold me, Linda! Hold me!" His voice was urgent as his hips pressed against her. "Hold me…here," and in a matter of moments, he screamed painfully into the darkness as the last of the ecstatic spasms rendered him weak.

He lay breathless beside her with eyes closed. *Dear Jesus!* He took a deep breath and looked at her in the dim light.

"Oh, Linda, I'm sorry!" She was only twenty-one, and other than when she'd gotten pregnant, she had never been with a man—and she didn't even remember that! He put his hands to his face and groaned. "I'm so sorry. I…I don't know what to say."

She looked at him in shock, then got up and went into the bathroom. When she finally emerged, Jeff was in the kitchen, tucking his shirt into his damp jeans.

"You listen to me, little girl!" He stuck an angry finger in her face. "Don't you ever let a stranger come into your house again! Don't talk to strangers and *don't* invite them in for tea!" He hurriedly slipped his belt through the loops. "I happen to be a hell of a nice guy, but to tell you the truth, if you weren't pregnant, I don't know *what* would have happened in there!" He pointed to the living room.

"For all you know, I could have been some kind of maniac! You listen to me: don't ever do anything this stupid again!"

He was angrier with himself than with her.

"One more thing," he added. "I just lost someone I love. So if you want this baby, you keep it! Tell your family they can all go to hell. Christ, I can't even have kids, and here you are, giving one away." He opened the door and started through it.

"Jeff, wait!"

He stopped, but didn't turn around.

"Stay," she whispered. "You don't have to go. Please. I'm asking you to stay."

He hung his head and sighed. "Linda, do you know what happened in there?" he asked quietly. He forced himself to look at her. "I'll tell you. If you hadn't been pregnant, I might have…"

"Made love to me?"

He turned fully around. There was something in her he had not seen before. "Is that what you would have wanted?"

"I don't know. All I know is that I've been told how worthless and despicable I am for so long that when someone needed me…I guess it was nice to be needed."

"I could have raped you."

"You aren't capable of rape!" she said angrily. "I just saw you in what was probably your most desperate hour, and you stopped to worry about a baby I can't even keep. You're not capable of rape!"

"You didn't know that when you picked me up!" he shouted.

"I didn't pick you up. I took you in!" Angry tears spilled down her face.

Jeff groaned and put his arms around her. "Shhh…"

"I'm not a whore, Jeff. I don't pick men up!"

"I know. I know…"

"Jeff, please stay. What happened a while ago, I understand. You're just embarrassed right now. Things will look different in the morning. Please stay."

He finally agreed and was secretly glad to take off the damp clothes and climb back beneath the warm blankets, though he felt awkward when she got into bed beside him. But after a few minutes, she moved closer and nestled into the crook of his arm.

"Is it always like that?" she asked, and he raised his head off the pillow to look at her.

"Like what?"

"When men have sex, is it always so intense?"

He put his hand over his eyes and winced with embarrassment, then suddenly laughed. It was the laugh he had longed for, the laugh he so desperately needed to reassure him that life would go on. "Go to the library and check out a few books," he laughed and gave her a hug. "Linda, you know what you've just done for me? I think you just saved my life."

The rest of the night was spent in quiet conversation. He finally told her about Anton, and they discussed the strict Catholic background in which they had both been raised.

"Why can't you have kids?' she asked after a while, and had to repeat part of their argument when he wondered how she knew.

"Vietnam conflict. I had an injury—"

"I read about Vietnam in history class," she said, and the age gap widened. "How old are you?"

Staring at the ceiling, Jeff tensed. "Thirty-five." *If only I were fifteen years younger...* But it was useless to think about. Soon he would return to Three Rivers, to his old job, his old life. He would see what kinds of strings he could pull to get Clay back as his partner, and he would see to Hope and the baby. That he was lying in bed with someone barely out of her teens, pregnant or not, was ludicrous.

"Are you going to marry Valerie?"

"I don't know," he answered. "We argue a lot. She came out of a bad marriage. Her husband used to beat her. It's almost like, now that she has someone who would never do that, she wants me all to herself. She's very possessive. She was furious when I came up here to take care of Russia and Hope. She liked them and all, but she couldn't stand that they depended on me. She was jealous of the time and energy I gave them and was mad when I didn't catch the next bus after I laid Russia in the ground..."

Linda watched as he talked, realizing he was hardly even aware of her. He simply needed to talk. He was an extremely decent man, she concluded, sensitive and giving, even when it meant having to drain away everything, leaving nothing for himself.

Jeff turned on his side and leaned on one elbow to look at her. "What would you do if you had a real choice about your baby?"

She looked pensive for a moment before answering. "I haven't allowed myself to think about it."

"What's the worst thing that would happen if you kept it?"

"Jeff, my brother and uncles are paying the rent because I can't afford it with my part-time job. If I worked full time, I would have to get day care, and that would eat up the extra money. I wouldn't be able to afford to feed a baby, much less have time to spend with it."

"Is that how they rationalized it?" Jeff saddened, and she touched the side of his face to comfort him.

"Don't let it get you down. I keep reminding myself that I'm giving a couple who can't have children a chance to have one. Like you and Valerie."

"Val doesn't want kids," he said quietly, then reached beneath the bedding to caress her melon-like stomach. "She might have to share me with them."

"And you?"

"I love kids," he answered, then grew very quiet. He nestled down in the bed and laid his head against her breast, gently caressing her stomach. It rolled and wiggled, and he smiled sadly. He thought of how Anton had grasped what little he could of fatherhood.

Linda left him alone with his thoughts but spoke again after a long while. "I have to get ready for work pretty soon," she whispered, and he realized they had talked all night. Dawn had broken, and he knew it was time to say goodbye.

He dressed in silence, and while she was in the bathroom, he put what money he had into an envelope and wrote her a note. *Thank you for being there*, it read. *Buy something beautiful for the baby.* He signed his name and put it on the counter by the stove.

"Jeff!" Linda caught him as he was going out the door. "Weren't you going to say goodbye?"

He turned for a moment, drank in the beautiful picture of the pregnant girl, and shook his head. "I gave my last goodbye to Russia."

CHAPTER 53

Within two months, Hope was packed and ready to leave San Francisco. Jeff helped her close up the house and arrange her legal matters concerning the Pavlova School of Dance. She couldn't bear the thought of putting it on the market. Anton had so desperately wanted the school. One of the instructors he had trained was hired as manager, and with that, she, Jeff, and the baby left for Three Rivers.

Little Anna was their joy. Both Hope and Jeff commented often to each other about how proud Anton would have been and found solace in keeping him alive in their conversations. Jeff was wonderful with the baby, though sometimes while holding her, he slipped into sad, dark moods. But Hope understood. After the terrible strain they had endured, she said nothing and always allowed him to cling to Anna until the darkness passed.

Before they left the bay, Jeff disappeared often and didn't return until long after dark. When Hope questioned him, he would only say, "Looking for a pregnant lady," then asked her with his eyes to let it go.

After their return, Jeff stayed on the mountain for a while until Hope was settled. He got his job back and, after a while, approached the chief about Clay. But eventually he left the mountain to reestablish his own life, leaving Hope alone for the first time.

She had thought living on the mountain would be easier than in the house in San Francisco, but soon she found that it, too, contained too many memories. She insisted that the portrait of Anton's grandparents remain above the mantel, saying they were Anna's great-grandparents. But everyone knew the real reason was that she hated to change the way the house had been when Anton was there.

Saturday nights became a tradition again, only now there were toddlers clinging to furniture and everyone's knees. As time passed, they started walking, and eventually running, around the house. Thomas and Anna played for hours while the grown-ups cried over old movies and ate popcorn, desperately trying to recapture something that each knew in their heart was gone forever.

Hope grieved interminably, Jeff thought, noticing she had had another snapshot enlarged and placed on the mantel. It was one of Anton and Alexis that had been taken in Paris. Jeff scolded her with his eyes, but she looked back at him stubbornly. Even though no words were exchanged, he often left the house feeling as though they had argued.

*****

"Leslie wrote and said Paul Sanderson got married to an eighteen-year-old," Hope told Jeff over Christmas dinner. He and Val had married a year after Anton's death, and Jeff never failed to invite Anna and Hope for the holidays. They were his family, he insisted, and this year was no different.

"No kidding?" Jeff laughed. "Wouldn't Russia get a kick out of that! After all the grief he gave him about Catherine." Valerie only had to look at him. He wiped his mouth on a napkin and kissed her cheek. "I know. Enough said," he whispered, and excused himself from the table to play with Anna.

"What was that about?" Hope asked.

"Nothing." Val got up to stack the dishes.

"It bothers you when we talk about Anton, doesn't it?" she said, a little hurt.

"It's just that you need to start seeing other men, Hope. It'll be five years come March…"

She didn't look up. "I see. Time to fix up the poor widow. Well, Anna and I are doing fine. We don't need anyone else, thanks. I know I can always count on Jeff and Clay."

"Jeff is *my* husband," Val said pointedly, and Hope looked at her, suddenly aware that she had overstepped her bounds.

"I'm sorry, Val, I didn't realize..." Hope glanced at Anna, who giggled merrily on the floor with her *Uncle Jeff*. "I wish you had said something a long time ago." She felt terrible. It was already common knowledge that Jeff and Val argued a lot, and she wondered now if she was the cause.

"Mommy, Mommy! Uncle Jeff is taking me to the ballet! What's the ballet?" Anna asked excitedly, and Hope glared at Jeff as he approached.

"It's her Christmas present, Bud," he said quietly over Anna's head.

"Why didn't you ask me permission before you told her that?" Hope shouted.

Jeff knelt down to Anna. "Hey, Pumpkin, I'll betcha Aunt Val has some ice cream in the kitchen." He glanced at Val, who gave him an icy glare. "Please?" he whispered, and finally Val reluctantly took Anna's hand and led her away.

"We both promised Russia," he said once she was gone.

"I can't, Jeff. We've been over this a hundred times. I can't!"

"Both of us promised him on his deathbed. Now, damn it, I plan to keep my promise, whether you do or not!"

Hope turned to get her coat.

"Damn it, Bud, why won't you just let me take her?"

"You don't understand, do you? She's almost five years old. She would talk about it incessantly. I couldn't handle it! I just couldn't!" Hope turned from him momentarily. "Anna! Come put on your coat," she shouted, and Anna appeared in the doorway.

"For God's sake, Hope, let her finish her ice cream."

"Come on, Anna, we have to go." Hope tried to put on the little girl's coat, fumbling with the buttons.

"Mommy, are you going to cry tonight?" she asked, and Hope looked up at Jeff.

"My God, Bud, look what you're doing to yourself! Look what it's doing to Anna. When are you going to let go?" He tried to stop her, but when she pushed his hands away, he swooped and picked Anna up in his arms. "Where's your daddy, Pumpkin?"

"He died," she said.

"Don't you see? Even Anna knows the truth and accepts it!"

"How *dare* you!" Hope tore the child from his arms and hurried toward the door.

"Bud!" he yelled, but it was too late.

He turned and found Valerie standing behind him with her arms folded. "Another Christmas shot to hell," she said.

"What's that supposed to mean?"

"It's not enough to argue with me, you need *her* to argue with too? I'm tired of it, Jeff. You're *my* husband and this is *my* home. I'm tired of ruined holidays, and if they aren't ruined, I have to sit through endless stories about Anton Pavlova, as if the man were sainted!"

Jeff frowned. "We don't talk about Russia that much. As a matter of fact, we hardly mention him at all anymore."

Valerie glanced toward the door. "I don't want you seeing them anymore."

"You've got to be kidding. That child is like my own. They're my family. They're a part of me."

Valerie stepped closer and looked Jeff in the eye. "He was a man. Nothing more. He wasn't your brother like you're so fond of leading people to believe. In fact, Jeff, he was nothing to you at all."

"How can he not be a part of me?" Jeff screamed, holding his arms out to her. "He died right here. He took his dying breath in my arms! And it's here that Anna took her first breath of life! Tell me, Val, how in God's name are they not a part of me?" He shook his head in disbelief and backed away from her.

"Why did you marry me? Why didn't you marry Hope instead? Is it because *Russia's* been with her, making her body sacred territory?"

"That's ugly. What's the matter with you?"

"I'll tell you what the matter is, Jeff Lansing. I can handle Hope Pavlova. At least I know how to compete with the other woman in your life. What I can't handle is competing with a dead man and his child!"

The silence was deafening as Jeff considered her words. *Maybe you're right,* he thought. Perhaps he had never loved her enough.

"Look at your hands, Jeff. The left one wears your wedding ring, the right one, Anton's. Take one off."

He stared at her. "Don't do this, Val. Now, listen, I'm going after Bud. I have to make her go back to San Francisco."

"Why, for heaven's sake?"

"She never had a chance to grieve, Val. The baby came too soon after Russia died. I have to help her, make her go back, and then things will be different. I promise."

But as he reached for his jacket, she moved toward him with an outstretched hand. "Give me one of the rings, Jeff. Give me the one you'll let me destroy."

He searched her eyes. She was right in a way. Russia had always been a part of him. Always would be. He searched his heart and knew that he, too, would always be a part of the people who had touched his soul—the people to whom he had given nicknames. Funny, he thought, he'd never given one to his own wife.

"The ring," she demanded.

He silently slipped the ring from his left hand and walked out the door.

*****

"Jeff, what are you doing here? It's four in the morning," Hope said from the bottom of the stairs. He had just finished decorating a small Christmas tree and was putting gifts beneath it. "How did you get in?"

"The key under the mailbox."

Hope stifled a smile. That had become his standard reply after picking the lock. "What are you doing here?" she asked again.

He grinned at her. "I found a twinkle in my eye, so I figured I must be Santa Claus."

"Does Val know you're here?"

His grin faded. "Yeah, she knows," he said. "I've left her, Bud. I think we should get a divorce."

Hope sat beside him on the couch, speechless.

"Don't look at me like that," he said. "I don't like it either."

"It's my fault, isn't it? I depended on you too much."

He shook his head. "It's nobody's fault. We argued even before we got married."

The arguments were about Anton even then, Hope thought, but said nothing.

"I brought some wine," he said. "Let's make a toast."

"To what?"

Jeff went to the kitchen and returned with two glasses and poured the wine. "To new beginnings," he said. "It's time you and I made some hard decisions in our lives. You need to go back to the bay and decide what to do with the house and the studio, and I need to decide what to do about Val."

"What do you mean about the studio?"

"Either run it or sell it." It was hard to be firm with her. Her eyes filled with pain, and she could hardly speak. "Bud," he continued gently, "stop hanging on."

"It's all he ever wanted. His whole life was sidetracked from the thing he wanted most. He finally got back to it the last year of his life."

"Then go up there and run it!"

"Jeff, just thinking about it makes me cry."

"Then cry. Crying never killed anyone. Keep crying until you just can't cry anymore. What you'll have left is the studio that Russia loved. Do you think he would have ever bought it if he thought it would cause you so much grief? Go and grieve. Go to his grave and scream at him for dying and leaving you alone to raise your baby." Jeff's voice changed. He put his arms around her and held her tight. "Bud, I've watched you grieve for almost five years. I can't watch it anymore."

Pulling away, he picked up the glasses and put one in Hope's hand.

"To good decisions," he said. "Cheers."

CHAPTER 54

"*One*, two, three, four, five, six, seven, eight, and *again*, two, three, four, five, six, seven, eight…"

With her eyes closed, Hope could almost hear Anton clap along as the young dancers bolted across the wooden floor, their arms swinging, then uplifted as they jumped.

"Up! Higher!" he would yell, the smell of their sweat filling him with energy and excitement. "No, Tony, it's all wrong. Do it again. Now, from the top…" In her mind's eye Hope could see the young man in the lead stop midbeat, disgusted at having to go through the routine yet again. Anton had been a hard taskmaster, and in the few months of his teaching, had earned a reputation. Anyone who could survive his instruction was worth their weight in gold. Hope had heard his students grumble, and Anton had smiled when she told him about it later. "Exactly what I want them to feel! It gives them character. It dares them to be great!"

She had loved watching him work. He had been the happiest then. It was when he worked that he forgot his life was slipping away. It was then that he felt well and complete, and life exuded from every fiber of his being.

"Mrs. Pavlova?"

Hope opened her eyes and looked at Tony Lavine, who now managed the studio.

"What did you think?" he asked. Several of the students crowded around behind him, awaiting judgment.

"It was wonderful!" she exclaimed but realized now that she hadn't even watched. The students pressed toward her, anxious to meet her, to be introduced to *the* Mrs. Pavlova—*the master's wife*, she heard someone say.

Tony saw her discomfort and led her to the small office toward the back. "It's hard on you to come here, isn't it? We've missed you," he said, taking a seat behind the desk. Hope started to speak, but before the words came, he jumped in. "Mrs. Pavlova, before you say anything, I want you to know, your husband's unique style is taught in this school. His techniques are drilled into these students. I was privileged to work under him, and even in the short time he was with me, he taught me more about dance…not just dance, but his philosophy behind it. This school is a memorial to him; to his style." He paused for a moment and studied her face. Her eyes were empty and sad. "Mrs. Pavlova, don't ruin your life by becoming a living memorial. Anton's memory won't fade as long as this school is open. The school *is* staying open, isn't it? Or have you come to close it?"

There was an uncomfortable silence while he studied her. She wished she could escape his gaze long enough to regroup. "I don't know, Tony. That's what I've come to decide," she finally said.

They spoke for only a few more minutes before Hope went home.

*****

Jeff had taken Anna to Golden Gate Park while Hope attended to business, and she ran him ragged. They went to the planetarium, the museum, the aquarium, and the Japanese Tea Gardens. It was like being with Russia, he thought. He, too, had always run Jeff ragged in his thirst for knowledge.

Jeff lay back in the scented grass and closed his eyes. The sun was warm, the grass fragrant and cool. The sound of Anna's voice mixing in the chorus of other children's play gave him great pleasure. *Life is good,* he thought, and he knew that he could be content if this was all he had left.

"Uncle Jeff! Uncle Jeff!" he heard Anna's sweet little voice. She landed square in the middle of his stomach, and he let out a loud grunt.

"What is it, Pumpkin?" He peeked out of one eye and saw that she'd found a playmate. "Who's this?" He rose up on one elbow, shading his eyes.

"This is Joy. Uncle Jeff, would you buy us an ice cream?"

"First, we have to ask Joy's mommy," he said.

"Why?"

"We just do." He turned to the little girl. "Where's your mommy, Joy?"

"Over there." The little girl pointed toward a woman who sat on a blanket beneath a tree.

Jeff rose to his feet and walked toward the woman as she turned another page in her paperback. "Hi." He smiled when she looked up from her reading. "Aren't you going to invite me for tea?"

"Jeff!" she gasped.

"How are you, Linda?" He sat beside her on the blanket. "I see you kept the baby."

"I can't believe it's you!"

"Have you been disowned?" he asked, smiling just a little.

"It's been hard. But keeping her is the best thing I've ever done. I have you to thank." She looked at him for a while. He looked older. A white wisp of hair now ran over his left ear. "And what about you? Did you marry Valerie?"

"Yes. But it didn't work out."

"I'm sorry."

"I looked for you, Linda," he said out of the blue. "I went back to find you, but you were gone. The landlady wouldn't tell me a thing, and a week later, there was a 'room to let' notice in the window."

Linda laughed. "I was in the hospital. Joy was born the next day. You kept me awake all night, and I was so exhausted I went into labor at work."

Jeff looked toward Joy. "Well, little Miss Walker is beautiful," he said, but when he turned back to Linda, he saw discomfort in her eyes. "What's wrong?"

"It's not Walker, it's…Lansing."

"What?"

"When they asked me to fill out the birth information, I didn't have the heart to put 'father unknown.' I thought if she had a father at all, I would have wanted it to be someone like you. I used your name and copied your signature from the note you left, because I honestly don't think I would have kept her if it hadn't been for you. Please don't be angry."

Jeff was speechless. He looked at the two little girls playing nearby, momentarily forgetful of their ice-cream cones. Joy was a dark-haired beauty with long legs and large green eyes. "You mean to tell me that Joy is my child, legally? That in a court of law, I'm her father?"

Tears welled in Linda's eyes. "I would never try to trick you, Jeff. I swear."

"Of course not," he said, taking her hand and squeezing it. "I just want to know what you've told her. What does she know?"

"She thinks her daddy lives far away because there are people who need him and he takes care of them, that he loves us too but they need him more right now."

A slow smile spread across his face.

"I know I'll have to tell her the truth someday, but it never seems the right time."

"Then I wouldn't even have to adopt her or anything, say, if you and I got married or something. She'd already be mine, and she'd just think I had finally come home. She would never know the difference."

"What are you saying, Jeff? Are you asking me to marry you?"

"I don't know. I was just sayin'..."

"But that's crazy. I met you once, five years ago!"

"Yeah, I know. But we lived a lifetime that night. You'll have time to get to know me. I'm back in the Bay Area for a while, and I have this little divorce thing to take care of first. We'll take our time...make sure it's right."

Linda looked from Jeff to Joy, then back again.

He leaned forward and brushed his lips against hers, and they tumbled backward onto the blanket, laughing and crying in each other's arms. He kissed her hungrily but soon began to laugh again.

"Uncle Jeff!" Anna's little voice reached his ears as she climbed onto his back. "Why are you kissing Joy's mommy?"

"Because I love her, Pumpkin. Because I've loved her from the first time we met."

*****

The moment Hope laid eyes on Jeff, she knew something had changed. He'd found the same childlike expression that had always been a part of his charm, but had somehow gotten lost after Anton's death. Now, his eyes were bright and mischievous as he led the tall woman into the house by the hand. Anna danced around his legs as always, but this time there was another little girl by her side.

"Hi, Bud. What's happening?"

Hope burst into laughter. "Apparently, I should be asking you!"

"This is my little girl, Joy." He put a paternal hand on her dark-brown hair.

Hope lifted an eyebrow. "Oh?"

"And this is Linda. We're a family." His innocent eyes warmed her heart as they had so often years ago, and his happiness filled the room.

"I'm happy to meet you, Linda," Hope said. She looked at Jeff as he stepped close. "You've made your decisions, haven't you?" she whispered, and he slowly nodded. She hugged him around the neck. "I'm happy for you."

"What about you?" he asked, feeling as though he had abandoned her.

"Tonight. I'll make my decisions tonight."

Tonight. It was the long-awaited ballet that Hope had dreaded for five years. After their argument on Christmas Eve, she had promised Jeff she would take Anna to the ballet by June, hoping he would forget. But the promise he'd made to Anton had eaten at him, and eventually Hope had come to realize Jeff would never rest until it was fulfilled.

A lot depended on tonight. Her reaction to watching the ballet was the standard by which she would weigh the sale of the studio. If she found it too painful, she would sell the studio and the house and move back to Three Rivers forever. If she enjoyed it, she would try to build upon what Anton had begun.

She had sat on the fence far too long. There were decisions to be made.

She would decide tonight.

CHAPTER 55

Hope went to her closet and picked out her most beautiful evening dress, one of the many Anton had bought her to attend the ballet. "My wife goes in style!" he had often teased when she scolded him for spoiling her. She slipped it on and stood in front of the mirror.

"You look beaudyful, Mommy!" Anna's little voice came from behind, and she turned around.

"You look beaudyful too!" she said and kissed Anna's cheek.

"Uncle Jeff says there's a big, fancy car waiting for us. Why are we going in a big, fancy car?"

Hope caressed the hair that lay in soft golden waves over Anna's shoulder. "Daddy wanted you to attend your first ballet in style," she said, then led her daughter down the stairs.

Linda and Joy sat with Jeff in the living room, Joy's arms wrapped tightly around Jeff's neck. He unraveled her arms and rose when he saw that Hope and Anna were leaving. "Bud," he began, but the lump in his throat forbid him to speak.

Hope smiled and put her hand on his cheek. "Please don't say anything. I already know."

He bent down and kissed her lightly, and she quickly disappeared. As the door closed behind her, Jeff knew she had begun a very long journey.

*****

Anton had died with only two regrets: one, that he had never held his children, and two, that he had failed to find Alexis. The latter had consumed him in the end, had forced him out of his sickbed even when his doctor advised against it. But he'd never failed to attend the ballet, right to the end. Now the smell of the auditorium, the chatter of the crowd, the sounds of the orchestra tuning in the pit stirred Hope's emotions as she and Anna found their seats. Jeff had arranged aisle seats so that Anna would be able to see better, and eventually the lights began to dim.

Anna had had a full day with her Uncle Jeff, but after the nap he'd insisted she take, she was excited and lively. Hope smiled at her anticipation. Throughout the ballet, it was Anna she watched, remembering her own excitement in Paris and the overwhelming awe she'd felt the first time she saw Anton dance. Alexis had taken her hand, saying, *"He should have never given it up. Never! He owes it to the world to teach! If only I had such a teacher!"*

The words haunted her now, and she took a deep breath.

Anna looked up, wearing an odd expression. "Mommy, you're squeezing my hand too tight."

"I'm sorry, baby!" Hope looked away quickly; her breath came out ragged and sad.

"Marry my brother, Hope," the voice came again. *"Marry him and give him children…for the both of us. You will make some beautiful babies for the brothers Vishnyakov, yeah?"*

Hope looked down at Anna, whose eyes were glued to the stage. She had indeed done what Alexis asked. Anna was an extraordinarily beautiful child, so much like her father.

"Does Anton really look like your mother?" she'd asked, and Alexis had laughed loudly.

"When I first saw him, I thought to myself, 'Alexis, that man looks like your mother!' And when I heard his name, there came a lump in my throat so large I could not eat. Then he opened his mouth and out came Russian words! I was so scared!"

She smiled to herself, warmed by the memory. But that night, the KGB had surrounded him and pulled him out of Anton's grip. Alexis had grabbed her hand. "Remember me!" he'd shouted, but then he was swallowed by the multitude of people.

"Mommy, why aren't you watching the ballet?" Anna's voice came again, and Hope realized she was crying.

"I'm okay, baby." She patted Anna's knee and wiped her tears. It wasn't fair to Anna, she thought, wondering how she would ever make it through tonight. How could she even think of keeping Anton's studio? What was she thinking?

A page discreetly stooped in the aisle and whispered, "Mrs. Pavlova? Mr. Samuels spotted you in the crowd and asked if he might see you after the performance."

"Hal Samuels? He's here?"

"Yes, ma'am. He is the new head of security. He said he knew your husband."

Hope nodded, and the page disappeared up the aisle. *Hal Samuels,* she thought. He had always been so kind, so caring. She'd wondered what had become of him after the dissolution of the USIB. She had seen his name in the registry of Anton's funeral, but she'd been in the hospital then and never saw those who had attended.

After the performance, an escort came for Hope and she and Anna were led backstage. The moment she saw Hal, she went to his arms. He had always been so good to her, so protective. Now it was like looking into the face of a long-lost friend.

"Hope, you look wonderful," he said, smiling broadly, but it didn't take long for him to see the pain in her beautiful eyes. He took her hand and kissed it. "I'm sorry I missed you five years ago. I came to the funeral, but I was called away before I could see you. I understand you had just delivered that beautiful little girl over there."

"Yes, I knew you were there. Thank you." She smiled, looking at Anna, who stood a few feet away, trying desperately to imitate the ballerinas she had seen. She twirled on her toes, and her pretty dress floated on the cool air.

Hal laughed, watching her. "Anton would be very proud," he said, and Hope nodded.

"Have you been in San Francisco long?" she asked.

He smiled, embarrassed. "I just got the job as head of security, and I thought I'd come tonight to have a look around. I don't actually start until next week."

"I'm so glad you did. I would have hated to miss you," she said, glancing in Anna's direction. "Where is she? Where's Anna!" Hope grabbed Hal's arm in a panic.

Anna was gone, had disappeared in the crowd.

"Don't worry. She can't have gone far."

*****

Anna was surprised that the rooms backstage were so cool and ill-lit as she passed through the dismal hallway. Men in business suits and dancers still in costume hardly noticed her as she ran her fingers along the cold plaster walls. She began to feel afraid until she spotted an open door that allowed a bit of light to splash against the pea-green color of the hall.

She peeked through the door and watched a danseur who sat on a wooden bench, still winded from his performance. "Hello," she said, pushing the door open wide.

He looked up at her from across the small room. "Hello," he answered, then looked back down to massage his ankles.

"I saw you dance," she said.

"Did you?"

"Yes," she said, taking a few steps into the room. "You were Prince Sig…"

"Prince Siegfried," he helped. He finally looked up at her again. "You are very young to know that."

"I watched you the whole time," she said, stepping a little closer.

He smiled, startled by her compelling blue eyes. "Are you lost?"

"No," she said matter-of-factly. She walked around him for a moment. "You look like the man in the picture with my daddy," she said. She stopped in front of him and put her hand on his face.

The powerful dancer trembled beneath her touch. Something about her triggered a wellspring of emotions, and he couldn't understand where they came from. He only knew that her inexplicable presence moved him. "You're very pretty," he said quietly.

She removed her hand and twirled in front of him, giggling. "I look like my daddy. Everyone tells me so."

A hard knot formed in his stomach, and when she stopped to look at him, he couldn't deny the resemblance. "Is your daddy here with you?"

"No. My mommy is here. My daddy died before I was born. Uncle Jeff says that's why Mommy cries." She looked at him curiously. "You talk funny," she said. "Are you from far away? My daddy was from far away."

The dancer nodded. "What is your name, child?" His hoarse voice could barely be heard.

Again, Anna twirled clumsily before him. "I'm named after a famous ballerina. Anna Pavlova," she said with pride.

The dancer closed his eyes, hearing his brother's voice ring in his ears: *"If I have to come back from my grave, I'll find you! Watch for me, Alexis! Watch for me!"*

"What's your name?" Anna continued.

"Alexis," he whispered. He opened his eyes and found Hope standing in the doorway.

Anna's tiny hand slipped comfortably into his as he struggled to his feet. "Mommy, this is Alexis."

CHAPTER 56

Jeff Lansing pulled the blankets over Anna's head.

"Uncle Jeff, I can't breathe!" she squealed, squirming beneath them.

"Sorry, Pumpkin, I didn't see you there!" He pulled the blankets back down, and she eyed him playfully.

"You did too!" she scolded, then sat up in bed and wrapped her delicate arms around his neck. "I love you, Uncle Jeff. You always play with me."

"I love you too, sweetie," he said, kissing her softly on the cheek. "It's two o'clock in the morning, young lady. Well past your bedtime."

Anna lay back onto the soft pillow but shot up a second time. "I forgot to say my prayers."

Jeff groaned helplessly and pulled the blankets down, motioning for her to get up. Once, he had suggested she say them in bed, but Anna wouldn't hear of it. "God can't hear you if you're lying down," she'd said. This time, he knew not to even try.

She climbed out of the bed and knelt beside it, her hands folded. She looked angelic in the lamplight as she peered up at his lanky form with those celestial blue eyes. "Uncle Jeff, aren't you going to pray with me?"

He knelt beside her and folded his hands on the bed. *We must make quite a picture,* he thought. But he didn't care. He adored her. At five years old, Anna was the only woman in the world who could bring him to his knees.

"Dear God..." she began. She watched as he made the sign of the cross. "Am I supposed to do that?" she asked.

"Well, I don't think…" Even at five, she could render him speechless. "I think saying your prayers is what really counts," he said at last.

"Oh," she said. "Anyway, God, thank you for Mommy and Uncle Jeff and for letting me go to the ballet tonight and helping me find that man."

"Uncle Alexis," Jeff whispered.

"It's not nice to interrupt when I'm talking to God, Uncle Jeff."

"Sorry."

"Thank you for helping me find Uncle Alexis. And thank you for the letter from Daddy."

Jeff paled. "What letter?"

"Shhh." She glared at him. She had nine "thank-you-fors" and eight "God-blesses," and Jeff watched her shiny blond head nod with each one. Each was precious and heartfelt, but he ached for her to finish. "Amen," she said at last, and crawled back into bed. Jeff crossed himself quickly and pulled the blankets back over her pink-flannelled body.

"Listen, Pumpkin," he said, sitting on the edge of the bed, "I know it was a conversation with God and all, but what letter? What letter did you get from your daddy?"

"This one. See? It has my name on it." She pulled a white envelope from under her pillow and handed it to him. "See?" She pointed. "That's my name. Uncle Jeff, if he died before I was born, how did Daddy know my name?"

Jeff turned the envelope over in his hand, silent. It was, indeed, Anton's handwriting. Elegant. Fluid. Almost like a woman's. "Your daddy always believed you would be a girl," he said absently. "Anna, where did you get this?"

"I found it."

"Where?"

"In my secret place."

"It says on the envelope that you are supposed to read this when you're sixteen, not five." He looked into her cobalt eyes. The resemblance to her father could be frightening at times. At moments like this, he felt it was Anton staring back at him, imploring him to do the right thing. "Does your mother know you have this?"

"No," she said and added in a confidential tone, "We don't talk about Daddy anymore. It makes Mama cry."

He nodded. "What do you suppose we should do with the letter?"

"You can keep it for me, Uncle Jeff, until I'm sixteen."

He marveled at her wisdom and kissed her good night. He went to the door but turned to her once again. "Where did you say you found this?" he asked again.

"A secret place," she said. "I'm five. Can't I have a secret place?"

He smiled. "You're a precocious child."

Anna frowned. "I thought I was Presbyterian."

*****

Alexis Vishnyakov was defecting.

From the moment Anna had found him backstage, he knew his life had changed. Never again would he cry out for artistic freedom. Never again would he be forced to dance only the classical ballets.

He was in America.

Only hours ago, he had bowed his way through twelve curtain calls exalting his performance in *Swan Lake*. The Bolshoi Ballet had been on tour in Canada, then the United States. Tonight's performance in San Francisco was their last before heading home.

"Did you know who the little girl was when you saw her backstage?" a reporter asked excitedly, pushing his way through the crowd of INS agents, security, and fellow reporters. "Did you know she was your niece?"

Alexis turned to the interpreter, then to Hope, who answered for him. "My husband died five years ago. Alexis hadn't seen him since a year before that. How could he know Anna was Anton's child?"

Alexis clutched her hand. From outside, he could hear the shouts of the Bolshoi director. "Don't do it! Don't do it, Alexis!" Mixed in, American fans clamored for a peek at him through the windows.

"You must not leave us, Alexis! Don't do it!" came the voice of a fellow dancer. He turned and peered through the sheers that covered the window. There stood Sonia, silent. It was still dark outside, except for the lights of the camera crews filming the crowd that had gathered in front of the Victorian house on Franklin Street.

"Alexis, do what you want to do. Don't be pressured." A heavy middle-aged woman from the Immigration and Naturalization Service sat before him, explaining his rights, while reporters both inside and out shouted into their microphones. "Tonight, after an electrifying performance, the *premier danseur étoile* of Russia's Bolshoi Ballet, Alexis Vishnyakov, was smuggled out of San Francisco's War Memorial Opera House to this residence in San Francisco's Pacific Heights district…"

Alexis felt like an island in the noise. He was full of terror and confusion, joy and relief. But when Anna had come to him, he'd known he had to follow.

*****

Upstairs, away from the confusion, Jeff stood in the dim hallway, clutching Anton's letter. "Jesus, Russia…" His eyes grew moist, and he sought refuge in one of the spare rooms.

Drop cloths still covered the furniture, and the room smelled musty. He leaned against the closed door and turned the letter over in his trembling hands, pushing the flap aside.

My Darling Anna,

Coming from a man who will never hold you or attend your birthday party or watch you get ready for the prom, that probably sounds strange. Forgive me.

I am writing because I want you to understand. I want you know who I am. The picture your mother will paint of me is blurred, and I want to set the record straight. I am not a hero. I have no desire for martyrdom.

THE PEBBLE AND THE MAN

I have loved two women in my life. My first wife, Catherine, and the child I bore with her are gone. I was not there for them. Nor was I there for little Rose. Now, only you and my beloved Hope remain. Again, I am not there. Life plays cruel tricks.

In my life, I've been a murderer and a thief. I've sold my soul in the name of patriotism. I've fought for my country in ways you cannot possibly imagine. I love the United States. I believe in democracy.

I am not a hero, but nor am I a villain, Anna. I am a man.

For answers, there are two people to whom you can go. There is your mother, of course, and the other is Jeff. Trust Jeff. He has literally given me the shirt off his back. He is our guardian angel.

I am a pebble at the seashore, Anna. As for my value, you alone must be my final judge.

Love,
Daddy

"Jesus, Russia…" Jeff whispered. He clutched the letter to his chest, bowed his head, and cried.

ABOUT THE AUTHOR

Born in the farmlands of California in the 1950s, Connie N. Hart, née Easter was raised by her father, who always encouraged her imagination and creativity. After marrying, she moved north of Chicago, where she and her husband, Ken, raised two sons, Matthew and John. Between working as a real estate agent, artisan, and interior decorator, as well as traveling frequently with her husband, Connie had the opportunity to learn about life from many different perspectives. An avid reader and writer of poetry, she began writing her first novel, *The Pebble and the Man*, in the 1980s.

As seen in the novel, life—and we ourselves—often get in the way of our dreams. The handwritten manuscript languished for years. In 2000, a period of personal upheaval, Connie and Ken moved to Southern Oregon, where they had purchased an old house on the outskirts of Wimer. Initially planning to tear it down and start fresh, they soon learned it was the dilapidated remains of the historic Bybee Springs Hotel. Learning of the structure's significance, they decided to renovate it into both a home and a monument to the community's history. After the years of work required, Connie's son John, an occasional editor, asked during a visit, "Mom, didn't you write a novel when I was about nine? Where is it?"

"In a box somewhere in the barn."

Over thirty years had passed.

"Mom. It's time to get it out."

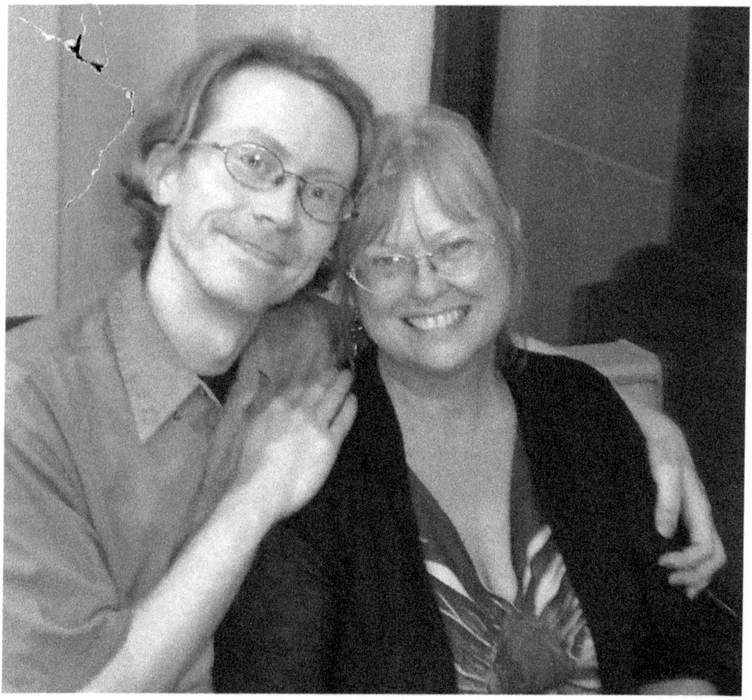